T0359698

HISTORICAL

Your romantic escape to the past.

The Earl's Cinderella Countess
Amanda McCabe

The Viscount's Wallflower Wager
Liz Tyner

MILLS & BOON

THE EARL'S CINDERELLA COUNTESS
© 2024 by Ammanda McCabe
Philippine Copyright 2024
Australian Copyright 2024
New Zealand Copyright 2024

First Published 2024
First Australian Paperback Edition 2024
ISBN 978 1 038 90580 2

THE VISCOUNT'S WALLFLOWER WAGER
© 2024 by Elizabeth Tyner
Philippine Copyright 2024
Australian Copyright 2024
New Zealand Copyright 2024

First Published 2024
First Australian Paperback Edition 2024
ISBN 978 1 038 90580 2

MIX
Paper | Supporting
responsible forestry
FSC® C001695

Published by
Harlequin Mills & Boon
An imprint of Harlequin Enterprises (Australia) Pty Limited
(ABN 47 001 180 918), a subsidiary of HarperCollins
Publishers Australia Pty Limited
(ABN 36 009 913 517)
Level 19, 201 Elizabeth Street
SYDNEY NSW 2000 AUSTRALIA

Cover art used by arrangement with Harlequin Books S.A.. All rights reserved.

Printed and bound in Australia by McPherson's Printing Group

The Earl's Cinderella Countess

Amanda McCabe

MILLS & BOON

Amanda McCabe wrote her first romance at sixteen—a vast historical epic starring all her friends as the characters, written secretly during algebra class! She's never since used algebra, but her books have been nominated for many awards, including the RITA® Award, Booksellers' Best Award, National Readers' Choice Award and the HOLT Medallion. In her spare time she loves taking dance classes and collecting travel souvenirs. Amanda lives in New Mexico. Visit her at ammandamccabe.com.

Visit the Author Profile page
at millsandboon.com.au for more titles.

Prologue

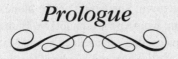

For love is a celestial harmony
Of likely hearts compos'd of stars' concent,
Which join together in sweet sympathy,
To work each other's joy and true content
—Edmund Spenser

1808

'*I'm afraid you cannot return to school in the New Year, Eleanor dearest. With your mother sadly gone, there is so much for you to do here at the vicarage. I do so rely on your good sense...*'

Eleanor St Aubin could hardly bear it another moment. Could hardly bear the walls of the old vicarage, whitewashed and hung with gloomy old paintings, the sound of her father humming to himself as he wrote his sermon in his library, where he stayed almost all the time. *Humming!* As if he hadn't just brought her world—what was left of her world after losing dear Mama—around her very ears.

She'd clung to the idea of going back to Mrs Meecham's School for Clergymen's Daughters in the bustle and colour of Bath, with her sister Mary. Clung to the thought that soon she would be with her friends, her books and her music lessons, walks across the hills and parks of the town. She would not be alone.

Now there would be no school. No Bath or music or friends. Papa needed a housekeeper, and Mary was only ten, no use at all. She would go back to school. Eleanor was fourteen and 'sensible'. So she would stay home.

Eleanor stood in the middle of the small drawing room, among her mother's dark-green-cushioned furniture and the scent of beeswax polish, woodsmoke and tea cakes, which she would now be responsible for providing. She listened to her father's humming and the thud of his books as he stacked them on his desk. She could hear the cook in the kitchen, clanging pots and pans, and imagined she also heard her chores in the still-room, the jam and potpourri and herbs calling to her. She imagined the parade of parishioners coming endlessly to their door, through the tangled garden pathway that also needed her urgent attention. They would want tea and cakes and would need placating as they waited for her father, who was always late.

Eleanor sighed. She didn't mind talking to the parishioners, really, even when it was about dull altar flowers and fetes to raise coin for the roof. In fact, she quite enjoyed that part, the organising and helping and the solving of problems.

Mama had been so splendid at it all, the church matters *and* the housekeeping. Chatting with people and bringing a tea tray in once in a while.

Eleanor's old chores were far from those she had being the lady of the vicarage and she already felt as if she was drowning. She had no idea how to do any of it! No idea how to manage their few servants, see to meals, tidy the garden and be gracious and smiling all the time.

She'd always half imagined that she might one day marry a curate herself and keep her own vicarage just as Mama had. But that was in some hazy 'someday', when she was older, more learned and not so very awkward and unsure. Not now, when she was still a school-girl.

Her frantic stare fell on a barley twist side table, its books and porcelain vases covered with a film of dust. Without her mother's close eye on every detail, things were descending into chaos. And now Eleanor was the one who had to pay the attention.

She closed her eyes against the dust. Against the windows that needed washing and the curtains that needed mending. She did not *want* to be the grown-up! She wanted to go back to school, to the pale houses and crowded streets of Bath. She wanted a little more time to decipher out her life, not have it thrust upon her without her say-so. She wanted to cry and kick something and rail about unfairness! She wanted…

She wanted her mother. That was what she wanted. She wanted Mary Ellen St Aubin to hug her close and tell her all would be well. But it would not. Not now.

'Eleanor,' her father called out plaintively. 'Have you seen my spectacles?'

The cook shouted at the scullery maid and Mary

shrieked from her chamber upstairs. Eleanor couldn't bear it another moment. The chaos *she* was meant to control now, the absence of Mama, the realisation that this was her every day now and there was no escape—she was suffocating.

She spun around and raced out of the drawing room, through the small, flagstone-floored foyer, and yanked the door open. Luckily, there was no one on the pathway, no poor soul seeking solace from the vicar and tea and cakes from the housekeeper—from her. She heard a hum of conversation from the churchyard just beyond the garden hedge, but she couldn't see anyone. She clutched at handfuls of her grey muslin skirt and ran. She ran down the overgrown path, veering a bit towards the church, its old Norman stone tower stretching towards the cloudy sky as if it watched her. She dashed through the lych-gate into the lane.

She didn't stop running.

Rather than head towards the village, a small but pretty place lined with shops, where everyone knew her and where someone was bound to see her and report her hoydenish behaviour to her father, she went to the woods that stretched in the opposite direction, cool and green and quiet.

The woods were part of the estate at Moulton Magna, the grand property of the Earl of Fleetwood, the greatest lord in the neighbourhood. Since the Earl was friends with her father, indeed had bestowed on him the living in the first place, no one in the Canning family—the Earl, Countess and their sons, plus a vast staff—cared when the vicar and his daughters walked there. It was a beautiful spot, with groves and streams, smelling of the fresh, green air and Eleanor usually loved it.

She enjoyed the company of the Canning brothers, as well, she had to admit. Especially the younger, Lord Frederick, he of the glowing sky-blue eyes and easy laughter. His teasing ways that made her blush and stammer, made her close her eyes and picture him at night and wish she had said something different to him, been someone different. She always sought him out there when they were both home from school, even if she told herself she did not.

But today she hoped she wouldn't see Fred, or any of them. She could feel drops of moisture at her temples from her mad dash, dampening her dark brown hair. Curls escaped their pins and clung to her neck, and she was sure her eyes must be red from crying, her pale cheeks blotchy. She would be a terrible sight, a disgrace to the vicarage. And she couldn't bear for Fred, of all people, to see her that way! To tease her and laugh at her, even in his light, joking way. She didn't want him to remember her that way.

She saw no one as she ran down a winding, mossy path, towards a small summerhouse that topped a rolling rise. It had long been a favourite spot for her, as well as for Mary and the Canning brothers. The view from its colonnaded portal stretched for miles—meadows and trees and the grand, glowing house of Moulton Magna. They would chase each other there, laughing and teasing. Today, she wanted to be alone. To not have to be the strong, sensible one everyone said she was. She had the rest of her life to do that.

She stumbled up the steps of the little, round, domed building and into the single room. Greyish sunlight filtered through the skylight high overhead, dappling the dried leaves that drifted over the mosaic floor, reminding her that autumn was lengthening and when winter came she wouldn't be at school. She'd be here. Alone in the summerhouse, which echoed now with old laughter.

She sat down on a wrought iron chaise, its cushions taken inside now. She didn't feel the hard press of the bare slats, though, or the chill of the marble walls. She let that silence wrap around her and drew her knees up to press her forehead against them. The tears fell then, until she had no more of them. There was only a sort of tired resignation.

She wanted to blame Papa, to curse at him, even though she couldn't. It was not his fault, not really. Her mother had been so superb at her job of keeping the vicarage and he couldn't begin to do all she had done. He didn't know how, and he had his own tasks of sermon-writing and consoling the bereaved, comforting the dying, celebrating marriages and new babies. She was the female. She had to cook and clean and manage servants. It was how the world worked. She was the eldest daughter. The duties were hers, along with helping Mary, and they had to be done.

But, oh! She had loved school and her friends and books. Loved Bath, glowing like honey in the light, the Avon bubbling past, laughter and people and shops.

She reached under the chaise and found the basket

of books she'd left there still waiting. Novels and poetry—things not suitable for the vicarage library. She
took out her favourite, Spenser's *The Fairy Queen,*
with its etched illustrations of the Redcrosse Knight
and his true love Una.

The door cracked open, letting in a bar of light and
a breeze that stirred at the leaves. Her stomach lurched
as she was suddenly dragged out of her fantasy world.
She dropped her feet to the floor and wiped at her
damp cheeks. Had her father caught her? She didn't
want him to feel even worse! Didn't want to put her
tears on anyone else.

But it was not her father or sister, or a Canning
gamekeeper come to lecture her against racing through
the park. It was Fred. The last person she wanted to
see. The only person she wanted to see.

He stood there in the doorway, half in the wavering
shadows, and studied her with a worried frown. Eleanor felt her tense shoulders ease at just his presence and
she clutched the book close to her with a sigh.

Fred, though he was much older than her at nineteen,
and *very* handsome indeed, with his waves of amber-
gold hair and sharp cheekbones, his bright blue eyes
filled with laughter was much sought after by every
eligible young lady within miles and miles, had always
been such a friend to her.

There was the flash of a deep dimple when he smiled
at her. He spoke to her not as if she was a silly child or
a sensible housekeeper, but as a lady who understood
poetry and history and who loved to run and dance
even when she shouldn't. He raced her through the

woods, taught her the rules of cricket, read with her, teased her, laughed with her. He was always quick to make her giggle when life at the vicarage was too dour, to run with her, read poetry with her, tell her tales of the world outside.

Yes—he was her friend. And if, in the quiet of her dark chamber at night, she dared to dream he might be more, might one day kiss her and hold her close—well, that was *her* secret. She knew he never would, not really. He was handsome as a god, as a prince in a poem, and the son of an earl. But the dreams were so lovely.

'Ella,' he said softly, kindly. 'Are you unwell? I was riding by and saw you running.'

Eleanor ducked her head, hoping he wouldn't see those red eyes and splotched cheeks. She was plain enough in comparison to him already! 'I—I'm all right, Fred, really. I just—my father told me I cannot return to school. He needs my help at the vicarage.'

'Oh, Ella. I am sorry,' he said.

His voice was full of sympathy and understanding and she feared it would make her cry all over again. He was one of the few who knew how much she really loved it at school, for she confided in him about her friends and studies. They read *The Fairy Queen* together while he told her about his own school and his hopes for the future away from his own family.

He gestured at the book she clutched. 'You could be Una.'

She felt her lips tug at a reluctant smile, even though she knew he flattered her just to cheer her up. 'And you shall always be the *parfit gentil knight*. The Red-crosse Knight.'

He smiled in return, but Eleanor sensed something rather sad and dark in the gesture. Something not like Fred, who was always so merry and ready to run and laugh.

She sat up straighter. 'Is something amiss?'

'Of course not. It's just…' He stepped closer, into the glow from the skylight. He wore a red coat, glittering with touches of gold.

'Fred…' she whispered, a cold knot forming in her stomach. 'Are you— That is…'

'I'm also leaving, yes. I have my commission in the Grenadiers and we're leaving for the Peninsula tomorrow. I was looking for you to say…'

'To say goodbye?' she choked out. Her eyes prickled and she warned herself sternly not to start crying again.

She had long known Fred was meant for the Army. His older brother, the dashing Henry, was the heir to Moulton Magna. Their destinies sorted them as surely as hers did for her and Mary. Fred would surely go far in the Army, flourish there where his bravery and gift for friendship would be valued and she was happy for him.

But—oh! He was one more loss, after her mother and her school and any foolish hopes she might have dared harbour about the future. That one day a miracle would happen and Fred could be hers, even though he was the Earl's son and she the vicar's daughter.

She rose slowly to her feet and took a step closer to him. He smelled wonderfully of sunshine and lemon soap and just *Fred*. She was suddenly achingly aware this could be the last time she saw him. It was certainly the last time she would see *this* Fred and be *this* Eleanor. So many images scrolled through her mind in a great flash—his smile, the blue glow of his eyes, the freedom of laughing with him.

She gently touched his hand. It was warm and slightly rough, so alive under her fingers, and she longed to clutch at him, hold on to him and this moment for always.

'I shall miss you,' she said simply. She could think of no other words.

He smiled at her, a flash of his old teasing grin, and turned his hand to hold onto hers. 'And I will miss you, Ella. Will you keep the book for me? Think of me adventuring when you read it?'

She gave him another smile in answer. It felt rather watery, weak, but she yearned to put all she felt into it. All she thought of him in her secret heart. All she hoped for him. She couldn't bear to send him off with a vision of red eyes and miserable weeping! 'Of course I shall. No one could ever read the lines as you do, though. Really, you should have been one to tread the boards rather than march in the Army!'

'I'm glad your father is here to keep an eye on Moulton Magna for me. I have the feeling my parents and brother will need all the prayers they can find!'

Eleanor shook her head, thinking of the Earl, of Henry and their carelessness. But it was Fred who would be in danger. She had the gnawing, anxious sense that it was Fred who needed the prayers, needed someone to look after him. And it could not be her.

To her horror, she felt those tears well in her eyes again.

'Oh, Ella,' he said, his sharply carved face crumpling in worry. 'Don't cry, please! I can stand anyone crying, but not you.'

'Because I am sensible and strong?' she whispered.

'You are that. But also because of your dear heart, your laughter and poetry. Your kindness. No one is kinder than you, Ella. I need you to keep watch for me here. You're the only one I can really count on.'

Eleanor nodded, cherishing those words. Trying to remember them for the long days ahead. But she hated the hint of worry in his voice, the tinge of some foreboding, and it made her shiver. She longed to cling onto him even closer, to not to let him leave her side. 'You *can* rely on me, Fred. I'll be—thinking about you a great deal and sending you all best wishes wherever you are.' Sending him her heart, even though he would never know it.

He gently touched her cheek, tracing the last of her tears. 'So, friends always, Ella?'

Friends. Such a pale word for what she felt for him, for her secret dreams. But it was a precious gift nonetheless. One she hugged close. 'Yes. The best of friends.'

To her shock, he took her hand in his, holding it tight and bent his head to press a soft, gentle kiss to her fingers. Then he turned and left and she was alone again.

Eleanor curled her fingers tight, as if she could hold

on to that kiss. The thrilling sensation of it all. The bright, sunshiny tingles. She wanted to remember it always, remember *him*.

She smoothed out his handkerchief, running her fingertip over the embroidered blue *FC*. She fancied she could smell his lemony soap there, the essence of Fred and his golden glow.

'The best of friends,' she whispered. She folded up the handkerchief carefully, tucked it in the pages of the book and stepped back out into the real world to face the future, carrying with her the memory of Fred and his kiss.

Chapter One

'And so that is it?' Fred asked the dour-faced lawyer who sat across the desk from Fred and Penelope, his father's widow. He could hardly absorb what the man was saying in his quiet, steady, solemn, oh-so-matter-of-fact voice.

Fred had seen much in his years in the Army, culminating in the hell of Waterloo. He had seen mud and blood and misery, biting cold and brutal sun. He had seen friends killed and maimed. He bore his own scars. A face lined with red wounds and a weakened hand. Sometimes all that had sustained him then was the memory of his 'Una', Eleanor St Aubin, and her sweet smiles.

Yet he never imagined he would return to all this.

His father had never been a man who loved, or could be loved, especially once Fred's mother died and all the softness and kindness and order of Moulton Magna went with her. And his brother had always cared only for hunting and fishing, not about the fact that one day he would be the Earl. Now they were both gone and Fred was the Earl himself. All the misery and death that he'd seen in battle had followed him, even to this peaceful place, and clung to him like a ghost. There was no time to grieve as he should. The estate and all who depended on it were his responsibility. He had to do his very best for them.

And now this. Not only was Moulton Magna his now—so were its debts. They were most considerable. For it seemed his father had enjoyed gambling while Fred was gone. Any sense of duty had been lost on the card tables.

For one long moment, he could say nothing else. Thoughts raced one after another through his mind, chasing and spiralling. How could this have happened? How had his father and brother been so far gone? All Fred knew was the Army. Yet now he had to fix this debacle. He had learned how to be a soldier, how to keep calm in the midst of battle, but this was something else entirely. This was something he never expected. Another kind of chaos.

He glanced at Penelope, sitting beside him in her inky veils. She looked deeply sad, but not surprised. Then again, she had lived in the crumbling house at Moulton Magna for years while Fred was away so much. Pen was young. She'd been married off by her family after her first husband died suddenly. No doubt when they thought an earl would offer her security. Now she, too, was adrift.

She gave him a quick, sweet smile, as if she tried to reassure him. His father had not deserved her, with her kind nature, her gentle humour and her pretty face. She'd been a good friend to Fred.

'Pen…' he began.

She reached out with her black-gloved hand to touch his arm.

'Oh, Fred, please don't worry about me,' she murmured. 'I know this is a such a shock. Your father…'

The lawyer cleared his throat. 'Indeed, Lord Fleetwood. I have here a list of the late earl's debts and a few of the assets of the estate. The estate manager will certainly have more detailed information for you. I suggest his lordship was not, er, entirely well in his final years.'

Penelope gave a little snort behind her black-edged handkerchief. His father never had been the most responsible of men, even before Fred left, but according to servants' tales he had grown far worse once Fred had gone. And Pen had had to deal with all that.

'But Lady Fleetwood does have her jointure, which cannot be touched,' the lawyer said. 'As well as a small sum from her own family.'

'I shall find a small place for myself, Fred. Perhaps in Bath, or someplace like that,' Penelope said. 'I will be quite well. Much better, in fact.'

Fred smiled at her. That was one good thing. Penelope did deserve a happy life now.

'I can help you,' she said.

He shook his head. 'No. You have helped enough. Too much.'

And she had. The people of Moulton Magna loved

her, even though his father had neglected them shamefully. It was Fred's job to see them all right now. No matter what it took.

Chapter Two

Bath, 1817

'I need a wife. The best! You must find her for me. Immediately.'

Eleanor exchanged a quick glance with her sister Mary and bit her lip to keep from bursting into laughter. Even Miss Muffins, their little terrier puppy, propped on her velvet cushion beneath the desk, looked startled by their potential new patron. Mary widened her pretty grass-green eyes, mouthed *Immediately!* and Eleanor shuffled a few papers about before she dared look back at Mr Higgleston-Worth.

The St Aubin and Briggs Confidential Agency was a most discreet, discerning and, it had to be said, successful place, where people who desired to be married but perhaps had a small difficulty or two could come for advice.

However, the agency didn't always attract easy-to-place clients. Oh, no. People who were easy to match had no need of their service. People who were handsome, pleasant and wealthy were not St Aubin and

Briggs' usual bread and butter. They had acquired a fine reputation for, so to say, finding a lid for every pot. The shy, the outwardly abrasive but inwardly insecure, the older and younger and plainer and choosier. Those were the people who came to the agency.

St Aubin and Briggs found fine marriages for them all—well, most of them—and their files were filled with grateful letters from those now ensconced in marital bliss.

Eleanor had learned in their work to never be daunted. Since she and Mary had opened their office with their old school friend Henrietta, the widowed Lady Briggs, they had found great success, beyond their modest hopes. When Papa had died and they'd had to leave the vicarage, the home they'd known all their lives, they'd been thrown into frantic worry. Their only choice had seemed to be separating from each other, going out as governesses or ladies' companions. Scraping by in a cold, lonely world. Until Harry had come to the rescue.

'I have my little bit of jointure,' she'd said as she had helped them pack up their meagre belongings. *'And a fine new house in Bath! No more dull country days for me.'*

'*Bath…*' Mary had sighed dreamily, as she'd often tended to be. *'I do long for Bath again!'*

Eleanor had laughed. *'School was delightful there, Mary darling, but after we last went there with Papa to take the waters, you declared you would scream if you saw one more wheeled, wicker chair!'*

Mary had bitten her lip, shaken her golden curls

and tossed a large volume of sermons into the 'to be sold' crate.

'That is only because we spent too much time in doctors' premises to have any fun! Poor Papa. But there could be dances and theatres, assemblies, garden parties. If only...'

'Then you must come with me,' Harry had declared.

She'd always been their leader in mischief at school. Tall, auburn-haired, full of confidence and merriment. Some of Harry's spirit had faded during her marriage but Eleanor had been happy to see the spark returning to her dark eyes. She'd drawn Eleanor and Mary in with her, despite their sadness and worry.

'I have the most fascinating plan to fill my time and I need your help...'

The plan turned out to be the St Aubin and Briggs Confidential Agency. Harry said she never wanted anyone caught in a marriage like hers if she could help it. She'd successfully paired up several of her friends at her marital home at Briggs Manor and her reputation had spread until people she barely even knew sought her out for assistance.

'My income is not as plump as one might wish,' Harry had declared. *'And how can I resist doing my tiny bit to bring some happiness into the world!'*

And so their business had been born and it had flourished. An office and lodgings in Kingston Buildings, right across from the Abbey and within walking distance of everyplace important. Pretty clothes for pretty Mary. Lots of books for Eleanor. Luscious Bath buns galore for Miss Muffins, who lived up to her name. They were all together, not to be parted despite the lack of any fine fortunes or grand connections. And Harry was proved right—the work was deeply satisfying, every new couple's blissful smiles a few drops of sunshine in a grey world.

The agency did nothing so vulgar as advertise, of course, or put out signs on their doors. They were strictly by referral. Past patrons giving letters of recommendation to those in need. Whispers at the Pump Room or the Theatre Royal to a friend who might need a tiny push in the right direction. Bath was filled with those seeking their perfect partner. It was as if being amid illness and uncertainty made people long for more from life.

Yes, it was fine work, and Eleanor enjoyed it. She'd long known that she herself would never marry. She had to look after Mary, be like a mother to her and make sure their family was safe. That was her task. Having work she enjoyed was a great comfort. But sometimes there was a potential patron who was just a bit—extra.

She made sure her expression remained serene, politely interested, *not* giggling and turned back to Mr Higgleston-Worth. He had been sent to them by Lord Kembleton, a gentleman the agency matched with a very pretty young widow several months ago, one of their first successes. So of course they wanted to help any friend of Lord and Lady Kembleton, though it was hard to imagine Mr Higgleston-Worth knowing such an amiable pair. Lord Kembleton was portly, amiable and quick to laugh. His new wife was sweet and funny.

Mr H-W was none of those things. He minced and chattered and demanded, constantly smoothing the few strands of his hair still clinging to his scalp and oiled flat, the copious gold buttons on his red and blue plaid waistcoat threatening to burst with every word. He purported to having retired from the Army as a wealthy man, but Eleanor had some trouble picturing him in a warrior light.

An image suddenly flashed into her mind, quite unbidden. Fred Canning in his fine red coat, as she last saw him, his golden hair shining in the faint glow of the summerhouse. The warm press of his kiss to her hand, the way he smiled at her. How often she'd thought of him in the years since then! *Too* often. As she went over the agency ledgers, or paid tradesmens' bills, thoughts of him would pop randomly into her head. His laugh, his lemon and sunshine scent and the touch of his hand on hers. The fleeting joy of his kiss on her hand. The deep, warm chocolate sound of his voice as he read poetry to her in their secret summerhouse place. It was maddening.

She'd heard wisps of information about him over the years, of course, when they still lived at the vicarage. The whole neighbourhood was shocked to hear of his wounding at Waterloo. They'd hoped he might come back to Moulton Magna when his mother died, but he did not. She did not see him again.

After Eleanor left for Bath, Fred's father and then his older brother died in quick, tragic succession and everyone knew he *must* return then. He was the Earl now! And Eleanor heard via letters from old friends in the neighbourhood the most shocking thing of all. Fred had become a notorious rake in his years in the Army. She knew then he had only and ever considered her a friend. She had not believed such rumours at first, not of the man who had been her friend. She'd clung to the memory of what they once had, until she realised from reading tales of battles how such things could change a person. She'd been forced to think it must be true, to put Fred out of her mind. She'd been so silly to ever think there could be anything between them besides friendship, neighbours!

Yet still she grieved for the man she thought she knew.

'Two thousand pounds a year! Surely I deserve the very best,' Mr Higgleston-Worth cried emphatically, pulling Eleanor back from her memories.

She blinked hard and focused on Mr H-W. It was not at all like her to be distracted when she was meant to be working. Patrons deserved all her attention, even ones as ridiculous as Mr H-W.

'Indeed, Mr Higgleston-Worth,' she said soothingly and glanced down at the papers on her desk.

Everything they asked potential patrons about their family—places of residence, age and appearance, income, wishes and hopes in a spouse—was asked about most delicately, of course. The ladies always desired a secure home, a guaranteed jointure for their future and someone kind. The gentlemen desired someone pretty and of sweet nature, adept at running a household. Mr Higgleston-Worth's list of wishes was perhaps a bit more, er, elaborate.

'A lady with a fine dowry. Good teeth. Shiny hair.

Preferably blonde, but a very light brown would be acceptable. No novel readers, they are too frivolous. A fashionable dresser, but not extravagant. Small feet. Not a loud laugher.'

Eleanor studied him again. Two thousand a year was nothing to sneeze at. Some of their patrons lived on far less and still found romance. But it was not the amount of grandiose riches a man like Mr H-W would really need to attract 'the best'. This was a challenge indeed.

Luckily, this was just a first meeting. No contracts had been agreed upon yet.

'I have much to offer,' Mr Higgleston-Worth said again, tapping at those shining buttons. 'And I would thus insist on the finest qualities in a lady. I must be wed by the end of the year.'

Eleanor considered this. It was late summer now. Not much time at all, especially for such a vast undertaking. Usually the arrangements for the agency's months were most careful and deliberate. Several interviews, references, things of that nature. It was a most personal business. But a business, nonetheless. Their reputation rested on making harmonious, durable matches.

'Thank you, Mr Higgleston-Worth,' she said. 'We shall be in contact very soon.'

Mr H-W spluttered. 'What do you mean, be in contact? I expected a match *now*!' He waved a pudgy, beringed hand at the rows of file cabinets lining the blue-papered wall behind the desk. 'Find one in there! I have two thousand a year.'

Eleanor heard Mary gasp. She feared her sister would burst into laughter, which in turn would make her laugh.

'Our process is very careful, Mr Higgleston-Worth. I am sure you must appreciate that as an organised military gentleman. We want all our patrons to have every success on this vital endeavour and that requires the closest consideration.'

She rang the bell that sat before her, three times—an urgent summons. Daisy, their maid, appeared at once. 'Daisy shall see you out and I assure you, we will write as soon as possible.'

Daisy, very well-trained in her job and practised in the ways of the agency, ushered a spluttering Mr Higgleston-Worth out. The door slid shut behind him to a merciful silence.

Until Mary burst into peals of laughter and Eleanor couldn't help but join her. Miss Muffins barked and twirled.

'Oh, heavens!' Mary gasped, wiping at her eyes, her upswept blonde curls trembling. 'I don't think we have seen quite such a specimen since—since…'

'Perhaps Mr Morris? That man who came here at Christmas, who claimed to be a widower of forty…'

'And was seventy if he was a day. But at least he had better taste in waistcoats.'

'Yes. And we did find a wife for him, remember? Lady Henderson. She was a most sensible and forthright lady, who would not put up with any nonsense. And we were handsomely rewarded. Surely, with two thousand a year, Mr Higgleston-Worth could equal that? With a lady of strong will?'

Eleanor frowned as she studied their precious file cabinets, going through those papers in her mind. There

were a few ladies who had lingered there a bit longer
than she would like, who were a challenge to match for
one reason or another. Perhaps one of them might suit
Mr H-W? Did they have a blind lady, mayhap?

'Mrs Miller? Or perhaps Lady Hayes? Or her companion! She was a pretty young lady, if terribly shy.
Though who could blame her with Lady Hayes as her
employer,' Eleanor murmured.

'Hmm, yes! Miss—Perkins, was it? I would love to
see her escape such employment.' Mary rose in a flurry
of pale blue striped skirts and hurried to open one of the
upper drawers, sorting through the array of carefully
curated files. 'Oh, there must be someone in here...'

Eleanor drifted towards the window, Miss Muffins
at her heels. She stretched her aching shoulders after a
long morning of interviews.

She glimpsed a man striding across the square between Kingston Buildings and the Abbey, taller than
most in the crowds around him, and supremely eye-
catching, even in a plain, dark blue greatcoat. His
wide-brimmed hat concealed most of his face, except
a square, adorably dimpled jaw and surprisingly full,
sensual lips. He was slim-hipped, broad-shouldered
and moved with an easy, loose, loping grace. He made
Eleanor think of a most extraordinary acrobat they had
recently seen with a travelling circus and she tracked
his progress with fascination, much like all the ladies
he passed.

'I shall go fetch some buns from Sally Lunn's for
our tea, Mary,' she said, suddenly feeling restless, and
took her dark green pelisse and plain straw bonnet from

their hooks. She glanced in the small looking glass to make sure her bonnet ribbons were straight, her dark curls still tidy in their plain coil. She would never be as pretty as doll-like, golden Mary, or tall, Greek goddess Harry, but she could be presentable enough. Not that she had such hopes for herself any longer. She had given that up long ago and now hoped only to help others find their romantic dreams. It had to be enough.

And she wasn't going out just for another look at the man in the wide-brimmed hat. She was *not*.

'Hmm,' Mary answered, buried in a stack of files. Once Mary became determined to find a challenging match, there was no stopping her. She looked delicate and sweet, but she was relentless. 'And some strawberry jam? I think it was all gone at breakfast.'

'Of course. I'll post these letters, as well.' As she gathered up the missives, Miss Muffins peeked from beneath the desk where she had retreated again with a hopeful tail-wag. She had been a rescue pup, found by Eleanor and Harry cowering half-starved under a bridge. She was usually an angel of manners, but she *did* love a good run. And a fine Sally Lunn's bun. 'Very well, Miss Muffins. You may come, too.'

She found Miss Muffins' lead and the two of them made their way down the stairs, past the elegant leaf-green and gold drawing room where patrons sometimes waited and took tea and out through the black-painted front door. It was a typical Bath day. Grey-skied, threatening rain, clouds scudding past overhead. Eleanor blinked at the sudden grey glare after the house, spots in front of her eyes, but Miss Muffins was in a great hurry. She ran to the end of the lead and yanked hard, catching Eleanor off-guard.

'Here, let me help you, madame,' a voice said. A most familiar voice. The voice that had so long haunted her daydreams. Surely this could not be real?

Eleanor blinked up and saw a dark shadow—the man she'd glimpsed from the window earlier. How could Fred's voice come from that gentleman? Had she conjured it from her wistful earlier, her memories? She felt so very slow and silly for a moment. As if she waded through molasses, through dreams, caught between *now* and *then*. Even Miss Muffins was silent with confusion and wonder.

He knelt beside her, his gloved hands reaching for the scattered letters. He even *felt* handsome, the sort of man a woman just wanted to stare and stare at and get lost in. There was such a quiet confidence about him. She dared to peek up at him, hoping it might actually be Fred even as she feared to see him again. Feared for him to see what she had become, a plain, quiet little spinster.

That hat, unfashionably wide-brimmed, hid most of his face as he looked down at his task, but she was sure it *was* Fred. That dimple, incongruously adorable above the hard, sharp line of his chiselled jaw. Those lips, even though they were bracketed with harsh new lines, were surely the same that had once kissed her hand so warmly, so lingeringly.

'Fred,' she whispered.

He suddenly went very still. Frozen like one of the carvings on the Abbey that rose above them. For one long, endless, taut moment she thought he might flee from her. He seemed quite as startled as she, but not in a good surprise way. Not in a *here is my old dear friend* way. In a *must flee...trapped* way.

Had she done something, said something wrong? She felt suddenly bereft, cold even in that warm day. Yet how could that be? They hadn't met in years. But now, so close to him again, she felt he'd only been away for a moment. That no time had passed between them at all.

He did not seem to feel the same. He was so very still, his head bent down. Slowly, ever so slowly, he turned to face her and her breath became trapped in her lungs. Those eyes, Fred's sky-blue eyes, glittered from the shadows under his hat. Every spark of that old humour, that old light-heartedness, had vanished from their depths. Even when she had tried to forget Fred, she'd sometimes dared to imagine how it might be to see him again. This did not seem like the man of her imaginings at all. He seemed a stranger.

'Eleanor,' he said at last, the word toneless. Distant. He stood and held out her letters and she scrambled to her feet. 'It's been quite some time.'

'Indeed. Many years. Yes,' she stammered, trying not to recall how she remembered every one of those years, every month. She hated how breathless and squeaking her voice sounded, when she wanted to be sophisticated, breezy, careless. Not like she longed to jump up and embrace him, hold him close. 'I—we heard you left the Army. After Waterloo. After—well, I heard you were wounded and then...' And then he raced and wenched through London, according to the gossip. Moved into a world so far from her own.

He still seemed so wary. 'Yes, I did leave the Army after Waterloo. I've been visiting my stepmother here in Bath.' He paused, glancing away as if he sought an escape. 'I was sorry to hear about your father. He was a good man.'

'Thank you. Yes, indeed he was.' Even though he ended her dreams of school and an independent life, needed her so very much to keep his house and nurse him. She'd loved him and thinking of him made her shiver. She started to tell him that she, too, was sorry for the loss of his parents and brother. But he seemed to silence any words like that. Didn't want to hear them.

'And this is where you have lived since his death? In Bath?' he asked quietly.

'Yes. My father's curate was granted the living and Mary and I had to leave…' She did not mention that the curate, Mr Neville, had made noises about wanting to marry her and make her the vicarage's permanent housekeeper, but she could not do that. 'Our friend Lady Briggs offered us a home here.'

'And what do you do here? Do you like it in Bath?'

'Oh, yes, it's a lovely place to live and I do…' She gestured helplessly, not knowing how to explain her strange occupation. She had given up hopes for a loving marriage for herself a long time ago, as long ago as the last time she saw Fred. She had to take care of Mary, be the head of their little family. Now she just wanted to help others who might be as lonely as she had once been. As she still was so often. He brought old dreams back too sharply, too painfully. 'I do things.'

A smile finally quirked at the corner of his lips. 'Things?'

Miss Muffins whined a bit, gazing adoringly up at Fred. Just like all the ladies he'd walked past.

Fred knelt down to pat her head, sending her into tail-wagging ecstasies. 'She's a pretty pup,' he said, his voice filled with an easy gentleness that reminded her of the old Fred. Not the distant new stranger. 'I only knew hunting hounds growing up, but my stepmother has a pug. I thought it a silly little, squishy thing at first, but…' He rubbed Miss Muffins' head, his smile widening. 'They are very good company. They ask no questions, have no expectations.'

Eleanor wondered with a pang if that was a hint. If he thought she had 'expectations'.

'Indeed, they are very dear. Mary and I quite dote on Miss Muffins. She…'

A sudden gust of wind caught at Fred's hat and sent it sailing from his head, barely caught in his fist before it escaped entirely. Eleanor couldn't quite catch her own shocked gasp before it left her lips. Half of Fred's face, once so unworldly and handsome, was scarred, puckered and pink. She felt appalled that he could have felt any pain, longed to make it all better somehow, some way.

'Oh, Fred…' she whispered.

'The war,' he snapped shortly and thrust the letters into her hand.

She reached for his face, the dear face she'd dreamed

of for so long, her heart aching for what he must have suffered. For the fact that she hadn't been there for him. But he flinched and her hand dropped away. 'Is it—painful?' she whispered.

His scowl faded and he seemed to soften a bit, swaying towards her. 'Not any longer. I barely think of it.'

Yet he hid it behind his hat, behind his fast, brusque movements. Beyond his eyes, that no longer sparkled with laughter.

Eleanor swallowed hard and glanced away. 'Lady Fleetwood lives here now?' she asked, reaching for any change of topic. She didn't want him to go yet. Didn't want to lose him again quite so soon. 'We only met her a few times before we left the neighbourhood, but she seemed very kind.'

'Indeed, she is. She has been a good friend to me. She was ill for a time after my father died, but the waters seem to have done her much good. She looks forward to mixing more in Bath society now.'

'And you? Are you looking forward to social occasions?' To finding a wife, maybe? She hated the pang such a thought gave her. But perhaps that really was what brought him back after all this time. To marry, start a family, be the Earl he must be. 'We are not London but there is the theatre, the assemblies, the subscription concerts…'

His expression snapped closed again, a shutter going down between them. 'I have a great deal of business to see to before I return to Moulton Magna.'

'Yes. Of course,' she whispered, embarrassed as she recalled the gossip about the current bankrupt state of the estate, thanks to the late earl's secret debts. That would all be on Fred's shoulders now. No matter he looked so much harder, so much older. No wonder everything in her longed to reach for him, comfort him. The one thing she could not do.

As if he could read her thoughts, as if he, too, yearned for some of their old connection, he suddenly reached out and softly, warmly, achingly touched her hand. 'It is so nice to see you again, Ella. You look— you look very well indeed.'

Ella. His old name for her. She smiled back and slid her hand away before she could seize him right there in the middle of the street, wrap her arms around him and never let him go.

'It must be the waters,' she made herself say with a light laugh. 'They say they are miracle workers! Do bring Lady Fleetwood to call on us soon. We should so much like to see her again. She was very kind when we had to leave the vicarage so quickly.'

'I shall. She would like to see you again, too.' Those terrible shutters came down again, hiding his thoughts and feelings from her. He bowed so politely, so correctly. 'Good day.'

She curtsied in return. 'Good day.'

She forced herself to turn away, to not look back even though everything in her longed to do just that. It was the most difficult thing she'd ever done, turning her back on him and walking away as if nothing had changed, nothing was wrong. That her heart did not ache. Even Miss Muffins dragged at her lead, reluctant to leave him.

'Did you fetch the buns for tea already?' Mary called as Eleanor stood frozen in the corridor, Miss Muffins watching her in puzzlement that they hadn't finished the promised walk. That they left her new friend behind. 'You must have run like Atalanta!'

Eleanor glanced down at the letters still in her hand and laughed wryly to realise she had entirely forgotten any errands at all. Forgotten everything about Fred and the golden glow of the past. 'Oh, Mary dearest. You will never guess who has come to Bath…'

Chapter Three

'Marriage would do you such good, Fred,' Penelope, his stepmama—though it still felt wrong to call her that, as she was only ten years his senior and looked ten years his junior—said with a wistful sigh. Pen filled a rose-painted teacup and handed it to him over the table, giving him that worried little smile he'd come to dread.

'It would *not*, believe me Pen,' he said. He took a sip of the tea and wished it contained something a wee bit stronger. It might help him get through this perpetual-seeming conversation. 'I do like my life as it is. Quiet and peaceful at last. And who would have me, as I am now?' He gestured towards his scars, his twisted left hand. 'No amount of visits to the baths can fix this you know.'

Penelope laughed, her brown eyes glowing. Fred's gruff old father really had been the most fortunate and undeserving of men to win her hand. She was so pretty. Petite and dark-haired, so kind and laughing. She had been a dear friend to him when he came home, wounded and wild as a bear. She deserved much better than what she had, a few years with a grumpy, debt-ridden man in a crumbling estate and now this tiny house in Sunderland Street on a small jointure. He longed to give her more. To repay some of the friendship she'd shown him when he so needed it. For nursing him when he returned home so damaged and angry, withdrawing from society and fed up with all people in general.

Fed up with all people—except Eleanor St Aubin. He could scarcely believe his vision when she appeared so suddenly before him again! Ella, whose memory had so long sustained him on so many endless, pain-filled dark nights. Her smile, the music of her laughter, the wild curl of her autumn-brown hair, the dreamy look in her eyes when she read to him from *The Fairy Queen* and talked of adventures.

He'd thought never to see her again, when he heard through Penelope's letters that Eleanor's father had died and she and her sister left the neighbourhood. The idea of her being lost for ever had pained him almost more than the scars on his cheek. To never hear her dreams again, never watch her dashing through the sunlight, always just beyond his reach. Her sweetness and innocence, things he'd thought vanished in the mud and blood of war. He'd had a wild notion to find her again once he returned to Moulton Magna and took up the title, then cold reality set in, as it always did now. He couldn't bear for her to see him this way, the way he had become. Couldn't bear to see revulsion and embarrassment in her eyes, as he saw in so many.

Then—there she was. In an instant, on that street here in Bath, like a dream bursting into bright reality.

It had been another long, dark-shadowed night, filled with nightmare visions of explosions, fire, death and pain. Friends blown to bits, the ground caving beneath him. At first, he thought he was still dreaming when he saw her, tempting visions of hope and light born of sheer exhaustion.

Once, she'd been his friend. His Fairy Queen. His haven of laughter and easy acceptance of life in a place where he never felt he belonged. A home that was empty and silent. He'd always wanted to be truly worthy of her approval, worthy of her goodness, even though he'd known that was impossible. Especially once he went to London and discovered the temptations there...

It was now even more impossible. As far away as the moon. If only he'd been given warning that she was near, so he could hide! So she wouldn't see him that way, so different from what he once was.

Yet, selfishly, he was glad he'd met with her. Seen her, touched her hand, smelled her floral summertime perfume. Known she was real again, that she truly was standing in front of him.

Like him, she was older than in his golden memories. The girl at Moulton Magna was a woman now. A beautiful woman, delicate and slender, with shining dark hair and sweet, sad eyes. What happened to her since last they met? The loss of her father and home, surely, but what he saw in those eyes was more than that. It was as if she was older than her years now, as he was, as if she had seen much. He longed to know everything, to ask her every detail of every lost minute. Just to hear her voice, sit in the peace and light that always seemed to surround her.

But he couldn't ask her to stay with *him* and what he was now. A scarred man who had done terrible things in the name of battle. A man with a house and estate falling down around him that was his responsibility to save now.

The silence in the drawing room had grown long and he was suddenly jolted by the awareness that Penelope watched him carefully, waiting for him to speak, to do *something*. She was always patient, always watchful, just like Ella.

And she saw too much.

He smiled at her and held his cup out for more tea, even if there was no whisky to go with it. 'Sorry, Pen. I'm no good at being an earl out in society yet.'

She refilled his cup and added more salmon sandwiches to his plate before slipping one of them to her puppy. She was quite sure Fred didn't eat enough, didn't look after himself and perhaps she was right. There were so many other things to do now, so much to worry him.

'Just one more reason you need a wife,' Penelope said. 'Someone to run your household properly, help you with your work, accept invitations. You cannot do it alone. And then there is—well, there is the money...'

Fred grimaced, remembering how extravagant Moulton Magna seemed in his childhood—always parties and hunts and new art and jewels around his mother's neck. All paid for with imaginary coin, it seemed. But the house and the family had been the centre of the neighbourhood, relied on by so many people.

'I cannot say you are entirely wrong, Pen. But there is a distant cousin somewhere, if I can't come up to scratch.' Not that the cousin wanted the blasted title any more than Fred did.

Penelope shook her head. 'He's not at all suited to the title.'

Fred gave a harsh bark of laughter. 'And I am?'

'You give yourself far too little credit. You are intelligent and resourceful. You care about the people on the estate. They need you!'

'You are not wrong about that,' he admitted, feeling supremely grumpy about it all. This was never meant to be his job. He hadn't been trained for it and now he was damaged in the bargain. The people of the estate deserved better. 'I do have duties now, as terrible as I may be at them. And a countess would be a useful thing. But as I said, Pen, who would have me? Looking like this, with no money, a shambles of a house...' He laughed, but there was shame there, too. Shame that he, who had been a fine soldier, couldn't solve this problem.

Penelope winced, as they both remembered that the once grand Moulton Magna, a showpiece of elegance and culture, had started to fall down around them. Leaking roofs, fading furniture, bare patches on the mouldy walls where paintings once hung.

'It would be a challenge to be mistress of Moulton Magna, that's true. I certainly found it to be so. But you would be a better husband than your father could

ever have been. You would be a true partner to the right
lady, a lady of taste and breeding. You used to be handsome as a god, Fred, and you are still a fine-looking
man! Three-quarters of perfection is still quite blasted
perfect, you know.'

He laughed in surprise. '*Blasted*, Pen?'

Her cheeks turned bright pink and she laughed, too.
'I am a widow, I'm allowed to curse sometimes. And
you *do* give yourself too little credit. You are young and
energetic and spirited now that you are regaining your
health. A hero of the battlefield! Moulton Magna is not
at its best right now, perhaps, yet it is an ancient estate
with much history and beautiful grounds and being a
countess is no small prize. Ladies of…'

'Ladies of fortune?' he said.

Penelope blushed again and turned away to feed
her dog another sandwich. 'I suppose she would have
to be, yes.'

'Taste, breeding *and* money. Where shall we have to
find such a paragon?' He thought again of Ella. Always
of Ella and her bursting, bright smile when she saw him
again. Her hand warm through her glove.

'Bath is full of ladies seeking marriage, you know.'

'Do you have any suggestions? Particular candidates
in mind?'

She fussed with the tea tray, rearranging the silver
pot and the cups. 'I do not have a certain lady in mind,
no. I am too solitary these days to know all the gossip,
I fear. But I do know someone who could help.'

Fred thought her determined expression, like an officer planning a campaign, was terrifying. Yet he sensed

there was no escape. What other solution could there be? Where could he turn? Other men married for advantage all the time, he knew that well, but he'd never thought to be one. 'Who might that be?'

She glanced up with a new, eager smile. 'I was talking to an old friend of my mother's last week, a Lady Hemston…'

Fred shook his head hard, horrified. 'I know her! I couldn't marry someone she would choose. Have you seen her army of nieces?'

Penelope laughed. She suddenly looked so young, as she had before her marriage. Young as Ella once had, as he had, before life turned all of them upside down. 'Oh, heavens, no! But one of those nieces was recently betrothed to a marquess. Everyone was quite sure she would never wed at all but she and her fiancé are utterly wild about each other! Lady Hemston told me, in the strictest of confidence so you must not breathe a word, that they had a bit of—assistance in the engagement endeavour.'

Fred was now even more worried. 'Assistance?'

'Yes. An agency of sorts, most discreet, with an excellent reputation. They are only to be found by referral, though I am sure word of their fine work has spread through Bath and beyond by now.'

'Agency?' That sounded ominous.

'Oh, Fred, do stop saying words in that way! It is an unusual organisation, yes, but we are in an unusual situation and we could use their help. *You* need their help.'

'Is this a brothel of some sort, Pen? Because I as-

sure you, despite my injuries, those things are quite,
er, in working order.'

'Frederick!' she cried. '*No*. This is a *marital* agency.
They help people find their perfect match. Their *respectable* match. When the usual channels of finding
a spouse do not quite work as they should.'

He laughed at the idea of someone marching around
Bath pairing people up. 'Matchmaking, is it?'

'Yes. They are quite good at it and as I said they are
very discreet. Discerning. We could at least consult
them. Ask their advice?'

'And have our family business known all over Bath
in a day.'

Penelope sighed in exasperation. 'Fred. Everyone already knows our business. But these ladies are hardly
strangers. They are known as the St Aubin and Briggs
Confidential Agency and two of them are the St Aubin
sisters. Daughters of our old vicar, perfectly respectable and commendable. Perhaps you remember them?'

'Eleanor St Aubin?' he whispered. The memory
of her eyes flashed through his mind, her smile, her
sombre dark green pelisse and plain bonnet. His Fairy
Queen. A matchmaker? 'She is the one who runs this—
agency?'

'Yes, Eleanor! Such a dear lady, they were so good to
me when I married your papa. I was sorry to see them
leave the neighbourhood so suddenly. And there is her
younger sister Miss Mary, along with Lady Briggs.
I saw the Misses St Aubin at the Pump Room a few
weeks ago, after I first arrived, but was not able to say
hello to them then. I have been thinking I should call

on them, now that my mourning is officially over. If they *could* be of assistance…'

Fred closed his eyes against a headache building inside of him like a vice at the thought of Ella of all people knowing *all* his business. Scanning the ladies of Bath to find him a wife. Ella thinking less of him than she probably already did. 'I should not like to put Miss St Aubin to such trouble. To presume on our acquaintance…'

Penelope gave a puzzled frown. 'But surely old friends would not mind! They would be happy to help. Everyone at Moulton Magna always spoke so highly of the St Aubin girls and Lady Briggs is such a leader of society here in Bath.'

'I saw Eleanor today, near the Abbey,' he blurted.

Her eyes widened. 'Did you? And she remembered you? Even better!'

'Pen…' he said. 'I don't want them to—that is…' He couldn't let an old friend assist him in such an embarrassing endeavour. Especially not one who had been his best friend once. Who he would wish could be more than that now.

She leaned forward and gently touched his wrist, just above his damaged hand. 'I say again, my dear Fred, you need a wife. If old friends, people who know you well, can be of assistance, I'm happy to ask them for their advice. Did you not like the St Aubins in some way, when you lived near them?'

Fred had another image of Eleanor running through a summer meadow, her curling hair flying behind her,

her laughter on the breeze. The sheer life and sweetness of her. 'Yes. I liked them very much.'

Penelope sat back, a speculative gleam coming into her eyes. 'Then let me call on them. I should do so anyway, as an old neighbour. I can see what their thoughts might be on our delicate subject.'

Fred pushed himself to his feet and strode to the window, feeling the surge of some of his old energy moving through his veins. As if just remembering Eleanor, talking of her, brought his old self back again. His old hopes and dreams.

'Very well,' he said at last and heard Penelope clap her hands in approval. At least he could make Pen happy for a while, and also have an excuse to see Ella again. To talk to her, see her smile, just for a little longer. 'We will call on them. But I do not want their help in finding a wife. Not at all.'

Chapter Four

'In short, Lady Briggs, Miss St Aubin—I fear if you do not help my poor, dear daughter, she will be quite lost! Entirely on the shelf. Alone in this cold and dreadful world. *Desolate* of all consolation!'

As Mrs Evans's voice climbed higher and higher, like a soprano straining mightily for a dramatic finale at the Theatre Royal, Eleanor stared hard at the notebook open in front of her and blinked. She feared if she looked at Harry she would giggle, which would then make Harry guffaw—Harry loved any opportunity to laugh—and then it would all be over. The Evans family would be lost as patrons, which would be too bad as Mr Evans had in recent years found rich seams of coal on his lands, and had a mercantile empire on top it all. Thanks heavens Mary wasn't there to giggle, too! She had gone to take Miss Muffins for a walk, luckily.

If the agency could help Miss Evans out of 'lonely desolation,' the greengrocers and the butchers would have their bills paid for some time to come and that could only be most desirable.

As Mrs Evans dabbed at her eyes with a lacy handkerchief and went on with her laments, Eleanor discreetly studied Miss Evans, and thought the girl did have much potential. She had a lovely, peachy complexion and large hazel eyes, honey-coloured hair peeking from beneath her flower-bedecked bonnet.

She'd said only about three words since they arrived, but who could blame her? No one could get a single syllable out with Mrs Evans there. But once Miss Evans learned to make the very most of herself, to speak up, and with such a nice dowry in the offering, she should have no worries in the marriage mart.

The challenge would be getting her away from her mother and finding out what *she* wanted. That would help her find the *right* sort of gentleman. Someone to make her happy, not just some fortune hunter.

Eleanor sighed. A challenge indeed, but they'd seen far worse at the agency.

'Will need a better dancing master, of course!' Mrs Evans was saying. 'And a new coiffure. Who does the Duchess of Raine's hair? We saw her at the opera last week, so charming. That hairdresser might do. If my girl would only smile more! Engage the young men with a bit of bright chatter, a smile or two. I've told her and told her…'

Miss Evans stared hard out of the window, her lips pinched together in way that would never 'engage the young men', but Eleanor couldn't blame her.

'I think Miss Evans should have no trouble at all in finding a suitable, indeed a very happy, match,' Harry said soothingly. She was so good at that, at appearing always confident and assuring no matter who the patron might be. Her elegant morning gown of purple striped silk and fine pearl earrings didn't hurt. If she could achieve such things, she could help anyone else do it, too!

Mrs, Evans frowned doubtfully. 'Are you certain, Lady Briggs?'

'Of course. A lovely young lady from such a good family? No trouble at all. It would have to be just the *right* sort of person, of course. One must be so careful.' Harry turned a page in her own notebook. 'Tell me, Miss Evans—what do you envisage in your future husband?'

Miss Evans glanced uncertainly at her mother.

'A vicar, perhaps?' Eleanor said, thinking of her own good-natured papa. 'Or a man with a small country estate, well known to all his neighbours.' A quiet young lady might well enjoy a familiar environment with a kindly squire.

'Oh, no! Our daughter can surely aim higher than that,' Mrs Evans cried.

It was rather a relief when they departed half an hour later, all their information entered in the agency books to be reviewed later. As their footsteps faded down the stairs and Daisy shut the door behind them, Harry collapsed onto the settee with a deep sigh and kicked up her purple satin slippers.

'Goodness me,' she said. 'I always longed for a mama, growing up with only my father after my poor mother died birthing me, but patrons such as Mrs Evans make me wonder if I was quite wrong in those dreams of motherly love and support.'

Eleanor laughed ruefully and flipped through her pages of new notes. 'Mary and I were certainly fortunate in our darling mother and I miss her vastly. But I can't help but think she might have been quite as anxious about the marriage mart as Mrs Evans, with two daughters to secure. Not that she would have gone about it this way...'

'Worrying is not really something Miss Evans needs to think about, with a bit of guidance. Though she must be extra wary of men seeking only fortune. Her dowry is truly a stupendous one. Really, all the Evans need to do is march her around the Pump Room after having our dear Master of Ceremonies spread a quiet word or two. And finding a better modiste, of course. That pelisse! But I suspect that was Mrs Evans' doing.' She laid back against the cushions and stared up at the ceiling as if envisaging a line of eligible young men. 'I'm glad they brought her here, though. No one deserves such a fate as being married for one's fortune. Especially not a girl who seems as shy as Miss Evans.'

A shadow seemed to drift over Harry's beautiful face, perhaps memories of her own unhappy marriage to a man much older than herself and Eleanor started to go to her. But then Harry just laughed and turned away, hiding her thoughts again.

'Perhaps we could winkle her away from her mother under the guise of a dance lesson or two,' Eleanor suggested. She took out another ledger—the account of all the people they employed when assistance was needed. Dance masters, music teachers, etiquette experts and modistes. One of them could surely be brought to the office and teach Miss Evans, along with some young men, the latest steps.

'What about that sweet Mr Monroe we met last week? Or Lord Perry? He is a shy young man himself. He'd be sure to be patient and kind with a lady like Miss Evans. His estate is nothing compared to Mr Evans, of course, but his house is very pretty indeed and in a quiet part of the country. And he has a respectable income and no wastrel habits.'

'Oh, what a good thought, Eleanor dear! Lord Perry is a darling boy. It's too bad about the shyness. It would be so nice to see him and Miss Evans ride off together to private country bliss.'

Eleanor laughed. It was her very favourite part of their work, when a thought, a fragment of an instinct, could lead to a happy lifetime for two people.

She only wondered, hoped…

She shook her head hard. Even beginning to wish for such a spark for herself was silly and futile. Her future had been decided long ago, when she was deemed the sensible one, the one who would look after her family. She had to take the bits of happiness from the people she worked for and warm herself in the glow of their happiness.

It had been enough, more than she could have expected in the days of her vicarage drudgery, that she might live in a fine town and meet so many interesting people. Help them in some way. She loved her work. The satisfaction of it and the life she and Mary and Harry had built there.

What was wrong with her today? She'd been terribly distracted! She needed to focus on the challenge at hand, yet her gaze kept drifting out through the window to the cathedral across the way and the crowds passing below. Her thoughts very far away from their ledgers and patrons.

It was the return of Fred. She was sure of it. Seeing him again after so very long. How changed he was! And yet his eyes, those wonderful sky-blue eyes, were almost the same. Her Redcrosse Knight.

'Do you think, Eleanor?' Harry asked.

Eleanor blinked, jerked back from her sky-floating daydreams into the daily routine of their office. 'I'm sorry, Harry, I was wool-gathering.'

Harry tilted her head, a puzzled little frown on her lips. 'I was just saying perhaps we could take Miss Evans to the theatre. Introduce her to Lord Perry there. Without Mrs Evans.'

'A fine idea. I hear they are doing *School for Scandal* next week,' Eleanor said vaguely, her gaze drifting back to the window.

'Are you quite sure you're well today? It isn't like you to be distracted and you do look a little pale. Should I have Daisy bring up a bottle of claret with the tea tray? The doctors do say it strengthens the blood.'

Eleanor smiled at her, hoping it looked reassuring. 'I wouldn't say no to a wee drop. I am just a bit tired. I didn't sleep well last night. I don't mean to be distracted with our patrons.'

'Of course you aren't! You never could be. You're always the soul of kindness and understanding. They love you. You are the backbone to this whole enterprise.' Harry lifted Miss Muffins onto the settee with her, still watching Eleanor carefully. 'Is there some reason you've been sleepless lately, my dear?'

Eleanor stared down at the desk, fiddling with the papers to keep from looking right at Harry. Her friend had always been so perceptive. It was a great strength in business but a nuisance when one had a secret. 'I just—well, I saw an old friend again, that's all. Someone I haven't met with since we lived at the vicarage. It's brought back such memories.'

'Ahh...' Harry nodded sagely. 'A man from your past.'

Eleanor laughed uncertainly, shuffling more papers. She only served to put them in disarray. 'Yes, he was one of the sons of our neighbour. And now he is an earl. He went into the Army and was wounded at Waterloo. It has—he has changed greatly. As he would have done, of course. But the change seemed like it wasn't just— not just physical.' Surely dreadful things had happened to him in battle. Things she ached to consider.

Harry's smile turned soft, sympathetic. 'You had feelings for this earl?'

Eleanor shook her head. 'Maybe once. Just a schoolgirl thing. He was so very handsome. Such fun. And he treated me like a person and not just a silly girl. We read together, *The Fairy Queen*, explored the estate and talked. Talked about so very many things.'

'And what was it like to see him again?'

Astounding. Wonderful. Terrible. 'Unnerving, I would say.'

Harry leaned forward, her expression solemn and

intent. 'Eleanor. You are so very good at our work. So caring with the patrons and careful of their happiness. Careful of everyone.'

'I do try, Harry. How else are we to pay for our soup and wine?'

'No, it's more than that. Mary and I like the agency, of course. We like the people and the romance of it all. But for you, I think it runs deeper. As if you wish you could make all the world happy.'

And that was impossible. She couldn't even make Fred happy, not now. 'It's the vicar's daughter in me, I suppose. I do want everyone to be comfortable and content.'

'And our files are filled with grateful letters attesting to your success! But what about *you*?'

'Me?'

'Wouldn't you like a match for *you*?'

Eleanor was shocked. 'I—I hadn't thought of such a thing. No. No, I am happy with the spinster life. Aren't you?' Once she'd been happy with such a life or at least resigned to it. She'd never met a man who made her feel as Fred once did and a marriage of convenience held no attraction for her. She had to look after Mary, run their business. But now—now maybe that life didn't seem quite so content as it once did.

'Certainly I am. Our work. The independence of it and not answering to anyone else at all. It's my dream come true after that nightmare with old Briggs. I have no desire to wed again.'

'Yet you think I would?'

'It would be different for you.'

'How so?'

Harry smiled sadly. 'I was just a girl when I married. I knew nothing of the world and had no choice in the matter. My parents arranged it all. They needed the money so much. You and I—we know how to make suitable matches, happy matches. It's our work, after all. We can see what makes two people compatible. What sort of lives they wish to lead together.'

'Our instincts do seem correct more often than not,' Eleanor said, thinking of the careful formulas they applied to their matches and the musing over personalities, wishes and wants. Yet none of that explained her feelings for Fred—the past, present and dreams all mixed up in a jumble.

'Perhaps we should try our instincts on you! I did hate being married but you would not, I'm sure. Not with the right person. You should have a comfortable home, companionship and fun.'

Once, she'd hoped for all those same things. She'd learned to put them out of her mind, never worried about them, until now. Until Fred.

'It's true I might not *mind* being married,' Eleanor admitted. 'Once upon a time. I would like a family. But never, ever with the wrong person. That would be terrible, to be trapped in that way.'

Harry nodded. She knew that all too well, after her own dismal marriage. 'What about this old friend of yours, then? Your expression just now when you mentioned him—such a soft little smile! And you'd make a wonderful countess.'

Eleanor laughed, thinking of the vast halls of Moulton

Magna, the grand gardens, the reception rooms fit to receive royalty—and how they were all starting to crumble. 'I would be a dreadful countess. I'm not nearly grand enough.' She gave a slow, dignified wave, a distant nod, making them both giggle.

'Is this friend of yours so very *grand*, then?'

'No. Not very.' She remembered Fred chasing her across the country meadows, his tawny hair tousled. Carefree and simple. Not that her feelings for him had ever been *simple*.

'Well, then…'

'It can never be, Harry, that's all.' Fred had vast responsibilities now and he needed money to fulfil them. A lady of fortune and breeding. 'His estates are in terrible shape now. His father turned out to be a secret gambler. He needs a fortune.' A sudden, startling thought struck her—maybe that was why he was in Bath. To find an heiress.

'Oh, well,' Harry said. 'He is not the only fish in Bath, Eleanor dear.'

But he was the only *fish* she might have wanted and he was beyond her. Like the moon and stars. 'I am content as I am. Now, what about Mr Ashington who came to see us last week? I have one or two ideas for him…'

There was a flurry of footsteps on the staircase, a quick knock on the office door. Daisy peeked inside, her eyes wide.

'I beg your pardon, Lady B, Miss St Aubin, but there's a possible patron at the door,' she whispered.

Eleanor frowned as she reached for their appointment book. 'I thought we were quite finished for the day.'

'She says she didn't write ahead, but she's an old friend who begs your assistance most urgently.' Her voice lowered even more, to an awed murmur. 'It's a *countess*.'

Harry sat up straight, making Miss Muffins bark. Their clients were usually well-off gentry, even knights and a baronet or two, but not often titled. 'A countess?'

'The Dowager Countess of Fleetwood.' Daisy held out an engraved card.

'Lady Fleetwood?' Eleanor gasped, remembering the old Earl's beautiful wife. Fred's *stepmother*.

'You know her?' Harry asked.

'She was married to the father of that man I told you about. The Earl.'

Harry's brow arched. 'Indeed? Well, Daisy, do show her in at once. And fetch some tea and some of those nice lemon cakes.'

Eleanor quickly smoothed her hair, hoping the curls weren't escaping their tight pins again, and smoothed her dark green skirt. Her heart was pounding as if she'd run a mile, to find her old life suddenly dropping into the new one.

Penelope, Lady Fleetwood, came into the room and Eleanor felt herself grow calmer. She'd only met the new Lady Fleetwood a few times before they left the vicarage but she had always been a kind, warm and welcoming presence. Even a bit shy despite her beauty and high position. Eleanor feared her years as Countess might have changed her, yet it seemed not. She was still very lovely, tall and willow-slim with shining, almost black hair just touched at the temples with a hint of silver. Her wide eyes almost matched the violet-blue of her pelisse and bonnet as she gazed around in obvious curiosity at their premises.

Eleanor remembered when Miss Penelope Preston, the widowed Mrs Elton, married the Earl. The whole neighbourhood was agog with the gossip of it. A man of his age with grown sons! And she so young, with such a small fortune. Yet the new Countess soon showed herself to be a treasure to the neighbourhood. Refurbishing the fusty old house and opening the gardens for teas and fetes. She was charitable, kind and always ready with a quick smile and polite word or act of assistance. The gossip soon became how did such a grumpy old man find such a fine wife?

After Eleanor and Mary moved away and the Earl died, everyone was shocked that he had left such vast debts and worried what might become of the dear Countess, still so young with no children of her own. She vanished from Moulton Magna, and Eleanor had heard she might be in Bath, seeking the waters, but she hadn't seen Penelope until now. Here, at their very own agency!

What could she be doing there? Perhaps she sought a wife for Fred? The thought made Eleanor long to sink through the floor and vanish.

But she couldn't. She had a business to run. She stood up with a smile and an outstretched hand. 'Lady Fleetwood. How very good to see you again.'

Penelope's smile widened with unfeigned happiness and she squeezed Eleanor's hand. 'And I am quite overjoyed to see *you*, Miss St Aubin. The church at

All Saints was never the same after your family left! I'm happy you're looking so well and what a charming premises for your work. You must be terribly busy.'

'We are indeed, yes.'

'So many people are in need of a little romance in their lives. I am glad you're here to help them.'

'We try our best.' Eleanor gestured to Harry, who watched them with curiosity. 'And this is my friend, Lady Briggs. I'm afraid Mary is out on an errand. She'll be sorry to have missed you.'

'So pleased to meet you, Lady Briggs. I hear such glorious word of your fashion. You must give me the name of your modiste now that I'm done with odious mourning. And I'm sorry to miss Mary, as well! She always livened up any gathering.'

Eleanor had to laugh. It was true that a large part of their success was due to Mary. Eleanor's sister was a born matchmaker and people person. She'd been engaged to two boys at once at the age of ten. She'd never lost the allure of her golden curls and wide, caramel-brown eyes, her ready laugh and the way she paid such close attention to anyone she spoke to, as if they were the only person in all the world. She was excellent at finding just the right people for each other, no matter how eccentric, slotting them together like perfect puzzle pieces. Eleanor had started out as more shy, more uncertain, not as instinctive. But marriage needed a pragmatic touch as well and she could do that.

Harry was a great businesswoman, organised, efficient, brisk. Adept at moving through society. Eleanor could see that shrewd speculation in Harry's eyes now as she studied Lady Fleetwood.

'Do sit down, Lady Fleetwood,' Harry said, gesturing to the cosy gathering of velvet-cushioned armchairs near the window, reserved for favourite clients. Daisy brought in the best tea set, arranging the plates and cups on a low, marble-topped table. 'Will you take tea?'

'Oh, you are kind! I don't want to take up too much of your time, if you are expecting callers,' Lady Fleetwood said. 'It was quite rude of me not to write ahead.'

'Not at all. Our books are open for the rest of the afternoon,' Eleanor said. 'I should so much enjoy hearing more of how you have been faring, Lady Fleetwood.'

'Do call me Penelope, I beg you! We're old friends and I do need as many friends as I can find right now.' She arranged the folds of her dark blue satin pelisse and smiled as Harry offered a cake. She glanced out at the cathedral, glowing mellow gold in the afternoon light. 'What a splendid view you have. One does hear such good reports of Kingston Buildings. So comfortable and so conveniently located. Do you live here as well as have your offices?'

'Mary and I have rooms upstairs and yes, it is a very comfortable situation,' Eleanor said, pouring out the tea. 'Lady Briggs lives on the Royal Crescent itself.'

'How glorious!' Penelope sighed and her gaze turned wistful as she studied the people strolling down below. 'I do wish I could join you somewhere like this. Where there must always be so much to command your attention. I am at Sunderland Street. It's not bad at all, but so short and quiet.'

Eleanor and Harry exchanged a quick glance, remembering how the houses there, though built to impress, were rumoured to be damp. The Earl's lost fortune again.

'How can we be of assistance?' Harry asked gently and passed the plate of lemon cakes from Molland's.

Penelope smiled. 'Oh, now I am afraid you will think me a horribly interfering old mama! But I hope we *are* old enough friends that I can speak with you most freely.'

'You may certainly be assured of every discretion,' Eleanor said.

'Well, you see, I am here on behalf of Frederick. The new Lord Fleetwood, my stepson.'

It was just as Eleanor had feared. Fred was looking for a wife. And she would have to find a way to watch him marry. To pretend that she did not care. That she was happy for him. How could she do that? She took a deep breath and tried to maintain an even, serene expression. 'Did Fr—? That is, did Lord Fleetwood send you here?'

Penelope looked horrified. 'No, indeed! He would not like that at all. He insists he has no need to marry. But I know—and you know, too, I am sure—that he must. I worry about him so much since he returned from Waterloo. Physically he has healed, but in his mind…' She shook her head. 'He has always been so kind to me. So welcoming when I married his father and came to Moulton Magna as scared as a goose. He often wrote to me when he was away with the Army and we became as close as a—well, perhaps not a true mother and son, but definitely as a favourite auntie of sorts. He's such a kind man. So aware of his duty now, despite how it might all appear. Despite any old gossip.'

Eleanor knew Penelope was right. *That* was not really Fred, the drinking and carousing rumours. Not *her* Fred. Her Fred was laughing and fun and kind. Now he was scarred, seemingly both inside and out, hardened. But surely her old Fred was still hidden in their somewhere.

Penelope leaned forward. 'He needs someone to help him in his new life. A wife.'

Eleanor and Harry glanced at each other again. Eleanor could see in Harry's face they would have to take this case on. Even if it broke Eleanor's heart.

'I'm sure, Lady Fleetwood,' Harry said, 'that a man such as your stepson, titled, a military hero, with a fine estate…'

Penelope gently shook her head. 'Moulton Magna is, I'm afraid, quite in dire straits. My late husband, for all his fine points, was no manager of money and the estate is in trouble. It will take much assistance to bring it to its former glory. To be honest, my dears—it will need a wife of good fortune, as well as the upbringing and spirit to oversee it all. And to put up with Fred, as he is now. Rather like a bear with a hurt paw, he does like to growl so.'

'His scars, they pain him?' Eleanor choked out.

'Not pain any more, no. But in his mind—oh, my dear Eleanor. He seems so different inside now, as well, so angry and quiet and solitary.'

Eleanor pressed her hand to her lips, trying to hold

back the tears at the idea of Fred being so unhappy, so lost.

'Is he ever—violent, Lady Fleetwood?' Harry asked carefully.

'No!' Penelope and Eleanor both protested.

'No,' Penelope went on. 'Never—except that one time he found a shepherd beating his dog and intervened most—strenuously.' Miss Muffins whined. 'I am not sure what he really saw in the war. He refuses to speak of it. He just keeps it all pressed down deep inside and I'm sure that cannot be good for him. How can he ever move forward? Find the beauty in life again?' She gazed down at the gloves in her lap, her eyes shining as if she, too, wanted to cry for him.

Eleanor's heart ached so much at the thought of Fred caught in such misery. Not her laughing, light-hearted friend. 'And you think he needs a wife?'

'Of course he does. One with a fortune, of course. Such an ancient estate, with so many people relying on it. It cannot be allowed to fall into ruin,' Penelope said firmly. 'But it's not just a wife for the estate dear Fred needs. He needs a friend, too. He would be furious to hear me say it, but he needs someone to care for him. Be kind with him. Patient. Loving and fun. As well as rich!' She laughed wryly. 'I don't ask for much, do I? It seems impossible.'

Eleanor and Harry laughed with her. They heard such lists regularly. Ones even longer and more specific and outlandish—hair colour, eye colour, the way someone pronounced 'supposedly'. Yet few from such a point of sweet, hopeful caring.

'We only take on clients of the best character here at the agency, Penelope, I promise you,' Eleanor said, 'while also keeping in mind the practicalities needed in marriage. I agree, Fred has endured so much and has a great task ahead of him still. He deserves the finest of partners. The—the best wife.' Her voice grew hoarse on that last word and she bit her lip again to hold back any ridiculous jealousy or longing.

Penelope relaxed back in her chair, the worried line between her eyes softening. 'Then you have a lady in mind?'

Harry hurried across the room to sort through one of the file drawers. She glanced at one, shook her head, moved on. Pulled a face at the next one. But soon she'd made a short, *very* short, stack of possibilities.

'Our methods are most careful,' Eleanor told Penelope. 'We almost never have a match in mind immediately. We look at the personalities and life situations of each person who comes to us very closely. What they say they desire…'

'And what they really need,' Harry said. 'Mary is especially good at winkling out that magical *something* that makes all the difference. We don't want to see our patrons merely wed, but very happy.'

Penelope clapped her hands. 'Oh, yes! I do want that so much for dear Fred. And he…' She hesitated. 'He need not know yet, if I engage your services?'

Quite against her will, Eleanor felt a tiny touch of hope deep in her heart. Fred didn't really want a wife yet? Maybe there could be some other solution to all their troubles? Yet she feared she was just being silly. Just letting hope creep in where there was none.

'I'm afraid that would be quite impossible, Penelope,' Harry said firmly. 'We have extensive interviews with every possible match, otherwise it is all too difficult. But you can definitely be with him, help him, when he speaks to us. And Eleanor and Mary already know him! It should be simple enough.'

Penelope still looked unsure and Eleanor couldn't blame her. Nothing about Fred seemed *simple*. 'I will talk to him, then. If you could have a few possible ladies to mention when we next call? If we can make him move quickly, so much the better.'

'Assuredly, yes.' Harry came back to the table to pass the cakes again. 'And what of yourself, Lady Fleetwood? Penelope.'

Penelope's hand froze reaching for a cake. 'Me, Lady Briggs?'

'Call me Harriet! Or Harry. I know we shall be great friends. Anyone Eleanor likes I definitely like and I can see you are a very good-hearted, caring person. Could you not also use the agency's services? We do have several fine gentlemen…'

'Oh, no!' Penelope cried. 'I have no thoughts of ever marrying again.'

Eleanor gave her a gentle smile. 'Are you quite sure? Any man would be so fortunate…'

Penelope laughed again. 'Oh, my dears. I am only thirty-one, but have been married twice. The first was an arrangement with the son of my father's friend—a man much given to the bottle. Fortunately, it did not last long, as he was killed racing his curricle on a bet. When my father died not long after that, there was little money and I was quite on my own until I met Fleetwood.'

Eleanor remembered the old Earl, red-faced, always irritable and another gambler to boot. He didn't sound like much of a fairy-tale rescue. 'He was also much older, I should think?'

'Yes, but he was rather settled in his ways by then. Tempted by nothing but the card tables. Too tired for other women. It was a quiet enough life, not a truly bad one and I had a home and position. Moulton Magna is a fine estate with much history and I loved being of help to the neighbourhood. And if I sometimes dreamed of something, well, more...'

Her words drifted off on a wistful smile.

'Dreamed of what, Penelope?' Eleanor urged.

Penelope gave a little wave, as if to brush away the thoughts. 'Oh, when I was young, I was very silly and romantic! I dreamed of a prince to sweep me off my feet, as young girls always do.'

'And you don't think of such things now? Maybe a younger husband?' Harry said.

'I am too old for such fancies now, I fear. I worry about Fred, that's all. Do you really think you can help him?'

'We can certainly try, Penelope,' Eleanor said, trying not to think of Fred marching down a flower-lined aisle to his beautiful, kind, rich wife. He did need a wife and it couldn't be her.

Penelope gave a relieved sigh. 'Thank you so much! I was certain I could rely on you.'

'Have Lord Fleetwood meet us at the Pump Room tomorrow morning,' Harry said. 'Just an informal greeting between old friends. We can look about and see what we all think.'

Penelope was all smiles when she took her leave and so was Harry. An earl as a patron of their agency! Such a grand thing. 'If we can find him just the right match, the perfect wife, our reputation shall be limitless!' she crowed as she danced about the office. 'Perhaps we shall have a duke on our books next.'

'Dukes would never need anyone's help to find a wife,' Eleanor argued. But even she had to smile to see her friend's joy. Harry had too little of that in the past and deserved every second. If only she could feel so excited about finding a wife for Fred. Of all people… She had to pretend to be calm, to smile, to not let anyone see the turmoil of her feelings. She was the quiet one, the reliable one. She could not let storms of emotion overcome her. Couldn't let her own feelings show.

And Harry was quite right. Matching an earl could do their business no harm at all. They were prosperous enough, it was true, but their books were mostly filled with people solidly respectable—lawyers, physicians, shopkeepers, mill owners. A few baronets who had some difficulties with shyness or eccentricity or whatever. Widows, young ladies who had passed several Seasons with no luck. Governesses and companions. There had been a milliner, who matched with the owner of a patisserie and they now created astonishingly beautiful cakes together. They were quite the rage of the town for every party.

Yet almost no nobility yet. That could be the real making of their business. If only it wasn't Fred.

'What about Miss Weston?' Harry mused, as she danced towards the files and sifted through them. 'She is so pretty and seems level-headed for one so young. Or Miss Evans from this morning? Such a fortune!'

'Miss Weston has a very small dowry,' Eleanor pointed out.

Harry frowned in thought. 'Yes, and Lady Fleetwood did say their home desperately needs a new roof. What of Mrs Gilbert? She has pots of money left from her late husband and surely Moulton Magna would have room for all her cats. How many does she have now?'

'Nearly thirty, I believe,' Eleanor sighed, picturing an army of felines traipsing up the marble staircase of Moulton Magna and scratching the parquet floors of the Long Gallery. But it was true Mrs Gilbert was wealthy and pretty. 'Is she quite young enough for children, do you think?'

'Oh, yes, the all-important heir business.' A cloud of sadness passed over Harry's lovely face for an instant. There had been no children in her own marriage. She smiled again, determined and tossed the files aside. 'We shall keep looking. We must go to the next assembly and see who has newly arrived. The Master of Ceremonies is sure to know all the freshest news.'

Harry tapped her fingertip on the ledger and went on. 'But what of Lady Fleetwood herself? She seems like prime matchmaking material. So beautiful. Such a fine dresser! And obviously caring. Look how she is concerned about her stepson.'

And Penelope seemed so sad.

Eleanor nodded. She understood why Penelope could be melancholy—two such dutiful marriages, no romance, no fun. 'Yet she says she doesn't want to marry again.'

Harry shuddered in sympathy. 'And who can blame her? The first two husbands sound dreadful! But not every match is like that at all. We should find her someone young. Someone handsome and merry...'

Daisy knocked at the door again. 'A caller for you, Lady Briggs, Miss St Aubin.'

'Ah,' Harry said, with a cat-with-the-cream kind of smile. 'Perhaps this is Lady Fleetwood's Adonis at last, heard us calling for him!'

It was not. It was Mr Parker. Eleanor sank down in her chair, barely resisting the urge to slide beneath the desk and be silent until he left.

Poor Mr Parker was one of their clients longest on the books. There was nothing really, truly objectionable about him. He was youngish, presentable if a bit on the short and balding side, possessed a prosperous estate as well as a Bath townhouse and was a good enough dancer and rider. Yet none of the ladies they'd found for him ever suited. Each meeting was an exercise in futility, as he found each lady too blonde, or too dark, too tall or too short, too talkative or too silent. If he did not pay them a very generous retention fee, Harry would surely have seen him off long ago. Eleanor wasn't entirely sure the fee was ever worth it.

At the end of every meeting, when a few new ladies' files were presented, he would sigh deeply and give Eleanor a long, sad, wounded fawn stare from his brown eyes made inhumanly large by his spectacles.

'Oh, Miss St Aubin, I do so fear *none* of them could properly suit, amiable as they all are,' he would say mournfully. 'I am expecting a lady exactly like *yourself*.'

Once in a while, patrons did come to imagine they might prefer one of the matchmakers to the matches. It was usually golden, laughing Mary or willowy, sophisticated Harry, but sometimes they glimpsed something in Eleanor they strangely preferred. Most were very easily moved along with an introduction to a lady from the files, leaving only gratitude behind. But Mr Parker was a tougher example.

He strode into the office behind Daisy and bowed low over Eleanor's reluctantly offered hand. Harry just raised her brow at them, no help at all. 'My dear, *dear* Miss St Aubin! And Lady Briggs. I do look forward to this moment every week, it is quite the brightest in my dull, sad existence.'

'Then we must draw you up out of your loneliness at last, dear Mr Parker!' Harry said with determined cheerfulness. She opened one of the files on the desk with a crisp snap. 'We have a lovely new lady. A Miss Evans…'

Mr Parker didn't take his moon-eyed gaze off Eleanor. 'Oh, no, I could not bear such a name as *Evans*.'

When he finally left, after discussing a few more possibilities, Harry tossed the files back into their drawers with a huff and some of them scattered on the floor. Miss Muffins barked in wild excitement at the unaccustomed chaos and sank her teeth into the corner of a paper.

'Impossible!' Harry cried. 'Sometimes I think you should just agree to marry the silly man yourself and get him off our books.'

Eleanor shot Harry a horrified glare that made Harry's frown turn into laughter. 'Not really, my dear, of course! How could Mary and I stand him as part of our little family? All his delicate little niceties to you, ugh. If only we could find him someone else!'

'We've tried everyone, really. And poor Miss Evans doesn't deserve that after living with her mother all her life.'

'True, true. Well, once we find a wife for the Earl, our coffers will overflow and we won't need Mr Parker's retainer. Now, let's dig deep into these files and find at least a few prospects who could be a countess before we go to the Pump Room tomorrow.'

Eleanor nodded. She vowed not to be tempted by Fred again. Not by his smiles, his sadness, the way he looked at her as if he understood all she hid in her heart and soul—no, not even by that. He was a patron only now, that was all. She wouldn't think about his sky-blue eyes. The touch of his hand…

Oh, no. She had to summon up every bit of professional calm she'd learned in running the agency. She had to conceal any emotion she had for Fred. She had to do what she did best. Be a businesswoman.

She was surely doomed.

Chapter Five

'**I** visited Miss St Aubin yesterday,' Penelope announced ever so casually over the breakfast table. She reached for the toast rack and a jar of marmalade and pushed them towards Fred. 'You should eat more, Fred dearest! The doctors say you must build up your strength.'

'I'm going with you to the Pump Room to drink those waters of hellfire, isn't that enough?' he grumbled. But really he only heard, only thought about, the first part of her statement. She had seen Eleanor.

His Eleanor. But not really *his*, never his. Only part of a dreamy, golden past. And a beautiful woman in the present.

He'd spent every moment since then trying to forget about her. About that past and all the things that could no longer be. And now here she was, in Bath, appearing like a tempting, rose-scented ghost even at his breakfast table.

'Don't tell me you went to that so-called agency of theirs,' he said.

Penelope's eyes widened in a too-innocent fashion

and she busied herself with spreading butter on her toast. 'Can I not call on old neighbours? It would be impolite not to and the St Aubin girls were always so kind.'

'So you were merely renewing an old acquaintance?' he said suspiciously.

Penelope tried to look even *more* innocent, but it didn't work so well. 'Well—we might have chatted a tiny bit about their work. So fascinating! Ladies making their own way in this harsh world. And such a helpful service they render.'

He tossed down his fork in exasperation. Everything in the world seemed determined to conspire to throw him in the path of Eleanor, when the pain of seeing her, longing to touch her, kiss her, absorb all her gentleness and warmth into his cold heart, was overwhelming. 'Pen! If I was going to seek out a wife, which I am not at present, I would do so myself. No need to involve the St Aubins.'

Penelope gave him a beseeching smile. 'But you refuse to seek out any ladies at all! You lurk about the house. Won't meet with anyone. Won't go to plays or assemblies. There is a masked fete at Sydney Gardens in a few weeks that would be perfect and you won't attend with me! You stomp in and out of the Pump Room quite like an old bear, sweeping out without conversing with anyone. This is no way to meet nice young ladies.'

'What nice young lady would want to talk to me at all?' He gestured towards his scarred cheek, his burned hand. 'I am hardly a picture of beauty. No lady wants this. Even I do not like looking in the mirror.'

Penelope's smile turned sympathetic. 'Many more ladies than you would think. Your scars have greatly faded under the doctors' treatment and you know your title and estate are a fine offering. You used to be so— so...' She broke off with a sigh.

'I used to be?' he said quietly.

'Such good fun. Always laughing. Always understanding and comforting. Always ready to be a friend. Of course, we all get older and more sedate...'

'So I am sedate now?' he said teasingly. She wasn't entirely wrong. He well remembered those days of exploring the woods with Eleanor, chasing through the fields, reading poetry, coming up with dreams and jokes. But even Eleanor seemed quiet now, her burdens bearing down on her as his did on him. He felt such a cold wave of sadness at losing that joy. At the way life had damaged him. 'Where is my stick? My bath chair? I require a nurse, not a wife!'

Penelope laughed. 'Not *quite* in your extreme dotage, maybe. But you must be careful. The years slip by before you know it, and your dreams have fled entirely.' She looked down at the damask tablecloth, her eyes shadowed as if she was lost in her own memories. Fred couldn't help but wonder if she could use the agency herself. She deserved love and happiness.

'You were such a merry lad when I first wed your father,' she continued, 'you brightened the gloomy halls of Moulton Magna to no end. I know that man is still in there, demanding to be free again.'

'I think I left him at Waterloo,' he said. That was a moment in his life he'd long wanted to forget. A moment that haunted his nightmares. But now, with her, he was surprised to discover the memories had begun to fade. He'd suspected Eleanor, the Eleanor he'd once known, could bring him out again, that joyful man. But there was not a chance of that now.

'You should not underestimate yourself, Fred,' she said. 'Just talk to Eleanor St Aubin! Their agency seems terribly well-organised, so efficient and they care so much about helping people find happiness. They could save you a great deal of trouble. Find a few suitable ladies for you to at least meet.'

Against his will, Fred felt a frisson of intrigue at her words. 'You had a peek at their files, then?'

Penelope shook her head regretfully. 'I should have so enjoyed that! Like a novel come to life. But they are quite locked up tight. Their rates are very reasonable. A small retainer, then the remainder on marriage. Everything always most proper and chaperoned. They could save us much time.'

'Time before the roof caves in on us?'

'Perhaps. Yes, to be brutally honest.' She reached across the table and gently squeezed his hand. 'Just have a chat with Eleanor. You and she were once good friends, I think. She can surely help us.'

He sighed. He knew Penelope, kind as she was, would not let go of a thought to help someone once it was in her head. And Moulton Magna did need a mistress. 'I only said we would call on them.'

'Excellent! Because I believe they may be at the Pump Room this morning. Now, eat up your marmalade. It's your favourite, sent from Molland's.'

Fred took a bite of his toast and had to admit it *was* excellent marmalade. Perhaps he was starting to enjoy a bit of the world after all, even against his will. Maybe the old Fred was still in there, just as Pen suggested. Just as Eleanor had once brought out in him.

'Such a lovely day! Not a drop of rain in the sky,' Mary said in delight as they made their way towards the Pump Room. They journeyed there nearly every morning, to peruse the book of arrivals for possible new patrons, study the crowds and check on the progress on some of their matched couples.

It didn't quite feel like an ordinary day, though. No days were ordinary since Eleanor had seen Fred again.

'No rain,' she murmured. 'Most unusual for Bath.'

'And smell that breeze! Bath buns baking, flowers on the stalls again, sunshine and light.' Mary took Eleanor's arm and drew in a deep breath, the pink feathers on her chop straw bonnet fluttering. Several young men turned to stare at her, but she ignored them. 'It's warm and bright now, perfect for romance. And you also look so pretty today, Ella.'

Eleanor self-consciously tugged at the scalloped hem of her new pale blue taffeta pelisse. She *had* dressed rather carefully that morning, in a white gown sprigged with blue flowers and blue moire ribbons fluttering from her bonnet, a colour she hoped suited her dark curls and pale skin. She always dressed neatly and stylishly for their work, of course. But she usually didn't think of fashion beyond that, as Mary and Harry did. She couldn't compete with Harry's elegance or Mary's porcelain shepherdess prettiness. Today, though, she'd been at the dressing table longer than usual.

She didn't want to admit the real reason was the possibility of seeing Fred again.

'Ah, Miss St Aubin! Miss Mary!' a voice called as they turned towards the portico of the Pump Room. 'So pleased to see you this morning.'

Eleanor plastered her most pleasant, professional smile on her lips and turned to greet Lady Hastings and her daughter. The Hastings were a new addition to the agency's books—a baronet's widow and her daughter. Miss Hastings had been through two London Seasons, was pretty and quite spry, unlike quiet Miss Evans, but her father had been a fisherman's son of all things and so many high sticklers turned up their nose at her. Yet her mama, much like Mrs Evans, wanted *only* high sticklers for her only daughter. A viscount at best and she guarded stringently against title-less fortune-hunters. As did the agency, of course. Their network of discreet investigators looked closely at any and all possible scoundrels.

Yet Miss Hastings seemed to find the careful process rather vexing and Eleanor worried about her impetuous ways. She remembered too well how romantic poetry gave a young lady dreamy ideas, especially since Fred came back into her life. Yes, it was best to find Miss Hastings a match as soon as possible.

She was all smiles today, though, pert and pretty under her pink, ruffled bonnet.

Mary took Eleanor's arm as they waved greetings to the Hastings ladies and continued into the Pump Room.

'Perhaps Miss Hastings might do for Fred!' Mary whispered eagerly.

Eleanor tried not to show her shock, her sudden pang at those words. 'For Fred?'

'Indeed. She has a fine fortune. Her mother wants a title for her. She is young and lively and does not seem to have a particular romantic attachment as yet. Perhaps she could help brighten up Moulton Magna for him!'

Eleanor started to protest, but she had to admit Mary did have a point. Miss Hastings was young, pretty and rich. It didn't matter how much the thought of Fred marching up the aisle with Miss Hastings pained her. It could not matter.

'We must persuade him to officially sign as a patron of the agency first, which I think might be no easy task,' Eleanor said.

'I am quite sure Lady Fleetwood can persuade him.' Mary glanced back thoughtfully at Miss Hastings. 'Harry says Lady Fleetwood is ever so pretty and amiable! Still young, too. And married twice. So sad. Perhaps we could be of help to her, too. Two for one!'

'Penelope would certainly be an easier prospect than Fred,' Eleanor agreed. 'Yet perhaps she does now *want* to marry again, after two such trials. It can't have been easy being married to Fred's father.'

Mary shivered. She had been young when they left the vicarage, but she remembered the Earl and the way the household was back then. 'Indeed. She deserves someone handsome and romantic this time!'

They joined the line to peruse the arrivals book, nodding to friends and to old patrons who strolled past in pairs, arm in arm, examining the fashions around them as they moved through the elegant, airy pale green and cream room, with its domed ceiling and columns. The sound of harp music filled the flower-scented air.

'Oh, look, it's Mr and Mrs Shipton!' Mary whispered excitedly. 'Don't they just look radiant with happiness?'

They did indeed. The Shiptons were one of the agency's great success stories. A romance at first sight when they were introduced. They had bonded over their mutual passion for collecting antique milk pails.

'The Misses St Aubin! How grand to see you today,' Mr Simpson, the Master of Ceremonies who controlled much of bath's social life, greeted them as they stepped inside. 'So many new arrivals, as you can see, all of them vying to be entertained.'

'So I see, Mr Simpson,' Eleanor said as she scanned the lines of names in the visitors' book.

'Mr Parker was just here, enquiring about you,' Mr Simpson said softly.

Eleanor glanced back in alarm. 'I do hope you did not—that is…'

He tapped the side of his nose. 'I said I had no indication you would be visiting us this morning and I believe he ventured off to a coffee house instead.'

Eleanor sighed in relief. She wasn't sure she could quite deal with Mr Parker today. Not after a sleepless night plagued with memories of Fred.

'That was kind of you, Mr Simpson,' she said.

'But I do hope nothing will frighten you away from

our little masquerade in Sydney Gardens. It shall be quite the event,' Mr Simpson said.

'Oh, no! We wouldn't miss it for anything,' Mary cried. Mary adored any ball, especially one that involved costumes.

They bowed to Mr Simpson and made their way into the midst of the crowd. It was the way of every morning in Bath. Meet with people drinking their daily glasses of mineral water, sip tea, chat, hear the news, then perhaps go on to take the heated baths, walk and shop. Above all, they had to find possible patrons for the agency.

Near the long tables dispensing the all-essential waters, Eleanor glimpsed Fred, half hidden by a blue satin window drapery. He scowled down into his half-empty glass as if he would toss the foul stuff across the room and she could not blame him one bit. It tasted like old eggs, no one liked it, of course. But he also looked as if he longed to make a joke of it all, as the old Fred would have and she couldn't help but laugh.

She pressed her gloved fingertips to her lips to hold back a snort of laughter, but he heard her anyway. He glanced up and actually gave her a *wink* and a white, naughty, wide, flashing smile. A conspiracy just between the two of them in the middle of the crowd. That smile that was always able to fell a lady at fifty paces. To make her long to dash across a ballroom and throw himself at her feet, begging her to be his.

Eleanor hadn't seen that smile in so long and never directed right at her. She had been young when they were friends and he had no rakish reputation then. For an instant, she was frozen, couldn't breathe at all. It had been so very long since she saw that old, wonderful Fred. He hadn't changed so very much, maybe. A fantasy come to life, brave and funny and with those gorgeous lapis eyes. Tall, self-possessed, making a lady long to just stand and stare and dream.

He poured away the last of the water into a potted palm and held his finger to his lips to beg her silence. A little secret between them. Eleanor made a zipping motion.

Someone bumped into Fred and said a few words to him, making him turn away. When he glanced at Eleanor again, her light-hearted Fred was gone once more, and the wounded bear warrior was there. She turned away, flustered. How wonderful it had been to see him again, to know he was really there. And then just to lose him again! She blinked hard against the prickle of tears, praying no one noticed.

'Oh, look, Eleanor, there is Lord Fleetwood himself! We should say hello,' Mary said and forged ahead as she always did. There was never stopping her.

Eleanor followed more slowly, trying to keep smiling, keep serene, nodding to acquaintances. Trying to pretend today was the same as any other day at the Pump Room. As if her world, the world she'd so carefully built around her, hadn't cracked and collapsed with Fred's return.

Luckily, by the time they reached Fred's side, Penelope had joined him and Eleanor didn't have to face him quite alone.

'Well met, indeed!' Penelope declared. She set her

own nearly full glass on a footman's tray and smiled at them brightly. 'Fred, dearest, you do recall the Misses St Aubin, I'm sure. It's been so delightful to find you will be our neighbours again. I declare I have been quite lonely since coming to Bath.'

'Indeed. Delightful. A surprise,' Fred said wryly. Eleanor noticed he kept his damaged hand close to his side, half hidden by his sleeve and her heart ached to see it.

'Miss Mary, I do adore your hat,' Penelope said brightly, distracting Eleanor from Fred. 'You must tell me where you found it. I must replenish my wardrobe after all this dull mourning. Do walk with me and let us chat?' She gave Fred a long glance. 'Fred, darling, do take the waters as the doctors said. A pint a day, remember?'

Penelope and Mary strolled off arm in arm, chatting merrily about hats and pelisses, leaving Eleanor to stand alone with Fred. 'You must take a *pint*?' she said, appalled.

Fred grimaced. 'Indeed. Pen has dragged me to several physicians and apothecaries and their advice does not seem to vary. Sadly.'

'I am quite convinced the doctors are in the pay of this very Pump Room itself and someone down in the cellars must add something to the water to make people feel *worse*. Then everyone must put their coin into longer and longer stays here.'

'Your theory has merit, Ella.'

Ella again. His special name for her. 'I know where

we can procure some cups of perfectly decent tea, if you like? What Penelope doesn't know and all that…'

Fred gave a blissful sigh and that wonderful old smile again. 'You are an angel, Ella. Do lead on.'

He offered her his good arm and she slowly slid her fingers over his sleeve, hardly believing they were there together once more. His arm felt solid, strong and hard under her touch. They made their way around the edge of the room towards the tea tables, silent together. She reminded herself sternly that she still had to find him a wife. That this could not last. But, at least, there was this moment. This comfort and ease.

'Are you—that is, do you have to see so many doctors, then?' she asked carefully, trying to not show her worry.

He shrugged, his muscles rippling under her hand. 'There is not so much they can do for me. I am as I shall be and I do not feel so terrible. Just a twinge of soreness now and then. Not a thing to worry about.' He flashed that smile down at her, making her feel warm and glowing all over again even as she feared he might just be putting on a brave face for her. 'And there is my wounded vanity, of course.'

Eleanor laughed. 'You always did have a surfeit of that.'

'Oh, you *do* wound me! How insufferable I must have been when I was young.'

'Indeed you were. Yet I did miss you when you were gone,' she admitted. 'The neighbourhood became terribly dull.'

'And I missed you,' he said quietly, making her cheeks feel warm. He had thought of her!

'I'm surprised you tolerate the Bath doctors, then,' Eleanor said.

'It gives Penelope a certain pleasure to fuss and I want to make sure she's happily settled here before I return to Moulton Magna,' he answered. 'She worries.'

Eleanor did not blame her. It was easy to worry about Fred, who'd always hidden any pain. 'She seems like a very kind lady.'

'Too good a lady for my father,' he answered. 'I have to say, Ella, I know she has visited you in your— professional capacity recently.' He gave a little cough, sounding almost embarrassed to mention the agency.

Eleanor swallowed hard. Did he think less of her for her work? 'I am sure she only wants to be of assistance.'

He smiled, that old, quirked, smile of his once more and Eleanor's heart dangerously stuttered. 'I am quite sure of that.'

'I'd like to be of assistance, too. To help you be— be happy,' Eleanor said softly, with such a pang that some other lady would make him happy in that way. She almost reached out to touch his hand, but curled her fingers tightly to hold herself back. Helping him in his matrimonial quest was never going to be an easy thing, she knew that, but it was proving more difficult than she'd imagined. Harder to keep her feelings for him hidden. 'If not through the agency, then as an old friend. With advice and such. If I can.'

He glanced away out of the window and was silent for a long moment. She longed to know what he was thinking. What he truly wanted. 'I know I must wed. My father left things rather in a muddle and it's my duty now. But to use an agency…' he shook his head. 'Forgive me if I have my doubts.'

'You could call it a muddle, yes,' Eleanor said with a sympathetic grimace. She thought of the shocked letters they had received from old friends, once the Earl died and the extent of his debts was revealed. Moulton Magna had always seemed the centre of their neighbourhood, their anchor. 'I assure you, though, our agency is completely above board and most professional.'

'Yet who would have me as I am now?' he said. He sounded matter-of-fact, even half joking, with not a speck of self-pity but just a certain reality.

'You are more handsome than you ever knew, Fred,' she blurted.

He glanced down at her quizzically. 'And you are a good friend, Ella. Better than I ever deserved. I wasted any attractions I might once have had in being a ridiculous wastrel. I wasted anything that might have been worthy of your friendship. And now…'

Now he had to marry a fortune. 'You must do your duty, which is something I understand very well.' For hadn't she, too, done her duty? Left school, taken care of her father, their home, her sister, their patrons at the agency. Forgotten about those days running free with Fred. Surely she should be able to keep those parts of herself separate in her heart. If he could do that, so she could she.

She made herself look away from him to glance

around the room at all the ladies gathered there. There were so many countess candidates in Bath. Young ladies of fine dowries, pretty faces, even kind hearts. Yet who was right for Fred? Who could be worthy of him?

'You have a professional look in your eye right now, Ella,' he teased. 'Have you a candidate in mind right now?'

'Ah, well, you must pay the agency's fee if you want to know,' she answered, trying to be light-hearted, to hide all her old feelings for him, her memories and silly half-hopes. All her thoughts about him now, in this moment.

He laughed, suddenly looking so much younger, lighter. As if being with her made the years vanish for him as they did for her. 'Quite right. Well, then, shall we take a turn about the room and look for Pen and your sister? You can tell me all I must know about how to make my way properly around Bath. I fear I have quite turned feral of late. Too quiet. Too much inside myself.'

Yet Eleanor had heard once that that was not true. That he'd gone rather wild with ladies and gambling, maybe after all the horrors he'd seen in war. Then the quiet feral ways, as he called it, were a way to dull the pain, too. How she wished she could bring him into the sunshine once again! That they could be free together once more.

He offered her his arm and she hesitated a moment before she slid her hand over his sleeve, fearing she might never want to let him go. When she did, she found he felt just like the old Fred—and like something new, something enticing and strong and, yes, hard to let go. 'Stay with me then, Fred, and you shan't lose your way in Bath.' Though she very well might.

Chapter Six

Ella often liked to venture out early on a fine morning, before Mary and Harry had even left their dressing tables. She loved the cool, calm silence before the rest of the town came to life. She and Miss Muffins would buy a tea and a Bath bun and stroll by the river to watch the water meander and twist along on its voyage. She sometimes wondered where it went, after it left Bath. What it saw. A few fishermen were there, catching their day's wares, and some housemaids were collecting the day's provisions. Otherwise, Ella was alone for a short, precious time.

She nibbled her Bath bun as she studied the pale morning sunlight, the small crafts that slipped past in the water, and let the blessed silence surround her. No one demanded she find them their 'One True Love For Ever' right now, no account books awaited. She could just breathe, take in the bridge and the water and the lights. And think.

Think about this new Fred. Ella sighed to consider it. Once, long ago, she'd thought she knew him well. But now—now she was sure she didn't know him at all. This Fred was harder, sharper-edged, more cynical than the young man she'd once known. He did not laugh as he once did. Did not enjoy the parties. Worry had carved new lines in his face, even beyond the scars.

Could she come to incorporate this new Fred into her old memories, her friend? She ached for what he'd suffered. Longed to help him even as he seemed to hold her apart. What could she do? She so longed for her friend again. The distance he put between them made her want to cry, to wail, to let out all the emotion she kept so carefully hidden. She wanted to wrap her arms around him and never let him go. To be with him always.

Miss Muffins seemed to whine in agreement.

They were suddenly interrupted by Ella's sister calling her name. 'Ella! There you are at last. You quite vanished.'

Mary glanced over her shoulder to smile at her sister, who hurried along the pier in the shade of her lacy parasol. 'Such a splendid day, Eleanor, don't you agree?' Mary declared, as they stepped from their door into the sunny morning. She popped open her lacy parasol, shielding them from the unaccustomed glare after so many grey afternoons. 'How I wish we could be out in nature somewhere, instead of going to the shops. Do you remember the woods at Moulton Magna, when we were children? How gloriously free it all was.'

'Indeed I do,' Eleanor said with a secret little smile, as she remembered running with Fred through those light-dappled woods. 'Living here in Bath has so many fine things—concerts and theatres, bookshops and milliners—but I do sometimes miss the quiet of the woods and paths, as well.'

They linked arms and turned towards York Street. They peeked into shop windows at ribbons and slippers, leather-bound books and lengths of fabric, greeted friends and chatted about new patrons.

'My dear Eleanor! Mary!' they heard a lady call as they headed towards the Gardens. Eleanor glanced back to see an open landau rolling to a halt near them, Lady Fleetwood and Fred seated inside. She had not seen him since the Pump Room and encountering him again so unexpectedly made her feel all warm and confused. So ridiculously young, as only Fred could do.

'How lovely to see you again,' Penelope said. 'And on such a fine day! Fred has taken the waters this morning...'

Eleanor gave Fred a sympathetic grimace, remembering how much of the sulphurous waters he was meant to consume, which made him laugh.

'So we hired this carriage for the day,' Penelope went on, pretending not to see his chuckles. 'The doctor says fresh air and exercise can be of great benefit, so we're off to Beechen Cliff for a picnic. There are great views to be had, I'm sure. They say there are ruins there! Maybe even a castle. I love a fine view of a ruin, don't you, Fred dear?'

'Oh, assuredly,' he said quickly and shot a glance at Eleanor, his brow quirked. It was her turn to laugh aloud, quickly smothered by her gloved hand.

'It sounds like a place in a poem,' Mary said wistfully. 'We haven't been able to venture out to the hills beyond town much of late.'

'Then you must come with us!' Penelope declared. 'I'm sure the doctors would tell Fred he would also benefit from time with friends, going about in society. He's become such a solitary old thing.'

Eleanor peeked at Fred from under the brim of her bonnet. *Solitary old thing* would never have described the old Fred at all. That Fred was always ready for a mischief. Now she feared she could see it there, that new loneliness, in incipient lines on his face, the grimace as Pen pointed that out. Perhaps he, too, wanted to leave that loneliness behind.

She longed more than anything to make him smile again. 'I do wonder if the climb would be too much...' she ventured, thinking of the steep pathways and the old wooden stairs at Beechen Cliff.

'I am sure it would not be. Oh, Eleanor, let's go with them!' Mary cried, giving Eleanor the melting, beseeching look that always swayed her when it came to her little sister. 'It is too fine a day to stay in town.'

Eleanor glanced about uncertainly. She didn't want to make a fool of herself if she was too long in Fred's presence, as she feared she might.

Mary squeezed her arm and whispered, 'And we can find out more of what Lord Fleetwood looks for in a wife! It will help us find him a perfect match.'

'I...' Eleanor began. She did want to be with Fred. Of course she did. She had to grab any moment she could with him! But could she conceal her feelings for quite so long? Chat about possible matches for him as if she worried about nothing else?

'Please, do come with us,' Fred said with a wonderful, coaxing smile. 'If only to give Pen another focus for her infernal fussing.'

'Yes, of course,' Eleanor said. She could not refuse that smile. 'Thank you. We would enjoy that very much.'

Penelope clapped her hands. 'Wonderful! How serendipitous to see you here today.'

The footman jumped down to open the door, but Fred alighted first and held out his hand to Eleanor. 'There is a seat here, Ella,' he said, gesturing to the spot next to his own place.

'Th-thank you.' She accepted his hand and let him assist her into the carriage. He helped Mary to sit next to Penelope and he pressed close to Eleanor as the door closed and the carriage jolted back into motion. He did smell the same as the old Fred, of sunlight and warmth and all delightful things. She longed to lean against him and feel him against her. She moved closer to the door on her other side.

But she felt half silly, being so very careful around Fred. In the light of day, a grown, sensible woman with many responsibilities and Fred could be a valuable patron for her agency. She knew that very well and wanted to help him, to be a good friend to him. To see the world as it was, not as she might have once dreamed it could be and do what must be done. Yet whenever she touched his hand, whenever he was close to her, she became a dreamy, giggly girl.

She thought of the rumours that Fred had gone rather wild in London, known many women, frequented gaming halls. Eleanor knew she couldn't quite compete with women like that. She knew much about human nature, she'd based her business on it, but of the marrying sort. Fred was still very handsome and had once been gorgeous beyond belief. She suddenly wondered if he thought her silly. If he compared her with them. If he sought a woman like those he'd once known as a wife...

The carriage lurched around a corner, towards the banks of the Avon River and the road that would lead away from the town, up a steep slope and Eleanor fell against Fred's shoulder. He took her arm to hold her steady, looking down at her with a dark, inscrutable look in his eyes. She straightened her bonnet and gave him a quick, rueful smile.

'Now, do tell us about the masquerade they say will soon be held in Sydney Gardens,' Penelope said as the crowds fell away around them and they bounced over a bridge. 'It sounds quite marvellous! I haven't been to a real ball in ages.'

'Oh, yes, everyone will be there,' Mary answered with great enthusiasm. She'd been planning costumes for several weeks already. 'There will be fireworks! And music—a famous soprano.'

'Then we must obtain tickets, Fred,' Penelope said. 'A dance would do us both good. And you need a new evening suit anyway. You shall be sadly out of fashion.'

'You must resign yourself, I fear,' Eleanor told him, all mock solemnity. 'You are in Bath now, Fred. Clothes must be commissioned. Fun must be had. It's the way of the town.'

Fred grimaced and then laughed. 'So I am discovering. As long as this masquerade doesn't involve drinking yet more water…'

'I'm sure there will be champagne instead,' Mary sighed. 'And so very much dancing! Royal musicians are coming all the way from London.'

'So, along with a new suit of clothes, I must procure some dancing lessons,' Fred said.

'I remember you were a very fine dancer,' Eleanor blurted. Once they had shared a country dance at the village assembly rooms and she had dreamed of it for so long after. The touch of his hand, the way they moved together.

'You danced with Fred?' Penelope asked. 'And yet he tries to declare he has *never* danced.'

'When we were young, at a village assembly,' Eleanor said. 'He was a much sought-after partner!'

'I'm sure we can find many amiable ladies who would be delighted to have you as a partner,' Mary said. The town spread far below them, honey-gold in the sunlight, beyond the vivid green of the trees.

Staring down at the sparkle of the glorious view before her, Eleanor stumbled a bit as she descended the carriage steps. Fred caught her before she could tumble down, lifting her high for an instant as she held tight to his shoulders, staring up in wonder at his familiar, unfamiliar, beautiful face.

He slowly, ever so slowly lowered her to the ground, a gentle slide, his gaze never leaving hers. Eleanor didn't want to let him go, yet the chatter of Penelope and Mary as they made their way up the path, the chirping song of the birds, pulled her back into the real world again.

She stepped back, flustered. 'Thank you. So clumsy of me.'

'The last thing you could ever be, Ella, is clumsy,' he said hoarsely. She noticed him running his damaged arm, as if he had wrenched it and didn't want her to notice. She felt so shy and awful that he had to worry about such things now! Her strong, funny old friend.

They walked together behind Penelope and Mary and the footmen, towards a spot where they could spread out their picnic with the glorious view all around them. Eleanor lost herself in the chatter, the wine and laughter and soon felt easy again, as if she was with the old Fred and was the old Eleanor, reading poetry in the Moulton Magna summerhouse. He'd known those women in London and she'd been immured with her family. How well could they know each other now? Especially as she so feared to show him her real emotions. Her real heart.

They were not those young, innocent people still. Not really. And there was a new, taut awareness she could not deny. He was at the other end of the blanket, far from her reach, yet Eleanor was achingly aware of him at every moment. As they finished their repast and grew quiet and drowsy in the sunlight, he glanced towards her and smiled.

'Shall we walk a bit, Ella?' he asked, popping a last

strawberry into his mouth. 'I fear if I sit here any longer, I'll quite go to sleep in this delightfully warm sun.'

Eleanor hesitated. She feared what could happen, how her feelings might escape, if she was alone with him again.

'Oh, yes, do,' Penelope urged. 'Mary and I shall just chatter on here for a bit and finish this wine. You two should go look for the ruins.'

She slowly took Fred's hand as he offered to help her to her feet and blinked as the sun behind his bright hair dazzled her. They made their way away from the picnic blanket, into the shade of a narrow pathway that led between trees and flowering shrubs, smelling fresh and sweet in the warm day. They walked in silence. Comfortable, comforting and close together, until they reached a cliff that looked down on the town between a break in the greenery. It all glowed and shimmered, just like Fred. Just like that moment she had with him.

He seemed to feel it, too, studying the view with a solemn, thoughtful expression on his face. 'For whatsoever from one place doth fall, if with the tide unto another brought. For there is nothing lost, that may be found, if sought.'

'Such beautiful words of Spenser's,' she whispered.

'They always make me think of you,' he said, his gaze so very blue and intense as he studied her. 'You are like a fairy queen.'

Eleanor stared up at him, wondering if the sun had dazzled her senses, sent her flying into another realm. He thought of her as fairy queen. She knew this moment between them, very still, sparkling, a time out of time, could not last; it would vanish like all dreams. Yet his compliments, the admiration in his eyes, made her feel so warm and glowing all the way to her toes.

'Me?' she whispered. 'A fairy queen?'

'Yes. Beautiful and kind. Someone for us mere mortals to look up to in admiration. But even better. For *you*, Ella, are real. You are kind and warm.'

He suddenly took her gloved hand in his, holding it very tightly. She curved her fingers around his, holding onto him as if he was the only thing that kept her from flying away.

'See?' he said, staring down intently at their joined hands. He sounded tense, hoarse. As if he was filled with some pain, some longing, just as she was. As if he was faced with something he reverenced and feared all at once. 'Warm and real. Not an icy queen at all. You always had such a kindness about you. Like a fireside on a winter's day. A place to curl up and stay, to be safe.' He pressed her hand close against his chest and she could feel the beat of his heart through linen and wool. As if it moved through her whole self and became a part of her.

'And so are you, Fred, though I know you never give yourself such credit. You are such a wonderful friend. So…' So wonderful. She'd always thought that and now she found it had not changed.

'I can only be that way with you, Ella,' he whispered. 'Once, I…'

Eleanor stared up at him, entranced, flooded with a bittersweet longing she'd never known before. She felt so dizzy. As if the whole world shifted and changed and rocked around her. As if there was hope and fear all at once. She dared to give in to all those feelings she'd long had for Fred and leaned closer to him, resting her forehead against his shoulder. It was so warm, that heat surrounding her, blanketing her against the world. He smelled of lemon soap and clean linen, of sunshine and Fred. And, for that moment, she didn't feel alone at all.

'What could bring us back to that, Fred?' she said.

His arms came around her, close and warm and she peeked up at him to see that he stared out over the hills, as if as lost as she was amid that honey-golden glow. Lost in their own world together. 'I know I went rather wild when I first went into the Army.'

Eleanor hadn't expected such memories as that. She gave a surprised little hiccough of laughter and thought of the gossip that had once reached her ears. Tales of cards and debts, women and whisky. She had always tried to ignore it all. Discount it and hold on only to her Fred. 'I may have heard a word or two.'

'It is true, I fear. I hate to think of it now. But once the regiment left England, I became friends with another young officer. A most amiable man who hadn't been married two years yet and had a new child. He talked so often of his wife and baby in the long, lonely evenings and I—I confess I began to see another way of being through his words. A real home. A place to belong. Someone who waited for me.' He'd sounded very far away just then, sad, and Eleanor ached for him.

She squeezed his arm, pressing close to his side. She only wanted to reassure him, to rush to tell him that he could indeed have that. Could have a home, a family, anything he desired.

She could help him find that with the agency. Even if she couldn't help him in the way her heart so longed for, help him by making that home, that family together. By comforting him always.

'And your friend?' she asked. 'Did he return to his home?'

Fred shook his head, staring out over the view. 'He was killed in battle. I glimpsed him, through the haze of smoke. I tried to save him, but I was too late. I went to call on his wife as soon as I returned to England, after I had been wounded. She was going back to her parents in Jersey. She was so brave, so kind, trying to reassure *me*, when I was the one who owed her so much. Her husband should have been there, not me.' He smiled down at her, sad, wistful. She could tell he tried to hide his emotions from her, but she was too long practised in reserve herself. She could see the raw torment in his eyes. Hear the anguish of that moment. 'She rather reminded me of you, Ella.'

'Of me?' she whispered.

'Yes. So very brave, such a warm heart. I've never forgotten her and her husband. Nor can I really forget the terrors of battle, though I try to hide that from Pen. But now—now I think I begin to forget a bit.'

She studied the trees around them. The green and gold. The sky arching overhead with only birdsong to be heard. 'Is this not the most peaceful place? A place for renewal, I think.'

'Yes.' He took a deep breath and stared up at the treetops. 'Peaceful indeed.'

'If only we could live in a hut right here in the hills. All alone in the quiet, with just the sky and these trees. Like shepherds in a poem!' They were quiet together for a long moment, standing close as they took in the view below them. Only the two of them in that never-ending, too-brief moment.

'Shall we take another turn along the path before we leave?' he said at last. Eleanor nodded and silently they made their way back along the trail they'd just trod. But it was no heavy, uncomfortable silence. It was peaceful, easy, filled with birdsong and the whisper of the wind in the trees. And he held her hand close in his, helping her over slippery patches of moss and loose stones.

'What of you, Ella? What did you do when I was gone? I know setting up your agency could not have been easy,' he asked.

Eleanor laughed, thinking of those days. 'We had nothing to copy, really, no business plan before us. We just had to rely on our good sense and on Harry's fine taste. We knew we were needed. So many people come here to Bath wishing to marry!'

'Then it must be easy for them to find each other?'

'Sometimes it is, of course. With so many assemblies and tea parties! Yet there are those who seek a bit—well, more. It is easy enough to marry, but it can be so hard to find the *right* person. Especially if one is a bit…er…different.'

'I think I see. Some people are not made exactly for

this world. They need help to find someone to see them through it all. Someone to understand.'

'Yes! Their missing half. And not all our patrons are wealthy. Some save up their coin—we see merchants, governesses, milliners. We sometimes give them a bit of a bargain rate, I admit. They deserve to find someone they can care for, too.'

'Lost causes, eh?'

'No one is a lost cause. I have never believed that.'

'Not even me?' he said ruefully.

Eleanor held his hand tight and studied his face. 'Especially not you, Fred. Never you.'

'You would certainly change your mind, Ella, if you knew how I have really changed lately. You would not wish to be my friend at all.'

'That is not true!' Ella declared stoutly. She remembered what she had determined before, that time changed everyone. Especially those like Fred who were unfortunate even to see war itself. Yet knowing that only increased her understanding of him and made her feel even deeper for him. Admire his strength that much more.

'I am always here, Fred, if you need someone to talk to,' she said. 'Whether you decide to partake of our excellent services at the agency after all. I am still your friend, always.'

Fred reached for her hand and placed a warm, tingling, alluring touch to her fingers that made her shiver. 'You have no idea how very much that means to me, Ella. No idea at all.'

She smiled up at him, tremulously, and hoped that this friendship could truly be enough.

'I think I may do something shockingly naughty now,' she dared to whisper, remembering the old days with Fred, the pranks they would sometimes get up to.

He tilted his head. There was a most intrigued gleam in his eyes. 'I can't wait to hear what that might be, Ella.'

'Remember when we were young and there was that enormous ancient oak out near the summerhouse?'

He nodded, looking doubtful but also interested, maybe even a bit excited.

'That tree over there looks very similar,' she said. 'I think I shall climb it, like I used to.'

His expression slid into doubt and that only made her feel more determined. 'Ella. I'm not sure that's a good idea.'

'You think I don't have it in me any longer?' she teased. If they were to be friends, she wanted it to be just as it was. Free and easy and simple. Before he could stop her, she dashed to the tree and found a foothold in the rough bark. She reached up and grabbed a thick branch, her muscles remembering what it once felt like.

Fred rushed over to her, his arms out as if he was afraid she would fall and he would be there to catch her. 'It could be quite dangerous.'

'Not as dangerous as riding into battle as you did, Fred,' she said. Her heart ached to think of him in such danger and she knew she had to try and be brave as he was. He was there with her and that made her feel confident. Certain. She kept pulling herself upwards.

She felt a touch on her leg, through her skirt, and glanced down to see he stood ready to catch her at a moment's notice. She smiled at him, sure she was brave now. He made her so. She kept going, higher and higher, until she found a lovely little spray of leaves. She snapped it off and dropped it to the ground, intending to keep it as a souvenir of this moment.

As she clambered back down, the toe of her half-boot caught in her hem and she felt herself tumbling backward with an instant of cold panic.

But Fred was there, always, to catch her. He held her against him, safe above the hard ground. She held onto his shoulders, feeling the hardness of him through his coat. She felt so very warm and breathless now. Safe.

'Th-thank you, Fred,' she whispered. 'It seems you have saved me again.'

'I'm always here if you need me, remember, Ella?' he said. He held her steady as she found her footing, but she noticed he winced as if his arm worried him.

'You're hurt,' she cried. 'Let me see…'

He laughed and flexed his arm again. 'Not at all. Parfit knights are never hurt when they catch their fair ladies, are they? It's merely a twinge.'

Eleanor wasn't sure she believed him, but she wouldn't embarrass him for the world. She nodded and they turned away from the tree, joking and laughing together again at last. As Fred waved at Penelope, perched above them on the slope of a hill, Eleanor scooped up her leaves and promised herself she would never forget that moment at all.

Penelope perched on a low, flat boulder between a stand of trees, looking out over the town below. Mary had wandered off to sketch a stream, since they hadn't yet encountered any ruins, and Penelope found herself alone. Fred and Eleanor were just hazy figures in the distance, moving in and out of the shadowed sunlight between the trees.

The sunlight filtering and drifting through the canopy of leaves was warm and delicious, flowing like summertime honey over Penelope's skin, chilled for so long, and she drank it in. She took her bonnet off, dangling it by its ribbons, and turned her face up to the light. She didn't care anything about propriety in that moment. That had ruled her life for too long. She kicked up her half-boots under the hem of her sombre lavender pelisse. How nice it would be to wear *real* colours again! To find a way to live once more.

She closed her eyes and listened to a distant song Mary sang as she sketched. Something about a shepherd and his pretty lass and the twitter of birds. Yes, she was truly alone, as she had been ever since she was widowed. Before that, even. Her first marriage had been over in a flash and her second had often been spent alone in her rooms. Yet this solitude felt so very different from all those long, grey, loveless days. This felt filled with sensation and heat and movement. The world gathering all around her once more. There for her to scoop up if she dared to.

Yet there was still that tiny, icy sliver of loneliness deep inside of her. That whisper of regret and yearning she was never quite rid of.

She opened her eyes and gazed out over the town again. The houses and churches, bridges and elegant crescents, like a scattering of toys. A place of play and

forgetfulness. All those days she had spent nursing husbands so much older than her, the crushing knowledge
of the Earl's debts, never knowing where she could
turn.

She'd imagined living in Bath would help her draw a
line under that old life and move forward. Her jointure
could not stretch to London but a small place in Bath
was possible. A place where she could slowly join the
flow of humanity again. Tiptoe into theatres and parties once more, make some friends, go for drives, have
tea. She hadn't quite realised what a marriage mart
Bath was! For people of all ages and situations. It was
as if being surrounded by reminders of one's health all
over, in the waters and doctors' offices, made everyone long to live.

Penelope swung her feet, wondering idly where
among those toy houses she could find a real place for
herself, which was what she longed for most. To decide
who *she* was at long last.

She glimpsed Mary skipping along the river pathway, her sketchbook in one hand and hat in the other,
singing. So young. So filled with spirit! When had Penelope ever felt young? She could barely remember it at
all. Yet once, before she had to marry, there *had* been a
few days. Some parties, friends, laughter and teasing…

And there had been that one moment. Yes, before she
married, before all her responsibility crashed down on
her, when she'd been allowed to attend a house party at
the house of distant cousins. For a brief fortnight, she'd
just been a young lady. Playing croquet on the lawn,

taking tea, charades after dinner, dancing and playing hide-and-seek in the attics.

There had been some young men, too, who wanted to joke and tease and dance with her. Who seemed to find her pretty and interesting. One in particular, maybe? Yes, indeed. Anthony Oliver, a man whose family had made fortunes in mercantile business and were on the edge of gentry. A young man of beautiful dark eyes and an enticing laugh, one who talked with her as if she actually had something to say and danced with her so gracefully. She'd never quite forgotten him.

But that was all. She had to marry soon after. Her father's debts, just like the Earl's, threatening to take away everything. And she, a lady with so few choices, had to save them. No more Anthony Oliver. That party was just a moment. A memory of bright joy.

She turned and glimpsed Fred and Eleanor walking down the pathway, so close to each other. Fred had been a good friend to her when she lived practically alone at Moulton Magna, though he couldn't be there very often. He wrote her letters from his Army postings. Amusing messages that carried her out of her small world and gave her tiny nuggets of advice and of hope. Now he had so many burdens of his own—his injuries, memories of war, restoring his estate. She longed so much to help him now, as he had once helped her. To find him a suitable wife to share his troubles. To shore up Moulton Magna for the future.

She'd heard such good reports of the work of the agency and Eleanor and Mary's family still had a fine reputation in the neighbourhood of Moulton Magna. Surely if anyone could help Fred, it was them.

Now, as she watched the two of them together, wrapped up in each other as if nothing else existed, she felt a touch of hope, just like that sunlight. Yet there was always that grey sense of disquiet. Eleanor St Aubin was the kindest of ladies, but she had no fortune. It was terribly sad, so sad that anyone so good as Fred should be left with such troubles.

Yet he *did* look happy now. Peaceful, as she had not seen him in so long. Surely estates, like people, needed more than money and titles to guard them against the rocks of the world? Surely affection and spirit could carry a great deal?

So the young Penelope had once hoped, but not for long.

She sighed and pushed herself reluctantly to her feet. She shook out her skirts, those drab folds of half-mourning, and turned towards the pathway to join Mary. They did all have to confront the real world again, but not just yet.

She stood, brushing down her skirts before she turned back towards their picnic spot in the distance. At the turning of the path, slanting down towards the stream, she heard a burst of laughter just beyond the curve. It was childish laughter, a shriek, and it made her smile. She swung her hat by its ribbons and prepared to wave at whoever it was and then hurry past.

As she came around the corner, she saw a gentleman and two little girls on the mossy path. The man wore no hat and his glossy dark hair shone in the sunlight.

'Oh!' one of the girls cried. 'What a pretty lady! Is she a forest spirit?'

Penelope, caught off guard, laughed.

'Natalie,' the man admonished. 'Remember manners, yes? Your mama would be very disappointed.'

'Not at all,' Penelope answered. 'Miss Natalie has quite brightened my day! I do think…'

She glanced up at the man—and gasped in shock. *Surely not.* The sun must have stunned her, pushed her back to those old, half-lost memories. That house party, those days of rare freedom and fun. It surely could not be *him.* Anthony Oliver.

For a long moment, they stared at each other in astonishment, as if they faced off over a games table and waited for one to make a move.

'Miss Preston,' he said, his voice as full of shock as she felt, and she knew it really, truly was him. Maybe thoughts and memories had magical powers in that beautiful place. Memories of youthful dances and laughter and the one moment in her life she'd felt free. His dark eyes were the same now as they had been then.

'I am Lady Fleetwood now. But yes, I was Miss Preston,' she said. 'A very long time ago.'

He smiled and those eyes sparkled. How delicious he smelled, too. Warm and woodsy and sweet. And young. So young. 'Not so very long ago as all that. Seeing you, I would vow it was yesterday. I remember that party so well.'

'As do I—Mr Oliver.' Yet in truth, it *had* been a long time since that party and she wondered what he did now. She glanced down at the two adorable little girls, all pink cheeks and dark curls, wide, curious hazel eyes. Her heart gave a sharp pang. 'Are these your darling daughters?' For surely he had a wife and a large family by now, all handsome and boisterous.

He laughed. 'Fortunately, no, for they are imps of mischief in disguise. They are my nieces, my sister's children. Natalie and Grace.'

Grace gave a wobbly curtsy and tried to pop her hand in her mouth, but Natalie grabbed the grubby digits and tugged.

'How do you do,' Natalie said. 'And, Uncle Anthony, Mama says you must not call us *imps* again! You encourage us too much, remember? You especially shouldn't say it in front of fine ladies.' She gave Penelope a beaming smile. 'Uncle Anthony is usually most proper, I promise.'

Penelope laughed even harder. They were adorable—and they were not his! 'Yet I recall a time he was not so very well-mannered...'

'Oh, please! Lady Fleetwood, no tales of my misspent youth to get back to their mother. She fusses at me enough as it is.' He smiled at her, a delighted grin, and the heart she'd been determined to close off so long ago cracked open again. 'It is very nice to see you again. I often wondered after that party how you fared.'

He had thought of her? As she had him? 'Did you indeed, Mr Oliver?'

'Yes. Do you and your—your husband reside here in Bath?'

'I do live here now, yes. I fear Lord Fleetwood is no longer with us.'

His smile dimmed and he nodded in sad understanding. 'I am sorry for your loss.'

'How kind. Tell me, have you and your—your wife been in town long?'

The two girls watched them avidly, their wide gazes swinging between them.

'I am not married, sadly,' he said. 'I am visiting my sister and her family.'

'He has *never* been married,' Natalie offered. 'Mama says there is no lady to suit him, though she tries to find one.'

Poor Anthony's face turned quite crimson and Penelope had to stifle another laugh. She longed to burst into giggles. To fall over with mirth! She hadn't felt quite so young and giddy in—well, ever since that long-ago house party.

She glimpsed Mary strolling up the path towards them. 'I believe I know someone who could help you with that…'

'Our mama would be *ever* so grateful if you could, Lady Fleetwood,' Natalie said primly, like a dowager gossiping over tea. 'Grace and I require cousins.'

Grace nodded emphatically.

Penelope studied Anthony, that gorgeous face of his, and couldn't help but picture *his* children. They would be lovely. 'I shall make the introduction, then.'

'Perhaps I could call on you to obtain this pertinent information?' he asked, shuffling his feet in a strangely hopeful manner. She did see those long-ago days in his eyes—the moments of being young and free and laughing. 'And renew our old acquaintance.'

Penelope felt a bolt of pure, warm pleasure at the thought of seeing him again. 'Certainly, Mr Oliver.' She un-looped her reticule from her wrist and took out a card to pass him, with her address, wondering if she was being foolish. He bowed, promising to call soon, and left again with the two skipping, giggling girls.

Penelope feared she, too, had a silly, schoolgirlish smile on her face and she wasn't entirely sure why. Or maybe she just didn't want to *admit* why. That she wanted to see this man again too much.

She dared to glance back over her shoulder at Mr Oliver's retreating figure. She hoped Mary hadn't seen the meeting. That she could hold it to herself like a delicious little secret for just a little while longer, but of course that was too much to hope.

Mary looked curious indeed when she reached Penelope, her eyes wide and shining under the frill of her bonnet. 'Who was *that*, Penelope? I haven't seen him around Bath before.'

Penelope laughed. 'And you know *everyone* in Bath?'

'Of course. It is my job to know them. And I'm quite sure I'd remember a face like that!'

Penelope pushed down a silly, jealous little pang. 'He is rather handsome, I admit.'

Mary tilted her head as she studied Penelope, who hoped her feelings didn't show too clearly. 'You are acquainted with him?'

'Somewhat. His name is Mr Anthony Oliver. We met at a house party, many years ago, before I married. He was—most amiable.'

Mary's head tilted even further. 'Indeed?' She looped her arm through Penelope's and they strolled along the path again, quite as if the world hadn't shaken around her. 'Tell me, will you and Fred be at the assembly rooms tomorrow evening? It's always a terrible crush, of course, but the dancing is usually of fine quality. Everyone can be seen there.'

Penelope smiled down at Mary. She was rather like Penelope had once been, in her younger, more optimistic days. 'Everyone you know.'

'Knowing people is my bread and butter. And it's a great deal of fun! I didn't know your Mr Oliver, though. I wonder if he will be at the assembly. If so, then you *must* come.'

Penelope thought over this, imagining dancing with Anthony as she had so long ago and almost giggled with a burst of excitement. 'Why?'

Mary twirled around. 'To dance with him, of course! Even from a distance I could see he admired you.'

'I fear my dancing days may be over.'

'What nonsense! You are in the very prime of dancing life, Pen.' They paused to watch Eleanor and Fred coming towards them, dappled in the sunlight as they laughed together. 'Do you think Fred could also be persuaded to come to the assembly? Or does he think his dancing days are past, too?'

Penelope studied Mary's expression beneath her straw, frilled bonnet. Mary looked like a china shepherdess, all blonde curls and pink cheeks, yet Penelope was certainly learning never to underestimate either of the St Aubin sisters. 'He might think that. He has born so many burdens of late. But I am of the firm opinion he is wrong and he must be persuaded of that. He must enjoy life again for a while.'

'I definitely agree. We must make sure you are *both* at the assembly. And that he mingles in the ballroom, not just disappearing into the card room.'

'You have a candidate—a lady in mind for him?'

'Perhaps. I must consult with Eleanor and Harry and hear their thoughts on the possibility.'

Penelope nodded, watching as Fred and Eleanor laughed again, their heads bent close together, as if they had always been just like that. Penelope saw the old Fred just then. The laughing young man who had welcomed her into his home and been her friend. The man who hadn't yet been stricken with pain and burdens. He looked…

He looked happy.

Penelope glanced at Mary to see if she saw it, too. That connection between Fred and Eleanor. Mary just watched, expressionless.

Penelope suddenly ached for Fred, as she once had for herself. A heart, no matter how well-guarded one thought it was, was a frail, vulnerable thing and she didn't want Fred to be hurt any more than he already had. Hurt by a love that couldn't be.

But if he truly loved Eleanor…

'Can you not give me some hint of who the lady might be?' Penelope asked.

Mary shook her head. 'We shall all know soon enough. Just come to the assembly and meet some people. It will be a pleasant diversion, if nothing else.'

Penelope sighed. They continued their walk, sunlight and shadow falling over them. 'I should certainly welcome a diversion, I declare.'

Chapter Seven

Eleanor St Aubin was a most unusual lady indeed. Fred had always known that. Her care and empathy for others had made her treasured in her father's parish and she had laughter like a sunny day. But now she'd grown even more into herself. Warm and caring, with her soft smile and magical laughter, she drew Fred closer and closer every time he saw her. She made his world a brighter place at long last.

He carefully studied himself in the looking glass as he painstakingly tied his cravat for the assembly. His scars seemed to have faded there in Bath, looking like mere pale streaks against his skin and he was as strong and fit as ever now that his strength had returned. Surely he was not *too* ruined for the ordinary joys of life now, for holding a lady's hand, laughing with her—kissing her.

Yet he knew very well the truth. There was really no use for such wishful thinking, for trying to remake the world. He was too old now. He felt so very much older than the Fred who was once Eleanor's friend at Moulton Magna. He was too changed by his years at war. Too weighed down by responsibility to think about a sweet lady like Eleanor. She was too kind to deserve his troubles—his crumbling estate, his nightmares from the war, the distrust it all left in his heart—and too caught in responsibility to family, just as he was. They wouldn't be good for one another. Not situated as they both were in life.

Yet the pleasure he felt when he thought of her, when he could actually be in the warmth of her presence, was there and there was no mistaking it. When she was near, it was as if the sun shone all the time. He longed to know what was behind those unfathomable eyes of hers and that little smile as she watched the world around her. Despite what she had been dealt in life, there was always that spark of humour, of delight in people, and in music, and in nature and in poetry, which made him delight in it all again, too.

Her sweetness was always unchanged, as was his craving for it.

Fred shook his head as he studied that slightly crooked cravat. Like himself, the lack of perfection and symmetry, couldn't quite be worthy of Eleanor. Yet it was all he had. He fastened it with a cameo-headed pin and smoothed his hair. He had no place for someone like her in his life now, nor she for him. When he went into the Army, he left his wild days behind him. He'd vowed he would change. That he would be a man his family and home could rely on. That he could be worthy of someone like Eleanor. But to be that he had to be apart from her.

He glanced out through the window at the gathering evening, purple-blue and shimmering. Surely, though, trying to be responsible and noble didn't mean he couldn't have the rare, golden pleasure of a dance with Eleanor on such a night...

Eleanor peeked curiously out of the window of their hansom as they joined the long line of vehicles and pedestrians snaking their way towards the assembly rooms, as they did every week. She'd been there many times before, of course. Meeting potential matches, playing cards, sipping wine, listening to valuable gossip—it was all an important part of her job.

Tonight, though, she felt quite unaccountably excited about it all. Nervous. She twisted her fan between her gloved fingers as she looked around, seeing things familiar yet new. She had barely been able to sleep last night, or concentrate on her work that day, for thinking about Fred there in the sunlight and Fred holding her hand. His smile, the touch of his lips on her skin, the sparkle of everything around him. Would she see him that night? She did long for that. And also dreaded it.

The familiar building, with its pillared portico, looked transformed in the evening. Golden light spilled from every window and doorway, a bright diamond shimmer in the purple-black night. Laughter rang out from the revellers making their way to front doors, with feathers waving merrily and jewels sparkling.

'Oh, look, Eleanor, there are Miss Evans and her mother,' Mary whispered, the ribbons in her hair nodding as she smiled at their newest patrons. 'Miss Evans *is* pretty, I think, even if she is terribly quiet. Who could blame her, with such a mother! I do think she would do well for Fred, don't you? That lovely dowry!'

Eleanor studied Miss Evans for a moment, trying to compose how to answer. She and Mary had spoken of Miss Evans, along with one or two other potential matches, and Eleanor had been a bit surprised by the notion. Surprised and, yes, discomfited, if she had to admit it to herself. Even if she knew in her head that Fred needed such a wife, her heart refused to quite co-operate yet.

On a professional level, Eleanor couldn't disagree with Mary. From an agency point of view, it could be a fine match. But her heart felt torn in two to put all her feelings aside and admit this, to be sensible again. 'Perhaps you are right, Mary. But shouldn't they meet first, before we decide she must be the one?'

'Of course I am right!' Mary declared. 'And they will meet, I'm sure, perhaps even this very evening. And speaking of matches, did you perchance see Penelope's old friend Mr Oliver on our walk on Beechen Cliff yesterday?'

Eleanor thought back and recalled glimpsing Penelope chatting with a man in a handsomely tailored blue coat, along with two little girls. Penelope had seemed most absorbed in the conversation, even from that distance, and she had not spoken of it after. 'The one with the two children? So he knew Penelope?'

'Indeed. All she would really say is they met at a house party before she was married, but I could see there must be much more. Such longing between them! So I did a bit of research.'

'In a day? How efficient of you, Mary.' But Eleanor wasn't really surprised. Mary was usually very efficient indeed, as well as being a romantic at heart. She had a sharp instinct for what would, or could, work. So if Mary saw something in Penelope and this Mr Oliver, she probably wasn't wrong. Though she was wrong about Miss Evans.

'Of course. Pen deserves someone truly worthy, doesn't she? Someone to win her heart and make her happy. After old Lord Fleetwood and his troubles...'

Troubles that had now landed on Fred. The estate and all its tenants and workers. The crumbling house that meant he had to marry an heiress. 'And what did you find?'

'Mr Oliver is quite well-off indeed, though he is self-made. He owns several business concerns, built up from his family's textile imports concern, and he just bought a fine house in Surrey. He has never been married. Too busy working, I'm sure, which means he needs a wife to manage his household and help him in society. He is also wonderfully handsome! I'm quite sure he fell deeply in love with Pen all those years ago and never married as no lady could compare to her.' Mary sighed happily at the thought.

Eleanor laughed. 'You should write novels! I agree Penelope deserves a happy match, but I fear neither of them are patrons of the agency. How can we help?'

Mary waved this away with a flick of her lace fan. 'We can surely assist a friend! I shall think of something. Oh, look, there is Lady Banks! Good heavens, what a turban, have you ever seen such colours? Would it look well on me? I shall have to find out her milliner...'

Eleanor smiled as she watched her sister vanish into the crowd. She took a glass of wine and found a quieter corner near the fireplace where she could examine the scene. The people finding their dance partners with shy smiles, the husbands slipping off to the card room, the friends calling greetings. This was one of the reasons she enjoyed Bath life and enjoyed her work. Helping people to find happiness and to enjoy their lives as much as possible in such congenial surroundings was a dream to her.

And suddenly, appearing in a gap in the crowd, was Fred himself, arm in arm with Penelope. He was smiling at something Pen said to him, his face alight and so young in that moment, the harsh lines of worry and pain erased. He had a new coat. A dark green superfine fitted perfectly over his broad, strong shoulders, the stark white of his cravat framing his square, chiselled jaw. A wave of amber-gold hair swept over his brow and he flicked it back.

In the glow of the candles, his scars could barely be seen and several ladies turned their heads to watch him walk past with avid interest. Surely they only saw his heroic, dashing *mien*. Penelope was soon claimed for a dance, and to Eleanor's surprise, instead of asking one of the young ladies to partner him, Fred came to her side, a smile on his lips that made her smile in return.

A rush of latecomers poured through the doors, racing to claim their partners for the next set and find places in the lines forming on the parquet floor beneath the sparkle of the chandeliers. The whole night had taken on a diamond-bright shimmer.

'Shall we join them, Eleanor?' Fred asked, gesturing to the dancers. She peeked up at him, to see he smiled at her ruefully, crookedly, a tiny flash of white that made her heart stutter. Was he really offering to open the dancing with her, to give her the first dance of the evening? 'My dancing skills have never been of the finest, but I'm sure I can manage not to quite disgrace myself.'

Eleanor laughed, put entirely at her ease with him again, as was always the way with Fred. He made her feel discomfited, fidgety. But then there was that wonderful feeling of ease and knowing. Of being with someone she knew. Or once thought she knew. 'It's been a long time since I did more than observe the dancing, but perhaps if we just follow the others we could muddle along.'

Fred offered her his arm and she slipped her gloved hand lightly over his sleeve, as she had many times before. But at this moment it all felt new. His arm felt so warm and strong under her touch, holding her steady as he led her into the crowd. Those ladies still watched him, whispering behind their fans.

She glanced up at Fred, wondering if he noticed them and he smiled back at her. The candlelight, the music and laughter, the scent of roses and perfume and wine. And, above all, the feeling of Fred beside her again after so long. Real and not a dream. Not a memory. Surely it was something, one small moment, she could savour? It couldn't last long, she knew that, but it was a wonderful, sparkling feeling all the same.

She longed to forget the agency, forget being sensible and responsible, just for one dance. She gave him a quick, delighted smile and vowed she *would* forget it all for this moment. She would just think of him.

They found their places at the end of the dance. In Bath, such gatherings always seemed meant for younger ladies than Eleanor—ladies who were fresh and innocent, seeking their futures, while hers had slipped beyond her before she even realised it. But now she felt truly a part of it all. Part of the fun and laughter and excitement of the dance.

The lead couple stepped off, skipping together then apart, twirling behind the next pair and everyone else in the line followed. Eleanor found her feet remembered the steps. Skipping right then left, turning, spinning and coming back to find Fred's hand again. How light she felt—as if she could float right out of her slippers! The music wound around her, carrying her forward. She couldn't help but laugh as Fred touched her hand, his fingers sliding over hers, and they cast off and around, meeting again. Their feet flew together, back and forth, light as whipped cream as she swirled around him. It was as if they'd always moved together just that way.

The lavish, glittering room with its pastel walls and domed ceiling, the jewels and silks and laces, all blurred together dizzily as Fred caught her arm in a turn. His bad arm was tucked behind his back, barely to be seen.

He stumbled a bit and Eleanor smiled as they righted themselves together and danced on, perfectly matched in their movements, bearing each other ever forward.

'I did say I was never much of a dancer, didn't I?' he said, his voice full of wonderful laughter. He turned them faster and faster as the music grew, until she giggled.

She, sensible Eleanor St Aubin, *giggling*! It was a magical, topsy-turvy night indeed.

'You do give yourself far too little credit, Fred,' she said. 'You have always been a splendid dancer indeed!'

'I am too out of practice,' he said.

He did not feel 'out of practice' one jot as his arm slipped around her waist for another turn. Eleanor felt so delicate in his arms, a true fairy queen born above the world by her knight.

They spun once more and the music, which had been winding higher and higher around them, crashed down in a great finale. Eleanor skidded to a halt, still holding on to Fred as she tried to catch her breath, tried to float down to earth once more. The blur around her slowed and turned solid again, other dancers bowing and curtsying, the chandelier going still above her head.

He bowed low to her and she curtsied in answer, trying to catch her breath. She didn't want to part from him, not yet. If only her moment could go on and on…

'Shall we take a stroll? Perhaps seek out some refreshments?' Fred asked. He sounded eager, even a bit unsure, as if he too didn't want the dance to end just yet. 'You can tell me more about Bath society and the people around us. Pen says I cannot go on being a grumpy old hermit.'

'I don't think you are grumpy and not *terribly* old,' Eleanor teased as they made their way to the quieter edge of the room. 'But if you want to find a wife, society is a necessity.'

Eleanor glimpsed Miss Evans near the doors to the card room, looking very young and pretty in a new, very stylish, pink-striped silk gown. Her mother was nowhere in sight for the moment. Miss Evans was speaking with a tall, slim, dark-haired, poetically pale young man Eleanor recognised as Mr Overbury, a young curate whose older sister had recently met her fiancé through the agency. He was handsome, true and beautifully musical, but not of great fortune. Surely Mrs Evans would not be happy her daughter was spending time with a 'mere' curate! Especially if she knew an earl was nearby…

'You see that young lady in pink just over there, by the card room?' Eleanor said.

'The one with the silver feathers in her hair?'

'Indeed. Now, you must not breathe a word that I spoke to you of any agency business, but her name is Pamela Evans and she and her mother paid us a visit in recent days. Her father has accrued a great fortune in industry and they wish for her to marry well. Mary thinks she might be a possible match for you.' She forced away that touch of cold reluctance and made herself smile.

Fred's eyes narrowed as he studied Miss Evans. 'For me?'

'Yes. I think her mother would be very impressed by a fine old title.'

'And what does the lady seek?' he asked quietly, still studying Miss Evans as she laughed with Mr Overbury.

Eleanor frowned in thought as she watched the young lady and the curate. It was rather hard to decipher what Miss Evans might want for herself as she was so quiet. So unreadable. Eleanor knew she or Mary would have to find a way to speak to her alone soon. 'To own the truth, I am not quite sure. She is a quiet lady and who could blame her when her mother loves to talk so much. She is very pretty.'

'And what of you, Eleanor?'

'Me?' she said, confused. 'I am not so pretty...'

He laughed. 'I do beg to differ on that. But I meant, Mary thinks Miss Evans would make a fine Lady Fleetwood. What do you think of that?'

Eleanor thought no lady would be worthy of being Lady Fleetwood now, not really. But he must marry. It was the way of the world. She had always known that. But she hadn't realised how much it would hurt to face those facts herself one day. To do what she must do. But she cared about Fred far too much to not help him. 'I think...'

They were jostled a bit by the growing crowd and someone stepped on Eleanor's hem making her gasp. 'Shall we walk outside a bit on the terrace I saw earlier?' Fred said. 'Get a bit of air.'

'Yes, I'd like that,' she answered, though she knew she shouldn't be alone with Fred like that. It was simply too tempting, the soft night air beckoning her with a gentle breeze.

They were alone for the moment under the starry

sky, only a few couples in the distance, and they strolled between the potted trees in silence. Eleanor studied him there in the shadows and a thousand things passed through her mind. Things she longed to say that she never could. That he should forget the Miss Evans of the world. That she, Eleanor, was right there! Yet she wasn't there, not really. She could only take the bits of his presence she could have now, while she still could.

'Have you never thought of using your agency to find your own match, Ella?' he asked as they stopped near the balustrade, staring out into the night.

Surprised by the question, she quickly shook her head. 'I couldn't do that! It's only a business, really, and no one I have met there would suit me anyway. I sometimes do wonder if it might not be good for Mary, though…'

Fred laughed softly. 'You St Aubin girls. Like the most attractive nettles, blossoms hiding prickles. In a sweet way, of course. It would be hard to get so close to you.'

She turned towards him, studying him in the moonlight. Yes, in some ways he had changed from the young man who had been her friend. But in some ways he was, he felt, just the same. She reached up and lightly traced the chiselled line of his jaw with her gloved fingertips, feeling a muscle tense beneath her touch. 'Yet you have always been close to me.'

They'd known each other so long, denied themselves so long. Danced away and around and beyond. She'd told herself it had to be that way and surely he had, too. But just now, none of that mattered. All that mattered was the raw longing that washed over her. All she could see was him, all she knew was him. She couldn't stay away now.

'And you to me, Ella.' His hands circled her waist, tugging her closer. She went, unresisting, curious, filled with the need to be close to him. It was dizzying and she clutched at his shoulders to hold herself upright. All her senses tipped and whirled and she knew only him.

As if in a hazy dream, far away but more real and immediate than anything she'd ever known before, his head bent towards hers and he kissed her.

The touch of his lips was soft at first. Velvety, warm, pressing teasingly once, twice. When she did not, *could* not, move away, instead she leaned closer to him and his kiss deepened. Became hotter, more urgent, answering her own need.

The world utterly vanished and there was only him. Only that one perfect moment. And she longed to seize it completely. Remember it for ever.

Yet it was a moment that shattered all too soon. A shout from the street below broke into her dream, dragging her back down to earth with a hard thud, reminding her where she was, who she was and what she risked there. Her reputation. Her heart.

She tore her mouth from his, tipping back her head to suck in a deep breath of night air.

'Ella,' he said hoarsely, stepping away from her. 'Ella, I—I cannot...'

'No,' she managed to whisper. Her heart and mind were in a jumble and she couldn't think at all. She longed for him, but he could not be hers. Never be hers.

Not really. She was losing herself. Losing him. 'Please don't say you're sorry.'

'How could I be sorry? But I must say…'

Eleanor shook her head fiercely. She couldn't speak. Couldn't think. Couldn't make sense of this moment. Not yet. Not when he was so close to her. 'I must go!' she gasped and ran away, leaving him there in the perfect night.

Just a bit earlier that evening…

Mary studied the cards in her hand, just as she studied the room around her, taking in every detail in one discreet, sweeping glance.

She especially studied the others at her table. Lord Coulton, a young poet who kept beseeching the agency to help him in his quest to find an artistic soulmate, a true muse, while also trying in vain to court Mary herself, she could dismiss for the moment. It was Penelope and Mr Oliver who held her attention.

Penelope had declared he was only someone she met once, long ago, at a house party. But Mary was certain there was more—far more—to the tale. Her matchmaking nose was itching.

'Have you resided long in Bath, Miss St Aubin?' Mr Oliver asked as he laid down a card.

'For some time, yes. My father was vicar at Moulton Magna village and when he sadly passed away my sister and I came here.'

'Her father was a veritable angel and so well-read. He knew all the philosophers and theologians and gave the most engaging sermons,' Penelope said. 'We were bereft to lose such a fine family, so I am happy to have the St Aubin sisters as neighbours again.' She glanced at Mr Oliver from under her lashes, a small smile hovering over her lips. 'It is such a pleasure to find old friends again, is it not?'

He smiled at her in return and, for an instant, Mary was sure they saw no one else at all.

'And how do you enjoy town life, Miss St Aubin?' he asked, studying his cards again.

'Very much!' Mary enthused. 'I love the assemblies and concerts. Sometimes I wonder what London must be like, with even more theatres and pleasure gardens.'

'Have you often visited London?' Mr Overbury said eagerly. 'I should love to show it to you...'

'How sweet of you, Mr Overbury! But when we find your muse at last, you shall want only to show *her* the sites,' Mary said, patting his hand. 'I fear I have only visited London once, when I was quite young and most overwhelmed by it all. I visited the Tower and Westminster Abbey and various other churches my father insisted on. I long to go back and see more. To see everything!'

'Perhaps you will fall in love with a London gentleman and be whisked away as his wife to a mansion in Berkeley Square!' Penelope teased. 'With so many visitors to Bath, who knows who we might meet?'

Mary laughed. The thought of marriage for *herself* always seemed such an odd and unthinkable thing. Her schemes were always for patrons. Her joy came from fitting them together like puzzle pieces and then seeing their happiness. She enjoyed making matches too much to become one herself.

Penelope, on the other hand…

She studied Penelope and Mr Oliver again as they murmured over their cards, their hands brushing. At the touch, Pen's cheeks went quite rosy, which Mary found fascinating.

Yes, a match for Penelope would be most satisfying. And one for Eleanor, though Mary wouldn't say so to her sister. Mary did often wish that dearest Eleanor would meet a man truly worthy of her and be swept off to a lovely life with a home and children, after all her hard work taking care of Papa and Mary herself for so long. She remembered seeing Eleanor walking with Fred along Beechen Cliff, their heads bent together, fitting together so perfectly.

Why did it have to be Fred, now?

Mary sighed. It was much too sad that Eleanor and Fred could not be, that Fred's duty took him away from them. Yet surely there was *someone* out there who would be just right. Who would be truly worthy of her sister. She glanced around the card tables, evaluating the gentlemen she saw there. Too old, too young, too flighty, too serious.

And too clergyish, she thought as she glimpsed that handsome young Mr Overbury strolling near the refreshment tables. No matter how lovely, Eleanor did not deserve to be a vicarage servant again. And Mr Overbury…

He seemed very absorbed by the lady who walked beside him, arm in arm. And that lady was Miss Evans.

'Mary?' Penelope said, studying the fallen cards before them. 'Are you well?'

Mary made herself laugh. 'Oh, yes, you were asking about marriage! Well, I have no desire to wed, at least not yet. I enjoy my life too much to change.'

'Mary has been telling me about a masquerade ball to be held at Sydney Gardens,' Penelope said. 'It should be most exciting! Costumes, music. Shall you be there, Mr Oliver?'

He smiled at her, wide and wondering, setting off Mary's matchmaking senses once more. 'If you will be there, Lady Fleetwood, I should enjoy it very much.'

'We should take a box,' Mary said. And she would be sure Penelope and Mr Oliver sat right next to each other.

'Anthony? By Jove it *is* you,' a deep, chocolate-rich voice, lightly touched with a Scots burr, said. The sound made prickles unaccountably tingle at the back of Mary's neck, like a fine opera aria could do. She shivered and longed to hear that voice again.

'Campbell!' Mr Oliver said, leaping to his feet to hold out his hand to the gentleman who approached them. 'How splendid to see you. When did you arrive in Bath? I heard nothing of your coming here.'

Mary glanced up and gasped when she saw the most extraordinary gentleman standing there. Very tall, broad-shouldered, with too-long, auburn-streaked dark hair falling over his brow just above bright green eyes. He wore the most fashionable, conventional evening coat of dark blue, with a cream waistcoat and well-tied cravat. But he might as well have been wearing a kilt as he strode over hills, a broadsword in hand.

Suddenly overcome with a ridiculous confusion and a warm flush spreading over her cheeks and throat as if she had been in the sun too long, Mary stared down hard at the new cards in her hand.

'Only this week. Adele declared she was in great need of society and I could not spare the time for London, so I thought to give her a little treat for a few days,' Mr Campbell answered, his emerald gaze sweeping over the table. It caught and lingered on Mary, a small frown on his lips as if he sought to read her thoughts.

Mary made herself smile back, carelessly, brightly. *Adele.* Was that his wife? For surely such a man must be married. The name 'Adele' made her sound like a dainty, china-doll-pretty creature. The two of them together would look like a pair from a novel.

'Bath is a fine choice, I'm sure.' Mr Oliver turned to indicate the others at the table. 'Lady Fleetwood, Miss St Aubin, Lord Coulton, may I present a cousin of mine, Charles Campbell? He lives in Scotland most of the time and I haven't seen him in some time. He's also been much occupied as guardian to our young kinswoman, Adele. Charles, this is Lady Fleetwood, who I once met when we were impossibly young. And Miss St Aubin, who is a resident of this fair town, as is Lord Coulton, a fine poet.'

'How do you do?' Mr Campbell said with a small bow. 'Miss St Aubin…'

'We are just finishing our hand, Mr Campbell and I fear I have lost most shockingly,' Mary said, hoping she sounded light and unaffected by this man's touch. By his night-dark eyes. By the intense way he looked at her. 'Will you take my place? I should go find my sister.'

'I would enjoy that, thank you, Miss St Aubin,' he said, his gaze never leaving her until she feared she would drop the cards in a flustered flurry again.

'Charles was a terrible sharper in our misspent youth,' Mr Oliver declared. 'We all constantly owed him our pocket money!'

'Anthony, you shall misrepresent me to these fine ladies,' Charles Campbell protested, though he laughed, a rough, low, rumbling sound Mary was sure she could feel all the way to her toes. 'I merely had more patience to practise than you. But I fear I must now decline and play with you on another evening. I left Adele dancing.'

'Mr Campbell!' Penelope cried. 'I am sure you shouldn't have left her alone in such a crush.'

Mr Campbell shifted on his feet, a look of chagrin on his dark, chiselled face that made Mary want to reassure him. Comfort him. Help him.

Oh, she was in trouble.

'You see what a terrible inadequate chaperon I am?' he said. 'I feel I am constantly learning new duties, new pitfalls.'

Penelope laughed, but Mary thought Mr Campbell looked so genuinely baffled she couldn't help but give him a reassuring smile as she folded up her cards. 'Dance sets do tend to be long here at the assembly rooms and Mr Derrick, the Master of Ceremonies, keeps a sharp eye on the proceedings at all times. I'm sure there is a very small scope for mischief, even if the young lady was determined.'

He gave her a little bow, a little, secret smile on his lips. 'I dare say you had much determination, Miss St Aubin.'

Mary tilted her head as she examined him, wondering if he teased her, criticised—maybe even admired? He was a wonderful puzzlement. 'I might have, once. Now I am an old spinster and can be a most devoted chaperon when needed. Shall I walk with you to find Miss Adele? I should look for my sister, anyway.'

'That would be most appreciated, thank you, Miss St Aubin.' Mr Campbell gave her a gallant bow. 'Anthony, shall I call on you this week?'

'Certainly. You owe me a chance to win my pride back at the card table.'

'I fear I am truly a poor chaperon—a poor guardian altogether,' Mr Campbell said ruefully as he and Mary made their way through the crowded room. She knew she should pay attention to what was around her, check with patrons, but all she could seem to focus on was *him*. Most extraordinary. 'I've always lived alone you see, Miss St Aubin, and I've become too set in my ways.'

He'd never married at all? Mary found that hard to believe. Surely every lady within a hundred miles had yearned after him! Yet there was certain satisfaction there, too. Not for herself, she told herself sternly, although not quite convincingly. But because he must have high standards. Maybe he wished to marry only for great love! So romantic. 'How old is Miss Adele?'

'Just now seventeen. Her parents, my distant cousins, sadly died from a fever a year ago and I became her guardian. I'm trying to bring her out in society. To give her a place in the world and help her be happy but...' He held out his hand in a helpless gesture and Mary's heart ached for him.

'I am sure she is very fortunate to have you. It is not an easy age for a young lady, especially one who has lost her parents,' she said.

'She seems more cheerful since we came to Bath. She smiles more and is more interested in what is happening around her, which gives me hope.' A tiny frown appeared on his brow as he looked at the crowd around them. 'But I fear I am ill-equipped to help her find something—well, more serious. She has a fortune, you see. Not the largest. But it could be of definite interest to more—unscrupulous elements. And she is pretty, of a trusting nature. She deserves so much happiness in life.'

'Then she is doubly lucky to have a guardian like yourself to watch out for her. Someone who cares for her.' Mary studied the couples strolling past, the knots of young ladies whispering and giggling next to the pastel pink walls. 'Which one is Miss Adele?'

'Just there, in the pale green gown, with the blonde hair,' he said, pride written large in his tone.

Mary turned to examined her. Yes, pretty. Golden hair, like fairy-spun silk, twisted atop a Grecian head and bound with a pearl bandeau. A heart-shaped face with sweet eyes. Not too tall or too short. Slim in fashionable pale green silk. She glanced around shyly but with interest. A small smile on her rosebud lips. Yes, very pretty. And with a fortune *and* a handsome guardian in the bargain. Mary wondered dreamily, hopefully, if one or both of the Campbells could use the agency's services. It would be quite a coup…

The dance set ended and as Mary and Mr Campbell watched, Miss Adele was quickly approached by two eager young gentlemen.

'You need have no fear of Mr Parker,' Mary said, gesturing at the taller of the two. 'I fear you can see his somewhat…misguided choice of waistcoats, but he is most respectable and has a fine estate. The other one—hmm, I am not so sure. Lord Teller has only just arrived in Bath but I would be wary. He is very often a habitue of the racecourses.'

Mr Campbell nodded, looking at her with an impressed tilt of his smile. 'You know much of Bath society then, Miss St Aubin?' he asked.

'Indeed. One might say it is even rather a—career.'

He laughed in delight. 'I should be very interested to hear more, then. Shall we go meet Adele and then perhaps join the next dance set ourselves?'

Mary studied him carefully and finally smiled and nodded. 'Thank you, Mr Campbell. I do enjoy a dance very much indeed…'

Chapter Eight

'After all our time here, Eleanor, I vow I do not know why it must always rain in Bath,' Mary sighed as she gazed out through the window of Molland's confectionery shop. Despite the steady downpour, people hurried past laden with packages, intent on errands, while inside all was warm and creamy with the scents of sugar and spices.

Eleanor studied the scene, too. But she didn't see the shop windows across the street, the bobbing umbrellas scurrying past, or the carriages casting up plumes of water to splash at those umbrellas. Instead her head was filled with visions of the assembly room, dancing with Fred, the stars wheeling overhead as she held onto his arm in the music-echoing night, the touch of his hand…

She shivered.

'Eleanor?' she heard Mary say, the words fizzy and echoing, as if they came from a long distance away. As if she was caught in those dreamlike moments she never wanted to end.

She blinked and glanced across the little round table

at her sister. Mary's face was creased with concern under her feathered bonnet.

'Yes?'

'Are you quite well, Eleanor, dear? You seem so pre-occupied. It's not at all like you.'

Eleanor made herself smile reassuringly. 'I'm quite well, I promise. Just a bit tired. You're right, it's all the rain. But at least we have Molland's marzipan!' She held out the dish of pink and green sweets and Mary popped one in her mouth with a happy sigh. Ever since childhood, Mary could reliably be distracted with confectionery. Miss Muffins, sitting at their feet, looked up with hope on her little face.

'It's no wonder you're weary,' Mary said. 'I am rather tired, myself. So much happening! Assemblies and theatres, and the masquerade to look forward to. I vow I counted at least five possible new patrons for the agency at the assembly rooms.'

'Five?' Eleanor asked sharply, wondering how many of them would be for Fred.

Mary ticked them off on her fingers. 'Lady Hertford and Mrs Miller-Forster, that charming young widow who just moved into the Crescent. Those two will be looking about soon, at least. And I saw Lord and Lady Amson! I am so happy for them. They just married last month and declared their undying gratitude to the agency.'

'Yes, of course. How charming they were together. I was very happy when they matched together.' Eleanor thought with a bittersweet pang of the bliss she'd seen on the newly married couple's faces when last they met. When Lord Amson first came to the agency, she wasn't at all sure who might suit him. But there was someone for everyone. Happiness waiting everywhere.

If only she could find that, too. She would just have to look for her joy in the matches they made, that was all.

'And Penelope and Mr Oliver looked so happy while they played cards together,' Mary went on. 'They could scarcely look away from each other!'

Eleanor laughed. 'Mary! I thought we agreed we should not yet meddle with people who aren't agency patrons.'

'I said they were not *officially* patrons. I did not say I wouldn't meddle just a bit! Penelope is so lovely. She deserves some happiness in life after being married to old Lord Fleetwood. And surely you saw how Mr Oliver watches her. So meltingly gorgeous!'

Eleanor had to agree. When they were in the same room together, Penelope and Anthony Oliver did watch one another when they thought no one was looking. Such longing. It made Eleanor feel so much for them, hope for them. 'But I am sure they don't need our help.'

'Maybe just a tiny push in the right direction, if the chance presents itself. Penelope has grown too accustomed to thinking of others all the time, not herself. She may need assistance in—thinking a different way.'

'Maybe if Penelope asks for our help or advice. Who else did you meet at the assembly that may be looking for a match?'

'A man named Mr Campbell, a cousin of Mr Oliver. Did you meet him?'

'I don't believe so.'

'I was introduced to him while I played cards with Penelope and Mr Oliver. Oh, and with Lord Coulton, we must find him a muse match *soon*, he is becoming so puppyish around me. Anyway, Mr Campbell is a widower with a fine estate and very good-looking indeed. But he is a new guardian to a young lady, Adele Campbell, something of an heiress. And I could see right away how overwhelming it must be for a gentleman on his own to steer a young lady to a suitable match. He surely needs a wife to help him.'

Eleanor glanced sharply at her sister. There was something rather odd, something soft and dreamy, in her sister's voice when she said that name. 'Have you someone in mind for Mr Campbell?'

Mary studied the bit of marzipan in her hand with an odd expression on her face—thoughtful and wistful. 'Not yet. It would have to be someone truly special.'

'We can go over our files as soon as we get home. Any other matches you considered?'

'Miss Evans and Fred, of course! I am still convinced of the possibilities there.'

Eleanor frowned. 'They barely spoke last night, as far as I could see. Miss Evans seemed to enjoy the company of Mr Overbury, that lovely young curate. He really brought her out of her shell when they were dancing.'

Mary waved this away, Miss Muffins avidly watching the bit of marzipan moving in her fingers. 'Her parents would never match her with a curate, I fear. A dance isn't a match, either, Eleanor, you know this.'

Eleanor nodded. She *did* know that. All too well. Just as she knew the sort of wife Fred required.

'Oh, look!' Mary cried. 'The rain has stopped. And is that a bit of sunshine I see? Let's take a stroll by the river, shall we? I am sure Miss Muffins needs to stretch her paws a bit.'

'Of course. A fine idea.' Eleanor could certainly use a breath of fresh air, too. Something to distract her from thinking constantly of Fred. The walk beside the Avon was a lovely one. Lined with trees and roses, and elegant stone bridges leading towards the green hills. Yes, a fine distraction for an hour. She gathered up Miss Muffins's leash and her reticule and watched Mary pop the last of the candy into her mouth with a happy sigh.

And then—disaster struck.

Miss Muffins, bored with so much standing about and looking at pretty views, darted off towards another dog in the distance, catching Eleanor by surprise. The lead snapped out of her hand and Miss Muffins bounded away in the direction of the river, making Eleanor's heart go still with cold panic. With a series of joyous barks, circling skirts and walking sticks, Miss Muffins became airborne and landed with a great splash in the muddy water of the river. Only her little head was visible as she drifted away, yelping with panic and alarm. A crowd ran towards the riverbank, pointing and crying out.

'Miss Muffins!' Eleanor screamed, filled with fear that she'd lost her little friend. She ran towards the river, pushing past the onlookers. She didn't even notice when her hat fell free from its pinks and the breeze caught at her hair, tugging it free.

'Eleanor! Be careful, you'll fall,' Mary cried.

'Miss Muffins, come back!' Eleanor called. She suddenly became aware of Fred beside her. His calm stillness, his watchfulness, steadying her. He always did seem to appear just when she needed him most and there he was, like magic. She was sure he must have looked just as determined before he charged into battle. He quickly stripped away his boots and coat, leaving him standing there in his bright white shirt sleeves, making a few ladies nearby coo with admiration even in the midst of emergency. He pushed the garments into Eleanor's arms and jumped into the waters after Miss Muffins. No one seemed to notice the scars on his arms at all.

It all happened so quickly. Eleanor felt all in a daze. One moment she was chatting with Fred and Mary, the day bright around them. The sun warm overhead. Miss Muffins frisking about as usual. Then, in a snap, the dog was gone. Carried away by the water.

Until Fred was there.

The ladies around them exclaimed in almost delighted fear and cries of 'how heroic' as Mary took Eleanor's arm and whispered, 'Don't worry, Fred will get her back.'

Eleanor could hardly breathe she was so overcome with anxiety. She stood still, so very still, sure she was turning into stone as she watched Fred wade out into the deeper water and then cast off with long, even strokes to catch Miss Muffins. Just like their days of swimming in the stream at Moulton Magna, when the sunlight would glitter on his head and he would laugh and dive like an otter. He'd lost none of his skill. He reached out and grabbed Miss Muffins by the scruff of her wet neck, tugging her towards and holding her against his chest. Miss Muffins thrashed and barked, frightened that her adventure had ended so very badly, but Fred held her fast. At last, he hauled them both free of the river and stood before Eleanor, dripping great quantities of dirty water onto the grass but safe at last.

'Fred!' she cried, kneeling down beside them, her heart pounding. 'Are you all right?'

He gasped, half laughing. But he winced when he rubbed at his bad arm, as if it pained him. 'Quite so, indeed. A fine day for a swim. I'm glad I happened to be passing, Ella.'

Eleanor suddenly realised that their little drama had drawn quite an audience. She laughed, a strange little hiccoughing noise of embarrassment. 'Oh, bad Miss Muffins! Very bad indeed. Thank you, Fred. Thank you so very, very much! You have gone quite above and beyond the call of gallantry.'

'What a great hero you are!' Mary declared and a murmuring chorus of agreement flowed around them. All the ladies stared at Fred with wide-eyed amazement, as if he was the hero in a grand romantic novel.

Eleanor very much feared she was doing the same. Gaping at him—in public!—like a moonstruck school-girl. It was just that she was hit, yet again, with the monumental realisation that Fred was quite, quite beautiful. Even dripping with mud, his waving, bright hair plastered to his brow, he was astounding. He was so tall, so strong-shouldered, his sky eyes glowing. He was the very epitome of 'heroism' and he did not even realise it at all. Which, of course, made it all the more attractive. He stared back at her, the two of them very still, pulled together by some wild force.

Until Miss Muffins gave a great shake, sending water and mud everywhere, and their onlookers backed away, exclaiming.

'We—we should take this miscreant home,' Eleanor said. 'She needs a bath in the worst way.'

Miss Muffins howled at the dreaded *b* word. Despite her glee at jumping into the river, she hated a pan of clean, soapy water with a passion.

Eleanor ignored her, and all the new admirers of Fred still gathered around and reached out to take the dog from him.

'You'll mess your spencer, Eleanor,' Mary protested.

'Indeed you will,' Fred said. 'Let's wrap her in my coat and I'll walk with you to your lodgings. I cannot mess my attire any further, I fear.'

Eleanor glanced around. The ladies still watched in sighing admiration. Their gentlemen escorts looking quite disgruntled to lose their attention to such a heroic gentleman.

'I think perhaps we should find someplace a bit, er, quieter where I could clean up a bit,' he murmured, his face a charming, embarrassed pink at finding himself such an object of attention.

'Of course, we can go to our house,' Eleanor said and Mary nodded. They marched out of the park in a soggy little procession. Miss Muffins, far too satisfied at the havoc she had wreaked. Fred, trying to stay dignified as his footwear squeaked. And Mary barely able to conceal her delight. 'We shall have a line of ladies beating down our doors to meet Fred!' she whispered in glee, and Eleanor nodded, wishing she did not feel so very disgruntled at such a thought.

Once in their kitchen, the cook and maid set about heating water, fetching towels, scolding the pup—and clucking in concern over Fred. They took away his damp shirt, leaving him wrapped in blankets near the fire. Eleanor busied herself with warming more towels and making tea. She had to stop herself from those whirling thoughts. Wondering just what he looked like under those blankets. The strong, muscled chest that had been revealed in the wet shirt as he emerged from the river...

'Eleanor,' he said, his voice muffled in the towel. 'We should talk about what happened at the assembly...'

That was exactly what she did *not* want to do. What she had been trying not to think about at all. What she could not think about, because it was no use sobbing over what could never be. What she could not feel again.

'What of it?' she asked, busying herself with dog brushes and fresh towels, not daring to look at him.

'Ella.' He yanked the towel from his head and reached out for her hand before she could turn away from him. 'Ella, what happened...when I kissed you...'

Eleanor swallowed hard, trying not to cry. She

couldn't bear to hear his apologies, hear what a mistake it had been, even though she knew it was wrong all too well. 'I know, Fred. Truly I do,' she said quickly, looking everywhere but at him. 'There was music and starlight…it can be quite overwhelming! And memories. We are such old friends, things like that are sure to happen sometimes.'

'It's more than that. Surely you felt it, too? Felt those old bonds between us. No one knows me as you do, Ella. No one *sees* me as you do.'

Eleanor buried her face in her hands to keep him from seeing the shine of her tears at such tender words. Words she'd longed to hear from him for so long. And no one saw her as he did. No one ever had. He thought her a fairy queen, not just someone sensible and useful. He liked her as she was, just as she did him. Just as she could love him for who he was.

'Fred, I do know you and I am your friend,' she said, struggling to find the words to bring both of them back to the real world. The world where he was an earl and needed a fortune to restore his home and where she was a vicar's daughter who worked for her bread. 'And I know you need a proper wife, a lady of position. I am here to help you find her. To find just the *right* one for you and for Moulton Magna.'

'To find me a fortune to marry, you mean?' he said quietly, tautly. He tossed the towel away with a snap.

'Not only that,' Eleanor answered desperately. 'Someone for *you*. Miss Evans is a fine young lady, intelligent and thoughtful, pretty…'

Fred reached out and grabbed her hand, holding her

close. She blinked hard to keep from crying at how much she loved his touch, longed for it.

'Ella,' he said roughly. 'You are right about all that. I know it too well. But a person can't help their small dreams, can they?'

No, they could not. She was so tired from trying to force her own dreams away all the time. To stay strong. Feeling his hand on hers made her long to crumble away.

He rose to his feet and stood close to her, so very close, for that one precious moment. She dared to look up at him and saw that she had been wrong to think him beautiful earlier. He was—otherworldly. A knight from a poem in truth. How easily he overcame all her years of being sensible and careful!

Yet it could not go on. She knew it very well and surely he did, too. So she turned, cowardly, spun around and fled.

'Eleanor. Please, dear. Are you well?' Mary knocked on the door again, frantic with worry after she'd seen her sister dash past the sitting room, heard the front door close after Fred.

'I'm perfectly well, Mary, just a bit tired,' Eleanor answered, her voice muffled by distance or tears. Mary hoped it was not tears. 'I'm just going to rest this evening. Keep an eye on Miss Muffins. Make sure she didn't catch a chill after her little swim.'

'I doubt anything at all could bring Miss Muffins low. She is indomitable,' Mary said. 'Are you sure you won't go with Harry and me to the musicale tonight?'

'No, no. You and Harry go ahead. I'm going to have some cocoa and read my lending library book.'

Mary was very concerned indeed. Musicales were a wonderful time to catch up with their patrons, to make sure the right people were sitting together, and Eleanor seldom missed one. 'Shall I send up some soup later? Something warm and soothing?'

'Yes, thank you, dear. That would be most welcome.' There was a long silence, a faint rustling sound. 'Mary?'

'Yes, dearest?'

'Please don't worry. I shall be quite myself by tomorrow.'

Mary turned away and made her way down the stairs towards the sitting room, wondering what could be wrong. Eleanor was usually so steady, so practical! Could she be so concerned about Miss Muffins. But no, that could not be the whole story. Eleanor had not been herself for some days and Mary couldn't fathom it. She'd been distant, daydreamy and not as involved in the agency as usual.

Mary tried to remember what happened of late. Was there an illness in town? A match gone awry? New friends? Penelope and Fred had come back into their lives. Maybe they'd brought old memories and Eleanor just couldn't...

Of course! Fred! Mary could have slapped herself for being such a fool. Eleanor must have feelings for Fred.

And she herself had been such an insensitive looby, going on and on about Miss Evans and Fred. How ridiculous of her! She should have realised. Fred was not at all the usual agency patron and Eleanor probably had cherished tender feelings for him for a long time. What a tangle!

Mary stepped into the sitting room and poured herself a cup of now-cold tea from the pot laid out by the window where she could watch the passers-by. She took a long sip, turning things over in her mind. She was rather proud of being good at seeing how two people could fit together and make a true match. Yet she hadn't seen the perfect match right before her own eyes.

'Eleanor and Fred. Of course,' she whispered. They both had such a sense of duty, of family. They both had such kind hearts and sly senses of humour not many saw. They had a way of looking at each other when they thought the other didn't notice. Looks that were so filled with sadness and longing.

Mary sighed and sat down next to Miss Muffins, who was wrapped tightly in blankets on the settee. She listened to Harry playing the pianoforte in the next room—an echo of a sad song that reflected her own thoughts perfectly. The world was sadly upside-down now.

She'd often worried about her sister. About Eleanor's tendency to help everyone else around her before herself. She'd worried Eleanor would feel lonely and never find someone who appreciated how wonderful she was. But Mary needn't have worried at all. They just needed Fred to come into their lives again. And now Eleanor could go back to their old home, their old neighbourhood. Be the Lady of Moulton Magna...

Moulton Magna. Oh, no.

Mary's head dropped to the cushions behind her and the warm wings of hope that carried her up suddenly dropped her all over again. There was a reason Fred needed the agency and that was to find a wife who could save his home.

Miss Muffins whined as if she sensed Mary's despair. Mary wrapped her arms around the dog and held her close. 'Oh, Miss Muffins. We simply *must* find a way to assist in promoting your mama's happiness. But how?'

'What is amiss?' Harry asked from the doorway. Mary had been so wrapped in her thoughts that she hadn't heard the music cease. Harry watched her closely, her arms crossed in her elegant purple afternoon gown.

Mary shook her head. She didn't know how to begin to say everything, but she knew Harry could help. Harry's cleverness saved the agency every day. 'Oh, Harry dearest. I am ever so worried about Eleanor…'

Chapter Nine

⟨ ⟩

The Theatre Royal was crowded. Every seat and box filled with flashing jewels and fluttering fans. *The School for Scandal* was still always popular and, just as at the Pump Room and assemblies, no one in Bath missed a chance to see and be seen.

Eleanor raised her opera glass to examine the throng beyond their box, taking in the swirl of pastel silks and muslins amid the scarlet velvet and gold braid of the theatre and the gleam of the chandeliers overhead. A mural of rustic Grecian muses dancing in a flower-decked circle glowed above the curtained stage. The maidens watching the furore with doubtful glares.

Eleanor, Mary and Harry very often attended the theatre, of course, as well as concerts at the assembly rooms. It was the perfect place to discreetly look in on patrons, evaluate matches, see who had recently signed the visitors' book and who might require just the right spouse. But tonight she couldn't quite focus on any of that. Couldn't stop her gaze restlessly flitting from one spot to another, one person to the next, the toe of her slipper tapping against the thick scarlet carpet. No one was the one person she most sought.

No one was Fred.

She hadn't seen him since Miss Muffins' disastrous swim, though Penelope had called to check on the pup's welfare. She'd said Fred was closeted with paperwork and agents. Eleanor longed to see him again herself, touch his hand, hear him laugh, make sure he was not exhausting himself with worry. But she knew, she told herself most sternly, it was better if they never met again at all. Not that such a thing was possible. Not if she was to find him the right match. Not if their old friendship haunted them. Yet surely, if he was truly beyond her sight, he would fade from her mind and she would one day forget him? He would be a memory, bittersweet maybe, but not a part of her life.

Eleanor lowered the glass and shook her head. Had his absence before, when he left her life and went into the Army, erased him from her thoughts? Of course it had not. She'd worried about him then. Dreamed of him. Longed for him. And she feared those things could not be ended.

Now he was even more vivid and more vital to her. More a part of her world and dreams. Even though she knew she had to help him find a wife.

'Eleanor? Look at Lady Russell's gown. Such an interesting sleeve design,' Mary said, pointing with her folded fan at the lady in question. 'Is that the latest London fashion, do you think? Maybe I should try something like that with my green striped muslin.'

'Hmm?' Eleanor murmured, blinking hard to clear

the clouds of worry, futile hope and dreams from her mind before she turned to her sister. Mary often saw far too much. 'Lady Russell's gown?'

'Those pleats on the sleeve with the gold satin insets. Perhaps it's just a cunning way to call more attention to her pearls. But I could still try it on my green. It does need some freshening up. Though I think the fashion would look better on you.'

'On me?' Eleanor couldn't help but glance down at the plain cap sleeves on her dark blue silk gown. It had been a serviceable dress for the whole season but now she wondered if it lacked any dash at all, any spark. What would Fred think if he saw her in it?

But that was beyond foolish. What did it matter *what* he thought? She had resolved to put away her feelings for him and she was going to do just that. Soon. Surely.

She *had* to.

Mary gave her a gentle smile. 'You have seemed rather preoccupied of late, Sister. A new gown always cheers *me*. Though perhaps you would prefer a new book? I am sure you've been working too hard this month.'

'No harder than you and Harry, dearest.' She pressed her fan to her lips to hold back a yawn, remembering all the late nights she'd spent recently. All the silly daydreams floating in her mind when she should be concentrating on work. 'Though I suppose I do worry about the people who are counting on us to help them find happiness.'

'As do I. It is certainly no ordinary work we do! I feel the weight of our patrons' futures, too. I want to see them all wildly happy.' She gazed pensively over the crowd, as if she matched each of them in her mind. 'Though I think there is little hope for a few of them no matter how hard we work. Can there really be a match for Mr Ormonde? And poor Lord Coulton refuses to see any lady but you. Yet we help so many! We must always remember that. See Lord and Lady Eberhart?' She gestured towards the newly married couple in their box across the way. The two of them smiling into each other's eyes as they leaned close, as if they were the only two in the whole theatre.

Eleanor couldn't help but smile to see them. Lord Eberhart had been the saddest of widowers when they introduced him to the pretty, sweet young governess and now they were as happy as two cooing doves. Yes, her work could be most satisfactory at times.

Yet there was still that tiny, sharp, wistful pang to show she would not have that with Fred. 'They *are* lovely together.'

'You knew they would suit right from the start. You always know. But you must look after *yourself* as well. Perhaps a holiday would be nice? We could take Miss Muffins to the seaside. Though I don't know if the naughty creature deserves it.'

Eleanor laughed and remembered how bedraggled and heroic Fred looked when he fished the dog from the waves. 'I am quite sure she does not deserve it! She had to have four baths to get rid of the river smell.' She wondered if Fred had needed the same. The warm, soapy water flowing down his bare back…

No. That was most definitely not a suitable image to dwell on!

'But think of how she helped us! We have had so many callers to see if she was well after her wee swim and new patrons as a result. Which is all the more reason for you to have a rest.'

'I am perfectly well, Mary. I promise. Perhaps we could go away in the autumn, once we have closed some of our files.'

And once Fred was betrothed to a suitable heiress.

Eleanor turned her head to hide her thoughts again, and caught sight of Penelope in a box down the way, her new purple and gold gown glittering. And she was not alone. Mr Anthony Oliver held out her chair for her, looking most attentive. Penelope laughed up at him, her eyes shimmering. 'Look, there is Pen! And it seems perhaps you were quite right about Mr Oliver.'

Mary gave a smug smile as she watched him sit down beside Penelope, his leg pressed to the fold of her skirt. 'They are sweet together, I think. I'm so hoping we receive an invitation to the wedding, even if they aren't agency clients. Weddings are always so lovely! Orange blossoms, cake, music, not a dry eye in the church. And when the groom looks into his bride's smiling face…' Mary sighed, a misty gleam in her own eyes as she conjured thoughts of lace and flowers.

Eleanor studied her sister in surprise. Could it be? Did Mary have match fever for herself? Her sister had always been so independent of spirit and so carefree. But did Mary actually long to wed? She did never give such an indication, even though suitors so often crowded their doorstep. Yet it did make some sense. Mary was pretty, young, vivacious and intelligent. She would make the perfect chatelaine to a fine house. A glittering hostess. If a man could be found who was worthy of her, which Eleanor doubted.

She would have to search through their files. See if there was anyone who might actually suit Mary after all.

'Oh, look, Fred is with them now! How splendid.' Mary waved happily at the box across the way, wistfulness vanished.

And so he was. Looking so handsome in his evening coat, smiling at Penelope as he took his seat beside them. Eleanor stared down at the fan in her hands feeling overly warm and flustered. How could she face him again after they let their emotions overcome them once more? How could she ever really look at him at all? Yet she had to. She could not stop herself. She peeked back to see they had all taken their seats, still watched by the ladies with their opera glasses all around the theatre.

'And who is that gorgeous giant of a man with them?' she asked once she was composed. She made herself raise her glasses to study the group again, trying not to focus only on Fred.

Mary fidgeted with her sash. 'Oh. That is a Mr Campbell, Mr Oliver's cousin. I met him at the assembly. He is a widower, guardian to a young lady who is about to make her bow in Society. He seemed rather apprehensive about the whole prospect.'

Eleanor watched him as he settled a young lady in her seat beside him and then turned to speak to Mr Oliver. The girl was very pretty, with strawberry-blonde curls and a gentle smile, but she seemed unsure of herself. 'They sound as if they could perhaps use the agency's assistance.'

'I am quite sure they could. We could surely find a wife for Mr Campbell in only a moment. Someone to help him see that Miss Adele is properly settled.' That was the sort of task Mary was so good at. Making things tidy for people. Yet Eleanor thought she saw something else in her sister's eyes as Mary studied the handsome Scotsman. Something misty and dreamy and most unlike Mary.

Penelope glimpsed them just then and frantically waved her fan at them, a bright smile curling her lips as she jumped to her feet. 'Shall we see you at the interval?' she called loudly above the roar of the theatre.

'Of course!' Mary called back.

'So much to tell you,' Penelope went on. 'Fred is quite famous!' Mr Oliver tugged her back into her seat and she turned to laugh at him merrily.

'Famous?' Mary whispered. 'What do you think…'

Eleanor studied the theatre again. There did indeed seem to be a stir rustling through the aisles and the boxes. People craning their necks and turning their glasses towards the Fleetwood box with whispers and giggles. Fred studiously ignored it all, talking to Penelope and Mr Oliver.

'He does seem to be something of an *on dit* tonight,' Eleanor said. 'What do you suppose it all means?'

'I hope it means our matchmaking task just became much easier. I didn't have time to read the papers today, so I just brought the Society pages to glance over at the interval.' Mary took a few torn bits of newsprint from her reticule and spread them on the railing. 'Hmm… The Harrison elopement. Betrothal announcements. Ah, yes, here is something!' She clapped her hands in delight. 'Look! Fred is deemed a great hero for rescuing Miss Muffins from certain watery death. Just look at this sketch.'

Eleanor was astonished. The sketch made him look like Hercules—vanquishing all opponents as he dove into raging ocean waters! She had always seen Fred's hidden gallantry, of course, even when he took pains to play the careless rogue. Now it seemed, thanks to his quick actions in rescuing Miss Muffins and the glimpse of him in a water-soaked shirt, everyone else saw it, too.

Now he would be inundated with ladies enquiring about him, pursuing him. So many thoughts passed through her mind in that moment. Delight that everyone saw what she had always known, but also sadness. Fred was wonderful and now they all saw it. She was proud of him, but also so very sad. She'd always known he could be with her, be her friend, only for a short time. Now she had to grasp whatever moments she still had. She turned away from the sight of him.

Eleanor watched the play for a few moments before secretly scanning the audience again. Perhaps that lady would do? Or that one? All pretty, all stylish, all eligible. She slowly lowered the glasses, her thoughts whirling. A decision would have to be made and soon.

She feared soon there would be one thing waiting

for them on their doorstep. A long line of ladies waiting to meet the 'Great Puppy Saviour'.

'I—I'll be right back, Mary,' Eleanor whispered quickly. She felt as if her whole being was burning with a blush, a warm yearning for something she dared not even name, and she couldn't bear for anyone to see it. To know her hidden feelings. It was as if a whirlwind picked her up and spun her about until she didn't know herself any longer.

Luckily, Mary was so enthralled by the play she merely nodded, not glancing at Eleanor, and she was able to slip out of the box into the dimly lit corridor. She hurried past a few footmen and a couple or two who lingered in the shadows. Past closed box doors until she found a quiet nook near a window looking down on the street. A carriage rumbled past. A light flashed in a building across the way. Otherwise she seemed quite alone.

She took a deep breath and opened her reticule to peek at the handkerchief inside. The folded muslin that Fred pressed into her hand so long ago and that she carried still, like a silly schoolgirl with a romantic talisman. She couldn't quite let it go. But soon, she knew, she would have to. Fred would have a wife.

She heard a footstep. A soft movement behind her and though it was so very quiet, she somehow knew it was Fred. There was a crackle when he was near. A change in the very air unlike anything else. She knew the sound of his walk, so confident and quick, the way he smelled of lemon soap and fresh linen and just that dark essence of Fred-ness. The emotions that swirled

around her whenever he came close. She quickly shut
the bag and pasted a smile on her face she hoped didn't
look quite as false as it felt. She feared her cheeks might
crack with it.

'Are you well, Ella?' he asked. His tone low and
deep, filled with concern. 'I saw you leave your box
so quickly.'

'Oh, quite well, thank you, Fred.' She turned to face
him and saw his tall figure in the shifting shadows,
the small frown on his lips. 'It was just rather warm in
there and I didn't find the play as diverting as Mary.'

He nodded. 'I understand. It's been hard to be in
warm, confined spaces like that since I returned,' he
said simply and Eleanor wondered what nightmares
lurked behind those few words. She twisted her hands
tighter into the cords of her reticule to keep from reaching for him.

Yet in the end she could not help herself. She *did*
reach out, gently touched his sleeve and he covered
her fingers with his. He raised her hand to his lips. A
kiss brushing across her fingers, hot through the thin
silk of her glove. She curled her touch around him, and
they stood there just like that for one frozen, dreamlike moment. A moment she wished would never end.

'I—I shouldn't keep you from your party any longer,' she whispered, slipping her hand from his and
stepping back even though it was the hardest thing she
had ever done. 'Surely Penelope will worry?'

A smile flashed across his face, rueful and delicious.
'She is with her old friend. I doubt she will notice.'

'And your admirers?' Eleanor bit her lip, trying to

hold back that sharp prick of jealousy that touched her heart thinking of all those ladies.

He laughed. 'Admirers?'

'The ladies who think you the greatest hero after saving Miss Muffins. Which you are, of course.'

'Anyone would have done the same.'

'They would not!'

'Well, they should. A life, even one of a spoiled pup, is worth multitudes. And I am hardly a hero for it. I think Bath society merely needs something to distract it and a different 'something' will appear tomorrow.'

Eleanor thought of the agency's patrons, and laughed along with him. 'Distractions are much appreciated here, that is true. Something different from tea-drinking and rainy strolls.'

'Different from plays in stuffy boxes?'

'Different and better. For you are real.' And he was. The most real, the most beautiful, thing she'd known in so very long. Something to cling to if only she could. 'I must go.'

'Yes,' he said, sounding suddenly distracted and distant. 'We shall see you soon?'

'Of course.' She gave into temptation and touched his sleeve again, one quick brush, before she turned and forced herself to walk slowly away.

'Where were you, Fred?' Penelope asked as he slipped back into their box, thoroughly dizzy and bemused from his encounter with Eleanor. From the kiss on her hand he could still feel, like an echo deep inside of him.

'Just a quick breath of air.'

'Well! As I told you—you are the Bath *on dit* of the moment,' Penelope whispered delightedly from behind her fan as the actors gestured and declaimed from the stage. 'Isn't it so exciting?'

Exciting was not quite the word Fred would use. A blasted nuisance was more like it. When he took his usual morning walk to the Pump Room to imbibe those vile waters, he'd suddenly become aware of subtle stares and whispers. A few bolder sorts even came up to him to claim an acquaintance. Not the usual embarrassed glances he sometimes received for his scars but wide-eyed wonder from young ladies, appraising admiration from their mamas.

Some of them even spoke to him right there in the Pump Room. Soft smiles, cooing words, sweet expressions of concern for Miss Muffins. Miss Evans, or rather her formidable mother, insisted on buying him a tea, eager to hear the whole story of the 'perilous rescue'. Miss Evans was still so quiet and awkward around her mother but Fred found he liked her quiet, understanding smile and her tentative but sensible questions about his time in battle—real battle, not just dog-swimming wars. She seemed a fine sort of young lady and her mother was eager to advance their acquaintance. Yet she was not Eleanor. No one was ever really Eleanor.

He had to admit, as he glanced around the theatre, he somewhat enjoyed the admiration. In his Army years, his connection to an earldom, handsome face and thick, bright hair meant he was never short of female company. He'd never really believed their words of ardent admiration, but it was all rather fun. Then, after Waterloo, after his injuries, that admiration greatly receded. Not that he could blame them. He had healed a great deal now, but had been nothing pleasant to look at and his fortunes were quite depleted. He had to do his duty now and he'd been determined on it. He had made peace with it.

Until he found Eleanor again. The way she looked at him, seeing only *him*, Fred, none of the trailing baggage of war and injury and worry. The way she understood all without even having to speak. He was becoming addicted to her nearness. To her entrancing face, her sweet smiles and feeling the soft heat of her touch. He needed it more and more. Craved it. He feared what would happen when she was gone again from him, snapped away like some life-saving cord. Would the cold memories of war be upon him again? Could he ever escape it all?

Penelope leaned close and whispered, 'Look, there is Miss Evans in that box over there. She seems to be enjoying the play. How pretty she is when she laughs!'

Fred glanced at the young lady, who did indeed seem very interested in the antics of the actors, her gaze rapt on the stage as her mother fanned herself vigorously and examined every face in the crowd. He turned away before Mrs Evans saw him. 'She is pretty, yes.'

'And such a fine fortune her father has, they say. They also say Mr Evans is intent on a title for his daughter.' Penelope watched him carefully, as if she wanted to read something in his eyes. He so wished she would not do that.

'And what does Miss Evans say herself?' he asked.

Penelope's lips pursed. 'Not a great deal. She is a young lady who seems to keep her own counsel, which seems wise when one has such parents. They say she is often wandering about gardens here in Bath. All alone.'

'She seemed talkative enough with that young curate at the assembly,' Fred pointed out. 'And I think a little bird whispered she'd been walking with him in a garden or two.'

Penelope dismissed this with a flick of her fan. 'A youthful flirtation, perhaps. He is a handsome lad, for a curate. But, like all of us, she must listen to her family's counsel when it comes to something more important.'

'Penelope,' Anthony Oliver said, taking Penelope's attention blessedly away from Fred and his marital prospects. 'Campbell was trying to think of someplace that might amuse the young ladies, Adele as well as Grace and Natalie. We thought we might walk to the cricket green on Wednesday, if the rain holds off, watch a bit of a game, have some cake and lemonade. Charles likes to play when he can. Would you care to join us?'

'I would enjoy that very much,' Penelope answered with a brilliant smile, one Fred had never seen from her before. She glanced over her shoulder at Fred and he realised she hadn't entirely forgotten him. 'Won't you come, too, Fred dearest? You did used to admire a good game of cricket. And you were so good at it.'

He laughed, and tapped at his weaker arm. 'I used to, yes. I fear I am far out of practice.'

'This is Bath, not King's Lawn,' Penelope scoffed. 'A friendly little match, a nice outing…'

'We could certainly use any assistance we can find,' Charles Campbell said. 'We are a sorry lot, I confess, but it's all mostly an excuse for a nice walk and a cream tea after.'

'I thought I might ask Mary and Eleanor to come along,' Penelope said. '*Not* Miss Muffins, however.'

'Then I will be most happy to join such a merry crowd,' he said. And to see Eleanor again. That made him all *too* happy.

'Splendid!' Penelope leaned closer and squeezed his arm. 'I am so happy you are peeking out of your shell into the sunlight again, Fred.'

He nodded. Perhaps he was indeed. And that sunlight was called Eleanor.

Chapter Ten

~~~

Court Street Circulating Library was always most busy, but especially so on rainy afternoons. Ladies and gentlemen strolled between the towering bookcases debating the merits of various new novels, while a clutch of young poets in their corner debated a certain rhyming scheme.

Eleanor perused a copy of *The Maid of Killarney*, her mind turning over and over the theatre last night, seeing Fred there. Mary had blessedly wandered ahead in search of some ladies' fashion papers from London. Luckily seeming too distracted to question Eleanor too closely about where she had been for so long at the theatre interval. The soft patter of raindrops against the windows, the soft rustle of turning pages, the arguments from the poets, the assistants suggesting titles to two dithering matrons—it all blended into something of a song. A rhythm that circled and meandered like a river.

She sat down in a window embrasure to look over the book in her hands, pretending to be engrossed in reading.

Oh, you must snap out of this dreamy state, Eleanor! Immediately! she told herself sternly.

She had much work to do, including the difficult task of finding a wife for Fred and losing him for ever. She had to snap out of this. There was no time for any more mooning about like a schoolgirl. She was a grown woman. A woman with a business to run and she couldn't neglect it.

Thinking of the agency, Eleanor studied the room again. A shy-looking young lady stood near a collection of sermons. Maybe she needed a match to bring her out of her shell? Yet such things as other peoples' stories, usually so engrossing to her, could not distract her today.

Then she turned her head and saw Miss Evans standing by the windows with her mother.

Mary strolled over to them, her ruffled muslin skirts swaying. They were too far for Eleanor to hear their conversation, but it seemed most amiable. Mary still seemed determined that Miss Evans was the right one for Fred and it seemed she was making some headway. At least with the mother, who nodded and smiled with great enthusiasm.

Miss Evans herself fidgeted with the strings of her reticule, glancing around the library, seeming rather bored. Until she glimpsed something and her thin face lit up, making her quite pretty indeed. Eleanor wondered if it was the handsome curate from the assembly, but it appeared to be a display of botanical tracts. Most interesting. Miss Evans started in that direction, but her mother seized her arm and in a clawed grip and held her fast. Miss Evans' pretty face clouded again and she went still.

Mary returned to Eleanor, shaking her head at the tower of books at Eleanor's feet. She hadn't even realised she'd discarded so many, or what they even were. 'Eleanor! How many volumes does one need on one trip to the lending library?'

'Oh.' Eleanor glimpsed a volume of recent fashion plates and said, 'Is this not important research? We must stay *au courant* with all the new styles.'

'Indeed. Though you might stay a bit more current on millinery, sister, for I vow I have seen that bonnet you are wearing dozens of times. We must find some new ribbon at least.' Mary smoothed her gloves and nodded at Mrs Evans. 'Never mind, though. Mrs Evans seems most satisfied with the agency's progress and she would be most happy if Fred were to invite Miss Evans for a short drive or stroll.'

'Oh, Mary,' Eleanor murmured, not daring to look at her sister. 'I am not so sure Fred and Miss Evans are quite so well-matched as all that.' But she feared she was just making excuses to herself. They might like each other very well, given a chance. She could not let her feelings and old hopes sway her now.

'Pah!' Mary cried, and waved her doubt away. 'They just need to know each other a bit better.' She gently touched Eleanor's arm and smiled. Eleanor did not know what to make of the great, shining sympathy she saw in her sister's eyes, the—was it *pity*? Oh, she did hope not. She couldn't bear that. 'My dearest. I know how fond you are of Fred and you must worry about him as you do all of us. But we must do all we can for him in this matter of a suitable match.'

Eleanor nodded. Mary was right, of course. If Eleanor could not be with Fred, he did deserve someone smart, pretty and quiet-mannered, as Miss Evans seemed to be. Someone of wealth. It was the way of all things.

The door opened with a jingle of bells and Fred himself appeared there, as if summoned up by her very thoughts. With him was quite a crowd—Penelope, Mr Oliver, Grace and Natalie, Mr Campbell and his niece Adele.

'Lord Fleetwood!' Mary called, waving madly. She caught the attention of several people nearby and a wave of excited whispers wound around the stacks and shelves. Ladies patted the curls peeking from beneath feathered and ribboned bonnets, mamas urged their daughters forward, and several men looked on it all with jealous scowls.

'You see?' Mary whispered to Eleanor with great satisfaction in her voice. 'Fred's favour does grow apace! He's quite the hero now. Isn't it quite lovely?'

Lovely. Eleanor wasn't sure that was quite the word she would use. Envious, maybe, or discomfited. On her part, anyway. But it was very clear he was the latest *on dit* and how could she blame other ladies for noticing what she already saw so very well? Fred, however, looked around him with astonishment and discomfort writ large on his face. Penelope held tight to his arm and urged him forward.

Mary hurried towards their group, drawing Eleanor with her. 'What a fine chance to see you all here!' Mary said. 'Such a glorious day for reading, is it not?'

'We were planning to take the children to the cricket green later,' Mr Oliver said, with a laughing grimace at the rain. 'If the weather decides to cooperate.'

'Ah, that is Bath for you,' Penelope said with a fond glance at him from beneath her lashes, a secret little smile. But not so secret that Mary and Eleanor didn't notice, and they exchanged a significant glance. 'It always changes in only a moment. I'm sure we will be able to continue our walk in an hour or so.'

'I do hope so,' Natalie said with a pout. 'We've been stuck inside for *days* and *days*.'

Mr Campbell laughed, a hearty, deep, whisky sound that made everyone else laugh, too. Especially, Eleanor noticed with a twinge of acute interest, her own sister. Mary's cheeks turned quite apple-pink with delight. 'Hardly days, my dear,' he said. 'And surely you have been kept occupied?'

Natalie shot a disgruntled glare at Adele. 'By helping Adele practise her dancing over and over.'

'I must know the steps perfectly by the next assembly,' Adele protested. 'Or I shall quite disgrace myself at my very first public gathering in Bath!'

Eleanor carefully studied Adele. The girl seemed entirely unlikely to 'disgrace herself'. She was very pretty with her pale, silvery gilt curls and wide green eyes, her careful manners and fine clothes. She wondered if Mr Campbell sought a match for her yet, though she seemed a tad young.

'We know a very fine dancing master we can recommend, if you like, Miss Adele,' Mary said. 'Though I hardly think you must be in need of much tutelage at all!'

'My mother was a dancer who eloped with Mr Campbell's cousin,' Adele whispered, her face flaming at such a scandalous admission. 'Though I hardly remember her.'

Eleanor gave her a gentle smile. 'I am sorry to hear of your loss, Miss Stewart. But you must find a new path here in Bath! It is a fine place for it.'

'I am enjoying it very much so far,' Adele said with a little laugh. 'Especially all these books! I have never seen so many in one place.'

'And you will be much admired, I can tell,' Mary said. 'Oh, look! The sun does seem to be peeking through at last…'

Penelope and Mary had been quite right. In only an hour, the sun had crept through the pale grey clouds and shimmered over the town, turning everything honey-gold and making the gardens glitter like diamonds with left-behind raindrops. The girls' dresses, pale blue and pink and sprigged with white, looked just like the flowers as they hurried past with Adele leading Natalie and Grace and everyone else trailing behind.

It was a very merry party that set out for the cricket green, laughing and joking. Natalie and Grace skipped and pushed and giggled, admonished ineffectually by Anthony. Penelope and Mary chattered and laughed, arm in arm like old bosom bows.

Eleanor trailed behind the noisy group, the poetry

still dancing through her mind. There could be no time
for poetry now. Mary was right—Fred had a job before him and so did she. The job of finding a suitable
match. One that she, Eleanor, could not be.

But they did have the day, one filled with sunshine,
and warmth and laughter. And she was determined to
enjoy it to the full. To put it up in her memory box to
take out on rainy future days.

They made their way to the cricket green at the park.
The lawn undulated towards the horizon like a soft, emerald carpet, lined with flowering hedges. There was
a small pavilion at one end set up with rows of chairs
and tables of tea and cakes. Players ambled about, idly
tossing balls, laughing and calling out challenges and
Eleanor felt her spirits rise even more at the delightful scene. Once, back when she had been a youthful
girl who could once in a while escape the vicarage,
she'd played cricket with Fred and his brother and other
young people from the estate and the village. It had
been great fun, running free with the wind catching
at her hair.

She sat down next to Mary on one of the folding
chairs, watching as Fred, Anthony and Mr Campbell
made their way onto the pitch. Fred was the first to bat.

'How can you follow what's happening?' Natalie
asked, a little frown on her face as she watched the
running and pitching.

'I think Eleanor knows,' Mary said, fanning herself
as she studied the green. 'She used to play when we
were children!'

Eleanor smiled to remember those days, running

free with Fred, the crack of the bat on a ball, the grass under her feet. How long ago they seemed now!

'Well, there are two teams of eleven players each, you see,' she said. 'With batsmen, bowlers and all-rounders. I was quite good at playing batsman and at running!'

'Like Lord Fleetwood?' Grace said.

Eleanor tilted her head to one side as she watched Fred. He had rolled his shirt sleeves up to make play easier, with no seeming thought at all to the pink scars on his skin. The strong, sinewy muscles looked as strong and as alluring as ever. There was just something about a man in shirt sleeves that made ladies' knees weak! The slight limp he sometimes showed from his war years seemed to vanish as he flew over the green and it made her smile to see him.

'Yes. The batsman and the bowler stand opposite each other on that line, the batting strip, and the bowler tosses the ball towards the batsman who then tries to hit it. If he does, he can try to run to the other end of the strip. That is called a 'run'. He scores one point for each run he can complete before the ball is returned to the field. If he's taken out, he must come off the field and can't bat again.'

'I'd like to try it!' Grace cried and Eleanor laughed as she stood up to show the girls a bit of what she remembered using a stick Natalie found in the grass.

'There are two methods to batting, really,' she said, demonstrating. 'Vertical, like so—drive or glance. Or horizontal, sweep, square. You must watch your stance, girls, before the ball is bowled. Watch your hands, feet, head and body. Line them up like so.' Eleanor remembered all the ways to set oneself up to take a mighty swing at the ball, just as Fred once taught her. She pretended to bat then ran as fast as she could, Grace and Natalie applauding and cheering.

Her bonnet flew off but she couldn't quite care. It felt so wonderful to run once more. To feel the breeze rush past her ears. She heard cheers, and glanced over to see Fred and Anthony Oliver applauding her, Fred's face alight with laughter. She waved, laughing with them and let her feet soar. When she made the run Fred caught her hand for an instant, squeezing it.

'Well done, Ella,' he whispered. She felt a glow of pride at his words, such as she'd never known before with anyone else. 'Well done indeed.'

Mary clapped enthusiastically, barely able to keep herself from jumping up and down as she watched the wild game play out before her. It had become a beautiful day indeed. Clear, sunny and azure-sky-perfect. With the green fields rolling before them like a carpet. Laughter and cries echoed on the breeze as every care seemed forgotten and there was just a world filled with fun before them all. It was exactly her favourite sort of day—something to take such pleasure in and store up for another rainy afternoon.

Best of all was seeing Eleanor enjoying herself so much as she dashed back and forth. Her pale blue skirts flying about like those skittering clouds in the sky. Reckless and laughing and pink-cheeked. As if she hadn't a care in the world.

It was a sight Mary saw far too seldom. In fact, she couldn't quite remember the last time. Mary had few memories of their mother. It was always Eleanor who cared for Mary and her father. Indeed who cared for everyone who made their household and their agency work so very well. Eleanor who'd made sure Mary went to school and that she always had what she needed.

Mary pressed her hand to her lips, fearing she might cry just to see her dear sister look so happy. It was how matters should always be. It was what Eleanor deserved. And Mary suspected she knew the reason for Eleanor's joy now. It was plain when she thought no one watched her and she gazed at Fred with such a glow in her eyes.

Well, Mary was no child now. She knew Eleanor wouldn't see it that way, but it was Mary's turn to take charge of things of make sure Eleanor had the happy future she needed and deserved. How to achieve it, though? Eleanor and Fred were both so duty-bound. And it was true, Fred needed someone to help him with his estate. Surely there had to be a way!

'Miss St Aubin, isn't it? How fine to see you again,' she heard a man ask and she pasted on her brightest 'agency smile,' wondering if it was some patron strolling the green on such a fine day.

She turned and saw it was Mr Campbell. She was struck by him all over again. Rather stunned, in fact, to come so close to him. He was really so very, very handsome. Tall and golden and strong. Like someone in a Walter Scott novel about the noble Highlands.

'Mr Campbell,' she said. 'Indeed, yes, Miss Mary

St Aubin. How lovely it is to see you and your ward again! Are you looking for your cousin?' She gestured towards Mr Oliver on the field.

'No, not at all. He would never welcome being interrupted in the sacred act of playing cricket,' Mr Campbell said with a charmingly crooked grin. 'I was merely hoping to renew our all too brief acquaintance on such a fine, strangely sunny afternoon.'

Mary laughed. 'I see you have been in Bath long enough to know to watch for rain at every moment.'

He smiled down at her with a teasing, admiring gleam in his eye. 'Indeed. Yet, I am from Scotland and thus much used to rain. I have found that Bath has many compensations to offer for its weather.'

Mary dared give him an admiring glance in return. 'Indeed it does, Mr Campbell.'

'You have met my ward, Miss Adele Stewart?' he said and held out his hand to the pink muslin-clad young lady who'd worried about her dancing.

'Of course, we were just speaking at the Circulating Library,' Mary said with a welcoming smile to the girl. 'She was telling me how much she enjoys Bath.'

Adele flashed a shy smile. 'I—I do enjoy it very much. I like the bookshops and the milliners. And I can't wait for more assemblies. And I have joined the library, of course.'

'You enjoy reading, then? As well as dancing? What do you most enjoy? Modern poetry, perhaps, or novels?'

'Novels certainly!' Adele said with great enthusiasm. 'I love tales of Highland history, especially, since it reminds me of home. But poetry is always most welcome. Especially Scott, of course. And Mr McCloud. Have you heard of him?'

Mary nodded. McCloud was a man of meagre poetic skills but great sentiment. His work was much enjoyed by young ladies such as Adele and much aped by poets like the agency's own client Lord Coulton. Mary wondered if Adele might like him and he her in return, thus removing his romantic attentions from Eleanor. She sighed to think that probably was no solution as of yet, given Adele's youth.

'It sounds as if Mr Oliver has known Lady Fleetwood for some time,' Mary said, watching as Penelope applauded for Mr Oliver, her eyes shining.

'Yes, I believe they met when they were quite young, at some house party, but have not encountered one another again until now,' Mr Campbell answered. 'He has often spoken of her though.'

'Has he indeed?' Mary watched Penelope and then Mr Oliver with great interest. Noticing how, just as at the theatre, they seemed to have eyes only for each other. As if drawn together by some force, unable to deny it any longer. 'I do wonder why such a fine gentleman has never married.'

Mr Campbell gave her a curious glance, his head tilted as his bright hair caught the sun. Mary had forgotten he didn't know about the agency—most people did not until they required their services—and surely wondered at her interest in matches.

'Anthony is one of the best men I have ever known,' he said. 'A fine friend. A good landlord. Liked by everyone. Also an astute businessman and ruthless card player, it must be said! He deserves to be happy in his marriage. To find a lady truly worthy of their life together. It's something not as simple to find as one might expect.'

There was something in his voice, a sadness and a wistfulness, which made Mary study him even closer. He seemed distant just then, looking at the game but seeing something far away. A memory perhaps? Had he been terribly disappointed in romance? It made her feel so sad. So filled with longing to comfort him and help him.

'I am quite sure he will find such a lady. Have you ever been married yourself, Mr Campbell?' She laughed to dispel any cold touch of discomfort. 'Do forgive me! My sister says I am too inquisitive by half.'

He smiled at her. A quick, merry flash that seemed to say any dark cloud of memory had drifted quite away. 'Not at all, Miss St Aubin. You are entirely charming and a great pleasure to converse with, I must say.'

Entirely charming.

Mary felt her cheeks turn hot, a little flutter deep inside, and she glanced away to hide her burst of silly pleasure.

'And I was married once, very briefly, when I was rather young,' he continued. He glanced back at Adele, who was laughing with a group of people she had met at the tea tent. 'Not much older than Adele, in fact.'

Mary, too, studied the girl, with her smooth, peachy cheeks and innocent smile. 'Heavens! Yes, a very youthful match.'

'She was the daughter of our neighbours on my family's estate and very beautiful. I admit I was most infatuated, as any callow youth can be! But we were not truly compatible. We hadn't lived together very long. She went to London on a visit to some friends and sadly passed away soon after.'

Mary felt the sharp prick of sympathy, of sadness, for that young husband. 'I am so very sorry, Mr Campbell. Do forgive me for bringing up such a subject.'

'Not at all. It feels so very long ago now. I've been too busy with my business concerns to think of marrying again. And now I am responsible for Adele. I admit it feels rather intimidating to be a man alone trying to manage such a task as a young lady's debut!' He looked once more at Adele, who was shyly smiling up at a young man who offered her a strawberry. 'She is such a sweet, dreamy sort of girl. I should hate to see what once happened to me happen to her.'

'Perhaps, once she is a bit older and thinking of such things as marriage, my sister and I could be of some small assistance?' Mary didn't usually approach such a new acquaintance about the agency, yet something about Charles Campbell did tug at her heart. She removed a small card from her reticule and handed it to him. His hand brushed her, warm and strong through their gloves, and she held back a shiver. 'You can speak to Lady Fleetwood about us, as well. I assure you our work is much respected.'

He studied the card and glanced back at her, one brow arched. 'You are a most interesting lady indeed, Miss St Aubin.'

Mary laughed. 'Oh, I do try.'

Chapter Eleven

Eleanor glanced in the looking glass as she smoothed her hair. The brown, caramel-ish locks had been pinned up in curls and fastened with new, sparkling combs and she had to admit she rather liked the effect. It was younger, more fashionable, that she usually attempted. As was her new gown of green and gold stripes with a small frill of gold lace over the sleeves and edge of the square bodice.

A benefit musicale at the assembly rooms was always an important occasion. She'd seen many a match solidified when two people sat beside each other listening to a moving romantic aria, or walked together on the terrace at the interval. It was important to look stylish and yet respectable at such events, in case anyone needed advice or a subtle push in the right direction at the last minute.

She usually did not fuss over her appearance so very much. Tonight, though, Fred might be there and the thought that he might see her brought such a silly flutter. He'd seen her looking wild at cricket, after all!

But since he had reappeared in her life, so much had changed in her thoughts. In her heart.

It could not last, she knew that. But she had her memories back again. When he left Moulton Magna to go into the Army, she'd lost that one beautiful little thing. Now she had it back again and the memories would have to last her for a long time to come.

She smoothed her hair again and reached for her small pearl drop earrings to slide them in. She did hope he would think she looked pretty. That he might remember, too.

There was a quick knock at her chamber door and Harry hurried in with a red cashmere shawl over her arm, Miss Muffins at her heels. The dog seemed to have suffered no ill effects at all from her swim, but would be very disappointed when she realised she would not be allowed at the musicale to make more mischief. She had quite enjoyed the attention, the little mischief-maker.

Harry, as usual, looked very beautiful in a Turkey-red and gold gown embroidered with tiny, sparkling gold sequins over the tulle skirt, small gold-headed pins flashing in her hair. Eleanor did often worry why Harry had never married again, though her friend did talk so seldom of her husband.

'Eleanor, I thought if you were wearing your red and white stripes this would look well with it but I am not sure about the green and gold...' Harry held up the shawl—a confection softer than clouds of fine cashmere shining with embroidery.

'How kind, Harry! I think it will do quite well. I shall be quite the rare bird of colour tonight.'

Harry draped it over Eleanor's shoulders, its whisper-soft folds drifting down. 'There! How pretty you look this evening.'

Eleanor laughed. 'I did try rather more than usual, I admit.'

Harry tilted her head to the side, considering. 'Because of Lord Fleetwood? He and Penelope will be there tonight, yes?'

Eleanor glanced at her friend in surprise. Was her infatuation so very visible, then? She had to take some lessons at the Theatre Royal. 'I—I don't know.'

Harry gave her a reassuring smile and a squeeze of the hand. 'Mary and I were just looking over some of the patrons' files and she told me all about how you once knew each other at your childhood home. His name does seem to be flying around town of late! The dashing military hero who saved this little miscreant from certain drowning.' Miss Muffins looked up at her with innocent, wide brown eyes. 'We have had several enquiries about him from eligible young ladies.'

'I'm glad,' Eleanor forced herself to say smoothly, glancing down to shift some bottles on her dressing table. 'Fred deserves just the right match. Someone wonderful. Someone worthy of him.'

'As do you! My dear friend, if you care for him…'

'I cannot care for him in that way, Harry,' Eleanor interrupted. She could not bear to hear such things any longer. She had this one evening. She didn't want to mar it, no matter how well-meaning she knew Harry and her sister were. 'You know why he came to the agency. The condition of his estate.'

Harry nodded, her eyes too understanding, too knowing. 'There is always more than one solution to a difficulty, I have found.' She picked up Eleanor's small strand of pearls and helped her fasten the clasp. 'Mary was also telling me about Penelope's old friend, Mr Anthony Oliver. She believes they are also very fond of one another. Very fond indeed.'

Eleanor nodded, relieved at the change of topic and the focus on someone else's romantic life. 'I do think they are. I have never seen Penelope look so happy. She had quite the burden with old Lord Fleetwood.'

'I made a few discreet enquiries about Mr Oliver.'

'Harry! You know he is not a patron.'

'Perhaps not, but Lady Fleetwood is a friend of yours, yes? Mary said we should help her if we possibly could and I agreed. We must make some use of our contacts once in a while.'

'Yes,' Eleanor admitted. 'I agree we should help Pen if we can.'

'Well, Mr Oliver has made quite the fortune. He is a man of property, quite daring in his investments. He owns a fine house in London and two country manors he has made very profitable. He is also highly respected by all his business acquaintances and employees and is considered very eligible. He is also, as we can see for ourselves, most handsome! If he and Penelope come together…'

'What do you mean?'

'I mean, surely he would wish to help his new wife's

family if he could. His fortune is quite great, all built up himself.'

Eleanor considered this and it was as if one tiny, shimmering ray of hope light broke through. 'Harry. I hadn't thought, that is...'

'It was just a thought, of course. An idea that we might help more than one patron at a time, which is always a pleasure.' Harry picked up Eleanor's small bottle of lavender water and gave her a spritz. 'Mary was also telling me she met a man called Charles Campbell, kinsman to Mr Oliver, and she wonders if he, too, might like to find a suitable wife. And one day a match for his ward.'

Eleanor considered his, her professional instincts taking over. 'Yes, Mr Campbell does seem a fine gentleman. Handsome with a Scots accent I'm sure many ladies would appreciate! And his ward, Miss Adele, is very mannerly and pretty but at a rather impressionable age. I would think he must be rather struggling with it all. A single man with a girl to bring out in Society. He seemed most amiable.' She remembered something else—how Mary looked as she laughed with Mr Campbell at the cricket green and her bright pink cheeks. 'Mary did seem to like him.'

Harry looked most thoughtful as Eleanor watched her in the looking glass. 'Did she now?'

The music room was already crowded when Eleanor, Mary and Harry arrived, sans the distracting company of Miss Muffins. The pale yellow walls shimmered in the light of dozens of candelabras from the glow of the

crystal chandeliers overhead and the air smelled of lilies
and roses from the silver-potted arrangements banked
around the low dais where the musicians warmed up.
The gilt chairs snaked in lines around the display. The
most well-known people of Bath sat the front, the ladies' gowns shining like stained glass and their jewels gleaming.

'Eleanor! Over here, do come sit with us,' Penelope
called. She sat on one of the back rows with Mr Oliver. The two of them leaning very close—or possibly
that was Eleanor's imagining, brought on by Harry's
romantic speculations about the pair. Yet they did seem
comfortable and happy in one another's company. As
if they had always been just so. 'Fred had another appointment this afternoon but he promised faithfully to
be here before the music begins, so I have saved him
a seat. Eleanor, do sit between us here. You can find
him when he arrives. Wasn't the cricket delightful? I
vow I miss a bit of fresh air at times! We must have a
picnic at Beechen Cliff again soon.'

Beechen Cliff—where Fred had caught her when
she fell, and she had never felt more safe, more cherished. But she was saved from having to answer, to
have her blushes noted, when the conductor appeared
on the stage. The musicians lifted their bows amid applause and launched into their first piece—a Handel
air. The notes were flying through the air like summer
swallows when someone sat down beside Eleanor. She
knew right away it was Fred. No one else felt as he did,
smelled of that lemony sunshine. She trembled knowing

this was it. This was the one last time she would truly let herself feel for him. Be with him. One last memory.

'Do forgive me,' he whispered to Eleanor, his smile rueful and bright as the sun to her. 'Pen will surely be angry I was so late.'

'They have only just begun. She said you had a business appointment?'

'Yes, with the family's attorneys. The estate agent is to arrive tomorrow.' Fred grimaced. 'I am sure he will tell us dire news and give me instructions to retrench most severely.'

Retrench—or marry well? Just as she, and everyone else, knew he must do. Yet the reality of it was so cold. Like a sudden, drenching rain. 'Do excuse me,' she gasped and dashed out of her chair and from the crowded music room. She hoped Mary or Harry would not follow, for she had absolutely no words to explain herself.

She made her way past a few couples strolling the corridors outside the concert room, nodding and smiling as if all was perfectly ordinary and her heart was quite whole and content. Or at least she *hoped* it looked that way. She'd had such long practice in hiding her emotions, making a smooth and smiling facade, surely it must work now.

She turned and moved onwards, half blindly, down a staircase, past a row of pale classical statues that watched her with blank, indifferent eyes. It made her feel invisible. Like she could crawl away and no one would notice except these gods and goddesses who did not care one whit. She wasn't quite sure where she was going, perhaps looking for a withdrawing room, but really she just wanted that moment alone. A moment where she didn't have to hide her feelings for Fred.

She turned once more, and found a half-open doorway to a dark room beyond. It seemed to be a storeroom of sorts, with crates stacked along the walls. Perfect. She tiptoed inside and leaned against one of the boxes, taking a deep breath as minutes ticked past.

Suddenly, she heard soft footsteps in the corridor outside, pausing as if they too looked for a hidey-hole. She held her breath, listening to them come ever nearer. A shadow loomed in the doorway, elongated against the flagstone floor. A hand reached out…

Eleanor gave a soft, involuntary shriek. But then she blinked and saw it was no stranger or ghost that had found her. It was Fred. Fred—the one person she longed for, the one she was trying to escape. He was shadowed by the luminous lamplight behind him, yet she knew it was him. No one else felt like that or smelled of summer sunshine like him.

'Blast it all, Fred, you frightened me,' she gasped.

He flashed her a rueful smile, white in the shadows.

'I'm sorry, Eleanor. I was worried when you left the concert so suddenly.'

'I—I needed a breath of air.'

'I agree. It was quite crowded in there. So much—noise.'

Eleanor remembered what he'd told her of his time in battle. The noise, the chaos, the feelings of despair. Perhaps he did sometimes feel overwhelmed now, and didn't speak of it. Couldn't escape it. She reached out and gently touched his arm, hoping he saw that she understood.

He covered her hand with his own and she felt the warm steadiness of him envelop her until she couldn't even remember her own fears.

His eyes narrowed and his expression turned serious, intent, as he studied her. He slowly, carefully, reached for her other hand and drew her closer, as if giving her the chance to draw away, apart from him. She could not. She seemed bound in a silvery net of enchantment. Fred wouldn't ever look like her everyday world, grey and practical, her feelings hidden. The feelings she had with him were as bright and wondrous as a vivid summer day.

She swayed closer to him, and wound her arms tightly around his neck so he couldn't fly away again and leave her alone in that dream. She wished she could stay in his embrace all night—every night! To forget about duty and families. Everything but him.

She stared up at him in the shadows, thinking how beautiful he was. Even his scars made him more so, with what they said about his honour, his heart.

'How lovely you are, Fred,' she whispered.

He gave a surprised laugh. 'Of course I'm not. I am quite a wreck.'

She shook her head. How could she ever convince him of what she saw, what she'd always seen, in him? She went up on tiptoe and pressed her lips to his in a swift, sweet kiss, as if it could say what she could not.

He groaned and pulled her closer, so close there was not even a breath between them. He deepened the kiss, his tongue gently seeking the taste of hers and she fell completely into him. Lost in that wild need to be just that close to him. Drawn to him by those invisible, silvery magic cords that had always seemed to bind them together.

She didn't question herself. Couldn't walk away. Not yet.

He pressed tiny, soft, fleeting kisses to her cheek, her temple, the tiny, ever so sensitive spot just behind her ear. She shivered to feel the warm rush of his breath on her skin.

'Oh, Ella,' he whispered hoarsely. 'How can we go on like this?'

She nodded, leaning her burning face into his shoulder. She tried to breathe deeply, but that only seemed to draw him into her even more, surrounding her with his very essence. He was the one true thing she'd always clung to. She saw that now. Yet soon he would have to go away from her, for always.

She imagined nights in the future, when she would lie alone in bed, listening to the silence beyond her window. When she would close her eyes and remember Fred just as he was now. Remember how this felt. She leaned her forehead against his chest and listened to the steady sound of his heartbeat. She let it flow through her and bind them together. She hoped it would be enough to hold them together at least in some way for a long time to come.

She kissed his cheek one more time, and spun

around to leave. 'Thank you,' she whispered and dashed away. At least she would always remember how his kiss felt. Always.

Chapter Twelve

'And this portion, you see, Lord Fleetwood, is quite a large parcel and is not part of the entail set up by your great-grandfather,' Mr Palmer, the estate agent who had travelled from Moulton Magna with parcels of documents and surveys for Fred to study, said as he pointed out a detailed map of the estate.

It was vital work. Under his father's lackadaisical final years of stewardship, the property had become very disorganised indeed. Farms required vital repairs, fields and structures were neglected. Finding any assets that could be sold was most important, it could tide them over until Eleanor's agency found him a suitable heiress bride.

Eleanor.

The sweetest, kindest, most beautiful lady he could hope to know. And one as far from him as the moon, despite the heated rush of her kisses and the way she felt under his touch. That kiss had been nothing else he'd ever known. It had sent him out of himself, out of the world entirely, and shown him a heavenly beauty and sweetness. A perfection. He'd thought of little else since…

'Lord Fleetwood?' Mr Palmer said, breaking into his longing, lustful thoughts.

'Yes, of course,' Fred said quickly. He studied the map before him and saw not what was now, the neglect and decay, but what had once been and what might have been. Fine farms, fertile fields, a home for so many. But all that would take funds.

He examined the outlined parcel to the north of the estate. It was indeed quite large, with properties to make up a fine manor of its own for a buyer or tenant. It would still leave Moulton Magna with its oldest portion, its grand house and the home farm that could be made productive again. Yet he remembered that land so well from when he was young. The stream, the fields and woodland. Running there free with Eleanor, the happiest he'd ever been.

'What was meant for this land here?' he asked, tapping his finger at the largest parcel of the north manor. He remembered when he was just a small boy and his father managed to purchase it from the neighbours as the last puzzle piece to the estate. His father had ridden there with small Fred in front of him in the saddle, pointing out the prettiest spots to him. There had been an old manor house, in need of repair but pretty, and empty meadows. 'I'm sure it was not meant to be left vacant when it was acquired.'

'Indeed, no, Lord Fleetwood. I believe your mother planned to make the old house into a school for the children of tenants and employees,' Mr Palmer said.

He took off his spectacles, gave them a polish before replacing them on his nose and harrumphing. 'A very kind lady she was. I remember your father's widow, the current Dowager Lady Fleetwood, was once minded to revive these ideas. It would be of great benefit to so many, but by then there were not the funds.'

'Of course,' Fred murmured. So many things left undone. So many regrets. 'But the land could be sold?'

'Certainly. The terms of the entail only include this central portion, the house and home farm, and these tenant farms here and here. These acres were acquired later, of course, as was this woodland. It would be a shame to lose them. I believe much could be made of them with the proper planning. But these unfortunate circumstances do happen.'

Fred nodded. Unfortunate indeed. They were all trapped by the past now. By choices others had made.

He suddenly longed to know what Eleanor would think. What she would advise.

The door opened, interrupting his thoughts and dreams. 'Why, Mr Palmer!' Penelope said as she hurried into the library, holding out her hand for the delighted estate agent to bow over. She was dressed to go out, in a dark blue redingote and feathered tilted hat *à la militaire*. 'What a lovely surprise to see you today.'

'And a pleasure to see you again, Lady Fleetwood,' Mr Palmer said with another little bow. Penelope had been so popular at the estate, even in the midst of his father's worst behaviour. 'I brought some of the newest surveys for his lordship to review.'

'Yes, of course,' Penelope said with a sigh. 'Always

the worry of Moulton Magna.' She leaned over to study the map. 'Is this portion where the school was once to have been built?'

'Indeed, my lady.'

'Such a great pity. It would have been of such value.' She looked most wistful for a moment, quite far away, before she gave her gloves a sharp tug and put on a bright smile. 'I am going to meet Mary St Aubin at Molland's. I shall be back for dinner tonight. Then to the theatre?'

Fred had forgotten about the theatre. He had been so much in crowds of late, so many people wanting to meet him now that he was the 'heroic celebrity' of the day for rescuing that silly dog and he longed for a quiet evening by the fire. But he knew he couldn't do that. A wife had to be found and contacts made if they were to dig themselves out of this mess. He rubbed wearily at his eyes. 'Yes, of course. And we can talk about that masquerade you're so excited about, as well.'

'Oh, my dear Fred. You've been working so hard,' Penelope said, gently touching his hand in sympathy. 'You must be so tired! But I promise the masquerade will be fun. Just what you need. Some music and light, wine and pretty ladies.'

'Maybe you're right, Pen.' Once, when he'd been young and careless, he'd thought *fun* would solve everything, too. It hadn't, of course. It had only created new problems. But maybe the music and noise would stop him thinking so very much right now. Stop him thinking too much of Eleanor.

Penelope took a parcel from under her arm and

handed it to him. 'Here's a black cloak and mask for you, as I know you won't wear a costume. Now, I really must fly. So charming to see you again, Mr Palmer.'

Once she was gone, Fred made himself study the maps and ledgers that so limited his future again. 'Now, Mr Palmer, do show me these figures again…'

Molland's was quite busy when Penelope pushed open the door, with every table and stool occupied. But Mary had saved seats near the window where they could watch everyone hurrying past.

'Penelope!' she called with a wave. 'Over here! I have marzipan.'

Penelope threaded her way across the room to sit down across from Mary at the high table, gratefully accepting a cup of tea. It was not at all a long walk to the shop, but every step had felt weighted with thoughts and worries. Seeing Mr Palmer and all his maps and papers just brought it back to her what a mess they were all in. How unfair it all was on dear Fred.

Mary smiled, and gazed out of the window as she waited for Penelope to collect herself, calm and unhurried. Penelope was happy to have such friends in the St Aubin sisters. She'd not often had female friends, except for Miss Collinwood who had once taken her to that house party where she met Anthony Oliver. Friends were the best part of her new life in Bath. A life she could create for herself for the very first time.

Now, though, she feared she and Mary together had got something very wrong.

'I'm sorry I was late,' Penelope said, popping a bit of

that divine marzipan into her mouth. 'Mr Palmer, an estate agent from Moulton Magna, was there with Fred.'

Mary gave her a sympathetic frown and offered
more tea. 'Is the news so very bad, then?'

'No more than I had imagined. But, oh, Mary! I do
fear so for poor Fred. For his future happiness.'

'Don't worry, Pen, darling, I beg you. I have a fine
idea for him, a very pretty young lady whose parents
came to the agency on her behalf, a Miss Evans. Her
father is a businessman, quite well-to-do, who is eager
to find a titled gentleman. She would help him to put
all things to right in no time. If they like each other.'

Penelope sighed. 'I'm afraid that is quite the trouble.
I know of the agency's fine work, of course, that is why
I sought out your help…'

'But?' Mary gazed at her curiously, not at all angry
or worried.

'But I quite fear Fred is in love with someone else.'

Mary's eyes widened. 'Is he indeed? But that is
lovely! Someone suitable, I hope? It is not a regular
occurrence, I admit, but we *have* had people come to us
in despair they should never meet their match and then
they find them all on their own. They merely needed
reassurance, I think. It's a good thing!'

'That is the very problem.'

'She is *not* suitable?' Mary gasped. 'An actress or…'

'No! No, the lady herself is most suitable. She merely
has no fortune and Fred feels he is bound to take on
the whole burden of his family and estate.' Penelope
took a deep breath and tried to find just the right way

to state her concerns. 'Mary—did you ever have any suspicions about Fred and Eleanor?'

'*Eleanor?*' Mary burst into laughter. 'Fred and Eleanor? No, I surely would not have...' Suddenly, her laughter broke off and her eyes grew even larger. 'Oh. Of course. Yes. I did wonder but then I thought...what a great fool I have been. How quiet she has been lately and how they look at each other. Oh!'

'Then you see it, too?'

Mary took a long, flustered sip of tea. 'I did not before. I was too intent on agency business. So sure my instincts would lead me to the right answer.' She pounded her gloved palm on the edge of the table. 'How silly! How could my instincts have failed me with my own sister?'

Penelope sighed. 'Perhaps our instincts are sharpest when we are not so very close to the situation.'

'I truly should have seen. At Beechen Cliff, the assembly, the cricket.' Mary shook her head. 'Poor, dear Eleanor. She has been so distracted of late. So distant and—and sad. I feared she had been working too hard.'

'Fred, too, has been distracted and solemn. Most unlike his old self.'

'Well, then, he cannot marry Miss Evans, or anyone but Eleanor! Love is truly the most important thing, if one is lucky enough to have it. I would never see my sister made unhappy.'

'Nor can I bear to see Fred sad. He was a true friend to me when we first met and when I needed one. But his sense of duty would never allow him to abandon his estate.'

Mary scowled. 'What a dreadful conundrum. Yet there must be an answer, if I look hard enough.'

'I have thought of one.' Penelope drew in another deep, steadying breath. She'd realised what she had to do on her walk to Molland's. And the sparkling, hopeful way she'd felt when Anthony Oliver didn't, *couldn't*, matter one bit. 'You must find me a match. The most wealthy gentleman you know. It does not matter his age or—or anything else. As soon as you can.'

Mary looked horrified. 'No, Pen! You must not rush into such a thing. You deserve happiness, too. I'll find you someone. Indeed I will. But not like this.'

'It *must* be like this. I can't let Fred and Eleanor give up their love if I can help them. I heard Mr Palmer say Fred could sell a parcel of Moulton Magna and use the money to repair the main house and revitalise the home farm. If I had a husband of fortune, surely I could include buying this land in our marriage contract and then I could be of help often after. Fred just needs some assistance to start his work. And Eleanor would make him the finest of wives.'

'Of course she would. Eleanor would make any man worthy of her love the most fortunate man living! Yet surely Fred would never see you make such a sacrifice.'

'Then we must do it without telling him. He'll only find out once the match is made, so we must work quickly.'

Mary still looked doubtful. She glanced wistfully into her teacup, as if she wished it could be something a tad stronger. 'I will go and look at our ledgers right away, and put off Miss Evans somehow. I can find you someone, Pen, I am sure. But working so fast…'

Penelope held up her palm. 'A fortune. That is all he must have.' She thought of her past husbands, old men who gambled and drank and who saw her as a prize to be displayed. And of Mr Oliver's kind smile. She had to forget that now.

Mary sighed, and nodded sadly.

'Now,' Penelope said with determined cheerfulness. 'Let us talk about the masquerade at Sydney Gardens! One last glorious burst of merriness for us all. I intend to dance my slippers off and consume an immoderate amount of rum punch. Tell me, Mary, do you have your costume yet?'

Half an hour later, Penelope departed from Molland's amid a light, grey drizzle, sad but most determined. She parted with Mary on the corner of a busy lane, and watched as her friend hurried back towards the agency to study their ledgers of patrons.

A flash of colour caught her attention and she paused to study a bonnet in a milliner's window. Bright blue, with purple and pale blue feathers and fluttering lavender taffeta ribbons, like an exotic bird suddenly alighted on a plain stone wall.

She imagined herself wearing it. That colour following her on her path to bring noise and commotion and *life* again. It had been so long since she'd had such things amid days of worry, helplessness and loneliness.

In fact, she couldn't quite remember when she last had such colour in her life at all. It had been a very long time indeed.

She tugged at the edge of her old grey hat, and smiled to imagine it turned to blue instead. That she was a young lady who wore the latest styles, who could laugh and dance and flirt without a care. She suddenly did remember when she last had such a life, if only briefly. It was that house party where she danced in the moonlight, played croquet and lounged in the sunshine.

With those memories breaking around her as if they were yesterday, Penelope turned and strolled on, thinking not of Lord Fleetwood and all those solitary days at Moulton Magna as his wife and widow, but of the present day and the present moment. Maybe she wanted everyone she cared about to be free and happy because once she had seen such things for herself. Felt the wonder of falling in love, the giddiness of spending her moments just as she liked. She couldn't have held onto them then, yet surely Fred could. Dear Fred, who gave so much in the Army, who cared so much about his home. He deserved happiness.

She came around the corner of her own street—and found herself face to face with Anthony Oliver. The Anthony of her memories and the man she longed for still. He smiled and swept his hat off to reveal wind-ruffled, glossy dark hair and she couldn't quite breathe.

His smile widened and for an instant she was flying right back to those days of youth and laughter.

'Lady Fleetwood,' he said with a bow. 'What a fine chance to see you today.'

'And you! But please—call me Penelope when we meet like this? It would make me feel rather like myself again. Not this stuffy old matron I seem to have become.'

'I'm honoured, Penelope. If you will call me Anthony, as you once did.' He paused, his smile turning wistful, as if he too thought of their sunny days at that party. How they seemed so close and yet so far away. 'And I dare say you are the least, er, stuffy lady I have ever known. I remember at that house party, when you insisted we slide down the stairs on silver trays as if we were sledding!'

Penelope hid her laugh behind her gloved hand. 'Oh, I do remember much about that dear party! It has always been a memory of such a happy time.'

'For me, as well. The happiest.' For a long moment, they merely watched each other. Silently. Intently. Watching time trace itself backwards between them.

He offered her his arm. 'Shall we walk for a while? I am still learning my way around Bath.'

'As am I. I should much enjoy a turn with you, Mr Ol—Anthony.' She gazed up into his eyes, like warm, amber sherry. He must have had many ladies in love with him since they last met. 'If I am not detaining you from an appointment.'

'Not at all. I promised Natalie and Grace I would take them for ices, but not until later. I am quite—free.'

Penelope smiled, wondering if that could be true. If they were both at last free. 'As am I.' She slid her hand over his sleeve, feeling his muscles tense under her touch, and she longed to lean into him. 'Your nieces are so charming.'

'Indeed they are. I fear they quite have me wrapped

around their fingers. They like to dress my hair in curling papers, use me to boost them up trees they are not meant to climb and make me a fourth at dolls' tea parties.' He sighed theatrically. 'I am much put upon.'

Penelope laughed, picturing him at a tiny table with a wee tea set, his hair curled. What a fine father he would make! It gave her a pang to realise he had no children of his own yet. 'You like children?'

'Very much. Especially clever ones like Natalie and Grace.'

'So do I. As often as I could at Moulton Magna, I visited our tenants' children, played with them and read with them, I loved it. They made me laugh like no one else could!' She sighed to think of the school she had longed to build for them, which could not come to pass.

He studied her from beneath the brim of his hat, those sherry eyes sympathetic and warm. 'You have none of your own?'

What would have sounded like the veriest impertinence from someone she'd just met merely seemed like empathy and understanding from Anthony.

'I should have liked to, but it was not meant to be.'

And, despite her disappointment, it was fortunate she had none with her dreadful husbands. She was not tied to them in any way but memory and that faded when she was with Anthony. 'But you, Anthony! I am sure you would make a most fine parent indeed. I wonder you have not married.'

He gave a wry laugh, looking away. She glimpsed a spot of red blush on his cheekbones—most intriguing and sweet.

'You and my sister! I am forever fending off her "helpful suggestions" and "chance meetings" over tea tables.'

Penelope thought of the agency and thought it was good his sister had not yet seemed to have heard of them. Anthony would be snatched up in a moment if he sought their services! 'You have met no lady to suit you?'

Their steps slowed, ceased, and he looked down at her without blinking. Without turning away. 'Indeed I have. That has long been my trouble.'

Penelope could not breathe. Her heart felt so tight, so hopeful, so panicked and wondering. 'Did—did you?'

'Yes. Long ago, I saw a young lady, with dark eyes and a sweet smile, who made me laugh as I never had before or since. Made me *feel*, as I certainly have not done since! I could not forget her. No one else has ever equalled her.'

'I—understand,' she whispered. 'When I was young, I also found a person I was most drawn to. Most—intrigued with, truly. I thought then it was only a dream. A vision that would fade in the face of reality…'

He stepped even closer, taking her hand in his. 'As did I. I worked as hard as the devil for years. Threw myself into my business. Built it to where it is, trying so much to forget.'

'And did you ever? Forget?'

His fingers curled tighter around hers and she hoped most fervently he would not let her go. Not let her fall. 'Never. And when I saw her again, at Beechen Cliff, I knew I never could have forgotten at all. She was all I remembered. All I longed for and more.'

Penelope gave a tiny, choked sob, letting herself believe again at long last. Letting herself hope. 'I never forgot, either. When I was unhappy, in despair, I remembered those days with you. The laughter and dances. The feeling that I could say anything at all and you would understand.' She rested her forehead against his shoulder, listening to the steady, reassuring beat of his heart, uncaring who might see them. 'I thought I would never see you again.'

And here they were, together, nothing between them now. She felt giddy, dizzy, so young again! She felt like herself.

He laughed, and raised her hand to his lips for a long, lingering kiss. The warmth of it flowed into her cold, lonely heart and made it summer again.

How could she ever deny such feelings to anyone she cared about? To Fred and Eleanor? She had to help them. Had to make sure the world was put right for them all.

Chapter Thirteen

'Oh, Eleanor, isn't it terribly exciting?' Mary whispered as they stepped through the gates of the gardens into the fairyland of the masquerade everyone had been looking forward to all the social season.

'It is,' Eleanor agreed, surprised at herself. She could seldom afford to be fanciful, to whirl around in girlish excitement, but she felt the fizz of it all inside herself tonight. The gardens, where they so often walked, had been transformed into something astonishing. A dream world. Equally dreamy creatures drifted past them— fairies, elves, queens and kings and knights. Mysterious men in black cloaks, faces hidden.

Here, she did not have to be Eleanor. She could be anyone at all. She could escape work and worry for a time. Though she found she could not escape thoughts of Fred. The memory of their kisses, the way he made her feel, the way he made her forget all she'd worked for, strived for and tried to be. With him, she was not sensible. She was—free.

Mary held her arm tightly as they followed the butterfly-bright crowd down the entrance pathway towards the main theatre set up near the centre of the gardens—their destination for the evening. Through the carefully spaced trees, thousands of coloured glass lamps faceted to make the lights sparkle like stars and cast amber, green, blue, red over the costumed crowds flitting between them.

Eleanor smoothed her own skirt, dark red and black velvet made to look like a Renaissance duchess's, and straightened her red satin mask.

'Oh, look at that man over there!' Mary whispered with a giggle. She tugged at the edge of her white, pleated muslin Greek goddess costume, looking like an angel of white and gold. Eleanor felt such a burst of pride in her beautiful sister. 'See? The one dressed as a medieval knight. Such delicious broad shoulders! Can we entice him to the agency if he is unmarried? He would be much sought-after.'

Eleanor laughed, but she was quite sure the knight's shoulders were not nearly so fine as Fred's. She remembered how those shoulders felt under her touch when he caught her at Beechen Cliff. And how strong he was when he saved Miss Muffins from the river, and made himself an idol to every lady in Bath.

Eleanor suddenly stumbled a bit on a loose patch of gravel on the pathway. Cursing her silly, distracted state, and her new heeled shoes, she yanked her heel free and hurried after Mary.

A stage surrounded on three sides by temporary wooden boxes was the centrepiece of the party. Four classical colonnades held the supper boxes, wrapped by more shadowed walkways and trees. An orchestra played on the stage, lilting dance music to greet the guests who cried out to friends and looked around for new flirtations, trying to guess who was behind the masks.

Even more of those glittering lanterns were draped everywhere, lighting up the colonnades so brightly it could have been midday. The magical costumed creatures floated through it all, catching Eleanor up in the dazzling kaleidoscope.

She was so distracted, she stumbled again and someone caught her arm before she could fall. Dazzled by it all, she glanced up to find it was one of those black-cloaked men. A plain satin mask covered most of his face, his head draped in a hood, giving him a slightly sinister air in the midst of that fairyland.

Instinctively, she drew back a little, startled. But then she glimpsed the eyes behind the mask, bright blue and realised how very familiar that touch felt through her velvet sleeve. Surely only one man felt like that. Smelled like that, made her heart race like that.

'Thank you, F—that is, sir,' she whispered. He nodded and let her go, disappearing into the crowd before she could stop him. She wondered if she had only imagined him there.

'Hurry up, Eleanor, we'll fall behind!' Mary called.

Eleanor shook away the strange, fantasy spell of the gardens, of the man who might or might not be Fred and followed her sister to their designated box. It was a small space, open on one side so they could watch the dancing in the centre, made even closer by the long table and close press of chairs. Penelope and Mr Oliver waited for them, dressed as Eleanor of Aquitaine and a knightly swain, along with Charles Campbell, dashing in his kilt and Adele in a pretty, ruffled pink shepherdess gown and beribboned bonnet. A few other friends had joined them and to judge from the clutter of empty wine bottles on the table and their loud laughter they'd already begun the revels. They called out merry greetings and offered glasses.

'Here, Eleanor, do try some of this punch,' Penelope urged. 'It's quite fine and they've brought us such a great quantity.'

Unlike the food, Eleanor thought wryly as she studied the scant, small platters of cheese and ham, with a bit of shrivelled-looking fruit. They clearly hadn't gone to Molland's for the catering.

She took a sip of the offered punch, which was an inviting bright pink colour in the Venetian glass vessels—and coughed as her eyes started to water. 'Yes, it's…er…quite good indeed.'

And it rather was, once she'd got past that first sharp kick. Rather sweet, really and most relaxing. She sipped some more as she studied the passing crowds. She wondered if each man in a black cloak—and there were many—could be Fred. Surely she should have followed him! But then what would she have done if she found him? She was meant to try and forget him, not chase him over the park! But if he spoke to her, touched her…

Eleanor sighed. She knew she could do none of the things she dreamed about.

The orchestra launched into an aria and the famous soprano Signora Boldini appeared amid enthusiastic applause and cries. She held out her arms and curtsied deeply, vast white plumes nodding in her upswept hair. She threw back her head and launched into her song. A tale of love lost, won and lost again. Of heartbreak and longing. A tale that soon had everyone sighing just to hear it, just to feel those words in their own hearts.

Eleanor's eyes suddenly prickled with tears that threatened to fall at any second. She stared down into her empty glass, blinking furiously in hope that no one would see her silly weeping. It felt as if the walls of the box were closing in on her. The press of other people was so much she couldn't breathe.

'I'll be back directly, Mary,' she whispered.

Mary glanced up from whispering with Mr Campbell, her eyes wide. 'Are you quite well, Eleanor, dear? You look rather flushed.'

'I'm perfectly well, just—just need the necessary,' she blurted, unable to think of a more dignified excuse. She slipped out of the box, away from the music and the well-lit walks. She glimpsed couples flashing in and out between the trees, so close to each other.

She felt dizzy and rather silly and so very sad. Could it be the melancholy song? The punch? She really didn't know where she was going. She only knew she had to be alone for a moment, to collect herself.

She saw a narrower, darker path just ahead and stumbled towards it on her new shoes. There were far fewer lamps there, just a sprinkling set high in the trees, and it was blessedly quiet. She heard whispers and soft laughter beyond the trees, yet could see no one else. A cool breeze brushed over her warm cheeks.

Up ahead, in a clearing, she saw the white marble of a little teahouse where Mary and Miss Muffins liked to stop sometimes for a respite on walks. It was much like the one she remembered at Moulton Magna, where she and Fred could meet secretly and be comfortable and happy for a little time. She turned towards it, sure it would give her a peaceful place to sit for a moment and her heel caught again in the gravel. This time, it caught her off-guard completely and snapped off to send her tumbling towards the gravel pathway.

There was no time at all to panic or scream. A strong arm caught her around the waist and lifted her up and up, the trees spinning over her head. Cold fear rushed through her like ice in her veins, freezing her in place. She'd heard the tales about such parties before, surely she should have known better than to wander off on the dark paths by herself! Now surely something dreadful was going to happen.

She kicked out wildly, but her feet caught in her heavy skirt and pressed her even closer to her captor. She twisted and tried to scream and by sheer luck her fist flew backward and connected with a solid jaw.

'Ella! By Jove, I think you broke my tooth,' a man growled in a low, rough voice. A familiar voice.

'Fred!' she gasped, appalled she had just planted *Fred* a facer. 'What on earth…?'

'I saw you walk away from your box and you looked upset I suppose. I wanted to be sure you were all right.' He slowly lowered her to feet, holding her steady until he was sure she could stand on her own. She wobbled a bit on the broken heel of her shoe and inhaled deeply, smelling the warm, comforting scent of his lemon soap. How could she have mistaken him for anyone else?

He rubbed at his jaw. His face was all sharply carved lines and angles in the shadows. His hair was tousled. 'Oh, Fred, I am sorry I hit you.'

He laughed ruefully. 'You do have a strong right hook, Ella, no doubt. And good for you using it! I should certainly have called out to you. I had no business surprising you like that.'

'Still…' She gently reached up and touched his cheek, feeling the prickles of his afternoon beard on her palm and the heat of his skin. 'It may be quite black and blue tomorrow.'

'I shall just tell people I rescued another pup from certain doom. It will surely enhance my heroic reputation.'

Eleanor studied him for a moment. The shadows were deep there amid the trees, but a stray strand of silver moonlight fell over him, gilding him, erasing all the years and trials that had stood between them, making him her young, darling friend Fred again. He had discarded his mask and his eyes glowed like a summer sky. She remembered her feelings when she arrived at the masquerade. That she could be or do anything for this one night. What if she was not Eleanor, the vicar's daughter, the matchmaker and he was not Frederick the Earl?

'Well, thank you for catching me again,' she said. 'How clumsy you must think me! It was just too warm in the supper box. I needed a bit of fresh air.'

'Most understandable,' he said. 'The crowds are overwhelming tonight.'

'Yes, exactly. And I'm afraid I let Penelope urge too much punch on me. I was quite giddy.'

He laughed, the most delightful sound, and it made her want to laugh, too. Made her want to spin around and dance! Everything did seem grander tonight. Larger. Brighter. 'Too much of the punch, eh? I fear I know the feeling well.'

She sighed to think of the two, or maybe it was even *three*, glasses she had consumed.

'What was in it?'

'Quite simple, I think, a few grains of elderflower mixed with sweet wine and rum.'

'Simple yet deadly. Is that how you came to stumble?'

'I am not as ale-shot as all that, Frederick!' she said indignantly. 'I stumbled because my new shoe broke. I knew I shouldn't let Mary persuade me to wear them, but she said I could certainly not wear my old dancing slippers with this costume. What a difficult time Renaissance ladies must have had!'

'Let me see. Let's sit down over there and I'll see if I can fix it. At least well enough to get you home without a turned ankle.' He gestured towards the little teahouse, which was softly lit by a few lanterns that flickered over its pale walls, making it look like a piece of the moon.

Eleanor nodded and leaned on his arm as he led her towards its open doorway. The one round room inside was empty, but furnished with a few cushioned chairs and settees, lit by those lanterns and the open rotunda over their heads. He helped her to sit down, and knelt before her like a gallant knight with his lady. He gazed up at her with steady expectation as her heart thundered inside her, his blue eyes glowing.

'Are—are you a cobbler, too, then? As well as an earl and a soldier?' she whispered.

He gave her a wide, flashing smile. The smile that always did such strange, twisty things to her stomach. 'I am a man of many talents, Ella.'

'That I do know.' She felt that odd, bemused spell he cast come over her again and she didn't feel quite in control of herself. She slowly lifted her hem a few inches, and held out her foot.

Fred slid a strong hand around her ankle, his fingers strong and warm through her stocking. She shivered as his caressing touch slid over her instep, tickling lightly as if he touched her bare skin. It was so shocking, so...

Delightful. Better than all her dreams of him had ever been.

He slid the velvet shoe off her foot and examined the cracked heel of it as he still cradled her foot in his other hand. She had never imagined she could feel that way from someone touching her mere foot. Feet were merely utilitarian, of course. Meant to carry a person about and not be very attractive. But Fred touched it as if *her* foot was something precious.

She felt so dizzy all over again, and reached down to balance her palms on his shoulders. Yes—they were finer than the man Mary admired earlier, for certain.

The feel of those hardened muscles shifting beneath her touch did nothing to steady her at all.

'I am afraid it is quite hopeless,' he said.

'Hopeless?' she gasped. Yes, indeed, *they* were hopeless and always had been. She could not feel this way about him.

And yet, at this moment, she had never felt more right.

'Your shoe is beyond repair,' he said.

She laughed. 'You truly are not a cobbler, I see.'

'I am a man of some talents, but master of none.'

'I find that hard to believe,' she murmured. He was truly a master in the art of touching a woman in a way that made her mind go all soft and dreamy. Every soft little caress he ran over her toes and the arch of her foot, made her shiver. 'How am I to walk on the broken heel?'

'Well, one of the talents I learned in the Army is improvisation.' He slid the shoe back onto her foot and gently placed it on the ground. Then he reached for her other foot, curling his fingers around her ankle. He removed her other shoe. 'Hold on to me.'

That she could gladly do. She curled her fingers tighter over his shoulders and he let go of her. He twisted hard on the intact shoe heel and broke off that heel, as well.

'There! Slippers. Very fashionable,' he declared.

Eleanor laughed. How very silly she felt suddenly! 'Then you are a master cobbler indeed.'

'I try my best to right any wrong that comes my way.' And Eleanor knew he truly did. He was an honourable man, no matter how he protested, and would never let anyone who relied on him be disappointed. She loved that about him, even as it kept them apart.

He reached again for her foot and Eleanor giggled, some imp of mischief that usually hid deep inside of her peering out. She tucked her foot further in the folds of her skirt, making him search through satin, velvet and lacy muslin petticoats to find it.

When he caught her ankle he drew her closer to him and her fists curled on his shoulders. She closed her eyes against the sensations his touch created in her, his hands sliding along the curve of her leg. She felt him press a shocking, heated kiss to her ankle and she gasped as her eyes flew open. She felt weak and hot and collapsed onto the floor beside him, sending them both off-balance and tumbling down.

Fred caught her before she could hit the stone floor and lowered her slowly, slowly, bracing his hands to either side of her head. He gazed down at her, silently and intently, and all she could see were those wondrous eyes.

No one had ever looked at her as he did. As if he saw all of her, right down to her heart. She reached up in wonder and touched his cheek, traced her fingertips over his lips. At last, he lowered his head and pressed those lips to hers. It was so soft and slow, almost gentle, as he brushed his mouth back and forth over hers pressing little kisses to her lower lip. Those slow caresses ignited something deep inside of her, some burning need only Fred ever brought out. She curled her hands into the folds of his cloak and dragged him closer, opening her lips under his.

He groaned deep in his throat and the kiss changed. Became more frantic, more filled with need. She could taste him. Wine, and mint and the night air. Her palms flattened and slid around his back to hold him with her as long as she could.

His lips traced from hers along her cheek, below the line of her mask, to the line of her jaw and then to the soft spot behind her ear that made her gasp. It was like ripe summer fruit bursting over her tongue and she sought his lips again, so eager for another kiss.

Barely had their mouths touched when something broke through her dreamy haze—an explosion high over her head. It took her an instant to realise it was a *real* explosion, not one in her heart. Her eyes flew open to see fireworks through the rotunda above them, red and blue and bright white in the night sky. The party was winding to its conclusion and the flames seemed to illuminate what she was doing. The mistake she was making.

She pushed him away. His blue, blue eyes, incandescent by that firework light, went wide with a shock that echoed her own.

'Ella,' he said roughly. 'I'm so sorry…'

Eleanor frantically shook her head as she pushed herself up from the floor. She never wanted to hear his apologies, his regrets. She was never drinking punch again that was for certain.

'I should find Mary and the others,' she managed to say. 'They will be missing me.'

Fred stood up and held out his hand to help her to her feet. She let him, but released him as soon as she could.

'Let me see you back to the supper boxes.'

'No, no!' Eleanor cried, gathering her gown closer around her, smoothing her skirts and her hair. 'I—I am fine, I promise.'

'I know why you wouldn't want to be seen with me,' he said. 'But let me follow at a distance and make sure you get there safely.'

Eleanor almost laughed. Dear Fred, always gallant and kind. But her most *unsafe* place was surely right here with him.

'You will not even know I'm there,' he said.

She knew he would do it anyway. 'Yes. Very well.' She spun around and left the little teahouse, turning back towards the colonnades. 'You're going in the wrong direction,' he offered.

'Of course I am.' She spun back around to study him one more time. Her tousled, golden knight. 'Oh, Fred. You should marry Miss Evans, you know.'

He frowned fiercely. 'Miss Evans?'

'The pretty heiress. You need her and…' And Eleanor needed Fred. Always. The one thing she could not have.

She turned on her broken shoe again and headed in the right direction towards the lights and music. Towards reality again. She dared to peek back to see if Fred followed her, but he was nowhere in sight. She seemed to be alone once more.

Chapter Fourteen

'Don't you think, Lord Fleetwood?'

Fred glanced down at Miss Evans as she walked beside him, distracted from his ever-distant thoughts. Sydney Gardens had been cleared of signs of the masquerade. The boxes torn down. The dance floor taken away. The lanterns had vanished. Yet he could not forget that night at all.

When Penelope and Mary suggested they might meet Miss Evans, the lady Eleanor urged him to marry, and begin to see if she might be a suitable countess, Fred gave in against his every instinct. They were right, everyone was right, that he had a duty. And Eleanor had her own responsibilities, even if she *was* the only lady he had ever longed for this way.

Yet Eleanor surely would not have him. Her sense of responsibility too strong. *His* sense of responsibility too strong. Miss Evans was a quiet, pretty and well-mannered lady of fortune. Eleanor's urgings made real-world sense, of course.

'I do beg your pardon, Miss Evans, I fear I was wool-gathering,' he said. He glanced up ahead at where Mrs

Evans walked, her purple-striped parasol bobbing, too far to hear them.

Miss Evans nodded solemnly. 'Business matters, no doubt.'

He laughed at her knowing tone. 'A bit, yes.'

'My father is the same. I am sure it must all be so worrisome.' She studied the paths around them in the weak, watery sunlight, twisting the handle of her parasol. 'I do often wish Father would teach me more about it all. His business that is.'

'Do you indeed?' he said, surprised. In his experience, young ladies rarely wanted to know about balance sheets and outgoings.

'It might liven things up. Things are so dull otherwise.'

Fred gestured to the crowds around them, the horses and carriages on the promenade beyond, the display of fashion and conversation. 'Is life in Bath so very dull, then?'

Miss Evans gave him another of her inscrutable, serious glances. 'Not dull for someone like you, perhaps, Lord Fleetwood.'

'Someone like me?'

'Someone who has seen so much of the world. They say you were in the Army. I envy you that.'

'You envy Army life? I fear it is nearly always a lot of dull, uncomfortable waiting with a few moments of acute terror in between.' To say the least. 'And very little good food. The salt beef and biscuits on march are appalling.'

She laughed, surely something she did not do often.

Her dark eyes sparkled and Fred could see why Eleanor might urge her on him. But he could only see her with a certain indifferent admiration, a sort of curiosity. She seemed different than what he might have expected.

'Not really the Army, I think, but just to *see* things. Other cities and lands, different people. Making choices for yourself.'

Fred nodded. Yet look what such *choices* had brought him and his family. To the edge of ruin, to the point of having no choices at all. 'It is not at all the glorious adventure books and poetry might say.'

'Of course not. But at least you have *had* choices. And you have the memories of those sights and sounds and experiences. I have never been able to choose anything at all. Not even this bonnet I am wearing.'

Fred, puzzled by her intense, almost despairing tone, studied the chapeau in question. 'It is—very pretty.'

Miss Evans nodded gloomily. 'But it is not *my* bonnet. All these feathers and bows! It's my mother's. I do hate the bows.'

Fred thought this over. Was he like the bonnet, then? Someone else's choice that she would have to live with? What did she want instead? Travels? Another gentleman? What did *he* want?

He knew what he wanted. Yet he could not have that. He assuredly empathised with Miss Evans. 'What would you choose to do then, Miss Evans?'

Her solemn expression changed like the sun from beneath a cloud, her eyes shimmering, a smile touching her lips. And her answer surprised him.

'I would *choose* flowers! I would travel the world

and find rare botanical specimens and record them in my sketchbooks. I once had a governess, you see, a wonderful lady called Miss Montgomery, who saw how much I loved our botany studies. She had a brother who worked at Kew Gardens and he came to give me a few lessons, too. He gave me books to read and the names of botanists I might correspond with who would answer my questions. It was all so wonderful! I was never happier. Then my parents found out.' Those clouds slid over her again.

'I am sorry,' Fred said.

Miss Evans peered up at him with a little frown. 'Are you?'

'I am. To have something that means so much to you taken away in an instant…'

Miss Evans sighed. 'I must admit, Lord Fleetwood, you are much more amiable than I would have suspected.'

Fred felt a warm little touch of amusement at her evident surprise. 'Am I really, Miss Evans? I am not called "amiable" very often.'

'Oh, but I am sure you are. I thought you would be like my parents. Consumed with your own needs and ambitions and unable to see anything else. Yet you seem very understanding.' Her steps paused on the walkway and she studied the ladies far ahead of them, the tall plumes on her mother's hat waving emphatically as she insisted on something to Penelope and Mary. 'Lord Fleetwood, may I be honest with you?'

'I wish you would.' He thought of all the artifice in life, the veil that covered too much. He wanted to shout his feelings for Eleanor to the world, to send everything else to perdition, but he knew he could not. He could not even speak of it to anyone.

'I know well that my parents wish us to marry. It's why they came to Bath, after all. I suppose they imagined it might be easier to secure a title here than in London.'

Fred stared down at her. She was honest indeed. He couldn't help but like her. 'I am not sure, Miss Evans, really. I think…'

She waved his words away impatiently. 'It does not matter, Lord Fleetwood, for I know them well enough to see their intentions. Yet I think you might have feelings for someone else.'

Fred felt all topsy-turvy suddenly, as if he had been tossed into the air and landed in a new, strange, honest world. 'I…' He feared he was stammering like a fool again, but he wasn't sure what to say.

'I vow I do understand, Lord Fleetwood. We all have so many obligations to our duties, to people we care about and they often conflict with our own hearts. And I do love my parents, even if they can be quite ridiculous about matters like these.'

'We do have duties, yes, Miss Evans.' Yet somehow those worries felt a little lighter, just to be able to say those few words to someone who seemed to see them for what they were.

'Then I say we try this, Lord Fleetwood. I know you have many admirers after heroically saving that little dog from drowning, I hear your name everywhere I go. As does my mother.' She waved at her mother, who was peeking back at them curiously. 'You can marry in a moment, yet I sense there are other things you might wish to pursue and I would not care at all. You could have my dowry, which really is quite large, and my father would have your title. I could study and you could return to your estate and be with your true love, whoever that might be. It could all work out so very well!'

Fred had to admire such a plan. Matter of fact, shrewd, rather brilliant actually. It would be a good plan indeed, if he loved a woman who could agree to be his long-term, quiet mistress. But it would not work with a respectable vicar's daughter like his Eleanor.

'Miss Evans,' he said. 'You are a wonder, truly. And I admit it is a very fine idea.'

Her eyes narrowed. 'But?'

'But I fear the lady I do love could not live like that. She is too respectable. And I couldn't ask you to live like that, either. For all that we have just met, I admire your spirit and independence. You deserve your studies and travels just as you wish.'

She shook her head, but her eyes were kind as she studied him. 'It is a good plan, I know. But it is also a bargain and I would want to offer you the chance to make free choices, too. If your love is a fine lady...'

'She is. Very.' And she was the only one he would want. The only one he had *ever* truly wanted, Fred saw that so clearly now, like a lightning bolt. He could never find even a shred of happiness if Eleanor was not near. He had to be with her. He had to find a way. Think beyond the strictures, as Miss Evans did. 'Just as you are.'

'Then we must be friends. I need as many of those as

I can find.' She went up on tiptoe and kissed his cheek. They heard a faint gasp and titter from her mother but Miss Evans just smiled coolly. 'Are we, then, Lord Fleetwood? Friends?'

'I would be honoured, Miss Evans.'

She took his arm and they strolled onward, amid all the watching, gossiping stares of the garden pathways. 'Do you perchance know of any other titled gentlemen in such a situation, then?' she asked, most practical. 'Someone kind, of course, who would not object to a studious wife. I have made the acquaintance of a very handsome young curate who might suit my purpose, but alas it would not be so easy for my father to accept him…'

Eleanor could barely believe what she was seeing. It was as if the sunny day had suddenly been covered by grey clouds, a wind sweeping coldly over her.

Miss Evans kissed Fred on the cheek, in the middle of the Gardens, and now they linked arms and strolled onward, laughing together most comfortably. Like old friends. Or a new couple.

She felt the sharp prickle of threatening tears at her eyes and she angrily dashed at them with her gloved hand as Miss Muffins peered up at her in concern, whining low in her throat.

'I am quite well, my dear,' she assured the pup, but Miss Muffins tilted her hear doubtfully. Eleanor even doubted those words herself, though she knew they had to be true. She had to be well. To move forward. She had told Fred he should marry Miss Evans. She couldn't be unhappy that he had taken her advice.

And wasn't matching Fred with an intelligent, attractive young lady like Miss Evans what she wanted? They could be a good couple, each having what the other needed. And a good-looking couple, too, producing fine new earls for the future.

She turned away and walked as quickly as she dared in the opposite direction. She could not give Fred what he needed for his estate, his title or his duty. She had only her own energy. Her mind and thoughts and imagination. She had her love for him, too. That love had always been there. Would always be there. Miss Evans had a fortune and she was an interesting lady. Eleanor liked her, too.

Yet those moments at the masquerade...

'Fool,' Eleanor berated herself as she walked. She'd always known this day would come, ever since Penelope asked for the agency's help in finding Fred a proper match. She'd especially known it since Fred rescued Miss Muffins and became quite famous. Every eligible lady in Bath admired him now!

Yet knowing it and facing it as reality seemed two different things. She'd dared to let herself dream for a moment. Surely she knew better than to do that? Hadn't she learned in her life that dreams were not for ladies like herself?

Any time she had with Fred, time to see him or talk to him, grew shorter and shorter now. She had to steel her heart to give that up. To go on with her life as before. She'd been content with that. With work and her sister and friends. She could surely be content again? Even though she knew, deep down as the truest thing ever, that she loved him and would always carry that love as her great secret.

And that love was exactly why she had to give him up. He needed so much more in life than she could give him. It was simply reality. And no moonlit masquerade would erase that.

She nodded and smiled at friends and agency patrons as she passed them near the gates. Trying hard to pretend, to them and to herself, that all was well. That her heart was not cracking to bits inside of her.

Chapter Fifteen

The next day Eleanor forced herself to rise, even though she'd barely slept a wink, and dressed quickly to make her way downstairs for a quick breakfast and then work. Work would surely distract her from thoughts of Fred. It *must* she determined and made her way out of the room, with Miss Muffins at her heels, turning towards the staircase in the still-quiet house.

She almost missed the step as she saw him in the foyer below, looking so radiantly handsome standing there in a ray of sunlight from the high windows. She clutched hard at the banister.

Somehow she'd thought, in the imaginings of her sleepless night after seeing him with Miss Evans, that she would encounter him again in a crowd. There would be no chance there of a private word and she could prepare herself. Put on her armour of dignity and duty.

Now there was no chance to prepare herself at all. He was *there*. He glanced up and saw her, staring at him with unguarded, starry-eyed, raw love.

She snapped her gaping mouth shut and tried to smile politely. She feared she failed terribly. So many emotions flooded through her. All the things she had denied, pressed down, for so many years. All the longing of her soul to reach out to his.

'Eleanor,' he said eagerly, hurrying to the foot of the stairs with a smile on his lips. 'I know it's very early to call, but I've been waiting for you. I have to talk to you.'

To tell her he was marrying Miss Evans? Eleanor swallowed hard past her distress at the thought. 'Have you?' she managed to say. She forced her feet to keep walking down the stairs.

'I have to say—so many things.'

'I know we must talk, yes,' she answered softly. It had been foolish to think she could ever dismiss her feelings for him in a crowd. This was *Fred* who had been her friend and her love for so very long. She couldn't hide from him.

'Shall we?' He gestured towards the door of the small sitting room just off the agency office.

The early-morning silence of the house seemed so large around them and Eleanor feared she couldn't trust herself to be alone with him there. To be close to him, alone with him. Yet she couldn't run. She nodded, and hurried into the room.

It was seldom used except when she, Mary and Harry needed a consultation over patrons. It was very feminine and frilly—all pale green and pink, small and close and friendly—and she knew it was a mistake to be there with Fred. He was too close, too warm and so strange and familiar all at the same time. The scent of his lemon soap flowed all around her.

She plopped down on a pink-cushioned settee and

folded her hands tightly in her lap, trying to look anywhere but at him.

'Eleanor, I...' he began, then broke off with a rueful laugh. He ran his fingers through his hair, leaving it standing on end, shimmering in the sunlight from the window. Eleanor had to clutch her hands even tighter to keep from giving in to her longings and reaching up to smooth it and feel the silk of his curls against her skin.

'I fear I am no good at this,' he said.

'You came here to say that you are marrying Miss Evans,' she blurted.

His eyes widened and for a moment he just stared at her in taut silence. 'What? I—no...'

'It is quite all right,' she rushed on, wishing so much this was all over. 'You need not say anything at all. I know how things must be. We do part as good friends, I promise.'

'Part?' He shook his head fiercely, and sat down beside her to reach for her hand. She dared to let him. Dared to feel his touch just once more. 'Eleanor. No. That is not what I want at all.'

Eleanor feared she would burst into tears. She tried to draw away from him, but he wouldn't let her go and she couldn't give him up. Not yet. 'Then what is it? You have found someone besides Miss Evans?'

He looked amused. *Amused.* 'I rather hope so. Oh, Eleanor. I told you I am terrible at such things, but surely we have known each other so long, so well, that we *know.* I—oh, blast it all. Eleanor St Aubin, will you do me the great honour of being my wife? I fear I have no ring yet, but I shall do. This very day.'

Eleanor was shocked, cold and hot all at once. She had never been so entirely at a loss in all her life. Surely she had not heard him correctly? 'Fred? Marry you? What?'

He frowned at her doubtfully. 'I know I have little to offer you, but we can start again once I sell off the land at Moulton Magna. We can retrench. Rebuild. And once I return to the Army there would be that income.'

'The Army?' Eleanor gasped through her daze of joy and despair. What was happening? Yet she could hear that—he intended to return to the Army. After what had happened to his friend? The terrible things he had seen? 'You cannot do that. Moulton Magna needs you. You belong there now.'

'But that is why I will return to my commission. To earn what I can. If you are at the estate all the time, I know I can do that.'

'And that is why I cannot let you do that! Even if…' Even if he wanted to marry her, which had always been her deepest secret dream. Her greatest hope. She loved him too much. 'Your duty is to restore your home and we both know I have no fortune to help you. I have nothing to offer you, as Miss Evans does.'

He shook his head again. 'Eleanor. You know that is not true. You're the kindest, sweetest lady I have ever seen. You love Moulton Magna, too. I need you by my side! After what happened at the masquerade, I know we both feel this between us.'

The masquerade. The finest, most wondrous night of her life. But that had to be behind her, a mere dream. She wanted to hold on to what they had as long as she possibly could. That invisible, silvery line between friendship and love had snapped, but which she longed to repair. To have something she could clutch at.

As she looked into his eyes, those sky-blue summer eyes she had loved for so long, she caught a glimpse of what life could be like with him by her side. Yet there was such danger in wanting something so very much it hurt.

'I will not use that to tie you down to something you will come to regret,' she said. She tried so very hard, with all her might, not to think about all the long years that stretched between that moment with him beside her and life without him. 'We can have no future together, can we? I will not let you return to the Army. You must find a wife who can be all you deserve. Which I am certainly not. You would come to resent me one day. I know it.'

His eyes shone like glass, as if he might start to cry as she longed to do. If he cried she knew she would be utterly lost.

'But I cannot live my life without you. You are my other half. You have understood me as no one else ever has or ever could. When I am with you, the world is always bright. Always just as it should be! With you—I know I can achieve anything. You do not have to tell me how I feel for you, Eleanor. I know very well. I have always known.'

'Fred,' she choked out, knowing she would be lost if she looked at him again. And they would both be lost if she gave in to what she wanted for so very much. 'You would hate me!'

'You know I could not. You are *Eleanor*. My friend. My love. My true love.'

'Fred. No.' She could say no more.

'Please,' he whispered. He reached again for her hand, but she buried it in her skirt. 'I *need* you.'

Unable to bear being near him a moment longer without throwing herself into his arms, taking what she wanted and not what was best for him, she leaped to her feet and turned her back so she couldn't see his face. 'I told you, Fred. I care about you too much to ever let you down in any way. To keep you from what you must do.'

She shook her head hard to be rid of what she longed to say—that she loved him. She loved him with a force and fire she'd never believed possible. Every time she saw him that love grew stronger. That was why she had to let him go.

She leaped to her feet and threw open the sitting room door to run out. Hurrying up the staircase, she dared to glance back, just once. Fred stood in the doorway, watching her with that tousled hair and desperate eyes. Could he, did he, love her as she did him? She had never expected that, hadn't expected that he would *want* her to stay with him and it broke her heart all over again.

She spun around and ran onward, past a gaping Mary and Harry and a startled Miss Muffins, and didn't stop until her chamber door was locked behind her and she could fall down in tears.

'Whatever are you doing, Mary?' Harry whispered.

'Shh!' Mary whispered back to her friend, not even

glancing over her shoulder from where she knelt beside Eleanor's closed door. She pressed her ear closer to the wooden planks and waved Harry closer.

She sat down on the carpet beside Mary in a puddle of pink muslin skirts. 'What is amiss with Eleanor?'

'I'm not sure, but I can guess. I just saw Fred leave with a face like a thundercloud and now poor Eleanor crying her eyes out.' Mary listened carefully to Eleanor's muffled sobs and she was sure her own heart would crack to hear her dear sister so destroyed. 'I fear it is all my fault.'

'Your fault, Mary?' Harry whispered. 'How so? You and Eleanor adore each other. You always do what's best for one another.'

'Yes—and so I should always have put *her* needs first!' She told Harry all about how she had urged Miss Evans and Fred together and that now Penelope was determined to marry a wealthy old man herself to make sure Fred was free. 'I should have seen it all along! I never should have tried to force things as *I* thought they should be. I have been doing this work too long.'

'Oh, Mary, no.' Harry wrapped a comforting arm around Mary and they sat huddled there together, longing to make all things right as they occasionally passed fresh handkerchiefs under the door to Eleanor. 'We run a *matchmaking* agency and our task is to assist the people who come to us for help. To give them what they say they need. We cannot read their minds! If Lord Fleetwood changed his desires…'

Mary nodded, still miserable. She knew Harry was quite correct. They were in the business of settling advantageous matches for those who couldn't do it for themselves. Yet she had always prided herself on her rare instincts and her intuition for romance. This time she had been a fool.

'Fred and Eleanor belong together! They've always been meant for one another. But I know my sister. She will never be selfish if she thinks it's for the best for him.'

Harry gave a little huff. 'Well, Eleanor *should* be a bit selfish for once! She's always been the kindest of friends, the most soft-hearted matchmaker of us all, but she's taken on too much responsibility for everyone else in her life. *She* deserves something now!'

'Exactly,' Mary sniffed. 'How can we make her see that? How do we get Fred back for her now?'

There was a brief knock at the front door and Mary sat up straight in a burst of hope. Perhaps Fred had *already* come back!

It was not Fred, though, who came hurrying up the steps but Penelope. Penelope—another kind soul who had tried to sacrifice herself for the people she cared about. To throw away her happiness for others. And Mary was sure now she had ruined everything for *all* of them!

'Whatever is happening?' Penelope cried, taking in the closed door and the bedraggled figures on the floor. She drew off her gloves and plopped down on the carpet beside them.

Mary disconsolately told her all they knew about Eleanor and Fred and Miss Evans, until they all collapsed in tears again.

'Oh, my dears,' Penelope said, leaning against them until they feel into a heap of muslin and wool and feathers. 'I do think that this once *I* can be of some help to *you*!'

Chapter Sixteen

'Fred, dearest! Do come in for a moment,' he heard
Penelope call as he tried to slip out of the house without being seen.

He knew he had been an utter bear for days, ever
since he parted with Eleanor, yet he couldn't seem to
stop himself. He was in no fit state for polite society.
Unable to think of what to say. Forgetting all he had
relearned after his recovery from battle wounds about
polite behaviour. Instead, he went walking alone all
hours of the day. Up and down hilly streets, through
parks and up into the hills. Prowling aimlessly. Trying to outlast his thoughts. But they wouldn't be left
behind. Wouldn't stop replaying memories of Eleanor
at every moment.

He did love Eleanor for so many reasons, one of
them being her kind heart. For as long as he'd known
her, she'd put so many people before herself. Her father, her sister—and now Fred. She thought she did
what was best for him. He knew very well that was her
reasoning. But how could any of it be right when it felt
like *this*? It was worse than being wounded and lying

on a battlefield. Worse than the cold rain of endless, lonely marches. Worse than the pain of sword strokes and canon shots. Eleanor was the brightest light in his life. In all the world. Finding her again had made him feel hope once more. Hope that there might be some happiness out there. Some contentment and fulfilment in life. A purpose. A family.

Eleanor knew and accepted him, as he did her. Surely that was rare—to be seen, cherished and accepted. Everything else could be solved as long as he had her and had her help. If only he could make her see that together they could bear anything!

Instead, he prowled the town alone, like that wounded bear and Eleanor seemed to have vanished.

He saw how Penelope watched him, with such concern in her large eyes. Yet he didn't know how to reassure her. Didn't have the words to make it all clear to her—or to himself. So he started avoiding her, too.

Now she stood in the drawing room doorway, catching him before he could vanish out in the grey day.

He glanced back at her, attempting a smile. He could see that she was not fooled. She tilted her head, studying him with that concerned little frown he'd come to dread.

'I was just, er, going out on an—important errand. Most important,' he said.

'Yes, so I see. This will only take a mere moment Fred and it is quite important.' She turned in a swirl of blue silk skirts and disappeared back into the drawing room.

Fred slowly followed. He knew he had been brusque

with Pen lately and he hated that. She'd always been a true friend to him, an ally in his family, and she deserved his confidences about all that had happened. If he could only find the right words. Perhaps he would be forced to do that right now.

Yet when he stepped into the sunny chamber, he saw Penelope was not alone. Mr Palmer, the Moulton Magna estate agent, sat behind a writing desk surrounded by papers and ledgers. Alexander Oliver was also there, standing near the windows. He turned, a pleasant smile on his face, his eyes glowing as he saw Pen and she rushed to him to take his arm. Fred felt a burst of hope that maybe this wasn't about his misery after all, but about some secret happiness of Penelope's.

'I am so glad you could join us at last, Fred,' she said. 'Anthony and I have several bits of news to share and Mr Palmer has kindly agreed to stay in Bath and help us with our business before he returns to Moulton Magna.'

'Mr Palmer?' Fred said, still puzzled.

Mr Palmer nodded before scribbling on.

'Indeed.' Penelope glanced up at Anthony, a radiant smile on her lips. 'I am sure you can guess, but Mr Oliver has asked me to marry him and I have agreed.'

'At last!' Anthony said with a merry laugh. 'I've waited for this glorious moment for *years*.'

Penelope laughed, too. They couldn't stop staring at each other, as if they'd forgotten anyone else was there at all. It gave Fred joy, as well as prickling jealousy, to see them.

'He is so patient,' Pen said. 'I, too, have waited. Though I was sure such a day would never come.'

'Pen, there are no words to tell you how very happy I am for you,' Fred said, leaning over to kiss her pink cheek, once so pale and thin. 'No one deserves this more than you.'

Penelope grabbed his hand. 'Except for you, Fred! You deserve all joy and happiness, too. You deserve to know this feeling—the promise of a happy family life.'

Fred shook his head. That feeling, that hope, had sunk away when Eleanor turned away from him. 'I am sure I will, one day, if I am very lucky.'

'No, *now*.' Penelope glanced up at her fiancé. 'Fred, darling, I know you shall think we are terribly interfering, but I know you do love Eleanor St Aubin. And that she loves you.'

Fred stiffened. 'Pen…'

'Fred, just listen. You and Eleanor should have every happiness. You have both given of yourselves for others much too long.' She gave a rueful grimace. 'I think we *all* have been trying to sacrifice ourselves to help each other lately! I'm so fortunate now that I can actually do something to help.'

'Pen, whatever you are about to do, I'm sure I can't let you,' Fred warned.

Anthony laughed. 'I don't think you can possibly stop her, man! I have learned very well that once Pen has an idea, she will not be stopped.' He gave her a teasing, smiling look that said he would never *want* to stop her.

'And this is hardly a sacrifice anyway. It is merely sharing my joy,' Penelope said.

Fred studied her suspiciously. 'I think you had best explain it to me, then.'

'Of course.' Pen waved towards the chairs grouped around the desk. 'Mr Palmer is here to help us.'

Mr Palmer glanced over the edge of his spectacles, looking almost cheerful for once. 'You are a most fortunate man, Lord Fleetwood,' he said, carefully arranging the papers around them.

'Am I?' Fred said, utterly bemused. He hadn't felt 'fortunate' in a very long time. Perhaps never.

'Oh, indeed. Lady Fleetwood and Mr Oliver have brought their marriage settlement for us to examine and there is one provision that should greatly interest you.'

Fred studied Penelope, who looked much too rosy and self-satisfied. 'Interest me?' He felt quite like a parrot now, repeating every sentence.

'Yes. It seems Lady Fleetwood and Mr Oliver wish to purchase the east parcel land at Moulton Magna to create their own estate. For a most generous sum. Quite high enough to set Moulton Magna on the firm path to self-sufficiency again. With the essential work from your side, of course. The estate requires much modernising.'

Even more confused, Fred turned to Penelope, who beamed back at him. 'We shall be neighbours, Fred! At least for part of the year.

Anthony laughed. 'If you can stand us!'

'Why would you want to be at Moulton Magna?' Fred asked her. 'Surely you were not happy there.'

Penelope shook her head. 'It is true I was not very happy in my marriage, but I cared very much about the people on the estate. Like you, they were so welcoming and kind to me. I always felt terrible I didn't have the resources to build that school as I wished. But now I can! With your permission, of course.'

'You wish to buy the land and improve on it?' Fred said, his thoughts racing over new plans as he studied the map and envisaged a new future.

'To build a school, yes. And see if any fields could be put back into production again,' Penelope said. 'We'd also like to restore the manor house to live in when we're there. I do want you and Eleanor as neighbours so much.'

'Me and Eleanor?' he murmured, the last, most shining part of that envisaged puzzle sliding into enticing place.

Penelope smiled radiantly. 'Yes! Oh, I know it would all be rather easier with someone like Miss Evans at your side, but you *love* Eleanor. And she loves you. You deserve as much happiness as you can find for as many years as you may. You shouldn't have to wait so long for it as long as I have.' She smiled at Anthony.

Fred felt that glittering shard of hope grow, slowly. He hardly dared it might really happen. 'Pen, you are the best of friends, but I cannot take your money...'

Pen held up her hand, stopping his protest. 'I absolutely insist! You would never want to wound my feelings by refusing me this. I need to repay you and Eleanor for all your great kindness to me and now I am at last in a position to do so. I want happy homes for all of us, close to each other.'

Fred was utterly overwhelmed. His father had ruined them all and now they were helping each other to rebuild from such selfishness and bitterness. There was a justice in that. A joy. 'Very well, Pen. I know when I am outmanoeuvred.' He gave her an exuberant hug, the two of them laughing while crying with the new joy. 'You are the very finest of all stepmothers ever.'

Penelope giggled, and wiped away her tears. 'Ha! Now—you must sign this agreement and go and find Eleanor at once. You must cease your prowling about town. And shave before you leave.'

Fred laughed, and did exactly as she said. He signed—and dashed upstairs to shave and find his finest coat. He had one more, very important, piece of the happiness puzzle to find.

Chapter Seventeen

Eleanor hurried along the garden pathway, not seeing the flowers and hedges, the children dashing past with their hoops or the clouds sliding above. She only saw how it had all been the night of magical, other-worldly masquerade. The lanterns and pavilions and music. The hidden little summerhouse of such grand delights. She twisted Fred's handkerchief between her fingers as she walked, as a talisman.

Now, the world had righted itself, spinning them all back into their proper spots. Fred had to marry. She had to concentrate on her work. That was how it was always going to be. Surely it always was? So why did it now hurt so very much? Why did she feel as if the tether to the world itself was cut and she was floating along, unmoored and uncertain?

She turned a corner of the pathway, and headed towards the walkway beside the river. The crowds were thicker there. Couples arm in arm, nurses wheeling their elderly charges in their wicker bath chairs and children floating boats on the waves where Miss Muffins had once tumbled in. Laughter echoed from a Punch and Judy show.

But Eleanor couldn't feel the joyful scene at all. Couldn't feel the warmth of the sun. She wondered if she would ever find her centre again. Her joy in her work and duty. Her care and responsibility for everyone around her. Or if she would just drift up and up into the sky until she vanished alone.

Eleanor paused to open her parasol against the glow of the light. The flowers in the manicured beds seemed to shimmer, pinks, blues and yellows, and rays of silvery sunlight filtered through the leaves of the trees along the walkway. Two little children dashed past, shrieking, waving back at her.

She smiled wistfully. She'd never really envisaged her own family or children. There had been no time for such dreams. Not with the agency. Not with taking care of her sister and making certain they were secure. She made other peoples' happy futures. It had given her much pleasure to do that work, but lately sadness, wistfulness seemed to overtake her.

And now she couldn't even really help herself. She could not forget about Fred. Couldn't push the memories and hopes to the back of her mind as she had for so long. Fred was always right there. All these new, wild, passionate feelings overcoming her. She longed for him, so much. There was so much she could not have.

She'd thought surely the past would fade if she could see him again. She'd see he was no longer *her* Fred. That too much time had passed between them and too much change. But that summer-blue gleam of his beautiful eyes was just the same as it ever was. The laughter. The sense of fun. Pushed down but still there and still glorious. Eleanor barely saw his new scars.

She only ever saw Fred, her dear friend. The man she loved. The man whose kisses sent her spinning up like a firework. The man she wanted to talk to, walk with, kiss and laugh with for ever and ever. The man she wanted to share her work with and his with her. The man she wanted to help bring Moulton Magna back to its real glory and make it their real home. A place for their children.

Children! Eleanor's heart nearly burst at the thought. *Fred's* children.

She could just almost picture them. Blue eyes and golden hair. Or maybe her dark curls. She smiled to think of a blue-eyed little girl running through their own garden, shrieking in delight until Fred caught her up in his arms and tossed her up into the air amid wild laughter.

'*Mama, Mama, did you see?*' the girl would cry with a giggle.

It was so very much what Eleanor longed for now, had suppressed any thought of for so very long, and now here it was right in front of her. Reminding her of what she couldn't have. The agency was all she had now. She wouldn't jeopardise her livelihood. Her sister's livelihood! She would see Fred properly married and then she would forget him and go to the next patron and the next match. Fred would go back to Moulton Magna to set his own estate to rights and once he was out of sight one day he might also be out of mind.

Taking a deep breath, Eleanor turned sharply away from the scene and turned blindly along the river. She turned a corner towards a bridge—and froze. Miss Evans stood there, looking so young and beautiful and prosperous in pink silk and pearls with her glossy hair shining and her smile brilliant.

'M-Miss Evans,' Eleanor gasped. Miss Evans was surely the last person she wanted to see just then. Yet there she was, standing so close Eleanor couldn't run away.

'Miss Evans,' she said, curtsying with her most polite smile. Was it possible for a face to crack in half? 'How lovely to see you today. You are looking—very fine indeed.'

And she was. Miss Evans was always a pretty girl, but now there was a satisfaction in her eyes. A comfort in her eyes. A glow of happiness.

Happiness because of her new betrothal? Eleanor's heart ached and she feared she couldn't draw breath.

'How kind of you, Miss St Aubin! I feel well today indeed,' Miss Evans said with a laugh.

'Am I to wish you happy in your engagement?' Eleanor whispered. Her throat was so dry she could hardly say the words.

Miss Evans laughed again. Eleanor was sure it was the first time she'd heard such a sound from the solemn Miss Evans. 'Indeed you can wish me happy. For I am *not* to be married!'

Eleanor was bewildered. 'You are—not?'

'No! Luckily.' She linked arms with Eleanor and they strolled together beside the river path, past the

Punch and Judy show and the shrieking children. 'Your agency does splendid work, Miss St Aubin, you must not blame yourself in this instance. It is all *me*. I have never had the desire to marry, at least not yet, not until I am far into my botany studies.'

'You are a—botanist?' Eleanor whispered.

'Well—no. A mere amateur right now, but I wish with all my heart to make it my life's work. I may marry one day, if I'm fortunate enough to find a man who really understands. Perhaps even another scientist, so we could work together!'

'I shall keep an eye out for just such a man,' Eleanor said, bemused. Whatever she'd thought about Miss Evans, she'd never envisaged this—Miss Evans wanting to find her own path, a career. To do work she found important and maybe not to marry. Eleanor admired her greatly.

But—oh, what about Fred!

'Does Lord Fleetwood know?' Eleanor asked. 'The agency can certainly inform him, in the correct way, and find him another match.' Which would mean even more time spent close with Fred. Eleanor sighed in despair. Just when she had imagined it all over, she must begin again! Steel her heart again.

But then she realised—really and truly realised— Fred was *free*! He was not to marry Miss Evans. There would surely be talk about it all, Bath loved nothing more than gossip, but soon enough a new *on dit* would appear. It all seemed most amiable on Miss Evans' part.

Fred was free, but Moulton Magna was still in trouble.

'You have been such a friend, Miss St Aubin, truly,'

Miss Evans said. She kissed Eleanor's cheek and gave her a radiant smile. 'I shall never forget you.'

'And I shall look forward to seeing your beautiful work at Kew one day,' Eleanor answered.

Miss Evans squeezed her hands one more time and dashed away, no doubt thinking of plantings. Eleanor's head spun with all she had just heard. She turned away—and found Fred watching her.

She felt freezing and burning all at once. Her thoughts refusing to move. Not able to speak or walk or think. He wore no hat and his hair gleamed gold and copper in the sun. She started to run away.

'Ella! Wait!' he called.

Uncertain and all a tizzy, she half turned to leave, to flee. But Fred was quicker than her, even with his limp. He hurried through the crowd to her side. So close she smelled the lemony spicy Fred scent that always made her giddy.

He reached out his hand as if to touch her arm, but it fell away when she stepped back.

'Ella. How have you been?' he asked so carefully, almost as if they were strangers and he was wary of her. 'I tried to call, but Mary said you were unwell. I was rather worried.'

Eleanor forced herself to smile. 'Just a slight cold. I am quite well now.'

He nodded, a smile of relief on his lips. 'I was concerned you might hate me, after—well, after our last meeting.'

The meeting where he offered her all she had ever dreamed of. All she could never have. 'I couldn't hate you, Fred, not in a million years. You know that well. I was just—surprised, of course.' To put it mildly. 'And scared.'

'Scared of *me*?' he said, sounding most shocked.

'Not of you! How could I be scared of you, dearest Fred? My darling friend.'

'Then—what?'

'Scared of wanting too much, I suppose. Scared of that horrible, sharp disappointment when you must leave again. Any more goodbyes between us and it will become impossible to ever recover.'

He frowned and shook his head, as if he could not fathom her words. 'But that is the thing, Ella! We need never part again. It will be hard work, but if we were together...'

Eleanor was bewildered. 'What do you mean?

His frown suddenly transformed into a beam, like sunshine through a cloudy, obscuring grey sky. 'I mean we have such fine friends who wish to help us make a start and give us a chance to be together.'

'I am so confused, Fred. Tell me what is happening.'

Fred held out his arm to lead her along the river path. And there, amid the splash of the water, the ancient bridges crowded with parasols and laughing people and the leafy shadows of sunlight, he told her a fascinating tale. One hardly to be believed. One of Penelope and Anthony Oliver's rekindled romance. Of their buying the parcel of Moulton Magna land and building a school there. Of the chance to put the home farm into production and a roof on the house. All for friendship. All for love.

'So you see,' Fred finished as they came near the slippery bank where Miss Muffins once took her fateful tumble, 'The money from Mr Oliver and Pen opening the school, will give us the means we've needed to revitalise the estate or at least make a fine start. Of course we can't fix it all at once and it will mean a great deal of work. But I know we can do it. And in a year or two, we might even see a profit, with good luck and good weather. I will just need help, for I cannot do it all alone. And I know no one more organised and efficient and intelligent as my Ella. No one I want more by my side as we bring our home back to life. You know Moulton Magna, almost as well as I do. I am very sure between the two of us...'

It sounded amazing. A dream. Exactly what she'd always longed for. To have Fred and have useful work, too. Could she really do it? Dare to make that great leap?

'Fred,' she said slowly. 'I know Miss Evans is off on other endeavours now, but there are plenty of young ladies of fortune who would...'

'Ella!' He seized her hands, holding them tightly against his chest so she could feel the powerful beat of his heart. 'You could find me four hundred heiresses. A thousand! I would only ever want *you*. Your beauty and kindness and thoughtfulness. I need only you. Moulton Magna needs you.'

Eleanor felt the most glorious, sun-warm joy wash over her such as she had never known before. To have Fred and work, too! A home, one that wouldn't be taken from her as school and the vicarage had. To not worry about everything all the time any longer. To never have that sense of impermanence. To live a different life— one of happiness and purpose. It seemed…

'Wonderful,' she sighed.

His smile turned hopeful. 'Then you will marry me?'

Eleanor laughed, laughed longer and harder than she ever had in her life before. 'Yes! Yes, yes.' And she longed to dare to jump into his arms. But all those years of caution couldn't help but hold her back.

'What if…?' she began.

Fred shook his head. 'No what-ifs! Not any longer. This is at last our own moment. Yours and mine, Ella.'

Eleanor, dizzy and hopeful and sad all at the same time, took a step back. Her heel caught in the hem of her muslin skirt, throwing her off her balance.

The soles of her half-boots, slippery and thin, slid across the muddy ground and her arms flung out as if to grasp onto—nothing. Her parasol went flying. Icy panic flooded over her as she tumbled down towards the waiting water. Her cries made heads turn, alarmed onlookers came running, exclaiming. Surely this was just how Miss Muffins had felt!

'Ella!' Fred shouted, though she feared she was too far away for him to reach her in time. Her feet seemed to be suddenly made of glass. But Fred fooled them all. Sleek and swift as a tiger, just as she tumbled into the cold waves with a dramatic splash and squeezed her eyes shut, he lunged towards her and fell into the river with her. His firm arm around her waist kept her from sinking in her heavy skirts and pelisse and he pulled her from the brink and back onto solid ground.

The momentum of their weight sent him sliding backward, to land on his back on the bank with Eleanor atop him. For a moment they both lay very still, breathless and stunned.

Until Eleanor began shivering and applause broke out around them.

'So romantic...' a lady sighed.

Eleanor definitely knew then how Miss Muffins had felt. Like she was Fred's for ever.

He slowly sat up, drawing her with him. She found she quite lost any control then, sobbing in great gulps of relief and fear and love.

'We are safe now, my love,' he whispered, holding her close and wrapping his coat around her shoulders. 'Shh. I am here. I shall never leave you. I shall always make sure you're safe. Just as you have always saved me.'

'So we must always save each other,' she hiccuped. She very much liked the sound of that. She had always been the one to save others. Now he was there, with her, doing just the same for her.

'Always. We shall be the perfect team for ever.'

His lips claimed hers in a passionate kiss, warm and all-consuming, as the applause and cheers grew louder around them. Eleanor never wanted to let him go. And now she never had to. Happiness, giddy and free, flooded her heart and she dared kiss him again.

Fred laughed as they realised the avid attention all

around them. 'I see we are quite the *on dit*! I fear you must marry me now or cause a scandal.'

Eleanor reached up to hold his face tenderly between her hands and studied every angle and line of his beloved features. All the scars seemed vanished and he was only her golden Fred. 'Yes, Fred. I will marry you,' she said, just as she had dreamed of doing so very many times. But this was real. This was true. This was their whole life together. She went up on tiptoe, careless of the river puddle they stood in, and kissed him again and again, as if she would never cease.

Chapter Eighteen

A few months later

'Oh, I do love a wedding day,' Eleanor declared, stretching luxuriously in the nest of sheets and blankets on her and Fred's rumpled honeymoon bed. She felt so warm, so tired and languid and perfect. 'And I have the feeling this wedding will be a particularly beautiful one!'

Fred laughed and burrowed deeper into the pillows beside her, burying his face in the loose fall of her hair. He gathered her closer and kissed her neck and bare shoulders until she giggled. 'Lovelier than our wedding?'

'Nothing could be lovelier than ours.'

White flowers and ribbons lining the altar. Rosy light streaming through the stained-glass window. Harry, Mary and Pen sniffling. Eleanor's new pale blue gown and veiled bonnet. Fred's hand in hers.

'But Pen's day will be just as beautiful. She deserves it so very much, after all she's been through. She and Anthony waited almost as long for each other as we did!'

And then, they would all travel to Moulton Magna to begin the hard work. To make a home. Surely the happiest home ever known. Mary and Harry would continue with the agency, of course. Mary was quite sure Mr Campbell needed a wife next.

'It's all too wonderful,' she sighed. 'Like a dream. I never want to wake up!'

'Beautiful Eleanor. My most glorious wife,' he said softly. He held her face gently between his large, callused palms as if she was the finest, most precious of delicate porcelain. A pearl beyond price. Despite their dozens of kisses, all the naughty, delicious things they'd devised to do together since they wed, every moment felt magical. Perfect. Like they had soared free of all the worries that held them apart far too long and burst free into the heavens together.

Clinging to each other, they fell back to the rumpled bed. The painted mural on the ceiling, of gods and goddesses and cupids in their filmy draperies and laurel wreaths, whirled around their heads dizzily. Eleanor spun on top of her husband, not able to breathe as she studied him in the first sunrise light filtering through the windows. His bare skin seemed gilded with the amber-tinged glow and his battle scars were hidden. How glorious he was. Vibrant and glowing with strength and with raw desire that burned in his eyes. How could he be hers now at long last? It was beyond any of her old dreams.

Her trailing fingertips traced the light, coarse sprinkling of dark gold hair on his naked chest and the thin line that arrowed enticingly to the band of his loosened breeches. His stomach muscles tightened and his breath went raged and harsh as her touch brushed across his skin.

'Ella, my darling,' he gasped. 'Be careful. If you're sore from last night…'

Eleanor laughed to remember the long, glorious night. Three times!

'I am perfectly well. If *you* have the strength.' She smiled as she touched every last, warm, silken inch of him. Yes, *this*—this was the most right thing she had ever done. The exact place she most wanted to be.

She fell back into his arms, their lips meeting, heartbeats melding as one. There was no longer anything careful, cautious about their kisses. They were as hot as the sun and filled with an urgent deep need, like the fireworks that once burst over Sydney Gardens. She felt the heat of his hands as he slid her light, silk nightdress from her shoulders and she pushed it away with no shyness at all.

'Ella,' he groaned, his hands tightening on her hips, so warm and strong. 'So very beautiful.'

How she hoped she *was* beautiful now, for him. Her husband, her only love. She kissed him again and he rolled her body beneath his, across their tangled sheets.

She laughed as her hair spilled all around them. She certainly did feel beautiful as he looked at her. She felt free at last. Burst out of responsibility and propriety and expectations. Only with him. There was only now, this one moment, where she was with the husband she loved. He kissed her and all other thoughts vanished.

She closed her eyes and let herself revel in the feeling his touch created. The press of his lips on her bare skin. Her palms slid over his back. So strong. So hot. Slick with sweat and sheltering her with all his strength. Her legs parted as she felt his weight lower between them and press forward to make them one.

'My beautiful Ella,' he gasped.

Slowly, so slowly, he moved again within her. Drawing back. Edging forward. A little deeper and more intimate each time. Ella closed her eyes, feeling all the ache and stretch ebb away until there was only that pleasure she had come to crave. A tingling delight that grew and expanded inside of her heart, exploding like the fireworks of the masquerade. Before Fred, she'd never imagined anything as wondrous at all.

She cried out at the wonder of it all, at the bursts of light behind her closed eyes, all blue and white gold. The heat of it was too much. How could she survive without being consumed with him to nothing?

Above her, all around her, she felt his body grow taut and his back arch. 'Ella!' he shouted out.

She utterly flew apart, clinging to him as she let herself fall down into that fire and be happily consumed.

After long, slow moments she blinked her eyes open, wondering if they had somehow tumbled into a deep volcano. But it was just their bed, the white sanctuary they had barely left since their wedding. Yet that wonderful sparkle still clung to her.

Collapsed beside her on the pillows, his arms tight around her, was her Fred. Her husband. He seemed to be asleep. His breath harsh. Limbs sprawled out in exhaustion. His hair was bright in the new daylight.

His face smooth and young as he had not been in so very long.

Eleanor smiled at the sight, like the painted Mars collapsed exhausted next to Botticelli's rather smug Venus, and she felt herself floating ever so slowly back to earth. Morning was even more glorious than she had ever dreamed. She always became someone different in his arms. Someone beautiful and bold and free. And she revelled in it all.

The ormolu clock on the mantel chimed, dropping her fully back to earth and reminding her where they were really were. What time it really was.

Eleanor sat up bolt-straight on the bed and reached for her wrinkled gown. 'Fred! We must hurry.'

'Why?' he groaned, muffled in his pillow. 'I'm happy right here.'

'As am I. But if we don't rush, we shall be late for Pen's wedding. And that would never do!'

She slid out of bed and hurried to the windows to pull the draperies open. The spires of the Abbey sparkled and crowds already hurried over the cobblestones. Shops were opening. Flower carts appearing. 'Happy is the bride the sun shines upon!'

Fred propped himself up on his elbow to watch her with a bemused grin on his morning-whiskers face. 'It rained on our wedding day.'

Ella laughed to think of it. The grey skies that had done nothing to dampen her joy, even if it had somewhat wilted her new hat.

'And also happy the bride the rain blesses! It will mean a fine harvest next year at Moulton Magna.' She kissed him quickly and tossed him his dressing gown. 'Happy every bride who loves her bridegroom. That is the only thing that really matters.'

'And Pen loves Oliver?'

Eleanor smiled to think of how Pen and Anthony secretly held hands all the time. How they smiled at each other, staring into each other's eyes. 'Assuredly. And this is going to be the most beautiful of days. Now— get dressed! There's not much time…'

'There! I think we have done quite a fine job here, don't you?' Mary said as she straightened the pearl-pinned flowers in Penelope's curls.

'You have indeed!' Penelope answered, turning her head one way then the other to study the effect of the white blooms against her dark hair and the gleaming pearl earrings that were the groom's wedding gift. The pale pink gown with its antique lace trim, the large bouquet of roses and lilies—both like something in a fairy tale story. Like a queen's wedding, mayhap. A queen who loved her prince.

So different from her first two weddings. Not least because of the new happy glow in her eyes.

Harry fastened the last detail around Penelope's neck, a triple-stringed pearl necklace clasped with a massive ruby. One more surprise last-minute gift from Anthony. 'There. Perfect.'

There was a knock at the chamber door and Eleanor appeared, holding Natalie and Grace by their little hands. They bounced excitedly on their slippered toes in their yellow and white bridesmaids' dresses and wreaths of flowers around their heads.

'I think all is in readiness now, Pen.'

'The carriage is waiting to take you on your honeymoon!' Natalie burst out. 'And it's *covered* with flowers!'

Eleanor laughed. 'I am sure every florist shop is quite empty in Bath.'

Penelope laughed, too. She carefully touched one dark curl, feeling a sudden touch of chill. 'Am I really entirely worthy of him, do you think, my dears?'

Mary grabbed her gloved hand. 'You two have been waiting for each other for years and years, my dear! Now you get to claim your prize. No one deserves perfect happiness more than you and Anthony.'

Penelope laughed again, this time filled with joy, half coughing with happy tears. 'And Ella and Fred!'

'And look at how disgustingly happy they are,' Harry said. 'We shall all be quite tired of hearts and flowers soon.'

'Until you find your own perfect knight.' Penelope rose from the dressing table and made her slow way down the stairs, Natalie and Grace carrying her lace-edged train. More flowers twined the banisters and waited below. Scenting the air like it was July at Kew Gardens. She could hear the faint strains of harp music, murmurs and laughter.

Her bridegroom waited in the drawing room, for the small ceremony a special licence had granted them. There, in the beam of sunlight before the makeshift altar of a lace-draped buffet table and silver vases of roses, she glimpsed that dashing young man who once so enraptured her. The man she'd thought she couldn't have. The man who had shown her the joy and fun of life.

She'd never dared dream they could be here now, together. And there he was. Hers.

She made her way up the Aubusson carpet aisle, smiling at her friends gathered there between the flowers. Mary, Charles Campbell, Adele, Harry, Miss Evans, Eleanor and Fred. Once, she could never have imagined so much happiness in one place. And now it was theirs. For ever.

She reached out for Anthony's hand, smiled and blessed all that Bath had brought them.

* * * * *

The Viscount's Wallflower Wager

Liz Tyner

MILLS & BOON

Liz Tyner lives with her husband on an Oklahoma acreage she imagines is similar to the ones in the children's book *Where the Wild Things Are*. Her lifestyle is a blend of old and new and is sometimes comparable to the way people lived long ago. Liz is a member of various writing groups and has been writing since childhood. For more about her, visit liztyner.com.

Visit the Author Profile page
at millsandboon.com.au.

Author Note

Years after my great-aunt penned her memoirs, I carefully read and reread every page, wishing she'd written more and thankful for the insight she gave into family history. This helped inspire me to write about the viscount's grandmother, a woman wanting to share her memories with future generations. I hope that if you have been thinking the slightest bit about writing your personal family story—and haven't yet started—that you begin. Family anecdotes can mean so much to your children, grandchildren, nephews and nieces.

DEDICATION

Dedicated to Maggie Bennett

Chapter One

The bedchamber door slammed into the wall, causing a lamp to rattle. Only one person in all of London would dare wake him so abruptly. His grandmother.

Gabriel's jaw locked. He opened his eyes, staring up into an amazingly innocent perusal.

His grandmother stood at his bedside. A woman who had to go on tiptoe to give him a kiss on the cheek—and who could make an executioner cry—smiled while her perfume hit him with the force of a sword blade.

A normal person in his presence would have trembled beneath Gabriel's glare, but his grandmother didn't notice.

'Good morning,' she chirped, marching back to the door. 'Or should I say good afternoon, slugabed?'

'How did you get past my valet?' he asked, knowing the man was assigned to stand sentry in his sitting room on the mornings his grandmother was in residence.

She ignored the question. 'We need to talk.'

'I have a perfectly good valet you could have asked to wake me. Where is he, by the way? Still alive?' he persisted.

'He's a bit stodgy. That turnip-head wouldn't let me into your bedchamber.' She waved a hand, dismissing his words. 'I had to take a circuitous route and someone left a mop and bucket in front of the entrance,' she said, annoyance evident in her tone.

She must really be determined if she'd used the servants' stairs.

She turned to his mirror, patting her silver bun and trying to make it taller, the rings on her fingers knocking together.

After adjusting her dress, which would have suited a virginal debutante better, she muttered to her reflection, 'Still got all your teeth, old girl.' She gave a grimace, inspecting them. 'Or at least the ones that count.'

She whirled to him. 'You need to get that valet of yours doing his duties. Making you presentable to your guests…' She barely paused. 'I meant to tell you eventually, but you know how Agatha is. She wants to see you. And you've slept much too long.'

Agatha—Lady Andrews—and his grandmother were friends…of a sort. Hissing and snarling friends, but close nonetheless. His grandmother had invited Lady Andrews to stay and he had thought it would keep her entertained.

Apparently not.

'Wear that black waistcoat with the embroidery on the buttons that I ordered from your tailor,' his grandmother continued. 'And try to look pleasant. Not like now.'

She pinched her forefinger and thumb together, then put them against her lips, scowling as she stared at him. Then she opened the draperies halfway and blinked at the light before turning back to him.

'And you could certainly use a bit of a hair-trim—that unruly mess is covering your face. Such a shame for that healthy head of hair to be wasted on a male. And don't let your valet give you any distressingly scented woodland soap. Use that ambergris I gave you. I don't care if it's from a whale's gut—it smells clean and tart.'

'Grandmother, why would Lady Andrews wish to see me?'

'That cauldron-stirrer should be horsewhipped for the way she cheats at cards. Don't let the lace handkerchiefs fool you—she uses them to hide the cards.' She gave an angry shake of her head. 'I had that king in my reticule— and she played it.' Her eyebrows flew up and she looked at him, chin down. 'And everyone knows how I manoeuvre, so it really *doesn't count*.' She stressed her last words. 'That's what I get for having such a disreputable woman as a friend. But I lost fairly. She out-cheated me.'

She moved, dashing towards the sitting room door, and then jumped back just after she'd opened it. His valet appeared, eyes wide, gasping at the sight of her. She peered at him and shut the door while still inside the bedroom. Her next words were almost hidden in a mumble.

'I lost you in a card game to Lady Andrews.'

Then she hurled herself out through the door at full speed.

'Watson!' he shouted. 'Stop her!'

He would never have told his mother he'd keep watch over his grandmother if he'd had any vision of the way his grandmother truly thought.

In his youth, he'd hardly seen her. The tales he'd heard had seemed humorous then, but now he understood the facts, and he realised his mother had sheltered him from many family upheavals.

The door opened again and Watson herded Gabriel's grandmother back inside, his arms outstretched, corralling her as if she were a sheep darting about.

'My pardon, sir,' the valet said. 'She… Your grand-mother—'

She slapped the servant's outflung arm, stopped moving, and peered at Gabriel. 'I do not want your valet learning about my misfortune at cards. It is not for his ears. If he will leave, I will explain. Agatha knew where I'd hidden the king but she didn't accuse me of cheating. Just let me carry on. Deceitful.'

'Do you know anything about this card game?' he asked Watson, seeking the truthful answer he knew his grand-mother would not provide.

The valet stepped towards him. 'It was last night. In her sitting room. A ruckus erupted late in the evening, and no one dared disturb them except a maid. She said the table was upended and cards were strewn around the room. Some had been ripped into pieces.'

His grandmother sneered. 'I have to give Agatha credit for her card skills. I would never have believed someone half my age could be so treacherous. The old bat…'

He stared at his grandmother. 'When she came to stay, you told me she was your dearest friend.'

She shrugged. 'Oh, let's be truthful. She's my only friend.'

She waved the valet away with a flick of her fingers.

'Get my grandson his clothing. I've already summoned someone to bring his shaving water. I need to introduce him to Agatha's niece, and he likely will want to wear breeches.'

'Likely,' Gabriel said.

'Don't sound so irritable.' His grandmother pointed a finger at him after Watson had left the room. 'No one would ever expect you to marry her, so no one will blame you when you don't go through with it. The poor thing is too thin, too tall, has no taste in fashion and reads books about plants…' She put a finger to her lips. 'I wouldn't call her a wallflower exactly. More of a wall weed.' She smiled. 'Yes. The child is a spindly weed, and it's easy to see how she's remained unwed.'

'Did you tell this mystery woman that I would wed her?' he asked.

His grandmother blew out a puff of air. 'Of course not.' She wrinkled her nose. 'I merely wagered a proposal on your behalf. How you get out of it will be between the two of you. It's not as if you aren't experienced in that.'

'Grandmother…' He spoke softly, but clenched his teeth.

She studied him. 'You inherited your grandfather's shoulders and height, and his ability to escape marriage until he met me.' She clucked her tongue in pride. 'And where would you be without me? Now, don't make a fuss. Causing a woman to end a betrothal should not give you any trouble.'

He clamped his jaw, worried about what he might say if he did not.

'The jest is on Agatha,' she said, laughing. 'You're too much like your father and me.' She slapped at her skirts, then paused, standing on tiptoe. She looked into the mirror and pulled the skin tight at one side of her face. 'Oh, I must stop laughing. It causes wrinkles.'

'Grandmother—'

'I think Agatha should explain to you. After all, I had every intention of winning that game, because I so badly wanted those pearls. But Agatha must have seen something, and she spilled her punch on my reticule—which concealed the winning card. Still, I thought I could brazen it out, and Agatha accepted the wager. But it was I who fell into the trap.' Her voice softened and she hid a smile. 'Or *you* who fell into her trap.'

He stared at her, completely flummoxed.

He'd seen two kinds of marriage in his life. His parents' bond, which had been one of incessant determined warfare, and his grandparents' union, in which his grandfather had waved away his wife's misadventures, oblivious to the detriment she caused. His maternal grandparents hadn't fared much better. They spoke only through intermediaries, such as Gabriel's mother. She lived with them—in part to keep the peace, but also in order to keep herself away from the upheaval his paternal grandmother caused. He'd tried to talk his widowed mother into visiting Town more, worried about her isolation, but she had refused, pointing out that it was best for her and her former mother-in-law to be separated.

'Really, all you have to do is propose to Marie. It's not even as if you have to kiss her or pretend she's lovely. And she's not going to accept your proposal, because she knows she is too unattractive and tedious to keep a man's attention. She's mentioned to me that she doesn't believe a woman should ever wed. I tried to tell her about my happiness. She didn't believe me.'

She put her fingertips together and rested them below her bottom lip.

'I know that I am generally not celebrated for my honesty, but I had a wonderful marriage with your grandfather and it would be lovely to see you find that same happiness—be it with Marie or someone else. After all, it is well past time you provided heirs.'

He knew that. That was why he'd considered the best

way to propose to the stunningly beautiful Rosalind. And considered it…and considered it. He was intending to act… eventually.

Flouncing to the door, his grandmother added, 'Agatha and her…um…passable niece are waiting in the main sitting room. Make sure you make a few jests when you meet Marie. I love it when Agatha laughs.'

'I refuse to have anything to do with this.'

He spoke softly, but firmly, and she took a step towards him, face crumpling in defeat.

'Gabriel, you have to,' she insisted. 'If you don't make good on this wager…'

'No.'

'You don't understand… I possibly had been drinking too much punch, and I might have written out a note stating the details—a sort of contract…' She looked heavenward and puffed a breath in the same direction. 'Which Agatha might have kept. She's so distrusting… Anyway, you really only have yourself to blame. Take this as a lesson to you on what will happen if you don't wed a suitable woman with due haste.'

'Grandmother.' He glared at her. 'You must get this sorted out—and without my being involved. I do not want any tales of it in society. It would devastate Mother. She cares very deeply about her courtship with the widowed Duke of Bellton, and he is a stickler for propriety—particularly because he has a daughter about to enter society.'

His grandmother put the back of her hand to her forehead, shut her eyes, visibly wilted, and then said, 'Very well. I will see what I can do.'

She left, humming some funeral dirge, and he rolled out of bed with a frown on his face. Perhaps *he* needed to worry about getting wrinkles while his grandmother was nearby…

He had known Lady Andrews had brought a niece with her on her visit, and frankly he didn't trust either of them any more than he trusted his grandmother. They were likely fortune-hunters.

Footsteps sounded and Watson stepped back inside.

'Find out from the maids which room belongs to my grandmother's young guest,' Gabriel instructed, taking his breeches from the valet and dressing. 'But don't let anyone know I'm curious about her—particularly my grandmother. Then get the maid to invite the woman to the music room and summon me. I don't want to hurt her reputation, but I think it's time I see what kind of woman Grandmother has brought into my home.'

'Of course. But perhaps you might wish to wait? Your cousin Pierce's mother has just arrived, and she and your grandmother are going to have tea. There is the possibility that your aunt might seek you out.'

'Fine. I will wait,' Gabriel said. 'After she leaves, however, we will need to move quickly.'

'I agree, sir,' the valet said as he moved into the dressing room.

Gabriel followed and took a comb from Watson's hand. 'I knew my grandmother had her friends visiting, but how long have they been staying?'

'I thought you knew, sir? Their stay has stretched for longer than a fortnight now. The younger lady has very little by way of baggage. At first the maids assumed she would only reside here a few days, because she brought almost nothing. Now the staff is all aflutter with speculation.'

Gabriel would have to get to the truth of the matter and

find out more about these women living under his roof. He knew of Lord Andrews, and was fairly certain his wife had wed him for financial reasons and brought her niece into her husband's home. Andrews had probably displaced them because they were draining his funds, buying fripperies and whatever else would waste money. Or they'd wagered everything away and were now worming their way into his grandmother's good heart—well, her not so good heart—so that she would pick up their bills.

He should have been watching his grandmother's activities more closely.

While he waited in the music room, with the scent of beeswax polish wafting in the air, Gabriel plucked at a few strings on his grandmother's harp. He winced at the sound he created, thankful that any so-called music from the instrument rarely carried to his rooms.

He looked up when Watson opened the door, and put out his hand to still the strings.

The valet gestured into the room with a wave of his arm and then left, the door remaining ajar.

A woman walked slowly through the door, her head bowed.

Her hair was about as severe as a woman could manage to make it, pulled into a knot and pinned onto her head in a fashion so tight he wondered if she had trouble closing her eyes. She wore a dress with flounces reminding him of strewn autumn leaves—which a few carriages had rolled over. She did appear thin, and her dress certainly covered her with plenty to spare. The neckline was puckered, and the round spectacles she wore sat primly on her nose.

The woman in front of him was perhaps fifteen or

so years older than he was and, given that until now his grandmother had always pointed out the virtues of women younger than he, he wondered if she was trying to send him a stronger message than she'd initially implied about her concerns about his unmarried state.

The woman greeted him more timidly than he could believe possible. This could not be the niece of his grandmother's friend—or perhaps she was. Perhaps her clothing was a ruse for a woman who was trying to hide her identity.

He realised he'd noticed another scent besides the beeswax. A flowery scent—lilac or lavender or honeysuckle, he wasn't sure which—was gently wafting into the air around him. He didn't know much about flowers, and until now one scent had smelled much the same to him as any other. This time, however, the floral scent captured his attention. It was fresh. Almost real. As if the blooms were in front of him.

He strummed a single harp string, the lonely tone resounding in the room.

'I'm pleased to finally meet you,' he said. He stepped away from the instrument, clasping his hands behind him, giving her the smile he used sparingly, and more with foes than friends.

Then he looked beyond the drab hair, the spectacles, the odd clothing, and without meaning too took another step closer.

Her skin was smooth. Apparently she hadn't laughed much in her life. Or she was much younger than he had initially assumed with a passing glance.

Letting the silence lengthen, he pushed all awareness of her as a young woman so far back in his mind that he hoped it might never resurface. He asked, 'How long are you planning to stay as our guest, Miss…?'

The niece's eyes locked on his face, and her chin lifted an inch. Her lips firmed, and he heard the soft inflow of her breath.

'Please call me Marie. And I have left any decisions about the length of our stay to your grandmother and my aunt. And you, of course.'

'Of course. You may call me Gabriel. Now, what do you know about a card game last night?'

Chapter Two

Marie hesitated before speaking. The man standing in front of her had the same look of the yeoman warders she'd seen guarding the Tower of London. Of course he didn't have a spear in his hand, nor a sword or any weapon. No, those were concealed behind his eyes…

Her aunt must have been drowning in liquor to have considered such a wager. They really didn't need to be making this man angry.

If she were a queen of yore, she could imagine choosing the Viscount to protect the crown jewels. He was sturdy enough… Plus he would be able to deflect any mischief with an emotionless blink—but one full of portent.

Shaking her head softly, she hoped her forced smile appeared unconcerned and pleasant. She touched the flounces on her dress before speaking.

'I daresay your grandmother and my aunt got carried away, drinking their punch. I completely release you of any obligation to anything that might have been agreed last night.' She clasped her hands together. 'I had no idea what was going on until I woke this morning.' She tilted her head, chancing a glance at his captivating eyes, and tried to give a dismissive shrug. 'I laughed it off and I hope you will do the same.'

She prayed he would. She'd never believed his grandmother would tell him about the wager, and was mortified that her doing so had brought them to this moment.

'They entertain each other with the strangest games sometimes…'

There was not a flicker of relaxation from her host.

She used all her strength to remain upright and keep laughter in her expression, although worry had tightened her throat. Once again she found herself having to cajole someone into a better mood so she would be able to maintain a roof over her head. She was proficient at it by now.

She forced herself not to ramble on. To choose her words carefully and control her tone. She bit the tiniest part of the inside of her lip.

'I hear there was a wager,' he said, raising his eyebrows in a display of unconcern that she would not bet a penny on. 'Do you know what it concerned…?'

Evasiveness wouldn't help. It would only make their conversation go on longer.

He moved to the floral settee beside which she now stood. 'Please…' He waved a hand, indicating that she make herself comfortable.

Well, she decided, easing herself onto the seat, it would give her a little more time to compose her words.

She picked again at the flounces on her dress, and arranged her skirts as her insides churned. She didn't want to answer his question, but the silence in the room seemed to swallow her whole, and she knew she was going to have to be the one to end it.

She'd never seen him except from a distance before, but now he was so close she could reach out and pat his knee. As he perused her in much the same way a Tower guard might appraise a suspected spy, she kept herself from trembling and forced out words she knew would seem an admission of guilt. He held all the cards, so she might as well put hers on the table…face up.

'The wager stated that you would make me a proposal. But I assure you I would reject it.'

She bit the left side of her lip. The right side was getting overused.

His expression relaxed. 'You would reject it?' he asked softly, and he put just the right amount of amazement and hurt—maybe even a tiny bit of humour?—into his reply.

'Yes,' she said, careful with her tone. She knew better than to offend the man providing the roof over her head. 'I've never been the sharpest arrow in the quiver, but I know enough to realise it isn't right to force a man into proposing.'

A glimmer of amusement passed behind his eyes. 'Have you ever tried archery?'

'No,' she admitted, confused at this sudden change of topic.

'Well, you never know… You might be the very best arrow in the quiver,' he said, and his voice altered when he spoke the last part of the sentence, making it sound almost like a compliment.

She forced herself to act nonchalant, and only by staying perfectly still could she hide the happiness that wanted to force itself onto her face.

Let that be a lesson to her, she decided. Given that her insides had already warmed, just from that hint of a smile, she knew that if he ever directed a fully-fledged smile her way they might just combust. And she was too sensible to tumble into a trap like that. She'd seen women who had destroyed their lives because a man had portrayed himself as some Romeo or Bassano or Orlando but turned out to be an Iago.

She could not tell him that she and her aunt were one spoonful away from poverty and that they'd been given little choice. Lord Andrews had made it clear that Marie was to wed his nephew or leave for good. Aunt Agatha, who wasn't even really her aunt, had told her husband to have the carriage readied and they'd both marched out that same evening, heads high, jaws firm, with Marie's insides fluttering like a flag in a windstorm.

'I'll marry him,' she'd whispered to Agatha, not wanting her aunt to be homeless.

'The blazes you will,' her aunt had said. 'I won't have you repeating my mistakes. I married that first old goat to get a roof over my head, and then I wed Lord Drippy Nose. I had thought he might have a thimbleful of affection for me, but he quickly started treating me like a used sofa…complaining of the lumps but refusing to buy new upholstery. A man will treat a horse well if he buys it. He will treat a carriage well, no matter what it cost him. But a wife… No, I do not want that for you.'

The driver had opened the door for them and they'd ascended into the carriage and left for good.

Agatha had reassured Marie that her friend the Dowager Viscountess would understand their plight, and after a warm welcome things had progressed well between the two friends…until that potent punch had been introduced into their card game.

The night before, Agatha had wagered her pearls. The only valuables she had left. And she'd planned to blackmail the Viscount's grandmother—if you wished to call it that—with the letter of promise she had signed, using it as ammunition to allow them to stay in the household. The Viscount was never to hear of it, her aunt had told her, when she'd stumbled into Marie's room to tell her the details. She had promised she would not give the letter to anyone, and she'd tucked it into her reticule for safety.

'But the servants may read it,' Marie had said.

'Well, I will keep my reticule close,' she'd replied, holding it high and weaving a little, before putting a hand over her heart. 'And we can trust Myrtle. She has a heart of gold…which she purchased at a good price! It's tiny, but it does fit on a bracelet.'

She'd laughed at her own joke and then stumbled off to bed.

But Aunt Agatha had played right into the Dowager Viscountess's hands. Because Myrtle Arthur won either way—either with a chance to pressure Gabriel into a marriage or a new set of pearls.

Marie knew she would eventually find a suitable way to support herself and Agatha—she hoped to write a book on botany—but she had to play her cards right while they were in society, in order to position themselves in surroundings that would maintain her aunt's reputation. And even Marie had to admit that having a bed with a feather mattress and an uncracked washbasin in her room was much to be preferred over the alternative.

They weren't homeless, exactly, but they were wobbling at the edges of it—which was a feeling she was familiar with. The woman whom her mother had paid to raise Marie since birth had reminded her daily that her father had deserted her mother and she'd had to be hidden away—with very little to her name, and certainly no paternal affection—so that no one ever knew. She'd loved reminding

Marie that the streets would be her home if the funds to maintain her didn't arrive.

When her real mother had died—a woman Marie had never even seen—her mother's companion, Agatha, had arrived in her life. At sixteen, Marie had shed the first and only tears she remembered shedding. She'd wept for so many different reasons and Agatha had reassured her, saying that from that point onwards, Marie would be her niece, and she'd continue to watch over her.

She'd kept her promise every day since, and had put Marie's needs over her own many times.

She took in a slow breath. 'Agatha is more than an aunt to me. She is the mother I never had. But we do differ in opinion on some things.'

Mostly their viewpoint about what was considered ethical. Marie never would have made the bet Agatha had in that card game.

Gabriel stepped towards the harp again, but he appeared unaware of it, his gaze still on Marie. His perusal of her face held a respect that seemed to say that no one in the world could be saying anything more important than what she was saying. Her thoughts—which had always clicked along like the inner workings of a timepiece, steady and with precision—reacted as if someone had wound them the wrong way, and she was aware of masculinity, and strength, and just how a woman could drown in the appearance of just the right man—or the wrong one.

And that irked her. He had to know that such gentleness would be dangerous to a female. He had to know that he had attributes that attracted women and caused their throats to dry and their hearts to beat faster. That his attentions would make it hard for them not to smile and simper and let all their fluttery feelings show.

Her anger grew. A man such as he could throw out charisma borne of generations of ancestors who had created the closed society that had forced her mother to keep her a secret.

Her life was precarious, and she was used to that. But his wasn't. He had the assurance of someone who'd never known a worry other than whether he should immediately purchase the best or wait for even better than the best to be procured for him.

She looked at her hands, rubbing her right hand over her left, stifling her irritation. When she met his eyes, she didn't waste any hesitation before speaking words fuelled in part by her anger. 'Your grandmother thought the card game a lark, and the wager a chance for her to get Aunt Agatha's pearls. They had both been drinking too much.'

She didn't believe she should tell him that her aunt had, in her foxed state, considered blackmail a good way to maintain their residence until they found another means of support.

But marrying was one thing Marie would not do.

Her aunt had already proved how marriage under less than ideal circumstances didn't ever lead to the happy ending one hoped for, and the woman she'd lived with in her youth had claimed harsh conditions made the soul stronger, and did much to improve one's fortitude. She supposed it had given her an invincible spirit—and now she had to use it to figure out how to put a roof over their heads.

'I don't know that it is a good idea to have someone in my house who considers a marriage wager a good idea,' he said calmly, peacefully, and much too easily for her liking.

Though two women had been involved in the game, she knew that this was not the time to ask him if he was speaking of his grandmother.

'I understand. Aunt Agatha knew she had a winning hand, and she wanted to wager something useful, she claimed. But you had no part in it, and…'

Perhaps her aunt had realised Gabriel wouldn't go along with it, but that haggling over the wager with his grandmother would keep her entertained until they could figure out something else.

She appraised Gabriel. He seemed to measure his responses, providing only just enough to keep her talking. And she had no choice but to do so—because he was the owner of the house she currently called home.

'I told her it was wrong but, as my aunt says, the biggest lie humankind believes is that we can change someone else's mind. Any attempt to change my aunt's mind is only going to make her even more determined to prove she has the best idea.'

He nodded. 'My grandmother is the same way…unfortunately.' A wisp of affection and warmth passed across his face. 'She's hard to corral, but we try.'

She had not been wrong when she'd first assessed him. He held a complexity behind his eyes that intrigued her. But she closed her mind to it, mentally backing away from him. Reminding herself he was a viscount. Reminding herself that the secret of her birth, and the society that he embraced, had deemed her someone who must remain in the background. It was only carefully constructed lies that made her welcome in his world.

She lowered her eyes briefly, and met his gaze when she lifted her head. 'I try to gently guide my aunt, but that requires changing an idea before it is set in her mind. Otherwise I seem to just make her more determined.' She touched the puckered hem on one of her sleeves. 'I barely slept last night,' she admitted, 'fearing the consequences of her evening's revelry.'

'I hope you barely slept because of the wager itself,' he said, glancing over her face. 'Not because I was the…shall we say prize?'

'Oh, no.' Her cheeks reddened.

'That would be a slap in the face, of a sort,' he said, his eyes a little too serious and his voice sounding almost… hurt.

Her mouth moved as she searched for a response. 'Er… um…'

He was jesting with her, she was certain of it, but nothing showed on his face.

She paused, studying that stone countenance. She peered at him. 'Out of curiosity, do you ever wager?'

'Of course.'

She closed her fingers into a fist and tapped her knuckles softly against her chin. Giving the lightest nibble to her lip before speaking, she asked, 'And do you ever…lose?'

His chin lowered just a bit. 'Not often.'

She could feel the air she breathed entering her body and warming her, caressing from the inside, just as that intractable stare relaxed enough to give her another glimpse of the real man. One she wanted to memorise—except she knew not to do so.

He bowed, just a bit, and she realised she was being dismissed. But she also comprehended that she was not being asked to leave his house—at least, not yet. Nor was she being held responsible for the wager.

The walls and the world around her turned softer.

For less than a heartbeat in time their eyes met—in a truce, or respect, or perhaps in the first heartbeats of friendship.

She left without saying goodbye. She didn't need to speak.

Without words, he had given her his approval to remain in his home for the time being—a kind of reassurance that made her think that perhaps she was staying in the most secure house she'd ever known…

Shaking his head, Gabriel exited past the butler, explaining that he would walk until he found a hackney. He didn't want to wait for a vehicle to be summoned and readied.

He'd only gone a few paces when his cousin's carriage rolled into view.

Pierce jumped out, leaving the door swinging, and grabbed Gabriel's shoulder to steady himself. 'You will not believe what Mother has said Grandmother and her friend Lady Andrews did last night!' He chortled.

'I might.'

Gabriel raised a brow and looked at Pierce, who laughed before punching Gabriel on the arm and stepping back.

'So, when's the wedding?' Pierce asked.

'February the thirty-first.'

'Fortunate for her. Who is the lucky woman?'

'Lady Agatha's niece… Marie.' Gabriel warned Pierce with a glower not to ask any additional questions.

'Ah, I've heard of her.' Pierce shuddered and signalled his driver to reverse the carriage. 'It's said that Lord Andrews' nephew finds her fetching—but he pants at every woman who crosses his path. I think even the lightskirts won't have him any more.'

Gabriel tensed while Pierce chuckled.

'She's pitiable,' Pierce said. 'My friend has said Marie would be improved only by standing behind a haystack, and he was surprised even Lord Andrews' nephew noticed her.'

'She is not pitiable,' Gabriel said.

'Well, I could get a look at her myself, if I wanted to, at Grandmother's soiree tonight. .' He leaned forward and his voice lowered. 'It sounds as if she's quite pathetic.'

'That's a lie.'

'No matter to me.' Pierce clasped the door handle. 'Just wanted to let you know why I'm going to be avoiding Grandmother's soiree tonight. Pressing business. I am planning to drink too much at White's, and I might not have enough time if I attend the soiree.' He paused, still holding the door. 'Want to join us?'

Gabriel shook his head, changing his plans in an instant. 'I will be attending Grandmother's event.'

'Oh, that should be *delightful*.' Pierce gave him a salute of farewell and stepped into his carriage.

Gabriel grabbed at the door and looked up at his cousin. 'Drop me at Aunt Susanna's house.' Then he stepped inside the carriage.

'Well, thank you for travelling with me,' Pierce said.

'You're welcome.'

He wanted to see what Pierce's mother knew about the two women living in his home, and he didn't trust Pierce's viewpoint where women were concerned.

Chapter Three

After returning home, Gabriel called for his valet. 'Were the servants able to keep the harp from being moved into the ballroom?'

'Of course,' Watson said. A look of nonchalance was chiselled into his face—which was not always a good omen. 'The musicians will be here, as you requested, and your grandmother does wish to dance. Lady Andrews is excited to be included in the event, along with her niece. The maids are hoping suitable attire arrives for the young lady before the event, but it doesn't appear to be expected. The niece is apparently steadily sewing away in her room.'

Gabriel stopped, noting the evening attire Watson held up for him. Watson was a valuable asset, who understood what went on in the rest of the house better than he ever could.

It perplexed him that the two women did not already have suitable attire. Lord Andrews was not impoverished—Gabriel was fairly certain of that, and would ask his man of affairs to verify that—but he also knew him to be a gruff, scowling man, always grumbling.

He knew Agatha was Andrews' second wife, and that his grandmother had known both women, calling the first 'a timid mouse' and Agatha 'more spirited'.

He continued his preparations for the event, feeling that for once his presence wasn't just to be an appearance to quieten his grandmother's antics. He wanted to find out more about Marie.

He'd agreed to let his grandmother have her soiree at his house, but their negotiations had been hammered out with him smiling graciously and his grandmother compromising where she needed to, in order to get the best deal she could. He'd made her promise keep the guest list circumspect, and the libations under control, but on food she could do as she wished. And he didn't have to worry about the event continuing overlong, as his grandmother would instruct the musicians to stop playing and the staff to start putting the refreshments away when she decided the time was right.

When he'd finished dressing, he trod his way to the ballroom and searched for Marie. She wasn't yet present.

As the musicians finished warming up their instruments and began their first tune, Marie stepped into the room. He found he was aware of her the moment she entered, even though she did nothing to bring attention to herself.

She'd been dressed plainly before, but now it was as if she had worked her hardest at appearing grandmotherly. Her dress was much like a puffball that had been gathered around her body, her gloves were too short and her shawl was an unsightly coil of clothing which reminded him of the rug in the entrance hall—only the rug was more fashionable.

Her hair was once again twisted painfully tight, and a feather hung crookedly from the band she wore around her head—which did not match her dress. It did match the shawl, however, which was a shame.

The only saving grace was the eyewear perched on her nose. The spectacles were cute. Impish. Framing eyes which, as she'd studied the room, were not cute or impish, but forbidding.

No wonder she did not have many suitors. In fact he would have said, based on her actions, her goal for the entire night was to be as discouraging as possible.

But her aunt was hooking a hand around her arm and dragging her off to speak with people.

An older male friend of his grandmother's—rotund enough to balance a drink on his stomach—approached Marie, handing her a glass of ratafia. The words of their conversation were well hidden by the murmuring voices around them, but it wasn't long before she pushed her spectacles up her nose, smiled, and put a foot behind her to retreat.

As the man leaned forward she kept moving away, creating an amusing picture.

Finally rid of the man, she went to speak with his grandmother.

'She is a beauty. Except I can't talk her out of wearing those spectacles,' Agatha said beside him.

The words gave him a start, because he'd been studying Marie so intently he hadn't realised anyone was near him. He could see Agatha's admiration for her niece in her face.

'And she is such a dear. Always watching after me most kindly. The daughter I never had.'

'Yes. She reminds me of a gem,' he said, appraising her. 'Uncut. Not in the correct setting. Easily overlooked. In plain sight, and yet hidden.'

Lady Andrews' eyes took on a new spark when she heard his words. 'Yes...' Her eyes were innocent, but her smile undermined the look. 'I would say that is an asset in a woman. I know I certainly do not like hearing tales of Rosalind Warton's many beaus, Rebecca Johnstone's unseemly behaviour in the Wilsons' fountain, Annabelle Logan's penchant for too many glasses of wine or Roberta Wiggins' inability to stop giggling…'

She stopped, smug with innocence. 'Have I forgotten anyone?'

'I believe you've covered every unmarried woman here.' He looked into her eyes. 'Except your niece, of course.'

At that moment Marie noticed them and her aunt beckoned her. The younger woman smiled, but didn't move nearer.

'She is a paragon of virtue.' Agatha gave a one-shouldered shrug. 'What can I say? She takes after the other side of her family.' She looked at him. 'You two have that in common, I suppose. We both know you don't take after your grandmother.'

'I don't know…' he said. 'Perhaps I just hide it better than she does.'

'I would hate your grandmother to be indebted to me… And the scandal sheets would so love to see our agreement…'

'You hide your participation in blackmail well. And it would hurt Marie more than anyone else.'

Agatha's expression changed again as she watched her niece. 'Yes, her chances to marry would likely be quashed. I know I can never use the contract, but I had to get your grandmother's agreement in writing. She's too conveniently forgetful—as we all are.'

'You should trust that your niece will find her own suitor if it is meant to be.'

'But she needs help in that area. No one truly notices her, and she does not seem inclined to put herself among people her own age. She doesn't know how to enjoy herself. And she thinks marriage is too much of a risk. She calls it "the guillotine of romance", and considers it a tragedy played out behind four walls.'

'Perhaps she is right.'

She waved away his words. 'I once thought that if we're both going to be miserable, we might as well be married and miserable together. But I can't see Marie marrying the man who asked her. One drippy nose in the family is enough.'

'A convincing argument for marriage.'

She grunted, then continued. 'My niece is upset with me for the wager. She thinks I went too far. But I think you'd make a good husband for her.'

She spoke the words so smugly Gabriel knew she expected him to feel complimented.

'I'm sure you have clean handkerchiefs…'

He disapproved of her words with a glance.

She frowned. 'Oh, well… I tried.' She patted her bun, puffed up her sleeves, gave him a mumble that relegated him to a lost cause, and then walked away to speak with another man.

Marie was a wallflower. And that was generous. She was avoiding everyone her own age and standing apart from the crowd, using the other guests as shields between herself and whomever might look at her.

But then, most of the attendees were his grandmother's friends, and the only younger people his grandmother had invited were potential marital prospects for him.

He watched Marie as another man approached her and

asked her for a dance. Moving closer, he was able to hear her rejection first-hand.

'I'm so sorry, my slipper is coming untied. I must go to the ladies' retiring room and see if I can fix it.' She darted away and disappeared into the corridor.

He realised she'd not danced at all, and when she returned she stayed on the perimeter again, talking with the older ladies and gentlemen. Hiding in plain sight as best she could. A part of society, and yet not really. One foot in and one foot outside of London's most elite, with her clothing placing her in some antiquarian setting not even suitable for dowagers.

He corrected himself. She only had one *toe* dipped in society, and even then was appearing to distance herself from that annoying appendage.

Some odd feeling stirred within him. Curiosity, he supposed. He certainly could not truly be attracted to such a beanpole of a woman, wearing more of an oversized dresser scarf than appropriate soiree attire.

He couldn't help but notice the parts of the dress that touched her body—a skill he'd acquired in his early teens which, at the time, had given him no end of frustration.

And now he felt a similar cauldron of desire igniting inside him.

Blasted celibacy was not doing him any favours.

He'd thought he'd left rushes of passion behind with his virginity, but apparently he was returning to virginhood and all the wretched longings that went with it.

He tried to focus on her spectacles, which drew his attention to her face and her eyes. He wondered if she truly needed them, or if they were a means of adding another layer to herself in a misguided attempt to keep people at a distance.

She was so different from the other eligible ladies of the *ton*.

He thought again of asking Rosalind to wed him. She could charm the buttons off a statue and was stunningly beautiful.

He turned in Rosalind's direction and was surprised when she scowled at him—until he realised she'd been watching him peruse Marie. He took a step towards Rosalind, feeling he needed to appease her. Rosalind was one of the few suitable brides for him, and it was time he sired an heir. Like some prize overpriced stallion…

He ground his teeth together.

But his second step stalled, and out of the corner of his eye he glanced at that vision of a woman hiding from society.

She pushed up her spectacles and somehow reminded him of one of those little bumblebees he'd dared to touch once. He had brushed a fingertip over its back, and instead of its hair feeling soft, as he'd expected, it had been rough. It hadn't stung him, but only because it had been happily staggering around on a thistle, covering itself in pollen.

Appearances could be misleading.

Curiosity kept rising and rising inside him—and then irritation slapped at him. Why was he paying attention to such a little mouse? Well, not a *little* mouse. She was tall, which made those blasted ruffly parts of her dress even more noticeable.

With a firm stance he moved to Rosalind and told her how lovely she looked—which was true. The man at her other side firmly agreed.

Gabriel asked Rosalind to save the waltz for him, and she apologised, saying she'd already promised her waltz to the Earl.

Gabriel hadn't known an earl could swoon, but the man almost did—right in front of him.

The Earl took Rosalind's arm and they strolled away.

Gabriel moved to speak to the musicians before catching sight of Marie again, and he kept his pace slow as he approached her, attempting to gauge where she would try to hide next.

He stepped nearer to her. 'I hope you are enjoying yourself?'

One really couldn't tell the host how miserable one was at his event.

'It's a beautiful night,' she ventured. Although she really wished to be relaxing in her room.

And now the Viscount had noticed her. She would likely offend him if she didn't speak glowingly, and she could not afford to offend him. Best she keep to herself. It was safer that way.

He raised his brows. 'You didn't answer the question. Are you enjoying yourself?'

She tried not to look at him, but she noticed that his voice was a rich caress to his words.

Studying the room, she said, 'The servants have worked hard to create a pleasant evening. The partridge was the best I have ever tasted. These musicians could play for any royal event. The guests all appear to be having a good time.'

'You are still not answering the question and that tells me a lot,' he said.

'I am having a...good time.' She put every ounce of acting that she could muster into her answer, trying hard to put truth into the words and feel happy.

'Then I'd hate to see you having a miserable one,' he said.

She tilted her chin down, crossed her arms, and words tumbled from her mouth, skipping her brain. 'It's not the event. It's just that I'd rather be alone in my room. Writing.'

He raised his glass, took a sip, and then asked, 'What was your aunt speaking with you about earlier?'

He'd seen those clipped comments. The instructive movements.

'Aunt was telling me about the men who are here tonight. The oldest ones. She told me of their flaws as she perceived them, and reminded me that she has not had the best fortune with men. Her first marriage was to an older man, and he died impoverished.' She clasped her hands in front of herself and spoke softly. 'She says the only thing that truly matters to a woman in marriage is coin, and that men prefer youth and beauty, but will sometimes settle for whatever is expedient.'

He could understand that perception. Men flocked around Rosalind. She was stunningly beautiful, and she knew it. As he saw the swooning Earl walk by and give him a superior glance, he decided she could dance with the Earl all night for all he cared.

'The older men invited tonight are friends of my grandmother,' he said, linking his hands behind his back.

'I know. But my aunt was afraid that one of your grandmother's friends might notice me, and I would be tempted because of…' She bristled a bit then, reminding him of a little cat when its tail was stepped on. 'She told me that if

I am to wed for funds, you should be my choice.' Her jaw jutted.

'Why?'

He hardly moved, more interested in her next response than he had been in the previous one, even though this wasn't the first time he'd heard of an older relative suggesting him as a mate for a young woman.

'Because you have a huge house and we'd never have to see each other.'

She peered at him as if she expected him to run from her presence.

'You have hardly spoken to anyone tonight. You might not need an estate in order to find solitude.'

Her jaw dropped.

'And I agree that if you court someone you don't want him to have grandchildren your age,' he said.

She gave the tiniest shrug. He wouldn't have spotted it if he'd not been watching closely. And when she glanced up at him he didn't see the fortress around her, but a glimpse of the somewhat uncertain young woman she was on the inside, evidenced by the way she was biting her lip.

'Your grandmother has not invited a lot of young men,' she said. 'She wants you to be the plum in the pudding. Evidently both she and my aunt believe in stacking the deck.'

'I would think,' he said softly, 'that my grandmother believes I could compete without assistance if I put my mind to it.'

'I did not mean to suggest otherwise,' she said. 'But you can see my point.'

'I can. And I understand you're not enjoying the event. Perhaps a dance will make it more tolerable. Shall we?'

Her eyes widened. 'Dance? Why are you asking me?'

'Because I want to.'

'You've not danced with anyone else here.'

'So you've noticed?' He spoke softly. 'I'm flattered.'
Her cheeks brightened.

'You're missing the point.' She whispered each word
firmly. 'I do not want to dance.'

'Neither do I,' he said. 'But it's my house, and you're a
guest, and these things seem to be expected.' He tightened
the side of his mouth before relaxing it and speaking again.
'I think people sometimes pay attention to who dances with
whom.'

'Yes, they do. And I don't want to offend anyone because they think I am overstepping my place. It's very kind
of you to ask me, but I'm certain there is someone else who
will take my place. Now, I must go to the ladies' retiring
room. Please accept my apologies.'

'I will pass the time until you return in watching people.'

'But—'

'I hired the musicians. I have spoken with them. They
will happily wait.'

'Very well.' She frowned, and pursed her lips again. 'I
don't need to go to the retiring room after all. I'm not the
best dancer, and I will likely tread on your boots, so please
remember that I did my best to get out of it.'

'I've not been injured in a dance yet.' He nodded to
the musicians. 'And you should perhaps drape your shawl
over a chair before we dance. It will only get in the way.'

She studied the cloth and placed it down gently, as if
she were bidding a friend who was going on a lengthy
journey farewell.

A few notes of music signalled to everyone what to
expect.

'I don't—' she said.

He questioned her with a raised brow.

'Very well,' she said.

As he put his hand on her waist her eyes widened, and she stumbled when he moved them into the dance. Then he took a step and had to practically pull her along, so he slowed, waiting to let her get into rhythm with him. She didn't have to make her reluctance so obvious.

They danced, unspeaking. He wanted to see if she'd break the silence, so he waited.

She danced on, her eyes looking into the distance, lips pursed. His grandmother appraised him, half glowering, and her aunt stood at the side, smiling, her body swaying along with the music.

'Your aunt appears happy,' he said.

She nodded, lips firm, and he could tell she didn't want to speak. Very well. He would give her the silence she wanted.

The feather on the band in her hair wafted as they danced, and it was the only thing about her that seemed happy with the movement—though it was a little off in its rhythm, just as she was. Her steps hardly constituted dancing.

As the music neared its end, he watched her still-silent, tense lips.

He supposed that was what he received for insisting she partner him. She knew how to get her revenge. By dancing like a rough-edged rock. She'd even trodden on his foot once, as he'd tightened his grip on her, moving her along.

He found he wanted to see a flash of that woman he'd glimpsed behind her carefully presented gaze. A spark of that happiness.

She continued to ignore him.

Miss Wallflower was likely to remain a wallflower for a very long time if this was how she acted when a man asked her to dance.

A flash of irritation unfurled in him. She could certainly have better manners…

The violins stopped and he led her to a deserted corner, which he knew she'd prefer, and let his hand slide from her waist, aware of the rustle of fabric beneath his fingertips. The feather gave one last flutter before it slid from the band, and he caught it and handed it to her.

But instead of rushing away, she let out a deep breath. She grasped the feather with both hands, and he saw happy, shining eyes gazing at him.

'That went beautifully,' she whispered. 'The dance was not nearly so bad as I feared. And I think I did rather well.' She twisted the feather. 'I did not know what to do when I stepped on your foot, and I so appreciate your righting me.'

'You're welcome,' he said, surprised at the emotion on her face.

'I am so relieved.' She bent her knees slightly, and bounced up, the feather bobbing as she gushed, 'My first true waltz and I don't think I mis-stepped much—except that once. I did have a bad beginning, but I caught up.'

'You have never danced a waltz before?' he asked.

Suddenly her happiness retreated.

'Of course I have.' She frowned. 'I misspoke.'

'Where and with whom?' he asked.

She sighed, and then answered softly, peering at him from under her lashes. 'My aunt instructed some of the servants to teach me. I danced with a footman, and the housekeeper hummed.' She shook her head. 'We did practise some reels, but they had work to do, and my uncle would have been upset to see them dancing instead of doing their duties. It would have been unthinkable for him to agree to my having a dancing teacher.'

'You did well.'

At least, well for someone who had never danced to music before.

'Thank you.' Her shoulders went back. 'It was frightening.' She peered around the ballroom. 'I tried to study the reels, and I think I could do one, but I'm not sure...' Her eyes widened. 'I might like it.'

The excitement in her face made him smile inwardly. Her enthusiasm was contagious, and he almost felt he had danced the first waltz of his life as well.

'You really didn't have a dance teacher or a governess? Someone who could teach you?'

He realised then he'd never seen her at any events. When Lord Andrews had been widowed he'd wed Agatha, but the couple had kept to themselves and the niece had not been mentioned much.

She put two fingers on the side of one spectacle lens, and pushed the glasses firmly. 'I didn't have any music in my younger life. Aunt has tried to expose me to dance it since I moved in with her, and others have helped, but it seems to just go in one foot and out through the other, to misquote Chaucer.'

Something about her eyes tugged at him, and he accepted the challenge inside himself.

'I have a challenge for you,' he said.

Her brows rose.

'To attend another event.' He studied her. That drab feather had been the most vibrant part of her attire. 'Perhaps a picnic. With no dancing.'

'I do appreciate the offer. And it would be pleasant. But I think my aunt needs me…'

He answered with the kind of stare that he would give a child covered in crumbs for saying she had no idea what had happened to the biscuits on the platter.

'Please… I am content in my room. Which is a very nice room. Very pleasant. An incredibly comfortable room. Thank you so much. The view is wonderful. The sun shines in so beau—'

'You needn't hide in it,' he interrupted.

He could see her evaluating his words.

'I can help you,' he told her.

If she truly hadn't danced a waltz before, and was so uncertain in social settings, perhaps he could help her feel more comfortable.

'Will you remain as a guest at my house for a while?'

The tension in her shoulders relaxed.

'Yes. Of course. I have nowhere— I mean, I am going to find a mirror.' She held up the feather. 'Thank you again for the lovely waltz.'

She scurried away so fast he was surprised she didn't leave a slipper behind.

Rosalind sauntered up beside him, and she had no trouble inserting herself in his line of vision and touching his arm. 'You know, I'm planning to wed soon…' she said. 'If the right person asks me.'

He smiled at her.

'The Earl is already dropping little hints,' she said.

'You would make him an admirable wife. A delightful countess.'

She levelled her eyes at him, then laughed before speaking. 'I will make the Earl an *incredible* countess.'

'I'm certain of it. You would make any man a stunning bride.'

'Thank you.'

Rosalind leaned against him, fluttering her lashes in a long goodbye, telling him that he did not know what he would be missing, and then she gave him a wave and sashayed away.

She would make a better wife for the Earl than for him, he decided. He studied the other women in the room, but noticed himself searching for someone else.

He thought of his other romances in the past—of how they always started with so much promise, and how within a few months his interest inevitably waned, and how within a year or so someone else caught his eye. If he was being honest, he had already lost interest in Rosalind—and she was the most beautiful woman in the room.

It was the way of passion—to burn, fizzle and fade. His father had once told him that no romance lasted more than two years, and that marriage was of little benefit to the male of the species aside from begetting heirs.

He decided to wait until the end of the event and see if Marie returned. But he knew it was futile.

The soiree was wrapped up quickly, with his grandmother practically walking everyone to the door *en masse*, and he stood sipping a drink, not wanting to go back to the silence of his rooms.

'Why are you still here?' his grandmother asked him after everyone had left. 'You never stay this long at my soirees.'

Then she answered for him.

'I saw you dance with Marie.' She waved her own mention of it away. 'That will make good on the wager, as far as I'm concerned. It was just a jest, and I let Agatha get the best of me. She'll have to forget about it now, because I'm letting her stay here, and they really don't have anywhere else to go unless they want to move back in with Lord Andrews. He's trying to force Marie to wed his nephew. I couldn't stand for that.' She puffed out her cheeks. 'I mean, it's fine for me to try to force *you* to wed. You're a viscount and my grandson.'

She waved her hands, emphasising the correctness of her own perspective.

'The niece doesn't have any other family?' he asked.

'Oh, don't get all soft-hearted. If she was any kind of niece at all, she'd try to find someone to wed and get a roof over their heads. But no, not her. She wants to find a way to support Agatha. She's trying to write a book on botany—as if that could help her. Next thing you know people won't be calling her a wall weed quietly any more, but loudly. Perhaps I should warn her...'

'Grandmother. Don't meddle in other people's lives. And don't be unkind to Marie.'

'I'm not,' she said, straightening her back and standing almost to his shoulder. 'I know she's unsightly. And she's much more fascinated by plants than people. Agatha loves her, though.'

'Like I love you?' he asked, patting her on the back.

'Much to your regret.' She beamed up at him. 'I have the best grandsons in the world. Sometimes they just need a little help in sorting out their lives.'

'Pierce might. But I don't.'

'Then why aren't you already married? It's your duty. Heirs and all.'

'I've thought about it.'

He had. And each time he had he'd discarded it. He'd heard from his mother the distress of being married to a man who could not remain committed to one woman. And he'd heard the rows of her parents, who were deeply committed to each other—and to disagreement.

Chapter Four

'Marie.'

No knock. No warning. Just her aunt's grey head poking around the doorway and an overly bright smile.

Marie wiped the sleep from her eyes and sat up. Her aunt moved to sit at her bedside, a soft vanilla scent following her. Then Gabriel's grandmother moved in behind her.

'Myrtle has a wonderful idea about how she can make good on her debt.'

'I know a publisher. For your book. Only it's not likely he will publish a book about plants…'

The wrinkles in Gabriel's grandmother's cheeks became prominent when she spoke, and she adjusted her ruby earrings while she talked.

'Sadly, I agree,' her aunt added. 'But you know how Myrtle and I had the duel? We were thinking you could write about that.'

'The duel?' Marie asked, straightening the covers around her waist. 'I can't imagine that will cover more than a few pages.'

'True…' Agatha said, putting a lone finger first on one cheek and then drawing it over her other cheek to rest there momentarily. 'True. But you know, I've had quite a life.'

'No. I don't know,' Marie said.

'And I did have an…um…adventure with Joseph Grimaldi, father of the clown, and he was quite a performer, if you know what I mean,' Gabriel's grandmother added.

'I don't want to guess,' Marie answered.

'You wouldn't have to. And since you're a virgin I could just add it in after you've finished.'

'She would,' Agatha added, nodding. 'And that will take more than just a few pages. A whole chapter, I'd say.'

'Plus, I did pretend to be a highwayman once, because I'd told my friends I was certain it wasn't that hard. But, well… It was. No one in that carriage realised that all I planned to do was take their handkerchiefs when I said, *"Stand and deliver."* I nearly ended up skewered, because even on horseback I am too short to make a ferocious thief.'

'Show her the scar,' Agatha said.

'Yes.' Myrtle lifted the hem of her dress and pointed to a small round welt on her leg. 'It went in here.' She moved her hand. 'And came out here. Luckily, the man's gun didn't go off, or it might not have ended so well, but he was prepared with his sword. I had the horse galloping like blazes, but the man was such a stalwart that he nicked me with the blade.'

'That's how she met her husband,' Agatha said. 'How fortunate that his was the carriage she stopped.'

'I thought he was the most handsome man I'd ever seen. I knew I just had to meet him again—if I lived. My parents were thrilled when I told them I'd met a viscount. I didn't tell them that I was stealing his handkerchief when I did so. You can imagine… They thought him a huge step up from Grimaldi, and would have paid any amount to impress him.'

'Her parents had already tried to interest Myrtle in a

titled husband,' her aunt added. 'She'd rebelled by having the liaison with Grimaldi. The next thing her parents knew, she was asking them if they could purchase the Viscount for her.'

'Is this true?' Marie clenched the bedcovers.

'Enough of it is,' Myrtle said. 'Some would say too much of it is.' She chuckled. 'My parents had not wedged their way into society at that point, and no one really knew me, but Father was making so much with his shipping endeavours and all his other investments... And I was getting enough pin money to purchase my chaperon's silence.' She looked heavenward. 'Those were the days...'

Marie slid her legs to the side of the bed, pulling her chemise properly into place, considering.

'So far it's all been rumours,' Myrtle said, 'and I have laughed it away. But now I'm getting older I would like to share my story with others.'

'What does Gabriel think of the idea?' Marie picked at the coverlet.

'Oh, I didn't ask him. He would likely be spitting fire.' She turned to her friend. 'Agatha, you will have to reconcile with your husband before this is published. I might need a place to live.'

'That's not likely to happen.'

'Don't worry. We'll just keep it a secret from Gabriel for the time being. No sense in upsetting him if we never finish it. His mother raised him to be a stickler. Which I appreciate.' She bit her upper lip before continuing. 'Did I tell you about the gunpowder experiment?'

'No...' Marie said warily.

'I'll show you a smaller version. Little bits of powder can make such a noise. You'll want to include the recipe in your book.' She held out her palm. 'About a fingernail's width in a clasped palm. I suppose the size of the person would change that somewhat, but then a bigger person would be able to run faster after lighting the fuse. We'll test the recipe now. And be sure to mention not to put it in a teacup. Those shards can sting…'

Gabriel was pleased that his grandmother had been so amazingly well-behaved at the soiree. A paragon, for her. She hadn't laughed too loudly or told any untoward jests. In fact, she'd been the kind of grandmother one would have hoped all grandmothers should be, and she'd not caused any problems in the past few days.

As soon as his hand touched the bell-pull to ring for breakfast, he heard female voices in the distance.

It was odd for his visitors to be about this early, but he stood, took a step to the window, looked out, and saw his grandmother, standing military-straight, with a lit torch in her hand. Lady Agatha was beside her. Marie was watching.

'No!' he shouted, palms on the windowpane.

'It's fine.' His grandmother raised her head, shouting back. 'I know what I'm doing this time.'

He lunged for the door and took the steps at jump.

Just as he made it out through the door, his grandmother was leaning over, lighting the fuse.

'No!' he shouted a second time.

She stopped moving at the sound of his voice, but the fuse was already lit.

Without a thought he jumped for Marie, grabbed her around the waist, and took several leaps with her in his arms, keeping his body between her and the mound of powder.

The explosion didn't even rattle the windows.

Marie stared at him, eyes wide.

He peered over his shoulder.

A big clump of grass had been removed, and the two elderly women were picking strands of grass and clods of earth from each other.

He kept a steadying arm around Marie and stamped out the last few embers from the torch his grandmother had dropped.

His grandmother stared at him. 'You could have started a fire, scaring us like that.' She practically sprouted a halo over the horns he sometimes imagined as she glared. 'You ruined a perfectly good demonstration.'

His voice matched the explosion in strength. 'I told you not to buy any more gunpowder.'

'I didn't. That was left over,' she said. 'Old. And it didn't seem to have its usual power. I don't know why you overreacted.'

'What if something had gone wrong?' he asked.

'It did,' she said. 'You rushed out of the house and terrified us all.'

'I told you no more explosions.'

'I would not call this a *true* explosion—just a small movement in the air. No windows broken. Although I still say that last time that one was already cracked.'

She dusted a few specks of earth from her arm.

'I wanted to show Agatha and Marie how simple it is to make fireworks. I told them it's best not to leave drinks about, because the falling debris doesn't really add anything to the flavour.'

Suddenly he realised he still had a grip on Marie's waist and she was tight against him, surprising him with the delicate femininity hidden underneath the fabric of her clothes. A vibrant burst of scent, springtime and gunpowder, hit him—two scents he would never have imagined going so well together.

His grandmother turned to Agatha and raised her chin. She said, a little louder than necessary, 'I was being extremely careful. You should have seen what happened last time.' She looked down and shook her head. 'One little window. Again, it was likely defective to begin with, but of course I received the blame.'

Then she side-eyed him. 'I noticed you didn't clasp Agatha or me to save us from the impending blast.'

'Marie was closer,' he said.

'I don't think so,' his grandmother answered.

'She's more innocent,' he said, glowering.

His grandmother snorted. 'Well, you have us with that one. Come along, Agatha,' she said, summoning her friend. 'I'm his grandmother and he should have rescued me. My feelings are hurt.'

Then she glared at him again, and the two older women trotted into the house.

He realised he was *still* holding Marie and her heart was beating against his.

He had only been concerned for Marie's safety.

And now he was concerned for his own.

Marie knew what it felt like to be held by gunpowder. She felt it in his clasp and in the little sparks inside her.

'There's not another explosion planned,' she said, her feet barely touching the ground, so secure was she against him. 'You can… You can let me go.'

He released her, but his warmth stayed with her.

She dusted down her arms, even though nothing was there. 'You nearly scared the breath out of me.'

'My pardon. I didn't want Grandmother to get you hurt.'

She took off her spectacles and blew over the lenses. 'I had no idea such a small amount of gunpowder could make an explosion,' she said.

'I did.' He locked eyes with her. 'Promise me you will not let her do that again.'

She put the spectacles back on. 'Once was enough. But I almost missed it because you rushed out of the house. It was very dramatic.'

And it had been. She had been caught up by him. Clasped close. Then the explosion had sounded and he'd shielded her with his body. He'd started his discussion with his grandmother and she'd just kept silent, clasped like a little bird in a nest of male strength, surrounded by the scent of gunpowder, fresh earth and clean male.

Oh, she would never forget it.

'As mentioned, she broke a window once, when she was testing gunpowder. If a little of something pleases her, she will use four times as much the next time. I have no idea how much powder she used previously, but this time I can tell she did reduce it a lot.'

'She evidently doesn't think the broken window was entirely her fault.'

His eye-roll convinced her of his opinion, and her wry smile told him she agreed with him.

'Promise me you will not take part in any more of my grandmother's schemes.'

Probably best not to mention the memoir...

'I'm sure you have tried to tell her no on many things? She just doesn't seem to hear it.'

He frowned, his eyes locked on hers. 'See me if you need assistance with that. It's much better than dealing with the after-effects.' He took her hand lightly. 'You seem to have her spirit of dangerousness. Don't let her lead you astray.'

No one had ever said anything like that to her. Other people were adventurous. She was the stable one. The one who kept her head down and did as she was told.

She reached out, pointing to the dust on his shoulder, wanting to ease the tension between them. After all, he'd just tried to save her from an explosion.

'May I?' she asked.

He didn't react, so she dusted the specks from his shoulder.

He thanked her with a smile that lit a completely different kind of fuse inside her.

'When you are with Grandmother you must take care,' Gabriel said.

'Of course.'

But she knew it was not just his grandmother she should take care around. It was him as well. He was as flammable to her as the largest barrel of gunpowder.

She rubbed at her arms, sensing the true jeopardy to her heart.

'Do you know about their duel?' he asked.

'Yes. I have heard about it.'

Her aunt had claimed it was merely a lark that had grown a little out of hand.

'I am not happy any time gunpower or swords are involved.'

She stood, staring up at him, possibly the strongest man she'd ever seen before, and yet she could see the dilemma he had. A grandmother who sought attention and explosions. The Achilles' heel in his life.

'They laugh about the duel now,' she said.

'I am not at that point yet. I was hardly twenty years old, and having to relieve my grandmother of a sword because the two of them had felt that a duel was the best way to settle an argument. I don't think they were even angry until I arrived—and then they were upset that I was stopping their duel. The crowd enjoyed it.'

'Wouldn't it have been worse if they had been angry?'

'More understandable,' he said. 'Grandmother just wanted the theatre of the moment.' He walked over, kicking at the earth to cover the hole left behind by the explosion. 'No one I've ever seen loves to be the centre of attention more than Grandmother. She probably hoped your aunt would send that wager contract to the scandal sheets.'

'I'm sure not.' She paused, then whispered, 'I tried to get it from Aunt Agatha, but she keeps that reticule close. She has the signed agreement and the pearls in it.'

His stare indicated that he didn't want to be reminded.

'I must thank you for trying to save me—though it wasn't needed,' she said, trying to change the subject back to something safer. 'You added a bit of excitement to what would have otherwise been quite a dull explosion.'

Goodness, the man was studying her as if she'd just slapped him for no reason. And she'd given him a thank-you.

'A dull explosion?' He gave a strong stamp on the earth with his boot, and then another final one.

Somehow she felt she must explain to him. 'Your grandmother is a dear woman. And she is fascinating. You are fortunate to have her near.'

His eyes met hers while he picked up the remaining

pieces of the torch. 'Will you stay away from her fireworks in the future? No more letting her light fuses?'

'Sometimes she's hard to say no to.'

'I don't have any trouble with it,' he said. 'Again, come and find me if you need any help with that.'

She knew he meant every word, and that if she didn't go along with his plans he would be more formidable than his grandmother. Best to keep him in the dark about some things. And surely his grandmother would lose interest in the memoir…

Gabriel studied her, pleased at the thought that she might search him out, and then gave a wave to indicate they go back into the house.

'Your grandmother expected you would still be asleep and would not even hear it,' she said, scrambling to keep up with him.

He stopped and raised a brow. 'She will tell you whatever suits her purpose. It doesn't make me feel any better to hear that you are aware Grandmother is hiding her antics from me and you are assisting her.'

'Oh…' She cupped her chin in her hand and rested her thumb against her lips. 'Your grandmother said she had used gunpowder before and was experienced. Although she did claim the people who create the gunpowder sometimes vary the strength.'

'*She* varies the strength.' He lowered his voice and didn't move any muscle unnecessary for speaking. 'Experience doesn't always equal safety. Not where Grandmother is concerned.'

'I don't believe she would do anything dangerous…'

The short burst of air from his nostrils contradicted her.

'Perhaps she knows her boundaries,' Marie challenged.

'Her boundaries are the earth, the sky and whatever else she can reach.' He nodded towards the side of the house. 'That lower window is the one which had to be replaced, and not all things can be fixed so easily. She should leave explosives alone.'

'But nothing went wrong with the experiment. In fact, I found it exciting.'

Exciting? Her eyes were bright behind the spectacles. She didn't realise how badly she could have been injured.

'She has some tall tales… Do you think they are true?'

There was a question in her tone. Uncertainty in her gaze.

'Sadly, they aren't all tales, I suspect,' he said. 'And I also suspect she is a bad influence on you.'

'I like her.' She pursed her lips.

'You liked the explosives.'

'Yes…' She moved closer. 'You didn't need to save me, but it was a nice thought.'

'You were too close to danger.'

'Nothing bad happened. Except we interrupted your day.'

'That is not the problem,' he said. 'You need to stand firm against their schemes.'

'Ho!' she said. 'You have a veritable army of people behind you, and what I suspect are unlimited finances, and yet you cannot corral her as you wish. Why do you think I can?'

'She might listen to someone who isn't a relative.'

'When you find someone she listens to I would like to be introduced to them.'

Steady eyes challenged him and she moved forward, the flounces on her dress billowing as she opened the door and left him to stare at the wood and remember the blast of having her in his arms. The feel of his fear that she was going to be hurt. And the steadiness of her eyes when she dared him to find someone his grandmother would listen to.

She might be nervous at social events, but she was not evincing any such emotion when she was alone with him.

He remembered their dance and relived it, smiling at his misinterpretation and the memory of her happiness afterwards.

Opening the door, he called out her name.

She hesitated, then turned to him, and he spoke one sentence before they both went their separate ways.

'I suspect you are as explosive as anyone else in this house.'

Chapter Five

Gabriel woke early, knowing he needed to study the details of a new property lease. His grandfather had told him over and over that a viscount needed to be aware of what was going on within the estate and consider the details of all purchases and properties sold. Trust was for the poor, he'd said. A wealthy man couldn't afford it.

Normally he slept late, but it was as if memories of Marie had prodded him awake. He summoned his valet, who appeared without so much as a wrinkle in his clothing and in his usual good humour.

'What has the morning brought us?' Gabriel asked.

As the man gave a nod of greeting, he answered. 'Miss Marie is in the library, probably for a respite, and the two ladies are still discussing your rescuing her before them.'

Gabriel raised a brow.

'Maids on duty, sir. The housekeeper assigned the most talkative one to your grandmother's rooms yesterday. She thought it best…particularly after the explosion.'

Giving a nod of approval, Gabriel dressed quickly so he could speak with Marie.

'And one other thing I thought odd,' his valet continued, 'is your grandmother's new love of botany.'

'Botany?' Gabriel paused, his hands on his top waist-coat button.

'Yes. Apparently Miss Marie is writing a book on botany. When the maid walked into the library Miss Marie had a notepad and they were talking about roots and tubers and daffodils, or some such. The maid thought it a bit odd… as if they'd suddenly changed their conversation when she entered the room.'

'Probably trying to figure out which ones are most poi-sonous,' Gabriel said.

The valet nodded.

'I wonder if we should warn Lord Andrews.'

'I will let the housekeeper know that the maids are to immediately alert her and she is to tell me if any dangerous plans are mentioned.'

'Thank you.'

'And I will see what else I can find out,' he said.

Gabriel left the room, pulling the waistcoat into place, and took the short walk to the library. He would have thought he saw Lady Andrews sitting in front of the open window if the valet hadn't said it was Marie, and he still had to take a second look to reassure himself.

Once more she was wearing a dress not made for her, and she had that disreputable shawl around her shoulders. But today it appeared to have been tied so she could write comfortably. Her skirts billowed at her feet, and appeared full enough to trip her.

She always dressed in a form-swallowing gown that ap-peared a bit faded and forgotten, and he wasn't sure that she didn't wear the same few dresses, with a few different bows and ribbons placed upon them.

She wore her hair in a knot, pulled back and with no

extra twists or turns in it, just the minimum care possible. The same as the maids. Then it dawned on him. She dressed like a servant. Hiding in plain sight.

If she remade old clothing she wouldn't flatter herself. She used her sewing skills to conceal herself.

He tried to recall all he knew about her. But nothing came to mind. She had slid noiselessly into his world. If not for the wager, he probably would not ever have been truly aware she was living in his home.

She saw him and her pencil stopped in mid-air. The pages of her notebook fluttered as she flipped them closed with the barest crisp sound.

Her spectacles sparkled in the light. The morning sunshine floated over her. But she was so shaded by her clothing that it might as well have been cloudy.

'You are up early,' he said.

'Aunt and your grandmother were comparing notes on the dinner they attended at Mrs Smythe's,' she said, her eyes darting away. 'Really, it was a chance for more wagering than for a dinner. But this time the cards were in your grandmother's favour.'

She gathered up the book on the table beside her, and he could tell she planned to leave.

'Don't go on my account,' he said. 'You should continue to enjoy the morning.'

'It is getting a bit warm,' she said.

Then she seemed to think better of exiting, and returned her notebook to the table beside her. Removing the heavy shawl, she placed it over the arm of her chair.

'How long have you worn spectacles?' he asked.

'Several years. Aunt Agatha saw me peering too closely at things and decided something must be done. It hadn't occurred to me that I would ever have an opportunity to have something so fine.' She touched the rim of the glasses. 'They are the dearest thing I own, and I will always remember she gave me such a gift.'

With both hands she took them off for a moment, peered at him, and put them back on. 'If they bother other people I don't care. I could hardly believe it when I received them. Some days I take them off and look at things, and then put them back on for the joy of seeing how much clearer everything is with them.'

'They are lovely.'

Her long stare and the brief upsweep of her chin let him know she didn't believe him.

But it was true.

'Lord Andrews was upset that Aunt Agatha had wasted so many funds on something so frivolous and he complained, telling her they would likely ruin my eyesight completely. Then he left to go to his hunting box because he was so angry with her,' she said. 'Aunt Agatha decided to use what little funds she had left to hire a coach and go after him. She took me with her. I'd never been to the country before.'

Memories wafted across her face.

'I was sad that Aunt Agatha was distressed, but everything seemed so clear and beautiful that I couldn't keep from looking out of the window as we travelled. I'd never seen leaves high on a tree, really. They were just masses of green. I saw a bird Aunt Agatha told me was a linnet, and it didn't fly in a straight line, but moved up and down as it flew. Before, I'd never been aware of anything like that.'

Then she appraised him, but took a second too long.

'So, what do you see when you look at me?' he asked.

Instantly, he saw a shutter go across her eyes.

'A viscount,' she answered. 'From head to boots. A respected member of society. Assured. Quite distinguished.'

'And what do you see when you look in the mirror?'

Emotions fluttered on her face. He wasn't sure if he'd hurt or angered her, but she seemed uncaring, and answered, 'I am a poor relation. I'm only allowed to attend social events by the barest thread. I don't mind, though. If I weren't to be invited it wouldn't upset me much. But I feel my aunt relies on my presence to make her feel better, and I'm pleased I can do that. I owe her so much.'

'I would like to give you a chance to see something else in your mirror. I don't want you hiding away at any gathering, particularly for the picnic. You are a guest of my grandmother's and are every bit as welcome as your aunt is.'

Her eyes flashed at him.

'What you see as hiding away is simply my knowledge of my place. I am making my aunt more comfortable if I am at her side.'

'And at the soiree? Weren't you trying to avoid people, and not giving others a chance to get acquainted with you?'

'If they'd wished to speak with me, they could have.'

'Not when you graciously excused yourself.'

She shook her head. 'I know Aunt Agatha wishes me to converse, and get on well with people, and I understand that.' She turned away. 'I know I should make more of an effort, and I do try to make enough to please her. But I am not fond of nonsensical chatter with strangers.'

He knew that the Marie in front of him now was presenting more of her real self than the illusion she had created to conceal herself within her surroundings, surviving as best she could. He wanted to know more about this version of her—the true woman.

'Besides, I don't have the right clothing to be in society. It would only cause speculation and cold shoulders if I were to try to be a part of that world.'

'What if you did?' he asked.

No answer.

Rain had begun pattering down outside, and she studied the window. 'I suppose I should close that.'

'Only if you want to. The cooler air feels good.'

She stood and walked to the window, putting a hand near the rain. The drops changed the smell of the gardens, and changed the feeling inside the house.

Her hand reached out into the rain. Her eyes studied the drops landing on her skin.

'I almost wish everyone could experience what I did,' she said. 'Receiving these spectacles gave me a chance to appreciate how green everything was. How alive. And I realised that nature should be noticed. Before wearing my spectacles, I wasn't able to experience much unless I could walk right up to it. In truth, if I saw someone at a distance, I often couldn't tell who they were.'

She stretched her left arm wide, her body still safely inside the house.

'Getting my spectacles was like lifting the lid from a magic kettle and looking inside to see another world. One that had been there all along.'

He moved to stand beside her, and study the view she saw, but really, he savoured the moment of standing alone at the window with her.

A burst of wind and rain splattered them both, chilling the air even more. She tilted her head downwards and he saw a hint of displeasure on her face, her spectacle lenses becoming dotted by water drops.

She stared up at him, frowning, and he hoped it was merely because of the water.

'I suppose it is time to close the window,' she said, tugging it with her dry hand, and he reached out and helped the frame snap into place.

'These water spots on the lenses do give me grief.' She touched both hands to the sides of her spectacles. 'Even the widest brim on a bonnet doesn't always help with that.'

'I have a handkerchief.'

He retrieved the cloth from his pocket and she took off her spectacles, causing a few strands of hair to escape her bun. She stared at the water drops and rubbed at her lenses carefully, to dry the moisture, and he saw the longest eyelashes he'd ever seen. She studied him for half a beat before returning the handkerchief and putting the spectacles back on her face, working to get the earpieces set as regally as if she'd been adjusting a crown.

His heart thudded at the sight of her.

Behind the agreeable, amenable countenance rested a woman who would try to escape conflict until she couldn't do it any more. But she enchanted him.

'I must go. My aunt will be sending a maid for me soon, I'm sure. Or your grandmother will.'

'My grandmother?'

She lowered her voice and her eyes. 'I think she considers me a good audience.'

Now he understood why his grandmother had been less likely to cause any upset these last few weeks. Marie and her aunt were providing companionship.

'Grandmother prefers all eyes to be on her and all ears to be listening.'

'I would agree. She has lived with a sense of curiosity and adventure and has no trouble stating her opinions.'

She gazed at him, as if she could see into his soul.

'I do try to keep the peace between my aunt and your grandmother. I have a lot of practice in keeping as many people content as I can.'

'I have already seen that in you. It's a good skill to have.'

It had never been one of his. He employed people for that.

Then he noticed one of the books she had put on the table: *The Herball or Generall Historie of Plantes*.

Indicating the tome with a nod, he asked, 'You're interested in botany?'

'Yes. I have been trying to read all the books I can on it. I had thought…thought I might write a book on botany and that would give me a way to support my aunt and myself.' She studied the cover, eyes downcast. 'But it is impossible for me to discover all I need to know…'

He stared at it, a hideous volume, and lifted it with both hands. He opened it. 'It's a book about…plants?'

Perhaps he'd looked at it a few times, but he'd never really been interested.

'Botany,' she repeated, taking the book from him and putting the notebook on top of it.

'Are you reading it?' he asked, nodding towards the book.

'I was, but I'm putting it back now.'

'Perhaps you could write about something else. Something more…'

She studied him, eyes suddenly widening. 'I suppose that is an excellent idea. Excellent…'

In a whirl, she put the book into an empty spot on the shelf and turned to leave.

'You appear very learned,' he said.

'My friend Polly's mother taught me to read, thinking she could teach two more easily than one and we would help each other.'

Her words were rapid. She darted to the doorway.

'Wait, wait,' he called to her back, taking one stride to catch up with her and another stride to pass her. 'My apologies,' he offered, although he didn't really see that he'd done anything wrong.

'I heard a man once say to his son that no education is ever wasted,' she said, hugging the notepad close to herself. 'I'm not so sure of that, because I see people all around me with an education and it was only a chore to them. But it was a luxury I could not have. If they'd had to struggle for it they would have appreciated it more.'

She looked at her notebook. Her voice softened. 'Please forgive me. I forgot my—'

He knew what she was going to say. She had forgotten her *place*.

'When the weather is right, your "place" is overlooking the garden or on a garden bench,' he said, walking to her and taking the pencil from her fingers, using it to point beyond the window. 'Claim it.'

'It's not my place,' she said. 'It's yours. You were trained for the role you have in life, and I suppose I was for mine, too.'

'I worked hard at university. Sometimes…' A pause. 'When I wasn't watching the liquor diminish. Or listening to wild tales. Playing cards. I suppose it has done me well.'

'I assume you are quite proficient at revelry, then? Although it's not apparent.'

'I suppose so. But then, most of the other students worked on that skill equally, so we were well matched. I also learned a lot about history. About how other people think. And I met people from different areas.'

She clutched the notebook as if it might preserve her life. 'It must have been incredible to have such an opportunity.'

'It was. But I don't think I appreciated it until this moment. I just wanted it to be over so I could get on with my life.'

Her lips tightened and she didn't speak.

'Forgive me. I've been up all night, mostly,' he said, 'so I suppose my manners have nodded off. I did not mean to upset you.'

'I know. I suppose I am sensitive about…some things. Most things, possibly. Truth be told.'

'I suppose many people are sensitive about something.'

'And you?' she asked.

'Can't think of anything.'

'Nothing?'

'No. Don't think so.'

She studied him while the silence lingered, but it was a comfortable quiet, with the rain pattering down harder outside, adding a background music to their words.

She took the pencil from him and used it to point at his neckcloth. 'What if I said that your cravat has too many loops?'

He touched the fabric. 'Beau Brummel himself trained my valet.'

She shook her head. 'Perhaps you should have found someone else to teach him. Someone who liked smaller bows. Or none. One floppy knot or just a small knot can be quite attractive.'

He touched the linen and laughed. 'As opposed to what you think of this one now?'

Her eyes opened wider. 'A simple one can be impressive.'

'This is a costly neckcloth. The finest linen.'

'The cloth is magnificent,' she said, by way of appeasement.

He moved to the window, away from her, and unbuttoned the top buttons on his waistcoat, then he untied his cravat, put it into a simple knot and grimaced at it. Now he had too much length at the end of the fabric. He opened his waistcoat and folded the ends inside. In his opinion, he appeared rumpled.

He did up the buttons and stood for her perusal. 'Better?'

'Now you look unkempt.'

There was just the slightest dip of her head and a blush on her cheeks, plus a small smile of acknowledgement.

'See? The cravat my valet tied was better.'

'Different. Not necessarily better.'

'Perhaps I'll try a smaller knot at this picnic I'm planning to have. I want you to attend and not stay in the shadows. I will wager that you will capture attention and like it. And I will wear a cravat without style, though it may be difficult…'

'One without a dozen loops?' she asked. 'Or even ten?'

'For you, I will,' he said. 'And I hope you will consider staying out of the background. I'd like to help you with that.'

He saw the puzzled look on her face, but he didn't give

her a chance to question him before he stepped away, bowing slightly as a farewell.

'My man of affairs is arriving soon. When he leaves, I will talk with the butler and he will help with my plans.'

She hid her sigh, watching the doorway after he left. How wonderful to have someone in your employ who could help with everything in the household, and someone else whose job it was to make money for you.

All that would have corrupted many people, but it didn't appear to have tarnished one hair on Gabriel's head.

He'd not seemed to mind her spectacles, nor even that she liked botany and birds.

No wonder so many women were entranced by him. At least, according to his grandmother. Marie could believe it. She'd seen the women vying for his attention at the soiree. All of them beautiful, accomplished at dancing, and wearing beautiful gowns.

From the corner of her eye she'd even noticed a few spiteful eyes on her when she'd waltzed with him, and that had interrupted her concentration, causing her to misstep. He'd been so considerate, and kept her dancing correctly, and her heart had fluttered more than any bird's wings.

A woman might easily lose her heart to him.

Just as a woman might easily float into a disaster she couldn't recover from. It would be a tragedy to care for someone who might not return the affection.

As Marie had been growing up her guardian had constantly reminded her that men only stayed long enough to father a child or two and then went on their way. She'd told Marie time and time again that she must remain on her own path. She must be true to herself. It was better to live alone than to live with a woman-chaser—and she should know because she'd known plenty of them.

Even Polly's father had left his family. Aunt Agatha's first husband had died, and now the second had pushed her out of his house.

In fact, she couldn't think of a single male who'd remained constant to the woman in his life. Even when she'd been very young, and had had her only true, devoted suitor, she'd known her sweetheart hadn't considered marriage overly binding. That was why she'd called off the courtship—a blessing in disguise, in the end. The realisation of how close she'd been to a tragic fate resounded in her. He'd wed someone else and been a tyrant to his wife— she'd seen the woman's bruised cheek.

If Gabriel found out the truth of her past he'd not have any qualms about ridding himself of her. It would be horrible if he tossed them out, so she should not risk antagonising him.

She and her aunt had moved in—temporarily—with his grandmother because they really had nowhere else to go. Aunt Agatha claimed she was certain her husband would soon realise his mistake, and they'd be able to return to his mansion again. But eventually his nephew would inherit, and Marie wasn't sure what would happen to her then, except that she'd again be scrabbling for a place to live—possibly for both her and her aunt.

Better that Gabriel remain unenlightened than realise what dire straits she was in.

It wouldn't matter anyway. She was about to become part of an even bigger scandal.

She'd not considered the ramifications of writing his grandmother's memoirs until she'd put pen to paper and seen the words flowing. But Myrtle had made Marie promise to be certain not to tell Gabriel anything about the memoirs, as she thought it best he did not know until after they were published.

That promise hung over her now—a dark cloud that would do more than make drops on the outside of her glasses. It might lead to tears on the other side.

Marie returned to her room and looked over the notes she'd taken from his grandmother's reminiscences. She'd not realised how wealthy women could behave when doors were closed…

Chapter Six

She'd worked all evening on her notes, and Gabriel's grandmother had just given her another anecdote she'd recalled, and sent Marie to her room to write it up.

The house always seemed quiet, compared to the other places she'd lived. She and her aunt usually seemed able to keep Myrtle calm, and Marie didn't count the gunpowder as a true explosion.

Letting out a breath, she moved towards Myrtle's room— but then she heard robust footsteps. Gabriel. She stopped, and he turned a corner and almost collided with her.

She jumped away, then put up a hand to straighten her hair. 'I wasn't expecting you,' she said.

Just the top half of his body moved forward as he almost whispered the words, 'It's my house.'

'You are rarely on this side of the house, from what I have seen.'

'It's true I don't visit Grandmother much, but she often stops by my rooms if she hears a scandal she thinks I should know about.'

'She probably sees you often, then.'

He chuckled. 'Will you join me in the music room? This will only take a moment,' he said, holding out his arm.

With only the briefest hesitation, she took it, surrounding herself with the crisp, clean scent of him.

He led her towards the music room, opened the door, and indicated that she enter. 'I wanted you to know the picnic plans have been finalised. Except for the plan to do with you.'

The harp was in the centre of the room, with several chairs placed conspicuously around it for an audience. She and her aunt had sat in those chairs several times.

'A picnic sounds pleasant,' she said, hearing a small waver in her voice which she hoped he didn't notice.

It did sound pleasant, but only if there were few attending. Perhaps if he were the only guest it would be grand. But to be among all those society people would mean watching every step, and every word, and being on her most perfect behaviour. And she had nothing new to wear. Or really nothing old to wear...

'I have not requested any musicians.' His lips firmed for an instant. 'I will instead suggest Grandmother plays her harp, and that will appease her on not being consulted over the details.'

'I listen to her playing sometimes. It's enjoyable.'

His eyebrows tightened.

'It really is,' she said, suddenly needing to convince him that she told the truth. It was so much better than hearing someone having a row.

He led her to the chairs, but they didn't sit.

'You really do act more like someone of your aunt's age than your own,' he said. 'You even dress like her.'

'I know. I like more comfortable clothing.'

The dress she had on had used to belong to her aunt, so it didn't surprise her that he thought so. It was better for all concerned that she did not stand out, and this clothing would serve her well if she was able to obtain a position on a housekeeping staff. A light day dress would not.

She continued to be pleased to take the older dresses her aunt could no longer fit into. But, since sewing wasn't her strongest skill, the flounces and things she'd added to help them fit better hadn't really improved them much.

Funds had been a struggle all her life. And now she and her aunt depended on Lord Andrews, and he was a penny-hoarding, miserly man. But still, he had provided a home for them, for a time, and she had appreciated it. Living with Aunt Agatha had been the best years of her life.

She saw Gabriel's eyes glance over her hair and she touched it defensively. She always pulled it back primly. It was the easiest, quickest way to style it, and suitable for someone in her station.

'Perhaps you could speak with my grandmother about a shopping trip? She dearly loves shopping trips.'

'I don't know,' she said. 'I'll think about it.'

She did, and dismissed it.

'Grandmother could help you. It would give her some-thing to do other than wager on me or meddle in my life.'

'I don't know that a shopping trip is the answer.'

It wouldn't be for her. She could not buy anything to wear for a picnic. She wore shawls sometimes, to cover her clothing better, but feared they didn't help much.

'Today my valet tied my cravat with less loops.' He touched the flowing burst of fabric at his neck.

'I can't tell.' She pursed her lips. 'It appears your neck-cloth is so tightly wrapped around your collar that if you dropped something you would have to bend at the waist to look down.'

He tugged at the silk, but didn't reduce its neatness. 'I have to give an appearance of maturity in order to be successful in conducting business.'

'You certainly do. But is it really necessary at your age?'

'My age?' he asked, eyes narrowing. 'It's not rare for someone my age to have inherited an estate.'

She studied him. 'How old are you?'

'Twenty-seven. Last month.'

'Oh.' Her mouth remained open. She studied his face. Peered at his hair.

'It's not thinning,' he said, his eyes giving her a straight glare. 'Or greying. At least, not noticeably. And anyway, I have been told it will make me look even more distinguished.'

She nodded. 'Your clothes work very well at giving you an air of maturity. I thought you were much older.'

'Appearing responsible is important to me.'

'You succeed.'

She hesitated, studying him right down to the last tiny wrinkle at his eye, imperceptible from any distance. She'd never have noticed it without the spectacles' help to her vision.

'I don't think either of us likes the clothing of the other very well,' she said, changing the subject from age.

A look of whimsy in his gaze told her he recognised what she was doing.

'If I wear a more simple cravat, would you consider dressing for a younger age?' he asked.

She didn't really know if that was a possibility. 'I would like to remain in what I'm comfortable wearing.' She crossed her arms. 'It is what is on the inside that counts.'

'Said the lady who has critiqued my neckcloth.'

'I thought it needed to be said and that you would not mind. It's such a simple thing to alter.'

He let out a whoosh of breath. 'Not where my valet is concerned.'

'Then I apologise for even mentioning it. It was entirely wrong of me, and I beg your forgiveness.'

'You're apologising for mentioning it, but you don't say you've changed your mind.'

Her teeth were almost gritted behind her smile, and she forced truth into her words. 'The neckcloth looks amazing. Mature. Respectful. Perfect for business.'

There—she hadn't lied. Still too many loops, though.

His smile told her he was reading her mind.

'Not all people look closely enough to see the inside,' he said, giving a tug on his cravat to increase the size of the loops. 'And the outside is considered a reflection of it. If you are considering suitors, the first thing you see is his outside. I see your dated attire, just as you see my impressive cravat.'

'I am not considering suitors,' she said. 'And I'll have you know that this dress was made with very expensive fabric…once upon a time.'

She couldn't tell him how strained her aunt's finances were, nor how new clothing had never been a consideration for Marie. A new dress was out of the question. Aunt Agatha had tried to keep their dire financial situation a secret, but his grandmother now knew all the details.

She took in a breath, seeing the image of something she'd never had right at her fingertips, tempting her beyond anything else. 'Perhaps a new frock would be nice, but I'm completely happy with my appearance.'

'As I said, my grandmother could assist you. She is always leaving fashion plates lying around, and she gets fraught if a servant moves them. She would help.'

His grandmother definitely wore the latest fashions. 'I am not sure what she would think of that offer. I shall have to decline.'

That hurt. The image of a new dress so possible and yet so far from her. She didn't think she'd ever had a completely new frock, but she'd been happy each time one was passed down to her. No one could have been happier to get a useable dress than she.

They walked a few more steps and she peered at him from the corner of her eye.

'Changing your cravat would be so easy for you, though. Just use fewer folds. It would take less fabric and save on funds.'

His eyebrow twitched.

She firmed her jaw.

Now both his brows nearly met in the middle.

'You would be impressive still with a plain cravat, a black waistcoat and coat and boots.'

'You wish me to vanish into the woodwork?'

'No. You'd never disappear into your surroundings. You claim them. You need no extra help. In fact, I think the opposite. I think you would appear more powerful in the plainest of clothing. And that is a compliment, and the truth.'

She wasn't speaking flattery. His movement was always purposeful. Intent. He never ambled, or meandered, or sauntered. She didn't think he planned his steps, but they were as strong as if he'd drawn up careful plans and moved precisely into them.

'I will happily wear plainer clothing if you will give

simpler gowns a chance, and at the picnic we can both see how we like the change in our appearance.'

He stepped away, so that her hand slid from his arm. 'The picnic is a week from today—surely a dressmaker can have a gown whipped together by then?'

'That's a short time,' she said, not willing to admit it had taken almost a month for her aunt to receive the last gown she'd purchased. 'My aunt's seamstress could never work that fast. I don't think it's possible.'

Particularly not with her limited funds.

'Grandmother could handle all of that for you. Her seamstress is skilled and quick. And I am sure she would make it a gift to you after the risk of your lighting the fuse for her.'

'Please don't speak with your grandmother about a dress for me. It would not be wise.'

She knew his grandmother might read more into such a simple idea than just the spirit of generosity, and would likely ask a hundred questions, determined to put a barrier between Marie and Gabriel. Recently the older woman had been talking about Rosalind as the perfect wife for him.

Marie imagined herself deflecting bolts of lightning-strong attention from his grandmother. If the slightest thing went wrong—such as anyone finding out she wasn't using her real name—both she and her aunt could be homeless.

'My dresses are fine. Just not elaborate.' She made a decision. 'I must thank you, but I cannot see me having a new frock at your expense.'

She touched the sleeve of her dress, running her fingers over the embroidery stitches she'd added. The stitches helped cover up the places where she'd made a mistake in taking in the garment and puckered it. She was no seam-stress, but she could get the job done. Just not perfectly.

'Do as you wish,' he said. 'But if my grandmother sug-gests it, will you consider it?'

She pursed her lips and didn't answer. Oh, it would be magnificent to have new clothing, but she did prefer to stay in the shadows. It deflected so much unpleasantness.

Nothing changed in his face, and perhaps that was what alerted her to the fact that she'd irritated him. He was used to others going along with his suggestions.

'I will go ahead with my plans,' he said, and reached into his pocket and held out a folded piece of paper with her aunt's name and hers written on it. 'My man of affairs has taken care of the invitations.'

Taking the paper, she perused the script for a moment, and then opened it up to read the date of the picnic.

She lowered her gaze and told herself not to be regret-ful. It was only a picnic and a dress…though a picnic with a written invitation.

His voice interrupted her thoughts.

'I have also come to see you this morning because the gardener is working,' he said, 'and I thought he could tell you about the plants while I check to see what changes I want made for the picnic.'

He held out his arm for her to hold, and something in his eyes dared her to take it. She gave him an answering blink, and he smiled.

That blasted smile was her undoing.

'Would you walk with me in the gardens?' he asked.

She put the invitation on a chair and took his arm. 'Since you ask… I was thinking of going that way.'

She couldn't hear his chuckle, but she felt it.

Together they walked outside.

A man was trimming plants with shears, and he had a scythe propped against a tree.

Gabriel walked over to look at the ropes coiled at the edge of the garden, and a wooden chair that had no legs. 'Excellent work on the swing,' Gabriel called out to the man.

The man gave Gabriel a nod and a smile.

'I wanted more activity than people just milling around having lemonade,' he told her, taking her to stand closer to the man. 'Henry has tended plants all his life,' Gabriel said, 'and he can answer any questions you have about the garden.'

'Could you tell me what kind of foliage that is?' she asked, pointing.

The gardener unleashed a torrent of information, telling her not only what was planted where, but also when, what had previously been tended there, how he worked the manure into the soil so it wouldn't burn the plants, and various other facts about the vegetation.

'It's no wonder this garden is so beautiful,' she said to Gabriel afterwards. 'He knows more about gardening than I can even ask about.'

'He constantly surprises me with the planting, and he is also an excellent carpenter,' Gabriel added, stepping aside. 'I sketched a drawing of the swing for him, and you will hardly believe how he has improved it. I'll fetch it to show you.'

Chapter Seven

⁓⁓⁓⁓⁓⁓

But he had another reason for going inside. In addition to giving Marie a chance to learn more about the plants, he also had a question to ask his grandmother.

Detouring to his grandmother's room, he knocked on the door and entered after she called out, pleased to find that she was alone.

'Grandmother. I'm planning a picnic, and my staff is taking care of the invitations.'

'Are you inviting Marie?'

'Yes.'

'Well, don't have a romance with her. She's not right for marriage.'

'You wagered me as her potential groom.'

She dropped her head to one side. 'I know, but I was positive I'd win. I had the cards put by.' She pressed her fingertips to her neck. 'I wanted those pearls. They're lovely. Agatha keeps them in that reticule and hardly lets it out of her grasp.' She puffed out her cheeks.

'Does she not trust you?' he asked.

'Of course she does.' His grandmother rolled her eyes. 'At least at a picnic there won't be dancing,' she said. 'I saw Marie nearly trample you.'

'She hasn't danced much.'

'I can see why. That pathetic little wall weed has not blossomed as I hoped.'

'Why—...?' He paused. 'Why do you call her pathetic?'

His grandmother grimaced. 'I saw her at the soiree. She didn't even take off her spectacles for the night. Don't let yourself become attracted to her. She doesn't have any idea about how to comport herself correctly. She can spell, I suppose, but she's nothing like Rosalind, or the other ladies who attended.'

'What is different about her? How is she not more than equal to Rosalind?'

'Can't you see?' she asked. 'I mean, she's a pleasant young woman, and I know she says she's twenty-four, but I don't believe it's possible she's that young. And really, that's too old for you. Also, she doesn't have any true skills. Not like Rebecca, who plays the piano wonderfully. Or Rosalind, who has all the men asking her for a dance.'

She strode over and slapped his arm.

'Don't be a dolt. Even you must see what a disaster Marie is in society. It was a little embarrassing for people to see I had invited someone who dresses so abominably to my soiree.' She shook her head. 'That is what I get for trying to help a friend.'

'I suppose she'll arrive at the picnic in a worn dress,' he said.

His grandmother gave a low grumble, much like an unhappy cat.

'Her dress at the soiree wasn't that bad,' he added. 'But it wasn't in the same category as anything your seamstress can make.'

'True,' she acknowledged.

'Why don't you have your seamstress make new frocks

for Agatha and Marie? Perhaps as a gesture of kindness and a form of repayment as I didn't make good on your wager.' He shrugged.

'I really do like Agatha… Almost as much as those pearls she has.'

'Be magnanimous.'

'Very well.' She put a hand to her temple. 'I must do the right thing sometimes, and I'll not raise a fuss. Just watch out for the wall weed. She would not be an asset to the family.'

'Yes, she does have a habit of letting people lead her astray with explosions.'

She shook her head. 'I know. I know… The girl is a little too amiable for her own good. That's another thing about her I don't like. She is so agreeable. Hard to get a cross word out of her. Never know what she's really thinking.'

His grandmother's lips and pupils were barely visible because she scowled so deeply. She waved him away.

'Oh, go ahead and invite Agatha and Marie if you wish. The jest is on you. The other ladies will make her look dreadful by comparison. And even if you put a new dress on a turnip, it's still a turnip. I'll see that they dress appropriately, if it is possible. Just because they're my friends.' Her eyes looked decidedly unpleasant as she closed one. 'But if I go along with your clothing ideas, you must have my harp put out at the picnic.'

He sighed. 'If you insist.'

'It's really not fair to her,' she said.

'The harp?' he asked, stopping.

'No,' she snapped. 'Your noticing Marie. You're not one to keep the same woman on your arm for long.'

'The picnic isn't about Marie. It is simply an occasion to invite my friends.'

'If you say so,' his grandmother said. She let out a cross between a sigh and a curse. 'You've always been a protector. Always. Now you're trying to protect Marie and… Well, I'm certain you don't know everything about her.'

'Are you going to tell me what it is you know that I don't?'

She pressed her teeth together for a moment. 'At some point I'll probably tell you everything.'

'You should keep some secrets, Grandmother.'

'We'll see.'

His grandmother was partially right, he thought as he left the room, but only partially. He had tried courting many lovely women, and could often be utterly fascinated by one, and then his attention waned.

The one time he had seriously considered marriage it had been to Rosalind, who was perfect at all social functions. She'd been groomed to be the bride of someone in society, and he'd sat at many dinners listening to tales of what her newest niece had done, or a new horse that had been added to her stables, or how wonderfully delicious the pheasant tasted—or the soup, or the duck, or the wine, or the potatoes. But no matter how 'truly wonderfully delicious' everything tasted, boredom had been the main course on his menu.

Marie was almost the exact opposite of Rosalind, and he wondered if that was what had caused him to notice her. She had been unfamiliar with attending a soiree. Uncomfortable.

He didn't want another occasion where she would not

fit in. He wanted her to feel at ease during the picnic. He would make certain she did.

In his room, he found the drawing he'd left Marie in order to fetch, and put it in his coat pocket. It was little more than a few lines of a sketch, but the swing Henry had created would be a nice addition to the garden.

Just as Marie was a nice addition, he thought, when he stepped outside and saw her talking intently with the gardener.

When she spotted him, and returned to his side, he showed her the picture, and watched as she compared it to the finished swing and complimented the gardener.

Then he took her back towards the house.

'Will you let my grandmother's maid arrange your hair on the day of the picnic?' he asked.

'I could not.' She touched the escaping wisps. 'I'm sure she keeps her servants very busy before any event.'

'Grandmother will be distracted by her harp. She likes it placed just so, and I will instruct the servants to have plenty of problems that will keep her occupied.'

He barely paused in speaking, not giving her time for a rebuttal.

'We should all try new things from time to time, I suppose. I will be having some new clothing made. Including a shorter cravat.'

He gave a bow, and then left before he could get into a disagreement.

'Wait,' he heard her call out.

When he turned he saw she'd stepped into the corridor, pulling the door shut behind her. They were alone.

'I wanted to thank you. It's very kind of you to let us stay. To watch over us. But please don't be disappointed if

I am not at ease among your guests. I am not accomplished at the finer points of conversation.'

'You don't have to be. This is a picnic. A chance to enjoy the day, the sunshine and the life at our fingertips.'

He took her hand, clasping it, and it seemed he felt the sun's rays shine upon him from within her eyes.

'You don't have to say or do anything—just relax and enjoy yourself.' He held her hand between them. 'Just this once, take in the day and see what it feels like to have fun in life. When you look in the mirror before the picnic begins I want you to see someone comfortable in society smiling back at you.'

'No matter what I wear, I'll still be the same Marie,' she said.

'Just as I'm the same man without the loops in my cravat? It might not be as hard as you think to change old habits,' he said. He placed a soft kiss on her knuckles before releasing her hand. 'And it can be worth it.'

He told himself he was doing this for Marie, because he'd seen the joy in her face after the waltz and wanted to give her a chance to have the same attention that the other ladies did. To see what it was like not to hide away.

But he wasn't sure he was telling himself the whole truth.

Chapter Eight

Something felt off to him. But it wasn't the game.

He put his cards on the table in front of him. Pierce had inherited their grandmother's love for gambling and had won this hand, but overall Gabriel had done well.

The clock struck midnight—a signal to the other men that it was time to end the game. They pushed back their chairs, bade Gabriel and Pierce goodbye, and left, clapping each other on the back and jesting about their wins and losses as they moved out through the door.

Gabriel didn't rise, but interlaced his fingers, put them on the back of his neck, and stretched. His carriage driver would have returned to collect him, but he wasn't ready to leave. The house would be so quiet upon his return. Perfect for sleeping. But too quiet.

'Getting older, old man?' Pierce asked.

Gabriel peered through half-open eyes. 'Yes. By the way, you're invited to my house for a picnic Saturday next. In fact, I insist you attend.'

'Is Grandmother going to play her harp?'

'Of course.'

He purposely didn't tell Pierce that she had ordered a toga, because she was going to present her compositions dedicated to Ancient Greece.

Pierce appeared to have swallowed something bitter. 'Oh.' But then he smiled. 'I'm sure you'll have a lot of marriageable ladies present.'

'Probably not.'

'What?' Pierce said. 'What is the use of having an event if you do not provide the best decorations?'

'The ladies are not decorations, and I'm not going to invite the usual set.'

'Well, Grandmother won't like that. She already thinks you are neglectful in your marriage duties. She blames your mother for that.' He fought a smile, but it emerged with a chuckle. 'Has she given you the names yet?'

'I know the ladies she has decided I am to choose from.'

'Not those names.' Pierce snorted in laughter. 'She's thinking of names for your future children. Thinks it is too important to be left until the last moment.'

'I'm too tired to kick the legs out from under your chair,' Gabriel told him.

'And I'm just tired enough that I'd fall.' Pierce sighed, collecting the cards, shuffling them, and straightening the edges, tapping them carefully into place after he put the deck on the table.

'Everyone has left earlier than you, which is unusual,' Pierce said. 'Nor did as many people show up for the card game as I expected. Did you notice…?'

'That it didn't seem the same without Robertson and Egleston?' Gabriel completed the sentence for him. 'Yes.'

Robertson was on his wedding trip and Egleston was so deeply besotted with his new beloved that he was most likely with her.

'Better them than us,' Pierce said, but he glanced up

with hesitation in his eyes. Then he yawned, and gave a half-laugh. 'So damn hard to feel sorry for them right now.'

'Give yourself a good night's sleep,' Gabriel said.

Pierce patted his waistcoat, a smile appearing and fading. 'I hate it that my friends are missing out on all the enjoyment.'

'I have said you're welcome to come to the picnic.'

Pierce snorted. 'I'm not sure I'm ready to settle into the tedium of picnics.' Then his eyes shone, and he leaned back in his chair, bouncing the front two legs off the floor. 'But if I'm awake I might stop by.'

'Oh, don't bother,' Gabriel said. 'It will just be harp music, lemon drinks in the garden. And maybe an archery contest.'

Pierce coughed, and the legs of his chair thumped down again. 'You are making this sound entirely too dreary. I may drop by just to see what you're up to.'

Gabriel laughed, rose, and strode out through the door.

The fresh night air hit his face as he stepped outside and his groom hopped down to open the carriage door,

Gabriel leaped inside the carriage, getting comfortable while the groom returned to his perch.

Card games were not the excitement that they'd used to be, but perhaps that was because his friends had aged and the tales of their tomfoolery had tamed somewhat—or he'd just became so used to them that they weren't fresh any more.

He pulled down the shade, crossed his arms, leaned into the corner of the carriage so he could stretch his legs to the opposite side, and closed his eyes.

He tried to sleep but he couldn't. He could only think

of Marie. Her spectacles and smile. The woman he saw beneath the severe exterior.

And suddenly he didn't want to sleep any more. He wanted to stay awake and think of her. And he wanted to rush home. To her. Only he wasn't rushing to her, but to his own bed. Alone.

The carriage stopped and he jumped from the steps, seeing his house loom before him, the same towering expanse he'd seen his whole life.

He looked up to the windows of the room his parents had once shared before his mother had decided that her parents needed her more. She'd left a long time before his father died, and nothing had really changed except his father had been home less. He'd had no reason to pretend he believed himself married any more.

True, his mother and father had come together for important events, but that had been dramatic. He'd grown to hate them being together. Separately, his father had been genial, charming and charismatic. Alone, his mother was thoughtful, discerning and caring.

Together, each had been capable of smiling while they struck out at each other with soft-spoken jabs designed to draw blood. Marriage had turned them into gladiators, fighting to the mental death.

Marie sat in the chair, biting her bottom lip, afraid that Gabriel's grandmother would return from checking on her harp and become upset that her maid was brushing Marie's hair.

She didn't like anyone else arranging her hair because the woman who'd taken care of her while she was growing up had always used it as an excuse to pull it. When the woman had decided it was time for Marie to wear her hair up, she'd grabbed her by the braids, sat her in a chair, undone the braids and pulled her hair up into a knot above Marie's head, given it a few tight twists that had nearly lifted her out of the chair, and stuck pins almost through her skin, telling Marie that this was how she'd best wear it from now on.

Agatha had appeared from time to time, bringing with her a much softer touch. She'd been sent by her employer so the woman's husband would not know about the child his wife had secretly borne long before they'd wed. Supposedly Marie's true father had died before even knowing she was on the way, and his parents had called her mother a liar. Her mother's parents had been equally unkind, according to Agatha, so Agatha had helped conceal Marie and had become a friend to her as she grew. Agatha might not be her true aunt, but she'd cared for Marie as if she were.

This time, however, the process didn't seem to take very long, and it didn't hurt. In only seconds the maid had put up a loose knot—so loose that Marie wasn't certain it would stay in place. Then she gave a few snips to the hair she'd left free, and fashioned some curls to frame Marie's face. The woman added some delicately scented pomade, and then stood back to let Marie look in the mirror.

'Oh, she's not finished yet,' Aunt Agatha said, stopping Marie from seeing her reflection and presenting her with a tiny case.

She looked inside to find some cosmetics. The maid whisked the case from her aunt's hands and insisted she would be best to apply it.

Marie looked at her aunt. 'You shouldn't have.'

Instantly, she knew when her aunt had purchased it—

while Myrtle's seamstress had been fussing over her she'd left them.

She met her aunt's eyes and frowned. 'You *really* shouldn't have.'

Her aunt shrugged and looked away. 'That's your opinion. I spoke with Gabriel and asked if his grandmother would mind if I added a few incidentals to the cost of the dresses, and he said most certainly not. I told him our wager was paid in full.'

Marie looked at her hands, clasped in her lap. She didn't want the wager to be fulfilled. It connected her to Gabriel and united them against the two older ladies' machinations. It wasn't that she'd expected him to honour the terms of the wager, but she would remember that waltz for ever. Perhaps it hadn't been perfect, but it would be perfect in her memory.

When the maid had finished, Marie studied herself in the mirror. A stranger stared at her—albeit one wearing her spectacles. She was a society woman with a beaming aunt looking on.

She didn't recognise herself.

She could not become accustomed to this. She was going to have to make her own way in the world, and the woman she saw looking back at her now would never be hired to work for others. She would provoke unwanted attention from the men of the household.

She forced herself not to run for her old clothing. For just this one day she could pretend. One day. She would enjoy the picnic.

Marie wanted to discover Gabriel's opinion of the changes in her, but she refused to search him out.

Chapter Nine

A few tables had been collected from the house and were now spread under the shade of the trees. The gardens appeared just as Gabriel wanted. The swing was sturdy, and his grandmother was sitting on it, using her feet just enough to give it a side-to-side movement. Her toga flowed gracefully, and the matching band around her head sported a few dangling jewels. Her harp had been given a small platform where it rested serenely, unaware of the beating it was about to receive.

His grandmother didn't care if the harp was considered something relegated to the lower classes. She enjoyed any opportunity to play it, and woe to anyone who might take a seat at the strings.

The soft scent of the rose bushes filled the air, mixing with a hint of smoke from the kitchen chimney. On the side away from the house a coiled rope target was in place, along with the quivers of arrows he and Pierce used to practice.

An older couple walked over to speak with his grandmother, and two of the men he'd made sure would arrive early stood by the table, its cloth billowing softly.

Pierce walked up to him. 'I'm not late this time. But where are Rosalind, Rebecca, Annabelle and Roberta?'

'My butler took care of the invitations. Not Grandmother.'

Pierce scowled. 'I should have known something was awry. For you any leisure activities are not about enjoyment, but results. You hardly care about gambling—you just want to keep abreast of other people's views.'

'If you are called away early I will survive,' Gabriel said. 'I only invited you because I had a momentary lapse in sense and was afraid I'd ordered too much food.'

'It appears you've provided enough for me, but are the others going to have anything?' Pierce indicated the relaxed group milling about, then gave a low whistle. 'Who is that?' he asked.

From the corner of his eye, Gabriel saw Pierce straightening his cravat.

'It is nice to see a new face. Who *is* that lovely woman?'

Gabriel turned to the woman and hesitated for a moment.

Marie.

Warring emotions battled within him.

Only it wasn't her. It was as if a society beauty had taken her place, and he found he was angry that this woman was there in her stead. He had caused the change, yet he found he wanted to see the old Marie.

Behind her spectacles he could still glimpse her, but he missed the way she'd looked before.

He spoke her name softly as she walked towards them. 'Marie… I would like you to meet my cousin Pierce.'

'Marie?' Pierce gasped her name loudly, and Gabriel turned in time to see her smile.

Pierce moved ahead, his vision locked on Marie.

'Gabriel did tell me I would not want to miss this picnic,

and I can see why,' Pierce said, before giving an elegant sweep of his free arm to indicate the refreshments. 'I'll fetch a glass of lemonade for you.'

Gabriel didn't hide the warning in his voice. 'Best be good, cousin.'

'Always.' Pierce gave an apologetic glance at Marie and shrugged his shoulders. He bowed his head and used his fingertips to rub his temple. 'Sadly, it's when I can't be good that I'm at my best.'

Gabriel groaned, and Pierce smiled before walking with her to the refreshment table.

Gabriel decided it had been a mistake to invite his cousin.

Then Lord Epperson and Foster Elway arrived and greeted him, and in the same instant he saw them both notice Marie.

'Who's that?' Epperson asked.

'Miss Marie,' Gabriel answered, seeing the wheels turning behind Epperson's eyes. 'Lady Andrews' niece.'

'We must make certain Pierce doesn't monopolise her,' Elway said.

'Epperson… Elway…' his grandmother said, walking up to them. 'Help me see if the harp is in tune.'

They both walked away, although neither looked where he was going, both sets of eyes still firmly on Marie.

Someone else stopped at his side, and he turned to see Agatha smiling at him.

'That was wonderful planning,' she whispered. 'I didn't grasp what you were thinking when you suggested these changes for Marie, but now I see that you are making sure she receives notice. How thoughtful of you.'

'Thank you.' He clamped his jaw.

'And you have invited Elway and Lord Epperson. It will

be wonderful to see what they think of Marie, as they are of marriageable age and mind.'

He'd not been thinking properly. He'd wanted Marie to be flattered, not devoured, and now the poor woman would probably be overwhelmed by all the attention.

'Epperson's low on funds, and Elway thinks himself much better than he is.'

'Thank you for reminding me—as I reminded you of the flaws in the ladies your grandmother invited to her soiree. But they're both kind men, and Marie would make a wonderful match for either of them.'

Agatha squeezed his arm, beaming at him.

'Marie will be receiving more than one invitation to go on a carriage ride, perhaps to the theatre.'

Gabriel smiled, and extracted himself from her grasp. 'I'm sure she will receive a lot of notice today.'

'Oh, and your sweet cousin is watching over her.' She studied him. 'I think Marie has met him several times, when he and my husband's nephew were traipsing here and there. I wonder if something is developing between them?'

'That's just his *modus operandi*.'

'That's Latin, isn't it?' she asked.

'Yes. It means he's always developing something somewhere with some woman.'

'Of course Marie is such a doting niece that I would hate to lose her to marriage. But if Pierce asked, I would understand. Because he is…' She shut her eyes briefly, smiled, and took in a deep breath. 'Not entirely unsuitable.'

'Yes. He has a winning smile, a way with words and a good tailor.'

Still dreamy-eyed, she answered, 'You do understand?'

'Marie would be better off with the tailor,' he mumbled under his breath.

Marie's aunt laughed. 'I didn't know you were such a jester.'

He didn't answer, but walked with her to Marie's side, where Pierce was talking, raising his hands, laughing, and commanding everyone's attention.

Then he heard the plink-plink-plink of several harp strings, and a few discordant notes as his grandmother tested her strength.

'And a glass for you, Lady Andrews.' Pierce gave Agatha the glass of wine a servant had poured, and then collected two more, for Gabriel and himself.

'It's a beautiful day,' Pierce said; staring at Marie.

'Isn't it?' her aunt said, trying to pull Gabriel away with her when she took a step.

He didn't budge.

Lady Andrews nudged him. 'We should go and see what your grandmother is going to play for us.'

He gave a warning glance at Pierce, and then followed Lady Andrews to his grandmother.

He spoke with them both, sharing idle chatter, but as he did, he turned slightly so that he could keep his eye on Pierce. Not that Pierce would try anything inappropriate or do anything questionable, but it wouldn't hurt to keep his attention on his cousin.

But then he realised he was lying to himself. It wasn't Pierce he was watching. It was Marie.

Then the music started and the conversation slowed, but the eyes on Marie didn't. He stood close enough to hear Pierce's comments to her during the pauses in the music.

So much praise for everything—from the beautiful harp to the lovely tendrils of her hair.

Gabriel smiled on the outside and cursed on the inside. He should never have considered suggesting his grandmother's maid help Marie with her preparations for the picnic, nor involved his grandmother in providing a seamstress for her.

Gone were the old-fashioned bits of cloth that had overwhelmed and swallowed her. This simple but perfect dress suited her, and made her appear anything but plain.

Epperson and Elway did not leave Marie's side, which he'd expected, but he'd not foreseen how it would irritate him.

The music stopped, and Pierce complimented his grandmother, then he saw Elway and Lord Epperson argue over who would get Marie her next refreshment.

Marie didn't have to worry about her conversational skills. She only had to stand there, nod, sip and smile. All the men were competing over who could garner her attention.

'Do you like archery?' Pierce asked her after she'd finished her drink. He bowed over the empty glass as he took it from her.

'I've never tried it,' she said.

In unison, all three men gave different responses.

'A shame.'

'You simply must.'

'I can't believe it.'

'We will be happy to assist you. I'm sure you're a natural,' Pierce suggested.

With the three men egging her on, Marie had no choice but to go with them to the bows and arrows. An umbrella stand had been taken from the house to use as a holder for the quivers, and three bows leaned against the target.

Pierce took one bow to Marie, another for himself, and Epperson grabbed the last one.

All three men were more than happy to assist Marie with her aim. It was indeed fortunate he'd invited men so interested in archery and so courteous, Gabriel thought wryly.

She took aim and shot, and her arrow hit the target but didn't get close to the centre. The men cheered. No one had ever got so much praise for such an errant arrow. Twice more she shot, the arrows once again going over the target, and they all commiserated, telling her that they had also had similar bad luck when they were learning.

Gabriel hadn't created a monster but he had unleashed one inside him—jealousy. The picnic had lost its lustre. And so had all the changes he'd instigated. He touched the one loop of his cravat and tried not to watch all the attention that was being showered upon Marie.

It irritated him that these men likely wouldn't even have noticed her in the ugly dresses. Although perhaps they would have. He wasn't sure…

Marie had taken a step back, and now Epperson was standing entirely too close to her for Gabriel's liking.

In a few quick strides Gabriel had closed the distance between them and inserted himself ever so slightly between her and Epperson, taking the archery bow from his friend.

Epperson stepped away.

Gabriel had not meant to put himself in the game, but once he'd seen Epperson so close to her, his feet had taken over.

'Care to shoot against me?' Gabriel asked her, taking an arrow from the quiver.

'You only say that because you have seen how untrained I am.'

Elway gave her an arrow and a warning. 'Gabriel's as good as Pierce. Their mothers started them with archery early, though she had to train them separately as soon as they realised they could injure each other with the arrows.'

'Perhaps you will be fortunate,' Gabriel said.

'It will not be a challenge for you,' she answered.

'Let's make a wager,' he said.

Her head tilted and her smile was whimsical. 'You saw how badly I am aiming.'

He nocked his arrow, placed his feet, and looked at her. 'If I hit the centre, consider it a marriage proposal.'

'Whoa…' Pierce said, stepping back. 'Gabriel has upped the ante.'

He pulled back the string, and no one moved but him. He let the arrow fly.

It was a little off the mark, but not much.

'If I were you, Marie, I'd take it as a complete miss,' Pierce said, and propped the end of his bow on the ground while he peered at the target.

'Let me try,' Epperson said, but Gabriel would not release the bow.

Marie stared at the arrowhead. So close to the centre. She turned to him, questioning him, wondering if he had missed by accident or on purpose.

She could tell nothing from his expression.

'If you hit closer to the centre than I, we will take it as a yes to my proposal. Or anywhere in the first two coils, let's say.'

Gabriel looked as if he were doing nothing more important than making an observation on the weather.

'Anywhere else is a no.'

'Anyone can have a lucky shot and hit the middle.' She bit her lips, studied the target. 'But you're on.'

She aimed, took a breath, and paused. She wondered how serious Gabriel was, and if she should sincerely try to hit the centre. But it didn't matter. She knew her chances of hitting the target were low—and even if she could do it, marriage was a farce. She didn't want to go through anything like that.

Still, she couldn't help rising to his challenge. She aimed for the centre, steadied herself, pursed her lips, and released the string. The arrow thumped into the last coil.

'I was right,' he said. 'You are hiding a great skill.'

'You could see the terror in her eyes,' Pierce said. 'She was afraid she'd hit the centre.'

'Try again,' Pierce said. 'I'm still proposing. And if you hit the target at all, we'll be married by Special Licence.'

She nocked her arrow, and this time tilted the bow. The arrow whooshed past the target and hit the ground behind it. She could not risk getting closer.

'Whoo!' Pierce said, jumping back. 'Who's next?'

'Not risking that,' Elway said. 'If she doesn't get us with the arrow, she might get us with the bow.'

The men chuckled.

Gabriel retrieved her arrow from behind the target, his from near the centre, and then hers from the last coil.

His lips turned up as he saluted her, tapping the wood of the bow against his forehead.

'That's all for me,' Gabriel said, handing his bow and

two of the arrows to Elway. 'I've been unfortunate enough for one day.'

'And I don't think I should risk hitting one of the guests,' she said, giving her own bow and arrow to Epperson.

Pierce looked at Epperson and Elway. 'Drinks next time at White's are on the loser. You men ready for a challenge?'

Gabriel left them to their game, and Marie followed him.

'I am getting more attention than I have ever received before,' she said. 'You certainly know how to manoeuvre a picnic.'

He glanced over at her, letting her eyes catch his, and bumped up his brows in agreement before he returned his eyes to the harp, even though awareness of her consumed his thoughts.

'You're the one who has made this an event,' he said. 'You're stunning.'

It was true, and yet he found the words took all his breath.

'Thank you very much. But this is just for one time,' she said.

The wistfulness in her voice threw an arrow shaft into him.

'And I don't know that the men would be so fascinated if not for the changes.' She touched the frames of her glasses. 'They've each said that it's my spectacles that intrigue them. I've never heard that before.' She took them off and stared at the lenses. 'I'd hate to think that they would not be so fascinated with me if not for—'

'Everyone wants to be attractive.'

'"Attractive" is in the eye of the beholder, and I haven't changed that much. I'm me—just with more costly clothing and cosmetics.' She fluffed the curls framing her face. 'I do like my hair, though. And I thank you so very much for the new dress.' Then she twirled around. 'But this is more *not* me than it is me.' She ran her fingers over the line of the bodice. 'I don't know what it is, exactly, but this is not how I see myself. It's confining.'

'Do you see yourself in those older, worn dresses?'

'They suit me more than this. I have to walk carefully in this gown. Small, ladylike steps. And if I am in a hurry I have to pull up the skirt to make more room for my legs, and it feels improper.'

'Not one of the men here would complain,' he said.

'Because they're courteous,' she said. 'I'm a person who needs to have more cloth. The seamstress promised me that I would like it, and I didn't have the heart to tell her it doesn't suit me. Do not get me wrong—I do like it. In fact, I adore it. But I could not sit about on a bench for hours in it. Or traipse through a woodland.'

'It suits you. Ask any of the men here.'

She looked at her feet, then at him. 'Are you playing matchmaker?' she asked, putting a hand over her heart, blinking her eyes as if to hold back tears.

'Perhaps I was at first,' he said. 'But not one of those men deserves you.'

Her face relaxed. 'They're all very kind. It doesn't matter, though. I'm not myself today. I do feel like I belong,' she continued, 'but the men are only giving me attention because I'm the only woman here near their age.'

'That's not the reason they're admiring you. I dare you to look in the cheval mirror in my grandmother's room and not note how beautiful you appear.'

She shrugged away his words. 'I would have expected

you to invite Rosalind. Your grandmother has told me the two of you are practically betrothed.'

'I'll let you in on a secret. *She* is practically betrothed—but not to me.'

'Why haven't you wed? Are you not anxious to produce heirs and so on?'

'It's a tough step to take,' he said. 'Marriage causes so much upheaval, and it can turn even the most well-ordered house into a shambles within. I know it's past time for me to provide an heir, and I'd really thought to ask Rosalind, but when I had to decide I knew I would not be marrying her.'

Rosalind would have been the perfect woman to be his wife. To produce heirs. She came from the right kind of family. Had the right manners. And he liked the way she sometimes wore a little flower tucked in her hair. But still…

He remembered when they were children, and Rosalind had carefully minded her steps around even the smallest puddle. Solemnly walking precisely behind her father, never rushing to catch up after avoiding a puddle, but calling out softly, 'Please wait…' when a particularly large area of mud was in front of her.

'Can't you walk closer to me?' her father had always asked.

'But your boots might splash me, dearest Father,' she'd answered, peering up, a smile in her voice.

'And we can't have that', he'd replied, tapping the carefully secured plait that had been set upon her head like a royal crown.

And with shoulders and chin high she'd continued on.

Years later, she hadn't changed, and she was perfect

for marriage. Perfect, but she took too damn long crossing a road.

'I keep giving myself excuses as to why I haven't wed, and I know time is forcing me into it,' he said. 'But when I knew I had to make a choice between marriage or letting Rosalind go I found I wasn't willing to take that step,' he said. 'It all boils down to the fact that marriage causes either boredom or upheaval. I would be bored because the woman has no mind of her own, or I would be upset because she does have a mind of her own.'

'Your grandmother describes your mother as having bored your father, and herself as never boring anyone.'

'True. But perhaps Grandmother is settling down now that she's getting older.'

Marie gave a tiny shiver.

'You should have a wrap. I can send someone for your shawl.'

She frowned. 'My shawl doesn't match this dress at all. But it's so warm and cosy.'

He imagined her, snug in it, with a happy smile on her face. Comforted. Alluring in her own way.

He raised a hand to summon a servant. 'I'll send someone—'

'No,' she whispered, and he dropped his arm.

He found he wanted to see her wrapped in it—because she was cold, he told himself. Not because he hoped it might discourage the other men at the picnic.

Perhaps he would fetch it for her later and they could sit on his sofa, talking as the day turned into night and the night turned into morning…

Blast! He knew he should not be giving her so much notice. He'd invited these men in an attempt to garner attention for her, and perhaps somewhat to play matchmaker so as to reduce the risk to himself.

He'd never been one to have mindless dalliances. He'd been faithful to each woman he'd had a romance with. And yet, no matter how much promise each one had started with, the romance had always turned sour before entering its second year.

He remembered a most polite but vitriolic carriage ride with his parents, during which they'd had a conversation as if he weren't there. His father had stated to his mother that he didn't understand why she was complaining because he'd never kept any woman in his life—except her—for more than a year. And then his mother had enumerated the many ways in which that made him a failure as a man.

He'd not believed it—his mother arguing with his father and taking him to task over how short-lived his romances were.

He had to acknowledge now that she had had a point.

When Gabriel had matured, he'd noticed his own attentions had wavered just as his father's had. But he'd made certain not to bring a wife into the equation. He refused to make any woman as unhappy as his father had made his mother.

Sitting in a carriage with Marie and realising his attention had waned would be unforgivable, and he would not do that to her.

He tensed. His thoughts had taken a gallop, running astray, and he felt as though he'd been bucked to the ground and trodden upon.

'That is what my aunt said. I could hardly believe my ears. What do you think?'

He'd been lost. Completely. 'I believe I think exactly as you do on that.'

Her face lit with happiness. 'Thank you. That's very kind.'

'Any time.' He didn't care much what he'd agreed to, because the happiness on her face put the same feeling inside him.

Then she studied him. 'As I suspected, you're still elegant, even without the extra flourishes on your cravat.' She smiled. 'It makes you look younger, as well. Dare I say boyish?' she asked.

Plain words—and yet they did make him feel like a youth.

'Thank you.'

'I wouldn't say it if it weren't true.'

Then Elway walked up to them and asked if she would be so kind as to go with him on a carriage ride the next day. Within seconds, they were surrounded by Epperson and Pierce.

Epperson challenged her to another test of her archery skills and Gabriel noticed something flicker in her gaze. He hoped it was a little dismay.

'Of course,' she said.

Afterwards, she wandered to a tree, inspecting a nest with all three men. Pierce commented loudly on the beauty of the birds.

His grandmother walked up to him. 'Stop looking at her,' she mumbled under her breath. 'I don't know what has happened. She doesn't look like a wall weed now.'

'Please lower your voice,' Gabriel said. 'I'm making sure Pierce behaves.'

'She's not so pathetic as I thought,' she grumbled. 'But I still say she's at least twenty-five. Still, she might make a good wife for Pierce. He needs a woman to settle him.'

Gabriel's head jerked sideways and he stared at his grandmother. She was studying Pierce, with a hawk's determination in her stare. Then she gave a slow blink, ready to swoop. 'I'll invite him to tea tomorrow.'

'She's going on a carriage ride with Elway.'

'Blast,' she said. 'Well, he'll have to stop by after that.' She crossed her arms, hands tight. 'I think I'll chaperon on that ride with Elway. I'd best not let Agatha know. I'll just invite myself after Elway arrives.' She chortled. 'There's more than one way to be a good grandmother.'

Off she went, with a compassionate, gentle smile on her face, and she moved straight to Marie, inserting herself into the group so that the only man standing close to Marie was Pierce. When Elway and Epperson moved, so did his grandmother.

Marie didn't seem to know what was happening, but she appeared radiant.

He'd known there was a beauty hiding under the tight knot of hair, the hideous dresses and the decrepit shawl.

Sometimes it didn't pay to be correct.

Chapter Ten

H‍e now understood why his grandmother put away the libations and sent her friends on their way at the end of her gatherings. Pierce, Elway and Epperson could not seem to tear themselves from Marie, even though everyone else except for her aunt, his grandmother and a few servants had already left.

Finally, his grandmother managed to wrap one hand around Elway's arm and one around Epperson's and lead them towards their carriages. It appeared to him that she would have tugged them each by the ear if they'd resisted.

Gabriel strolled next to Marie, giving her a respite from Pierce's ramblings about the beauty of swans and how Marie reminded him of one.

Gabriel stared at his swan-sotted cousin. 'It appears that everyone is leaving.'

Pierce would likely want to spend the night if he found out Marie and her aunt were staying with his grandmother.

'Ah, yes.' Pierce's head swivelled around. 'I was enjoying speaking with Marie so much I didn't notice.'

Then he spotted her aunt. 'Would you two lovely ladies like a ride home in my carriage?' Pierce asked.

'We're—'

'That's already taken care of,' Gabriel said.

'I'm sure,' Pierce said, his eyes meeting Gabriel's.

Finally, Pierce gave her a longing glance, bade them all farewell and said he hoped to see them again soon. Of course, Gabriel noted, he was gazing directly at Marie when he said that.

'Oh, it's been so nice since your grandmother invited us to stay here,' Lady Agatha said. 'You will find us on the side of the house where she has her own entrance.'

'Wonderful,' Pierce said, straightening his cravat. 'How fortuitous that I'd been planning to visit Grandmother more.'

'Yes.' His grandmother stepped up beside him. 'He is so devoted to me... I don't know what I would do without him.'

Pierce took his grandmother's hand and gave her a caring glance. 'I'll visit again tomorrow, Grandmother dear.'

'I'll look forward to seeing you,' his grandmother answered, 'as you always brighten my day. I'm so fortunate to have a grandson like you. And I do like it when you stop by the confectionery shop on the way here...'

'Of course.' Pierce winked at her and then strolled away, all but twirling his hat.

'Ah...' Lady Andrews smiled. 'Such a nice young man.'

'Perfect,' his grandmother answered. 'Mostly...' she added more softly. 'And he would make such a good... um...husband for the right woman.'

'Or an even better one for the wrong woman,' Gabriel said. 'If his actions are to be taken into consideration.'

'The right woman.'

His grandmother corrected him with a stare. Then her lids rose, as if a thought had just occurred to her, although to Gabriel's eye she overacted a bit.

'Someone like Marie.'

'Oh, they would be perfect together,' Lady Agatha said.

Gabriel could almost feel it when Marie's eyes darted to him, but he kept his face devoid of expression. Something must have leaked through, however, because Marie smiled.

'Please don't accept him on my behalf,' Marie said to her aunt.

'Of course not. You can do that yourself,' Lady Agatha said, as she watched Pierce's carriage roll by and they exchanged waves.

Her aunt reached out, patting Gabriel's arm after the vehicle disappeared from view.

'Our debt is more than paid in full. A picnic today. Tomorrow a carriage ride. And a visit from your cousin also. Instead of a proposal from you, perhaps there will be one to be accepted from your cousin. Indeed, you have made good on the wager many times over.'

She gave him a pat on the back of the hand as the group moved towards the archery field.

Gabriel's brows lifted, and his lips rose as well, in just the smallest acknowledgement. Then he went to the quiver and heard the arrows rustle inside.

Gabriel took one and put it in Marie's hand. 'A memento.'

'You should have been listening before, Aunt,' Marie said. 'Gabriel proposed. In front of the others.'

'He proposed?' His grandmother's voice went up two octaves. 'Gabriel?'

'Yes,' she said, 'and I refused politely.'

Her aunt squawked. Eyes open wide. 'She didn't shoot at you afterwards, did she?' She turned to her niece. 'Oh, Marie. Say you didn't.'

'I didn't,' Marie said, laughter in her eyes.

'She refused quite emphatically, though it was charming.' Gabriel put a hand over his heart. 'My first proposal. Shot down.'

Before she could chastise him, his grandmother's attention was caught on the harp being moved.

'Oh. Oh. Oh!' She ran to the servants, directing them. 'Small steps. Small steps. Be careful.'

'It would be horrible if such a beautiful instrument were broken,' Lady Agatha said, and then followed her friend into the house. 'Never to hear those melodious strains again…and again…and again.'

After the two women had left, Marie patted the arrow. 'Apparently you like to wager as much as your grandmother.'

He shrugged, turning up his palms. 'Sometimes wagers are just too tempting to ignore.'

'The picnic was enjoyable,' Marie said.

'The parts with you in it were. Elway, Epperson and Pierce, on the other hand…' He let his face tell her what he thought of them.

'They were kind,' she said, tapping the fletched end of the arrow on his shoulder.

'I tell it as I see it. By the way, Grandmother plans to be your chaperon tomorrow.'

She studied him. 'Do you think your grandmother is going to try to further a romance between Elway and myself?'

'I don't think so.'

She sighed. 'He is a nice man…'

Frowning, he held out his hand, palm down, and then tilted it back and forth several times. 'Hmm…'

'I don't think two chaperons would be a good idea.'

'Not for Elway, at least.'

He knew that would be his grandmother's plan. To disrupt any chance of a romance between Marie and her suitor so that she might become more aware of Pierce.

He studied the puffs of clouds overhead. He hated to say what he was about to say next. 'I suggest you send a note to Elway and tell him you wish to leave an hour earlier than planned. Then take a maid or your aunt with you and sneak out. I really don't think you'd want my grandmother chaperoning you.'

Marie nodded. 'She has a lot of stories to tell.'

'My earliest memory of Grandmother is when she wrapped herself up in my bedclothes and pretended to be a ghost. She jumped out to frighten me one night. She claimed she was trying to make me brave.'

'That is an unkind thing to do to a child.'

'My dog went after the ghost, which stumbled, and I attacked it with a candlestick. Luckily my father heard the uproar and saved her. He thought it was hilarious, but I'd actually hurt my grandmother. She said she'd just been playing a game with me.' He paused. 'I wasn't afraid of ghosts, but someone hiding in my bedclothes was certainly a threat. It was rough to see her black eye. She sported it for weeks. Mother wanted it added to Grandmother's portrait.'

Marie brushed her fingertips against his arm. 'I did not hear any family stories when I was growing up,' she said. 'Nor live them. At least not stories of my own family. I have little knowledge of my past.'

'What do you remember of your family?' he asked.

Marie could easily answer that honestly. 'Very little. I remember Aunt Agatha would arrive and sometimes recount to me a story about my mother.'

After she'd given funds to the lady who had cared for Marie.

'But I was too young to realise the import of that. I was more concerned with any treats she might have secreted away for me.' She ran her fingertips over the feathers on the arrow, smoothing them. 'I had to content myself with only her short visits. I couldn't live with Aunt Agatha as long as she was employed as a companion.'

Because Agatha hadn't been able to take Marie into her mother's house.

Agatha had told her later that Marie had probably been better off not living with her mother, who had been Agatha's distant cousin. She'd also once said that Lord Andrews probably wouldn't have been so cantankerous if she'd married him first. Apparently his initial marriage had thrived on conflict and made him the man he was when he entered his second union.

'When Aunt Agatha married she finally had a place for me, and she took me in.'

Marie peered over her shoulder, seeing the target, the swing, and the maids gathering up the remaining refreshments and the tablecloth. Two male servants were at hand, to whisk the tables back inside.

'I've had such good fortune,' she said, remembering the endless hours of laundry and errands she'd done for the woman who'd cared for her, knowing that not every orphan had someone to shelter them.

She'd been able to meet her aunt's society friends after moving in with Agatha—not a docile one in the group, but none as cantankerous as Gabriel's grandmother. But then Aunt Agatha's husband had complained about Marie living in his house when she should be married, and a huge disagreement had erupted—particularly because his nephew needed a wife and Marie refused to take on the job.

So Aunt Agatha had turned to her old friend Myrtle and asked for a respite until things were sorted, mentioning to her that her marriage was not the happiest.

Marie had expected her aunt's husband to come searching for them the next morning and demand they return, but he'd been quiet. That had incensed her aunt, and she'd determined to return home immediately, but Gabriel's grandmother had told her that would be playing right into his hands. That she must stay and make her point.

They'd had a fifteen-hour discussion on strategies with husbands, during which Marie had ended up feeling more empathy for her uncle than anyone else.

Her aunt had noticed how Gabriel stayed on his side of the house, and didn't seem inclined to berate the women around him, and had wondered aloud if he might make Marie a good husband.

A few days later the women had been drinking too much punch, and late that night her aunt had burst into her room to tell her the details of the winning wager.

Marie had been incensed, but she loved her aunt so much that she'd kept her ire to herself and tried to maintain her composure, knowing she would not accept any such proposal or go along with the wager in any way.

'I'm thankful that your grandmother invited us to stay,' she said now.

'I am too,' Gabriel responded.

She raised her eyes to his, surprised at the sincerity in his voice. 'Because my aunt and I keep your grandmother entertained?'

They paused while a servant went past them with the

umbrella stand and the quivers, and Marie stepped forward and put the arrow away. Then more servants bustled by, with the remainder of the picnic supplies, and they were left alone, with only a soft breeze and the scent of a neighbour's cook baking drifting over them.

'If you wish to think that, then yes.'

'I'm pleased that you've given us respite from my uncle.'

'Your uncle must surely have noticed his wife is no longer in residence.'

'I'm sure he has.'

She hoped he had not injured himself in his celebration dance.

'He should show understanding for his wife.' His voice hardened. 'It isn't that I mind your living here,' he said, 'but your aunt should be in her own house, with her own husband.'

'So she won't be experimenting with more explosions in your garden with your grandmother?' she asked.

'Explosions are never good.' He scrutinised the trees overhead, from where a shower of leaves was descending. 'Except maybe this kind.'

She reached out, dusting some flecks from his sleeve, and he stopped examining the leaves and watched her. She captured the cloth of his coat and tried to pull him closer, but instead she stumbled into his shoulder and he turned, catching her with both hands.

'Were you drinking the lemonade or the wine?' he asked.

'I was drinking in the sight of your manly cravat.'

He released her arms. 'Well, I suppose my valet will have to get used to it.' He tugged at the single loop.

'Perhaps you should continue wearing all those coils when you are out and about.'

'I've been enjoying staying at home recently, and I have just figured out the reason for that.'

'Explosions?'

'You could say that,' he said. 'But now the problem is that Pierce will be visiting more. I should not have let him know about the picnic.'

She heard all the different inflections in his tone. When he mentioned her staying it was warm, but it iced over when he spoke of Pierce. That pleased her more than she would have expected.

Having a place for her aunt to stay was important, but what made her happiest was the fact that Gabriel didn't seem to mind having them in residence.

'Your grandmother has been so gracious…and she's fascinating.'

One brow went up and he challenged her with an innocent blink of his eyes. 'Gunpowder?'

'I didn't see how such a small amount could cause such a large bang.' She ducked her head. 'It was louder and stronger than I expected.'

'That's Grandmother.'

'She's fascinating.'

'Yes. Like gunpowder.'

'True…'

'Those men were doing a terrible job when they were showing you how to shoot arrows,' he said. 'They were so busy vying for your attention that they hardly had any time to teach you how to do more than hold one. Preening peacocks.'

She laughed, and waved away his words. 'It might not have been just them. I truly am not interested in the hobby. I am much more interested in just being outdoors and in the garden.'

Standing near him emboldened her senses. Every breeze caused strands of her hair to brush her skin, and she even felt taller. Not as tall as Gabriel, but close. And he stood there so relaxed. Perfectly dressed.

In that moment she was happy that she'd worn the new dress and looked similar to society ladies. She doubted the men would have noticed her otherwise—not like Gabriel. He'd been aware of her even in the dowdy clothing.

He'd wanted to change her, though, and now she was dressed exactly as he'd planned. She suddenly didn't feel proud of herself because she'd altered her appearance.

'I appreciate the efforts you have made, and the results, but I like my old clothes and they make me how I wish to be.'

'You didn't enjoy all the attention at the picnic?'

Quiet words this time. Studied.

'It was more enjoyable than I expected, and I did have a grand time. But I like solitude even better. Routine moments.'

Every man *had* noticed her, she knew. And she'd wondered if it was because they were seeing her or just someone new.

'I like my hair freer, though,' she said, reaching up and fluffing the curls around her face. 'I do. But the clothing is more restricting.'

This experiment in her appearance was a success for her, and a learning experience in many ways.

'I would do it again, but I don't really need all the notice. I mean…' She shrugged. 'It doesn't change anything about me. I suspect it is the kind of thing that is important to others. Much more important than it is to me.'

'You are entrancing either way. A sweet nose. Big eyes behind the glasses. Long lashes. An elfin smile.'

'I've never seen an elf,' she said. 'So I am not sure if I should take that as a compliment.'

'You should. And even if I were never to compliment a thing about your appearance, your mirror should smile back at you every morning for the opportunity to see your face.'

'Silver-tongued,' she said, 'with no additional help.'

If one could be rough-edged and silver-tongued, he was. And when he chuckled softly the sound filled her with something she'd not felt ever before. She didn't dare look at him. He might be able to read her expression.

'If you enjoy gardens,' he said, 'then come with me. My neighbour's gardener is just as knowledgeable as mine, and he has different plantings. He's always working, and he can talk for hours about plants.'

She looked into his eyes and felt as if she was about to take a grand adventure, even though it was nothing more than a walk at his side. But maybe it was more than that. She had a feeling it would change her life…

She strode forward and ignored the little wound that felt like an arrow in her heart. Gabriel had been trying to find a husband for her from among his friends. That was so… Unpleasant.

He had walked on ahead of her and she put it out of her mind, hurrying to his side. He was just a friend, and his heart was in the right place. He didn't mean anything by it, and she didn't have to wed anyone anyway. Especially if these memoirs went as well as she hoped.

Chapter Eleven

'You're right,' she said, strolling with Gabriel back to his home, sniffing the small rose that his neighbour's gardener had given her. 'Between him and your gardener, they know everything there is to know about the plants they tend.'

She shook her head. When she measured herself, she realised she truly knew nothing about botany. She had thought she'd scented lilacs, or honeysuckle, but then she'd noticed huge mounds of flowering roses.

She did love nature. All the vibrancy of seeing green burst out after the rain, the feel of raindrops cooling the air in the heat of summer, and those days with her aunt at the hunting lodge had been beautiful.

'I told you about my dream of writing a book about botany,' she said, 'and you suggested I might try writing about something else. I've now decided to take your advice and give up the subject of botany. I don't know enough.'

'That doesn't mean you have to give up your love of nature.'

'True…' she muttered, watching a butterfly land on the hedge.

She didn't dare ruin the afternoon and tell him she was writing his grandmother's memoirs.

But apparently her conflicting emotions showed.

'A book about botany is surely not your only option,' he insisted, trying to reassure her. 'Perhaps a fictional story?'

'I really don't like the darkness in some of the stories everyone is reading these days,' she said. 'I suppose it has its place, but not for me.'

'Grandmother knows a publisher,' he said. 'More or less. She once threatened him with his life if he mentioned a word about the size of her derriere.' He paused. 'That might not be a route to take, though. He might bear a grudge.'

'I have made it my vow to take care of my aunt, and I will. She still has the pearls, and if we sell them it could help us get by.'

'Just don't jump into a marriage with Elway.'

She laughed. 'We're only going on a carriage ride. And he and Epperson were both nice to me. I appreciated that. You didn't tell them to do it, did you?'

'Absolutely not.' His eyes narrowed. 'I would never invite a guest whom I had to tell to be nice to someone.'

'So did you stack the deck, so to speak?' She lifted her brows. 'With marriage-minded men?'

'My cousin Pierce is not in that category.'

She shrugged. 'What about Elway and Epperson?'

'It was only an opportunity to show you how much attention you could get if you wished it.'

'I am completely happy with my plain ways and with not being noticed. This dress—' she held out the skirt with her left hand '—is nice for parties, but it isn't practical. I feel a bit like a flower in it, and I suspect the other gardener wouldn't have been so kind as to give me a rose if…' She paused. 'No. He was nice. He would have happily given me a rose even if I'd approached him wearing my serviceable clothing.'

'I'm sure he would.'

'But I don't know that Elway would have invited me on a carriage ride. And although I know Pierce somewhat, he's never noticed me as he did today. He didn't seem to re-member me at all, and yet I'm certain we've talked before.'

'Maybe that only proves he's not the sharpest arrow in the quiver,' Gabriel said, emphasising the words and mov-ing closer to her, sharing the jest.

Gabriel knew without any question that Pierce would return to see her, and that Elway would pursue her. And he knew without a doubt that Elway would propose if she gave him half a chance. He'd never been wrong when he had a feeling as strong as this. Never.

And he only had himself to thank. At least Elway was a mostly reputable man. He would not be the best hus-band in the world, but he would not be the worst, either. He would show off Marie on his arm. Happily welcome their children. Provide for Marie's aunt. She would have a respectable and comfortable place in society, and she would probably be happy.

In fact, he'd done an admirable job of being a match-maker. Only he wished he'd left it alone.

'Elway can be sullen from time to time,' he said, by way of warning.

She laughed. 'I was raised by one of the most sullen women I've ever known. I didn't try to cheer her out of her moods—I only tried not to worsen them. I don't think Elway's moods will concern me on our carriage ride.'

'I wasn't thinking about tomorrow's carriage ride but the next one, and the next one and the next one.'

'Your imagination is running amok.'

'Amok?' he said, leaning closer. 'No one has ever said anything like that to me.'

'Ah…' she said, resting the rose briefly on his sleeve. 'Perhaps it's time they did.'

He took the flower from her hand, sniffed it, and lightly ran the petals down her cheek. 'Amok…' he said. 'Perhaps it is because of you.' He returned the rose to her.

'You're jesting.'

'I wouldn't make light of something so serious.'

She turned, leading the way into the house.

His heart was taking over, and he didn't know if he would ever be the same. And he didn't know why he had so foolishly made certain to introduce Marie to eligible men.

Then she hesitated and turned back, approaching him with timid steps.

'Thank you for giving us a place to stay while we consider our future,' she said. 'Uncle has written Aunt Agatha a very hateful letter, and she was crying last night because she'd never expected him to become so vicious. He never treated his first wife this way, and Aunt Agatha can't believe he has turned against her so much.'

'I'm happy to have you here.'

He'd never had a guest like her. Someone he wanted to search out and encourage, see flourish. In the short time he'd known her she appeared to have become stronger. More self-assured. A different person from the woman he'd first seen.

'Perhaps Grandmother can give you some ideas for a story,' he said. 'She was, after all, once imaginative enough to put the bedclothes over her head and jump out at me.'

Dismay flickered behind her eyes, and he hoped hearing of his grandmother's antics didn't upset her too much.

'Just take care around Grandmother. As you know—given that she talked you into lighting that fuse—she can be persuasive,' he said. 'She causes people to do things they would not ordinarily do.'

Just as Marie had done to him. He had planned a picnic with her in mind and invited potential suitors. Only to regret it. But he didn't regret seeing Marie carefree and coveted. He was happy for her that she'd received the attention, even though jealousy simmered inside him.

He wasn't used to that. In fact, he'd never felt it before meeting Marie. At least, that was what he thought he felt. He wasn't sure. Perhaps the sun had affected him. Or the harp music. Or the reflection glinting from her spectacles.

Her stunning spectacles.

And that rose scent.

He'd never smelled a rose so beautiful. Or seen such a beautiful day.

He stood for a moment, savouring the scents, the sun and the nature around him.

The world had never seemed so alive.

After Marie had returned to her room, a maid knocked on her door, saying that Gabriel's grandmother and Marie's aunt requested her presence. They were curious to know which suitor she'd preferred.

Both women refused to believe that Marie wasn't interested in Epperson, Elway or Pierce.

'What of Gabriel?' Marie asked.

'Oh, he went to such an effort to see that other men noticed you,' Aunt Agatha said.

'True,' Myrtle added. 'He dearly cares for me—even if he hides it well. He planned for me to play for everyone, and he invited eligible bachelors. And during our discussion of the event we spoke of Rosalind. I know he didn't invite her because there were so many unwed men there.'

'True,' Aunt Agatha said. 'If he were really interested in Marie he wouldn't have invited Pierce. That man is decidedly more handsome than Gabriel.'

Pierce was decidedly *not* better looking than Gabriel. If her aunt hadn't been so dear to her, Marie would have offered her the spectacles.

'I know,' his grandmother added. 'Gabriel is the steady one. Pierce... Well, he just makes hearts flutter.'

She studied both women's faces. They were not saying this to gauge her reaction. They truly believed such nonsense.

'I would say Gabriel is better-looking than Pierce,' she ventured.

His grandmother raised her brows and then looked at Agatha. 'Does she need new spectacles?' she asked. 'I will certainly be happy to make sure she has them.'

'Oh, thank you,' Agatha said, patting her hands together. 'That would be wonderful.'

'I do not need new spectacles. I can see perfectly well with these.' She touched the frames.

Both women glanced at each other, and their mouths thinned. Then his grandmother started telling tales of her own romantic pursuits, and recalled the great number of men who'd pursued her—although she was certain her dowry had had a lot to do with that.

Her aunt chimed in occasionally, to remind Gabriel's grandmother of a suitor she'd forgotten to mention, and then the woman would be off on another tear.

Perhaps Gabriel wouldn't mind that she was writing his

grandmother's memoirs, Marie thought. She looked at her notebook, took out her pencil, and started writing notes on the stories. His grandmother wasn't only interested in lighting fuses on small amounts of gunpowder, apparently. She preferred, figuratively, to light the whole keg. Or several.

She knew she would have to tone down the tales, because no one would ever believe them. In truth, the ribald stories had shocked her, and she wondered how the older woman had acquired such an imagination. Not that she would ask. When his grandmother had started telling her about the explosion Marie had doubted it aloud, claiming it wasn't possible to do such a thing, and that had led to the demonstration. She couldn't risk that happening again.

Myrtle had been telling the truth, and if she always told the truth then she must have been a trial for Gabriel, his father and her husband.

She took a few notes and tried not to think of Gabriel. Or his reaction when he learned about the memoirs…

Chapter Twelve

'Grandmother said I'd find you here.' Gabriel walked into the room of his house in which the maids stored items no one wanted.

He'd known when Elway had arrived. Known when he'd left. And had waited, wanting to see Marie again. Particularly when he knew Pierce would likely be there in the evening.

When Gabriel hadn't been able to resist any longer, he'd searched her out.

He'd known which room to find her in when his grandmother had said she'd sent her to 'the Battle Room'. Unartistic paintings of Roman centurions adorned the walls, along with a few garish battle scenes which were mainly splotches of colour, and one costly but useless sword was propped in a corner.

Other than that, the room was furnished with two trunks, a nightstand and a crate, and various other household items.

Marie peered up from the book she was studying while sitting on the overturned crate. She was dressed in her serviceable clothing again, but her hair was still wisping around her face. The window's light shone on her, bathing her in a way that made her appear innocent—except for her eyes, which contained a whimsy he'd never seen as she peered at him from behind the spectacles.

He navigated through the doorway into the room—which must surely have only been created because of an architect's mistake.

'What are you reading?' he asked.

She held the book out to him and he opened it in the middle, revealing blank pages that smelled of dust and old paper.

'It's an abandoned journal. Your grandmother's.' She took it back and put it aside on the floor where she now knelt, dismissing it, obviously more impressed by the trunk and its odd collection of contents than by the journal. 'She sent me to look for it.'

'Blank,' he said. 'Nothing like her life.'

She reached into the trunk again. 'Interesting things inside this trunk, though. A treasure trove.'

He walked closer, his gait relaxed, wanting to stand near her. 'This is my least favourite room in the house. I always try to relegate Pierce to it when he visits, and he laughs and takes another.'

'It feels…preserved. As if no one has seen it in a long time.' She rummaged in the trunk again and held up a wooden toy. 'A little carved horse. Amazing…'

'I remember that,' he said, taking the smooth wooden toy. 'Didn't know what had happened to it. But I never played with it much. I had real ones to ride.'

'You started riding early?'

'Of course. Our country estate has stables.'

'What if you had fallen off?'

'I did. And Old Joe stepped over me. It hurt when I hit the ground, but I learned that way. Grandmother always said, "Fortunate you didn't hurt the horse." But she picked me up, dusted me off and sat me back in the saddle. Old Joe stared at me as if he couldn't believe I'd fallen off. Every time I tried to saddle him after that, he would swat at me with his tail while he moved away, or he'd place his hoof over my foot—not putting all his weight on it—as if he didn't know what he was doing. But he knew.'

'Your grandmother always said that she was glad you hadn't hurt the horse?'

'Yes. But, as I said, she always ran out, picked me up and checked me for injuries, all the while saying that a good horse couldn't be replaced, but I could. As the "spare", Pierce could get away with anything, and he spent his days and nights in revelry. Whereas I had to learn to manage the estate and could not be so rash.'

'But I know that you sometimes go out wagering with him and arrive home in the early hours.'

'Sometimes… Not long ago, while most of my friends were at the card table, I slipped away for a conversation with the Earl of Westcott. He was a good friend of my father's, and it was pleasant to hear his memories. To talk with him. Discuss views. He even told me some stories about my grandfather I didn't know.'

'That must have been so pleasant,' she said. 'All those family memories and that heritage. And learning about it.'

'Yes. Grandfather was a good man, and I have fond memories of him. He was gruff sometimes. And he hated his valet shaving him. I remember his white whiskers, always showing on his chin. His clothes had all seen better days. Except for when he went to Parliament. He might have been mistaken for a tenant on his days in the country—unless you looked into his eyes. His eyes could have carved through stone without a chisel. He was a wealthy peer and he knew it, and he made sure everyone around him did as well.'

Gabriel must have inherited his grandfather's eyes, Marie thought. She would wager on that.

He returned the toy horse to her and she carefully placed the little wooden creature back into the trunk, keeping her eye on it. And then she closed the lid, putting the latch in place and running a finger over it to remove a speck of dust.

'I haven't heard many stories of my parents,' she said. 'Aunt Agatha wasn't overly fond of my mother, even though she was her companion for years, but she has shared a few good memories. She told me about the duel with your grandmother. Is that the sword?' She pointed to the golden hilt.

'Yes. The infamous sword from the infamous duel. It's been in my family for generations. Grandmother achieved what the swordsmen of the past had kept from happening and made certain it would never again be used in combat. She nicked the blade and gave it the curve it now has.'

He lifted the sword, his hand hardly fitting under the knuckle-protecting hilt, and gave it to her.

'It's beautifully crafted,' she said.

As she touched the gold, her fingers brushed his. '

'This was the only sword in our family, and Grandmother decided she needed it.'

'I've never met anyone like her...'

He wanted to tell her that while his grandmother was truly amazing, he preferred to be with someone like her. Someone who didn't crave attention or too many wild adventures. Who liked a simpler life. A calm presence.

'I do care for her, but not for everything she does.'

'She loves talking about her adventures.'

'Far more than I enjoy finding out about them.'

He remembered his friends often raising a glass to his grandmother's antics. He'd laughed it off, because after all they were cheering her. But he'd been mortified that his grandmother relished attention so much, and could seemingly find endless ways to attract notice.

He put the sword back into the corner. He reached out a hand and Marie took it, and he lifted her to her feet. She didn't take her hand from his clasp, comforting him in his memories of all the unsettling adventures of his family's past.

'Sometimes it is best you don't have to hear the exploits of your family,' he said. 'Cherish that. The knowledge that you are making the chronicle of your own life.'

She squeezed his hand. 'You are fortunate to have a family. So much heritage. When your grandmother told me I'd find her journal here, I expected a volume filled with all the adventures she's mentioned, but it only has two entries. One is *Today I started a journal.* The other is a statement saying that she hopes whoever reads it is visited by the plague. She didn't tell me that when she sent me to fetch it.'

It seemed natural to keep standing there with her hand in his, the room surrounding them like a cloak.

'I do appreciate my heritage,' he said, but at this moment he felt more than the antiquity of his past. He could see the possibility of a future he'd not really imagined before. A partner at his side. Someone to share his life with.

He didn't think he'd ever just stood in a quiet room, holding someone's hand and feeling so connected with them. They were alone together, and that made him wonder how long the attraction would last. Perhaps she was someone with whom he might feel an attraction beyond a year.

His concept of marriage as nothing more than the union of two separate individuals who had meals and children together as they continued on with life wavered just a bit. Probably because of the silence around them.

He moved a hair's breadth closer. 'I'm sorry for the misfortune that brought you here, but I'm pleased to have you staying.'

'That is kind of you to say.'

'Not kind. Simply true.'

She squeezed his hands and leaned closer, putting the tiniest kiss on his cheek. It was as if that rose petal had brushed him again, and the softness reached deep into his heart, robbing him of speech.

'Forgive me for being forward,' she said.

He stepped away, his fingers sliding from hers. He didn't want to be close to her when next he spoke. He wanted her to understand, and to take his words lightly.

'Miss Marie.' He stood by the door and gave her a slight bow. 'You can be forward with me any time you want. I assure you I will let you know in the kindest way if I ever think you are stepping into impropriety.' Then he paused. 'It will probably be in the next day or so, but I'll let you know.' He hesitated. 'Possibly…'

He stepped to the other side of the door, closed it softly. Waiting, he examined his thoughts. He seemed to be carrying a bit of her spirit inside him. A calmness that he'd not felt before. A peacefulness.

He opened the door again. She was touching her lips, looking pensively out of the window.

'If I overstep, you must let me know as well,' he said.

Her reverie ended and she smiled. But then it faded and she swallowed, and her gaze darted downward.

'Of course.'

'What's wrong?' he asked.

'Nothing,' she said. 'I do wish to thank you for being so kind.'

She took in a deep breath, and then a deeper one. She held on to the trunk latch, her knuckles turning white.

'I want you to know that your grandmother has said she has made amends with the publisher she had the fracas with,' she said. 'She has been telling me story after story about her past, and I am writing her memoirs.'

His mouth refused to speak. And perhaps it was best that it didn't.

The wonderful feelings she'd engendered swirled into a maelstrom, spinning out of control, surrounding him and pummelling him into another kind of awareness.

He gathered his resources, giving himself a chance to consider carefully what she'd said and weigh his response even more cautiously.

Story after story about Grandmother's past? Oh, he knew full well some of the things his grandmother spoke of behind closed doors—he'd heard plenty of whispers—and it would certainly get other doors slammed if she spoke about them publicly.

To hear rumours was one thing. To see her misdeeds listed one after another in print would be damning.

The family name would be ruined.

His financial partnerships might flounder.

His mother's new beau would be offended, and the beau had a young daughter who would learn of it.

His maternal grandparents were frail, and did not need to know the sordid details of his grandmother's life.

He forced his jaw to unclench. Surely he'd misunderstood. He stepped back, his entire awareness on her face. He enunciated his words with precision.

'You are doing what?'

'Writing a book. About her experiences. Your grandmother thinks it is a grand idea. She's anticipating the chance to complete her memoirs and I am helping her.'

She bit her lip.

He heard someone in the distance. A servant moving about? Or the ghost of his father laughing?

He could not let anyone overhear this. He softened his voice.

'You cannot write about my family,' he said.

'I already am.' Her words were measured. 'Besides, it was almost your idea. You told me to write about something else.'

'Not my family.' His voice wavered in its intensity. 'Not my grandmother's life.'

The room was silent.

'I only plan to tell the exact stories your grandmother gives me.' Her voice was all innocence and light.

Oh, he could imagine that. 'I forbid it.'

She put a hand to her chest. 'You cannot do that. You will be destroying my chance of supporting my aunt and myself. My future.'

'And if you publish that book you will be destroying my family heritage. My life. I know what tales Grandmother has to tell. Other people in society will have their secrets revealed, and they will never be able to forgive that. Grandmother is already half a pariah.'

Gabriel reined himself in. He had managed to keep so many things from being discussed. His title had value, and he had power. But now she stared at him with determination.

'You can't ruin my family name,' he said softly. 'You have overstepped.'

With that, he shut the door softly.

Outside, he made two long strides towards his grandmother's room before he heard the door he'd just shut opening and pattering footsteps behind him.

She darted around him and stopped. 'Please don't be angry,' she said.

'Oh, I left anger behind quite some time ago.'

Soulful eyes studied him.

'My mother felt she had to move from Town because of Father's unfaithfulness and Grandmother's way of bringing unpleasant attention to the family,' he said. 'To have my grandmother's memoirs published will destroy my mother. She'll never feel able to come to London again. She has tried hard to shield her family from the whispers and tales, but if you write this book it won't be whispers, but fresh shouts.'

A horse neighed in the distance, the sound carrying through the open window, and a muffled command followed. Gabriel went to the window and slammed it, uncaring if he broke the glass. His hands remained clenched on the wood.

'I thought Grandmother would be a bad influence on *you*, but now I am not sure the reverse is not true.' He stared out through the window.

'I am not a bad influence on anyone. I can't be. I am always the least important person in a room. Even the maids have more say in where they go or stay and what they do in their free time. I have no employment, and I must always fit my needs with those around me. I love Aunt Agatha dearly, and I am thankful for her every day of my life. I must help her survive now.'

He released the window, relaxed his jaw, and turned to her. 'You are learning to mix your own form of gunpowder—and this is more volatile to my family than you could imagine.'

His mother and grandmother already barely tolerated each other. To bring the past into the open—a past that he had tried to protect the family from—was unthinkable. He could imagine the flare-up between his mother and his grandmother. His maternal grandparents would be aghast. And his grandmother's stories were always slanted. More like half-truths. Leaving out the parts that didn't portray her in the light she wanted.

Marie would be emphasising events that he had spent his life trying to diminish.

He calmed himself. Drew fresh air into his lungs.

He was approaching this all wrong. He needed a chance to gather his resources and consider the path to take. Besides, his grandmother had a short attention span. Short except when she was the subject of conversation.

'You must understand. I need a way to support my aunt,' Marie repeated. 'I do not want to have to depend on my uncle's largesse, and now it is as if he is waiting my aunt out. Refusing to help her financially and expecting us to return to his house and put up with his wastrel nephew destroying everything he touches.'

'Wait,' he said. He needed to tread carefully. 'I was hasty. I would not want you and your aunt to be without refuge. You are a guest of my grandmother's and that has been good for her.'

Or it had been until the blasted memoir idea had surfaced.

The eyes that stared at him were not reticent. His grandmother's influence was corrupting her. He wasn't sure he knew this woman. This Marie.

'You are keeping Grandmother mostly calm and quiet,' he said. 'She's not been asking for gambling funds. She restrained the last explosion to our gardens. The sword has stayed in its hilt...'

'I talk them both out of most of their newer ideas.'

'Don't unleash the secrets of my family's past, nor fabricated tales which will be taken as the truth.'

She responded quickly. 'I suspect you have heard most of them before.'

Oh, he suspected he had not. His friends had often asked if certain rumours were true, and it always pleased him to say he'd never heard of them before.

His words were soft, but they couldn't have been more direct. 'Have you already put pen to paper?'

Her eyes darted down and to one side too quickly. He didn't need a verbal answer.

'Will you let me read what you've written?'

'I don't know that it would be a good idea.' She went to the doorway. 'But come with me and I'll show you something I've started. You should know it anyway. It's about you.'

Gabriel wasn't smiling.

She took him into her room, and handed him the sheaf of papers on her desk.

He read of a young grandson who was almost standing on the back of the horse, letting it gallop over a stack of hay. A magnificent feat.

'She's talking about Pierce,' he said, returning the papers to her. 'Can I see the others?'

He motioned to those she hadn't given to him.

'Certainly.'

They were just a few pages of notes telling of his grandfather's proposal, and the dilemma it had caused when she would not accept or reject it. In part, because his grandfather had believed he loved someone else. She had also believed she loved someone else…but she could be a viscountess. The one thing his grandparents had agreed upon was that they wouldn't let love for others stand in the way of their union if they both decided it was in their best interests.

He read a little. Then looked at her. 'This is not true. My grandparents had a good marriage. Tumultuous, sometimes. But one with love.'

She looked at the desk, then sat down and dipped her pen, and drew a small heart on the top corner of the blank page in front of her. 'She told this to me as the truth, and she did say the marriage was wonderful.'

'You're describing him as mercenary and her as a woman only after a title. You have the facts wrong.' He held out the papers, half crumpled in his grip.

'She says this is the truth, and I believe her.'

He shook his head. 'I've not heard this before. She's embellishing.'

She stood, taking the papers back, straightening them. 'Let's ask her.'

He opened the door for her and she moved by him, suddenly aware of the masculine shaving soap he must have used, the crispness of his clothing, and the irritation on his face. Walking beside him in the corridor, she could feel his intensity, and hear it in the distinct steps he took.

After a quick rap on his grandmother's door, they went inside.

His grandmother had a small pencil in her hand. She dropped it when she saw Gabriel, and gave an overly innocent blink.

'Grandmother, Marie has told me about the memoirs.'

'Well…um…good,' she said, but she gave a quick glare to Marie. 'I have a few more things I want to cover with her.' She touched the handkerchief on her desk. 'I have just remembered a disagreement I had with my husband the morning before we were wed… We had such a row.' She laughed, lifting the handkerchief and dotting it to her eye. 'I'd just found out he didn't intend to go through with the vows, and it set me off something fierce. Particularly as we had just spent an intense night together.'

Gabriel cleared his throat. 'Grandmother. Marie is writing about you meeting Grandfather and claiming he wanted only your dowry and you the title of viscountess.'

'It's true,' she said, standing, her laughter fading.

'You've never said such a thing before.'

'Well, it's good that I'm getting it out in the open now.' She crossed her arms.

'Is it fact?' Marie asked her.

The older woman's eyes opened wide. 'Of course.' She uncrossed her arms, studied her left hand, fingers folded, and used her thumb to flick at her wedding ring. 'I fell deeply in love with the way he looked and his title. Then I fell in love with the man attached. He was in love with the nice amount he would receive from my parents, and he fell in love with the woman attached.' She studied Gabriel. 'A man doesn't find out his true worth until he is married.'

'Grandmother, that's mercenary.'

'It's not a perfect world.' She examined him. 'But you're already settled. You don't need a wife except for an heir.' She pulled a face. 'Let's not speak of that. I wouldn't want to see this conversation in my book.'

Her gaze locked on Marie.

'But Pierce does need a wife. You're much more presentable than I thought. Pierce will fall in love with you faster than a hat pin can fall to the ground. I could have everything ready for your vows just as fast. Think about it. Maids of your own. Footmen. A butler. A carriage.'

'I don't need you trying to marry me off,' Marie said, with a tiny shudder hidden in her words. 'And I don't need that kind of excitement. From what I've heard, your marriage was considered good—up to and including the time you had your husband locked in a tower with you to prove to him that the two of you were truly meant to be together.'

'What?' Gabriel's voice broke the calm.

His grandmother rolled her eyes. 'Don't act so shocked. I've not told you everything about myself. If you think back, I've hardly told you anything. You've listened to others instead, and they don't know what went on in the privacy of my home.'

'At least not yet,' Gabriel said.

'I have no secrets,' his grandmother said, scrutinising her pencil. 'Just things I've not yet mentioned. And I need a little excitement. My life has been dull lately, and having these memoirs published will give me something to talk about at social events.'

Gabriel peered heavenward and muttered something before turning to Marie.

'You cannot aid my grandmother,' he told her. 'Let her write the memoirs herself if she is so inclined. Don't put pen to paper against my family.'

'It is your grandmother's wish. And it is her story to tell.'

Gabriel's eyes narrowed, and she saw the rebuttal in them.

There was a brief knock, and Pierce opened the door and walked in. 'Grandmother… Miss Marie,' he said, giving a deep bow. Then he turned. 'Oh, Gabe. My valet is moving all my things into my room here. He saw a spider at home, and I didn't want him to live in fear, so we have come here for safety. I knew you'd be thrilled.'

Gabriel took in a deep breath.

'So, what has everyone been up to?' Pierce asked.

'Marie is writing my memoirs,' his grandmother said. 'Isn't that thoughtful of her?'

'And the pages are not bursting into flames?' Pierce asked, walking forward to bend and give his grandmother a kiss on the knot of grey hair.

'No,' Myrtle answered. 'But I wouldn't stand too close to your cousin just now. He's in a bad mood.'

'Well, that's fine. I really came to see Marie.'

Gabriel thought he heard the sound of an explosion again, but didn't say a word as left the room.

Chapter Thirteen

The house was so quiet he would have thought himself alone, but the butler would have alerted him if anyone had left.

He had to let Marie know that he had enough power in society to prevent his grandmother's story from being printed. It was unfair to let her invest time in a project that she expected to benefit from financially and would not.

According to a maid, she was were playing cards in his grandmother's rooms. Leaving his desk, he walked to the other side of the house.

Within a few moments he'd rapped on his grandmother's door and entered after she called him to come in. He wanted to see Marie, and there she was, sitting apart from everyone else, studying a piece of paper in front of her. Pierce and her aunt were playing cards with his grandmother.

A quiet, contented little domestic scene.

Marie appeared unaware that anyone had stepped into the room, so intently were her eyes focused on the paper, but he knew she was conscious of him. The pencil wavered. Then her teeth touched her bottom lip.

'It's too late for you to join us, and I know it's probably too boisterous for you,' his grandmother said, holding a hand of cards, the box for them open beside her. 'We shall stop playing.'

'It's only half past eight,' he said, standing behind his grandmother so that he could see her cards. They were dismal. No wonder she wanted to end the game.

'That's late for some of us. Particularly if we get up at first light.' She snapped her teeth together, tapped the cards, and put them face-down on the table.

Her aunt yawned, gave everyone a little wave, and then rushed from the room.

Pierce stood, pulling his coat from the back of his chair. 'I've had my carriage readied and I have pressing business to attend to.' He winked at Marie. 'I hope you can use some of the tales I've told you.' He waved, and headed for the door. 'Goodnight, all. I should return about first light.'

Gabriel forced himself to concentrate on his grandmother, the table and the room, but in truth he only saw Marie.

If he continued to tell his grandmother he didn't want Marie writing the memoirs, both women would become more determined. His grandfather had told him more than once that the quickest way to get his wife interested in something was to speak against it.

His grandmother studied him. 'Time to sleep. Goodnight, everyone.'

Gabriel gave her a nod and spoke to Marie. 'Can I have a moment of your time?'

'Blast!' his grandmother said. 'Don't worry her. It's not a good idea to get on a bad footing with her, because Pierce is going to fall in love with her and they'll probably wed—and you know how I want everyone in the family to get along.'

'I'm not going to wed Pierce,' she said.

'You will break his heart,' his grandmother said, standing. She yawned wildly and raised her arms high, then pressed a hand against her lower back. 'Oof... That was a stretch. Pleasant dreams,' she said, closing the door to her bedroom behind her.

'Would you like to continue the game?' he asked.

'The card game?' Her brow flicked up. 'I wasn't playing.'

'Perhaps you are playing. With more explosive materials than a simple fuse and gunpowder.'

She reached for the deck, but he put his hand between hers and the cards. 'Let's find a more private place.' His eyes indicated the door. 'I can assure you it's highly unlikely any conversation here will be ignored.'

He moved his hands away from the cards.

She lifted the deck and spoke softly. 'Your sitting room?'

Nodding, he stood.

He didn't speak as they walked down the corridor, forcing his mind to remain detached.

Inside his sitting room, he led Marie to a chair and helped her to be seated. He was shocked at the emotion the simple action unleashed inside him. Other than family or cousins or close friends, he'd always welcomed guests into the main sitting room. Never in his private quarters. But she didn't seem the least aware of this departure from his normal routine.

Marie reached out, took up the cards as if they were strangers to her, and shuffled, biting her lip.

'What shall we wager on?' he asked.

'Perhaps we could just play a few games for the joy of winning?' she said. Then she fumbled the cards.

He put the back of his chair against the table and straddled it. 'Deal. I know the game, and I play with viscount's rules—which means no handkerchiefs, no reticules, no hats, no mirrors, no feigned illnesses or other surprises that might alter the course of the game.' He paused. 'Did I leave anything out?'

She shuffled again, pursing her lips. 'You do make it more challenging.'

So did she. Lamplight shone around her, and although she wore one of the older, frayed dresses, it somehow merely accentuated the contrast between her beauty and the garment's dowdiness.

She didn't deal the cards as smoothly as he would have expected. It was more like the way she danced. Hesitant. Stumbling.

But she paused for a moment, raised her brows, and said, 'I feel the cards are in your favour.'

'Are they?'

'I would think so.'

And then she fumbled them again, almost dropping them onto the table.

No one had ever captured his attention with a card shuffle and a flick of the wrist the way she did. She passed out their cards slowly, deliberately, as if it were her first time.

He looked at the faces of his cards. Four aces.

'You probably should have wagered,' she said.

He examined the cards a second time, and then looked into her amused eyes. 'You're good.'

She laughed, and reached out, taking his cards and shuffling again. 'I suppose you would like a more traditional game. With the usual cards in disarray.' She turned them face-up and spread them on the table. 'When I was younger, and the stakes were high, I learned that I needed to win if I wanted to eat, so I found a way to increase my odds. I made the cards my friends. Then, after I moved in with Aunt Agatha, instead of embroidery or music or dance, we used the cards to amuse ourselves. Her husband was upset, but it was an inexpensive way to spend our time.'

Gathering the cards again, she shuffled.

'Do I need to cut the deck?' he asked.

'You don't. But I'm going to request that you do so,' she said. 'And you may shuffle every time.'

'You trust me?'

'You've apparently not played cards a large amount, and your grandmother said that she tried to teach you a few tricks and you were incensed.'

'True. Wagering usually bores me. I only play cards because otherwise I will not see my friends.'

'Perhaps the wagers aren't right for you.'

As the night lengthened their games seemed to more slowly, and became more of an afterthought to their companionship.

Finally, after a win on her part, she put the cards on the table, grabbed her pencil, and tallied the score—or tried to. He found he didn't want to see her stand, stretch, and yawn, say that she must be going. He wanted her to remain with him.

'I'm so tired I can't seem to count,' she said. 'I stayed up late last night writing, and your grandmother woke me early. You might need to check these totals.'

He moved to her side briefly and checked her figures. Except for a few scratchings-out, she'd made the correct sums.

They were tied. 'One last game?' she asked.

'No,' he said. 'I would like us to end evenly.'

'That sounds so final.'

He didn't speak at first, but then he saw the waif-like sadness in her eyes.

'Would you like to take a walk?' he asked. 'Now? In the moonlight?'

He peered out through the window. Under the stars, perhaps he could explain to her again how much it meant to him not to have his grandmother's life in print, and she'd understand and agree.

He studied her, willing her with his eyes to walk with him, to comprehend how important it was for him to remain above idle chatter and to move beyond his grandmother's misadventures.

In answer to his unasked question she leaned across the table, stopping only a fraction from his lips. He moved forward. Just enough. Their lips brushed. It was a small kiss, but it blasted through his body, giving him the feeling of being enveloped in something stronger than he was.

'We should say goodnight now,' she said. 'It's late and I'm sure you're—'

'I can fetch some wine and cheese and we can sit under the stars.' He stilled, eyes locked on her.

A fanciful smile. 'I'll be waiting. Perhaps sleeping, but I'll still be here.'

'The sofa is yours,' he said. 'And I can always wake you.'

'With a kiss?' she asked.

'If you're asleep when I return…'

He didn't want to ring for a maid, so he slipped downstairs and gathered what he needed. Talking to someone might ruin the wonderment of the night.

After he'd gathered the items, he made it back up the stairs two at a time.

Opening the door softly, he found her with her arm propped up on the sofa and her head resting back, eyes shut. Her glasses were still perched on her nose. She didn't move.

He wanted to kiss her, but he didn't want to wake her.

Quietly, he put the bottle of wine on the table, and the cheese. Then he poured himself some wine and sat, finishing the drink. Perhaps he should let her sleep for a few moments. He stayed in the chair across from her, relaxed and stretched back.

Such a delicate woman…and someone who could ruin his family name.

He propped his elbow on the arm of the chair and his cheek on his fist. He stretched a little more and shut his eyes. It was as if he was in the middle of a dream. A dream with sunshine, and a laughing Marie dealing cards from the bottom of the deck, all of them winning ones for him.

'Gabriel.'

He looked up. He'd not heard her move from the sofa nor felt her nudge his arm.

'We can put off the walk until another time,' she said. 'Pleasant dreams.'

'Wait,' he said, standing. 'I don't want to put it off.'

Somehow he knew that if he did, he might never again get a chance to be with her like this.

He went to his dressing room, pulled out a coat and returned, wrapping it around her shoulders, taking his time, enjoying the slumbery scent of her. The sight of her with his coat draped against her and her hair more tousled than he'd ever seen any woman's arrested him.

'This is better than my shawl,' she said, running her fingertips up the lapel. 'Thank you.'

The kiss she gave him was more than a brush of lips. It was a soft, moist moment that he shared with her, ending on a promise of more.

'Do you think we need a lamp outdoors?' she asked.

'No. I know the way.'

He led her outside and they sat in the middle of the garden. He spread the food between them and then lay back, interlacing his fingers and using them to cradle his head. His back was against the ground and his eyes faced the stars.

'Do you do this often?' she whispered, taking a bite of the cheese.

'Usually just once or twice a year. It's harder to find perfect nights than I would have imagined. But they exist. Like tonight.'

She finished eating and picked up a twig from the ground. She used it to scratch at the earth a few times, even jabbing the stick into a dried leaf and lifting it.

'You're not eating or drinking?'

'I brought it for you.'

She tossed away the stick, propped up her knees, and pulled his coat closer as she looked overhead.

'On a cloudless clear night, in the summer,' he whispered, his voice a low rumble, 'if you listen closely you can hear the sounds of the night.'

'Owls?' she asked.

'Mr Glenn next door. Snoring. At least, I think it is him. Who knows? It could be Mrs Glenn or a servant. But I think it is him, because once I heard her shout out that she wished he would stop that awful noise.'

'Do you snore?' she asked.

'The neighbours have never complained.'

'They would not dare.'

'You don't know Mrs Glenn. Our families have been neighbours for decades. And across the way is the Earl and Countess of Bennington's home, which has been in their family for generations.'

'I cannot imagine such history.'

'My heritage is important to me. And if you put Grand-mother's memories and moral lapses and buffoonery into written form, then it will be alongside that heritage for ever. A long reminder. Write something else. I'll even speak with the publisher and make sure you have all you need to be published.'

'I promised your grandmother. And besides, I don't like secrets.' She pushed herself to her feet.

'Are you going in?' he asked.

'If you are only here to try and talk me out of writing the memoirs, then yes.'

He stretched out his arm and put his hand over his heart. Being with her at that moment was more important than anything else. 'I will not mention it again until that little cloud gets past the moon.'

He saw the toss of her head, and knew it meant she was staying.

'I can't believe you lie out here like this,' she said. 'On the ground. With nothing between you and the earth.'

'You should try it.'

'My dress will get dirty.'

'It's just a few blades of grass.'

She didn't respond.

'It's warmer here, beside me,' he added.

She stepped to his side, tapped her slipper against his boot. 'Are you inviting me to lie beside you?'

He rose from his reclining position. 'The outdoors is plenty big enough for two.'

She sat beside him, their shoulders touching. 'I'm surprised you don't lie on a bench.'

'Too narrow. Too short.'

He put an arm around her, and suddenly the night wasn't cold any more.

The clouds moved over the moon, and he watched them, but he was more aware of her at his side. 'I've always watched the sky alone. Never had a night like this before.'

The kiss happened without his expecting it, and warmth filled him from head to toe. Her hand was on his chest. The night air was changing from cool to tinglingly comfortable. He felt the crush of their clothes joining.

She pulled away. 'I…'

'Let's not talk about it,' he said. 'Things happen without people meaning them to.'

He stood and put out a hand to help her rise. She seemed to fall into him.

'Things happen,' she said. 'My aunt has told me that. Over and over. But…'

He could tell she was lost in her thoughts when she lowered her eyes and studied the ground that was all darkness.

Like the memoirs. Like aloneness.

Marie stood unmoving. She should leave. One kiss might lead to two, and she was fairly certain she'd surprised him. That kiss wasn't something she'd expected to do.

She stepped away, hugging his coat close and surrounding herself in the scent of him. Leather, shaving soap, and delicious maleness.

He kissed her forehead. 'You've made this night one I will never forget.'

He lifted the bottle and glasses from the ground. The soft clinking sound was like a cymbal, signalling the end of their time together. She didn't want it to end.

'That's true for me also,' Marie said.

It was. She felt she could say anything she wanted to him.

Then he put his arm around her, the bottle and glasses still in his hand, and the tenderness of his lips surprised her. Tender and bold at the same time. He held her with one arm more securely than anyone else could with two.

She rested her hands against his chest, not ready to move away. But he didn't seem to have the same reluctance. He let her go, led her to the door. She supposed she could have put herself back into his arms, but she didn't.

'I'll be watching the sky tomorrow night,' he said. 'If you wish to join me.'

'I will,' she said.

'You could give up the memoirs,' he said, 'and stay here while you work on another topic. Let me know what you truly wish to do tomorrow night.'

'And if my viewpoint doesn't change—as it won't—will you still want to see me?'

'Of course.'

Chapter Fourteen

All day Marie had taken careful notes of his grandmother's tales, and she was determined to tell Gabriel that she wasn't going to give up on Myrtle's story.

The funds from publishing such a book would give her and her aunt some security. Besides, his grandmother had had a truly amazing life, and had not let the boundaries of society define her. She'd been her own woman and fulfilled her own wishes, sometimes at risk to herself and at risk to her happiness at home—but her husband had always forgiven her, she'd claimed.

And Marie hated secrets. Like the secret of her birth. Perhaps if people did not keep things so hidden, she would know her ancestral history.

She had grown up without parents. Without anything like the little toy horse Gabriel had taken for granted. The closest she'd come was when Polly's mother had made Polly a rag doll, and then a second smaller one from the scraps for Marie. Her first toy. The first thing she'd ever really owned. The woman who'd cared for her had burned it. She'd never reacted, but it had felt good when she'd been able to leave her house in the carriage, and had heard the woman had had to wed for money.

She almost felt bad about that. Almost. And she was

going to do all she could to keep the same thing from happening to her.

Marie had decided that if Gabriel was going to insist she give up the memoir, she must get as much information as possible before he cut off her access.

But even as she wrote Gabriel stayed in the recesses of her mind. She could hardly wait until the sun set and she would see him.

The temperature was perfect. The night was still and dark when she stepped out. But she could navigate her way into the garden easily.

Gabriel waited on the bench.

'I only plan to stay for a moment,' she said, having decided to go back in to work on the manuscript.

'Why?' he asked.

It would be best to tell him now. Best that he truly believed she wouldn't abandon her dream of being able to support herself. And writing a book such as the story of his grandmother's life would help tremendously.

Her place in society might be damaged, of course. She wasn't sure. Perhaps she could publish it anonymously? No, she wouldn't do that. She wanted to live a life without secrets.

'Perhaps I will stay out a little longer,' she said, absorbing the delight at having him at her side. 'I think I will.'

He took her hand. 'I'm pleased you have decided not to go in.'

'It is a magnificent night.'

He was responsible for that in so many ways. He had the garden and he understood her wish to enjoy the outdoors around her.

His hand covered hers, and even though the touch was innocent, it felt as though he was holding her in his arms.

She checked. 'Only one loop on your cravat again?'

He tugged at the small knot. 'Yes. My valet is deeply concerned, as I am taking so little care with my appearance, but in time I expect him to grow used to it.'

She hesitated. Leaving his home would be hard, because she would be putting him in her past. She liked being in Gabriel's house—not only because of him, but also because there was less friction here than anywhere she'd ever lived. Her aunt had taken her in without hesitation, but Agatha's husband had raged at her. Most often about Marie. About keeping secrets. Making his life a lie.

Her stomach had lurched when she'd realised the whole story. She doubted she would have ever moved in with Agatha if she'd known it in advance. Oh, she knew she wouldn't have. That explosion in the gardens had been minor compared with the fury unleashed by Lord Andrews. And, truly, she didn't blame him.

When Lord Andrews had told them Marie needed to marry his nephew or leave he'd known what he was doing. But Gabriel's grandmother had taken them in, and she seemed to like Marie well enough. She didn't really see her, though.

She didn't think Gabriel had truly seen her either. She was merely there—someone who would easily fall in with his plans. When she didn't fall in with people's plans they did what he had done—acted crushed, bereft, as if she'd turned into a beast and attacked them with no cause.

Only Agatha had ever really seen her, sacrificed for her. In fact, she'd supported Marie's decision twice when she hadn't wanted to wed. She'd claimed it untenable that

Marie take such a risk to try and improve her circumstances. She'd also claimed Gabriel's grandmother was the only woman she knew who had actually mourned her husband.

'Did you know your grandfather well?' she asked now.

She hoped Gabriel wouldn't get upset when he discovered that a few of his grandfather's errors were included in the memoirs. Gabriel's grandmother had told her that her husband had been a rake before they'd wed. In fact, he had claimed that men were not supposed to be faithful, but to be discreet. She'd responded by telling him he'd best keep his 'sword' put away, because she didn't want it to be sporting scars. She'd not been jesting.

She had also admitted, sadly, that she'd been so concerned with keeping her husband faithful that she'd not had a lot of time for her son, and she worried that Gabriel seemed to be following in his father's footsteps. At least where his heart was concerned…

'I remember him as a man who didn't take things too seriously,' he answered. 'I watched him shoe a wild horse once. A farrier had dared him that he couldn't do it and my grandfather accepted the challenge. You should have seen it when he let the horse go. He wasn't happy, and was intent on biting Grandfather's ear off. Or his nose.'

'Probably why your grandfather didn't live a long life?'

'He was already in his seventies when that happened, but he didn't act a day over sixteen most of the time. We had some good adventures. Grandmother was a lot younger than him, but they were well suited.'

'She told me she had to keep an eye on him.'

'She was the one more likely to cause a rumpus just because the calm bored her. Mother hated that. She's now watching over my other grandparents, who are gentle-minded people. Both frail. Living just outside London. I have several aunts and uncles, and their families are scattered about as well.'

'I didn't know either of my parents,' Marie said. 'I find it odd that you have so many family members.'

Listening to his grandmother's tales had made her feel better. She wasn't the only one with a secret, and her parents hadn't been the only ones who didn't adhere to propriety.

'But you have your Aunt Agatha. And Grandmother has mentioned that Agatha has some sisters…also some distant cousins in the peerage.'

'Well, yes.' She touched her bottom lip. 'But I suppose it's that I don't have any stories of my family that I took part in. The stories are all about other people. None with me involved. It's similar to seeing a play. You watch the characters, and at the end everyone goes their own way.'

Marie would have liked to know her parents, but she supposed it would never have been possible. Supposedly her father had died without knowing about her, and her mother had refused to acknowledge her other than by paying a woman to take care of her. Which she'd resented, Agatha had said, and was why she'd sometimes neglected to send the woman funds if she wanted something new for herself that was costly.

During her childhood she'd imagined her parents were travelling together somewhere, and one day the lady who'd cared for her had discovered that, and laughed so hard she'd cried.

'Do you believe your parents were content in their marriage?' she asked Gabriel.

There was a too-long pause.

'No. I don't know that my parents even spent much time in the same room. I did see Father furious with one of his sweethearts once. He had apparently ended their meetings and she hadn't taken it well. She wrote Mother a letter. Mother delivered the letter to him, after she had written notations on it and added her own viewpoints. I was with him when he came home and found the letter on his desk. Father was furious and Mother, strangely enough, was smug.' He touched his forehead. 'I learned all I ever wanted to know about their marriage that day.'

He'd had a whole plethora of family members growing up. A mother, a father and both sets of grandparents. So much more than she'd had.

And yet she still thought that she'd been so very fortunate. The woman who'd been paid to care for her might not have been kind, or loving, but other than a few times she'd not been outright cruel. Of course Agatha had told her that the funds would stop if Marie was mistreated. That might or might not have been true, but it had helped.

That was how she remembered her childhood. That and the cold winters. Putting on all the clothing she owned in order to stay warm. Gloves that didn't match and were beyond mending . Water freezing in the pitcher on the nightstand.

She couldn't complain about the woman being unkind on that measure, because they'd lived in the same house and she'd been sparing with her coal to save a few pence. They'd eaten together, and frozen together, and scrubbed their clothing together.

After Marie had moved in with her aunt, Agatha had kept on giving the woman funds, and Marie hoped the woman was doing well. But she and Agatha might have to resort to selling a frock or some stockings if Marie didn't manage to find a way to earn some money soon. She did not want Aunt Agatha to sell her pearls until she could get a top price for them.

In the darkness, Marie's voice floated across the night, more melodious than the most beautiful songbird, and Gabriel wondered what his grandmother had said to her about his father, or about his other grandparents, whom she disdained. They were tedious and wearisome, she'd told him, and had thanked him for taking after her instead.

His mother had admitted to him once, while throwing up her hands in consternation, that she'd been blinded by his father's smile, his title and his funds. She said he'd had the most attractive smile she'd ever seen. No one else had even come close, in her opinion, but sometimes she'd wondered if he might have been a better person if some woman's husband had dislodged a few of his teeth.

She'd told him privately that she'd thought his father had had the wrong mother. She'd never given her mother-in-law more than the weakest of upside-down compliments, saying she didn't want to say anything if she couldn't say something nice.

'She has nice ears,' had become her usual statement. 'Yes. She has beautiful ears.'

Otherwise, whenever his grandmother was mentioned, her lips would tighten and she'd reach up and tug her earlobe.

After his father had died he'd been surprised when the rest of the world had seemed more peaceful and to go more smoothly. Everything had been relatively quiet. Oh, he'd had to rein in his grandmother, but sometimes she'd seemed to have lost interest in creating a stir. She'd stopped staying out all night, and other than purchasing some rodents from the docks, in order to release them into the carriage of an enemy, she'd been happy to confine herself to creating more minor upheavals.

Marie took his hand. 'What are you thinking of?'

He rubbed a thumb over her knuckles, aware of the softness of her skin and the delicateness in her features. 'Taking on the duties of a viscount was easier than I expected after all Father's concerns. I had been raised to do it.'

'Your grandmother says that you are magnificent in the role.' She squeezed his hand. 'And she has admitted that you are not afraid of the dark, or even ghosts.'

He laughed, giving her hand a tug 'No. Grandfather always warned me that anything scary usually has a person attached.'

'I wasn't afraid of the dark when I was a child,' she admitted. 'But it is easier to trip over things, especially if you don't see well. The room I have now has such a lovely window, which prevents that from happening.'

'It does?'

He knew that he had the best rooms, and his grandmother had the biggest, in the opposite wing of the house. His mother had a set of rooms reserved for her visits, and Pierce always stayed on the side closer to Gabriel's rooms.

Lady Agatha had one of the nicer rooms, from what he could discern, with the fireplace that served both his grandmother's bedroom and hers, and Marie had a usually unused room near it.

'I thought the room you are in was mostly bare,' he said.

'Your grandmother has let me move things about. I can

show you how comfortable it is,' she said, pulling him up and leading him back into the house.

Once inside, she went towards his grandmother's rooms, but stopped at a bedroom he'd always considered little more than a storage room.

'There are much better rooms,' he said.

'I'm a guest, and this is closest to my aunt. I like it. If you always take the smallest space you are less likely to be displaced,' she said, laughing.

He frowned. 'You must move into another one.'

'No,' she said, opening the door. 'It's cosy.'

He walked in behind her. She'd left a lamp glowing, and it showed a dim room. He remembered the lumpy sofa from his grandfather's smoking room. The small desk had a chair snug against it, with a rip in the arm. If he remembered rightly, the chair had been the subject of an argument over which colour upholstery should be used for mending it, and the discussion had never been solved.

'You're comfortable here?' he asked, but he could see the answer in her eyes.

'This is my favourite room. The best I've ever had. Aunt's rooms are elegant and fine, but this one is so comfortable for me.'

'That sofa…?'

'Sit,' she said. 'But not there.' She pointed to a spot with a spring poking through.

'This should be mended,' he said. 'Or burned.'

'It's wonderful.'

She nudged him to the other end. He did sit, and it was comfortable enough. She sat beside him, turned towards him, her arm along the back of the sofa and her knee perched between them, almost as if she were alone, and suddenly everything about the room became cosier.

'See? It is relaxing and pleasant.' She turned. 'The chair has seen better days, but both are so comforting. I know the rest of the house is more elaborate, but this feels perfect for me. Everything is a little mismatched. And if something does need a new patch, it's not a concern.' Her eyes lit. 'Like a home. Not so much a mansion or an estate or a palace. But comfortable and a little well-worn.'

He heard the truth in her words and saw it in her expression. Time seemed to wrap around the look in her eyes, and it took everything else from his thoughts.

The silence connected them, and it seemed to be telling him all about her. He felt he had known her all her life. All his life. Even before they were born.

Then she put both her feet on the floor and moved closer, snuggling against his side so that he had her in the curve of his arm. Her head fell to rest against his chest, tickling his skin in a way that infused his body with awareness of her.

'I should go,' he said, and at those words she seemed to pull him closer.

'But this is nice. Maybe even nicer than lying on the ground looking up at the stars. Although on that night they'd never seemed so vibrant to me.'

They'd never been that vivid before for him either. They'd dazzled the sky.

And all because she had been with him.

She didn't want him to leave. She didn't. He'd been so kind, and he had let both her and her aunt stay in his house, and now she had invited him in to tell him the truth about her plans with his grandmother.

'I can't count on your kindness for ever,' she said. 'I have to make my own way.'

He took her fisted hand in his and studied it, holding just the fingertips and rubbing his forefinger over her smallest finger. 'Sometimes you have to trust someone.'

'I don't want to have to trust anyone.' She put her palm over his knuckles.

'I understand.'

He moved only a hair's width. Or that was what it seemed to her. And she relaxed against him. Or perhaps she slipped, as if she'd been standing on ice and the sun had touched them both and she'd no longer been able to remain upright.

She didn't even know the moment he stopped holding her hand and touched her chin, but the whisper of his lips against hers caused her to cling to him, amazed that another person could cause such a revitalising sensation in her. He'd taken the night and turned it into a sunrise.

She touched his cheek, feeling the strength in his jawline, the masculinity under her grasp. Stubble that should have been uncomfortable was blasting a wonder.

'You... I thought... When we kissed before, I thought it amazing.'

She stumbled over the words. Her mouth didn't want to speak. It only wanted to caress him.

'It was. It still is.' His lips touched hers as he spoke. 'Only more so.'

Then she remembered what she'd wanted to know. She'd not planned to ask him, but the words formed.

'Will you remember me? After I leave?' she asked.

'I will remember you. Never doubt that.'

After kissing her fingertips, he held her face in both

his hands, and she didn't feel confined but adored, as if she basked in his presence. She'd never felt so revered before. So cherished.

She removed her glasses and led him to her bed. She knew she could never wed him, because he didn't truly know who she was, but she could have the memory of these moments with Gabriel, which she would treasure for the rest of her life.

He ran his hands down her face and the strength inside him seemed transferred into her, as if she could feel not only his hands, but his entire body behind them. But then she realised it wasn't strength she was feeling from his touch, but from his eyes.

His lips, feather-light, belying the strength she'd felt, brushed hers, and then he moved away, just enough to take one more lingering look before returning to the kiss, softly and only enough to connect them. Until she wrapped herself around him, pulling herself closer. She could not be near enough to him. Not just his lips and his hands, but all of him. The distance was too far. She needed more.

His body pressed against hers, and their clothing was a wall between them, creating friction but not satisfying her, leaving her bereft.

She held herself away to touch his cravat, her fingers tangling in the fabric as she tried to untie it but only made a knot.

He paused, removed the cravat and slipped it and his coat away, tossing them to the floor so they landed with a soft fluttering sound. The fabric of his sleeves billowed out, and she realised she'd never noticed the true width of his shoulders before.

Long fingers undid each of the seemingly endless buttons of his waistcoat, and the adoration in his eyes for her appeared just as infinite as the fastenings.

Then he clasped her shoulders, lowering his head to kiss the pulse at her neck, and she heard him whisper her name.

She clutched his chest, her fingers gripping his shirt to hold herself erect, and when his arms went around her they enclosed her in a masculine scent that she would happily have lost herself in. She didn't need to hold herself upright. He did that for her with no effort.

A breath later he had touched the clasps of her dress and slid it from her shoulders. Then he placed it over the chair at the foot of her bed, moving delicately.

He stopped for a moment, his eyes changing, heating and melting at the same time. 'You remind me of a fragile figurine,' he said. 'Something too delicate to even be on display.'

She turned, letting him undo her laces, and when the corset dropped to the floor she fell into his arms, her chemise blending with his shirt, and her body feeling the thinness of their clothing. She wanted to be beyond that fabric. Closer to him. Wrapped in the sensation that she knew only he could give her.

She reached for the ties of his shirt, quickly undoing it. She asked him with her eyes, and he nodded, and she slipped the shirt over his head, amazed to see continuing evidence of his strength, and the difference in the planes of his body compared to hers.

Tentatively, she touched his sides, amazed at the vibrancy that flowed through her as her senses adjusted to the sensation of his masculinity, and then she ran her hand over his chest, following the small path of hair that contrasted with the smoothness of the spot where the dark stubble ended at the base of his chin. She slipped her hands around him and rested her cheek on his shoulder, savouring the feel of him.

His breath touched her ear, causing her to clasp him closer, and she felt the trail of his kisses and tongue and put her head back, so he could find her lips before moving away again.

He pulled the bedcovers back and she ran her hand down his arm, pressed the hair under her fingertips, and then she clutched his hand before slipping between the coverlet and the sheet.

'Lovely,' he whispered, studying her face while he removed his breeches and joined her in the bed.

She tugged at her chemise and he helped her pull it over her head. And then she could pull herself against him completely, feel his hardness between them, waiting for her.

He kissed her shoulder, the bristles of his beard caressing her skin, causing the intensity inside her to spiral. And then they joined together, feeling heartbeats and desire, and finally reached a place where they could be sated.

She lay on his arm, not exactly basking in the glow of lovemaking but thinking about what she'd done. She'd let her passions overwhelm her. The same thing that she'd inwardly criticised her mother and father for. She'd been weak.

She rolled away from him.

'What's wrong?' he asked, putting his hand on her arm, moving closer to hold her and put a kiss on her hair.

'I've not been truthful with you,' she said.

She didn't want to tell him, but she also didn't want to hide her past. She knew he would turn his back on her for her deceit. She would have her belated integrity, but she would not have him.

It was a risk she had to take.

'What do you mean?'

'I've not been honest.' She held the covers to her chest and moved so that their eyes locked.

'About what?'

She took in a breath, slowly exhaled. 'About…about my past.'

'Have I asked you to tell me?'

'Our lovemaking. It is a commitment to honesty.'

'I'm not sure that's written in stone. Or even in sand.' He gave her a kiss on the shoulder and lay back in bed. 'I almost wed once, but it would have been a mistake for both of us.'

'You?' she gasped, his revelation derailing her planned confession.

'Yes. Jane Brock. What could go wrong? I thought. I wasn't particularly ready to wed, but she was a peer's daughter, and I knew she was a respectable woman. A good person. But then one day we were sitting in her house, and our chaperon fell asleep. Jane and I were at a loss for what to say to each other. We laughed about it, thinking the chaperon must be having a better time than either of us.'

'What did you do?'

'We parted as friends and I wished her well.'

'Did you intend to wait and wed for love?'

'I thought I was in something close to love with Jane.'

He sat up, propped himself on one arm, and looked at her. The light was dim, but his words were so direct that it seemed she could see into his soul when he answered.

'Jane was a nice person, and at first I assumed we would

eventually fall passionately in love. But I doubt we would have. I enjoyed talking with the chaperon more than with Jane.'

Marie rose from the bed and put on enough clothing to be decent, but not enough to go out in public.

She stood by the bedside, and at first he seemed unwilling to break the silence.

He half smiled. 'Don't look so upset.'

'I'm not. Just assessing things.'

And understanding more than she had before.

Then she remembered her aunt's husband, tossing them out, and how Agatha had made her promise never to wed if her husband didn't truly love her. *Never.*

'But surely Uncle does love you? We're leaving in his carriage,' she'd told her aunt. 'Not on foot.'

Agatha had crossed her arms. 'And if I don't have the courage to step away I might as well be throwing my body underneath the vehicle. That's how it will be every day until he respects me. Either he takes me back on my terms or we risk starvation. You'll be able to find respectable work, and I'm completely happy being a beggar on a street corner. Better than being a beggar under my husband's roof.'

The words reverberated in Marie's mind now.

Gabriel would always be a peer. He could court so easily, and all the women would fall in love with him—as she now realised she had. She had no guarantee he would not become like his father...like all the other men she had seen. Chasing from one woman to the next. She could not live with that. She could not be a beggar under her husband's roof.

Gabriel's grandmother had said that had been the root of the problem between Gabriel's parents. His father had thought his mother a lesser person, and that she would have no choice but to put up with his straying. Which was true.

She had seen women so happy with their new husbands, thrilled to be gifted with so much love, and then it had all changed, leaving those women scrabbling about for a meal, or a new roof over her head.

It would be better for her to leave with parts of her heart intact, rather than stay with him and have her spirit bashed into a thousand pieces. They had made love, and she would have that happy memory for ever. But now she must walk away—or risk being pulled into the mire, where she would be an unwelcome addition to the household.

She paused, and then formed her words carefully. 'There's something you should know. About me.'

'I already know,' he said.

'You know?'

'Grandmother told me. No one really knows who your parents were.'

She deliberated for a moment. That was for the best, she supposed. She didn't want to cause Agatha and Lord Andrews—Drippy Nose—more distress.

She lowered her chin, and her gaze, and bit her lip.

'It doesn't matter.' He caressed her face. 'It doesn't change one lovely hair on your head. One flutter of your lashes.'

After seeing the upsets between Agatha and the husband who had claimed to love her aunt so very much before they wed, she was wary of marrying for love. Love was less dependable than anything else. It seemed too fragile to withstand day-to-day nearness. Or even week-to-week.

* * *

Gabriel left the bed and gathered his clothing, donning his shirt, waistcoat and breeches quickly. He lifted the cravat, studied it a moment and smiled, then tossed it to her.

She grabbed it from the air and held it in her hand, then she brought the neckcloth closer to her body, looking beyond the fabric. Her eyes were searching and she appeared dazed, lost in thought.

He almost hated himself. He should have been stronger. He shouldn't have made love to her. He'd not meant to. He'd not planned it. And now…

He didn't want to leave, but knew he should. And he would.

But only after he asked her again to forget about the memoirs.

'Will you stop collaborating with my grandmother?'

She shook her head.

'Why don't you write a fictional story in which you disguise the incidents about my family so much that no one will know who you are writing of?'

She touched the fabric of his cravat. 'I want to pay homage to your grandmother's strength and force of will. She is a strong and admirable woman.'

He snorted. 'She is a rebel.'

'Well, yes,' she said softly, raising her head. 'She rebelled against society and did as she pleased and thrived. She's a Boudicca with a happy ending and without the terribly bad parts.'

'To me, it's an embarrassment. She is my grandmother. You cannot take advantage of her like that. She deserves to be respected in her later years.'

He spoke softly, wanting her to understand. Wishing

they could stop talking about his family and crawl back into bed and spend the night together.

'Take advantage of her?' She shook her head. 'I respect her for her courage. Her honesty. She has told me she calls me a wall weed.'

He wouldn't even have thought his grandmother would be so rude to Marie as to let her know of the nickname.

'A wall weed,' she said. 'And it fits me. I imagine myself a climbing plant, moving up the walls and towards the light, holding close to whatever I can to make my way.'

'It was wrong for her to tell you such a thing. You can see how her judgement is clouded.'

'It's not her judgement. She has little of that. But she says if we write this book together I will turn from a wall weed into a warrior woman, with a home of my own. I will be making my own way for my aunt and myself. Aunt Agatha agrees. She will sell the pearls and get a house in my name, so her husband cannot take it. The money from the book will put food on the table. And your grandmother assures me that if we put enough fascinating stories in the first volume, we can hold out enough to make a second volume.'

'*Two* books?' The embarrassment would go on for ever. 'You do not have to put your energies into that,' he said.

The columns holding up his mental truths concerning her were slowly crumbling into dust. She'd worn the new dress, but she'd quickly returned to the frumpy dresses that were from the past and didn't suit her. He'd thought she was hiding behind them, but perhaps she was staking her place in her world by saying that she would wear the clothes she wished to wear.

'I suppose you mean I could wed? Instead of making my

own way?' she said. 'I don't want that. And I wasn't impressed to find that you were trying to find suitors for me just as your grandmother is trying to find suitors for you.'

He didn't regret showing people how beautiful she could be. Showing *her*. He'd wanted her to know that she could shine in the middle of a social event. That she didn't need to hide.

'You'd prefer to write a book that will destroy my heritage?' he asked. 'Bring to light—for ever—the things in my grandmother's past that I have worked hard to get beyond? Hurt my grandparents? My mother?'

He could not believe she seemed so caring of everyone but him and his family.

Gabriel fell asleep in his own bed and woke to the scent of springtime, though he wasn't sure if it was real or if it was caused by the memory of Marie. Then he realised he had been awakened by the valet opening the door.

'You have a guest in your sitting room,' his valet said, his voice disapproving.

Gabriel moved only his eyes.

'Your cousin. He is propping his boots on the furniture.'

'Kick him out of the house.'

'I have tried. Gently. But I suspect you will have to do it. I also think the butler will be happy to help. The three of us can make it more memorable for him.'

The butler was not soon to forgive Pierce for the mud tracks he always left in the entrance hall, and thought his personal habits caused too much demand on the staff.

Gabriel finished dressing and went to his sitting room, where Pierce was sprawled. Asleep. How could his cousin have fallen asleep in the time it took him to sit?

Gabriel walked over, and with the toe of his boot moved Pierce's leg. 'You know you're supposed to be staying in your own rooms when you're visiting.'

Pierce sat up, hair rumpled, clothes rumpled and expression unrumpled. 'Yes. But your sofa happened to be closer, and I didn't feel like taking another step.'

'I am sure the butler would have been gracious enough to put you in a wheelbarrow.'

'Straight out to dump me in the garden. I don't think your staff enjoy my being here.'

'They don't.'

'You should speak to them about that.'

'I'm fine with it. You need to be neater—and not demand things at odd hours of the night.'

Pierce ran a hand through his hair, smoothing it. Then he tugged his cravat into place. 'Since you mention it, I think I should stay for a while longer. I'm not getting any younger and I miss Grandmother.' Pierce winked. 'And there's something intriguing about Marie. The spectacles, I suppose. I keep thinking about her. Her aunt is married to Lord Andrews, so she has a viable connection to society. I'm feeling courtship-minded.' He leaned forward, hands on his knees. 'Unless, of course, you two are having a romance. Which would explain why she is living in your house.'

'Marie and I are friends, and you are not to mention her.'

Piece jumped up, walked over, and gave his cousin a punch on the shoulder. 'I should have known when she was at the picnic, looking so lovely. Keeping the best beauties for yourself.' He frowned. 'Because she has spectacles it will make it easier for you to court her. She can take them off and pretend you're handsome.'

'Do you plan to go down the stairs feet first or face first?' Gabriel asked.

Pierce gave his cousin another half-hearted punch, before tugging on the bell-pull. 'Romance is in the air! Gabe has a new romance with a reputable woman. He's all aflutter. I can tell by the way his teeth grind when I mention her.'

'You're about to lose the ability to grind your teeth if you don't watch what you say.'

Pierce clasped a hand over his heart. 'I will be silent. Quiet as a mouse. Not even a hungry mouse. They make too much noise.'

He lifted his boot and gave it a polish with his hand. 'Why did you invite Elway and Epperson to the picnic? That wasn't very well thought-out, now, was it?'

Gabriel kept silent.

Pierce moved to lift the glass beside the decanter. 'Grandmother's memoirs should turn the whole of Town on its ear. So I can understand your being irritable—not that it's any great change.' He took in a deep breath. 'Every little stumble and crash of our family splashed out for all to see... I'll revel in it, but it will kill you. And it will upend your mother and her family. I don't envy you that.'

A maid rapped on the door and Pierce opened it. 'Please have a meal brought to my room.'

'You can eat in the dining room,' Gabriel said. 'You don't need to be making extra work for the servants.'

'Fine.' Pierce peered over his shoulder. 'I forgot to tell you that I saw your mother last night. We were at the same event—imagine that. I did let it slip that Grandmother had been gambling, using you as a wager, and she didn't see the humour. Expect her to visit, as she said she would be here today. She fears you need help with Grandmother, and she wants to see the person she lost you to.' He grinned. 'Don't worry. I didn't tell your mother about Grandmother's memoirs. I'm saving that.'

A man could be a viscount. He could be a duke. He could be a king. He could control countries. But a man could not control his family.

Chapter Fifteen

❧

He didn't like eating in the formal dining room, but he had to attend so he could make sure his mother and grandmother didn't brawl.

His mother had arrived just before dinner, giving him two lectures on being wary of people who did not have his best interests at heart. Then she'd glared as she tugged at her ear.

She'd also asked what was going on under his roof, and then told him to please spare her the details and get straight to the part about his grandmother's gambling.

He had reassured her that all was well, and she told him that she shouldn't have taught him not to speak badly about family members. And although she hadn't torn her earlobe off after speaking, it wouldn't have taken much more effort.

She'd said she would be at dinner and expected his grandmother to be in attendance, and that she would assure that would happen by telling her former mother-in-law she hoped to have a quiet conversation with Gabriel.

He was leading her to the table when his grandmother strolled in, lacking all but royal robes and a sceptre to go along with her commanding arrival. She was never the tallest woman in a room, but she acted as if she were.

His grandmother and mother greeted each other with

perfunctory almost-kisses on the cheek, and then his mother stepped away—much in the same way two boxers would eye their opponents.

'Don't look so glum, Flora,' his grandmother said. 'I've been having a wonderful time with Gabriel, and he's so happy to have me staying with him—although I doubt there's anything of interest going on here for you.'

'I don't want you trying to get him married off,' his mother said.

'Another woman in this household would be one too many,' his grandmother said. 'She might think she runs the place, and as the matriarch of the family I'm perfectly capable.'

'Capable? At dealing cards, I'm sure. And how much have you lost at gambling overall, would you guess?'

'I always manage my cards well. Besides, you don't expect to win every game. The sport is in the playing. The camaraderie. The friendships earned.'

His mother snorted.

Then Pierce arrived, and both women seemed to try to outdo themselves in showing their devotion to him.

When Agatha and Marie appeared, the room quietened. Marie wore one of the old dresses, but Pierce almost tripped over his boots rushing to her. She appeared to want to stay in the background, but it wasn't possible. Her dress was plain, overly simple, but among his family she stood out in her lack of adornment.

His mother certainly noticed her, and her eyes turned to him, as if to ask *This one?*

He gave a quick nod of his head.

Pierce made himself available to the only women in the room he wasn't related to, flirting equally with Marie and her aunt. But that was Pierce. He'd once said that if a woman wasn't flirtatious then surely she must have friends who were, so there was no sense in ignoring the possibilities.

'Let us sit and enjoy our meal.' Gabriel extended an arm to the table.

'This is a wonderful evening,' Pierce said. 'Good food. Good company. And Gabriel.'

'And I'm equally pleased to have you here,' Gabriel said.

'I'm all for his staying unwed,' Pierce said, and gave Marie a smile. 'To keep you informed, that makes me next in line for the Viscountcy—after my two brothers, one of whom has been wed ten years and has no children, the other of whom has three lovely daughters.' He turned to Gabriel. 'I want you to know, Gabe, I would make a good viscount. I will be happy to taste all this food first, so you can be sure it is safe. In fact, I've heard that the wine could be tainted, so I'm going to make sure you will not get ill from it. I've been told a criminal will only poison the best wine. Are you sure this is it, Gabe? I wouldn't want you to get ill on a lesser drink.'

'That is not humorous,' Gabriel's mother said, and glared at her nephew.

'I'll test it for both of them,' his grandmother said. 'I could be on my last legs anyway.'

'Oh, please...let me pour for you,' his mother said.

Marie looked at his grandmother, and then his mother, and then at Gabriel.

He gave her the merest flicker of an eyelash, acknowledging the verbal duel.

'Well, cousin?' Pierce said. 'Have you been lost in any card games recently?'

'He was won,' Marie said. 'And it's obvious that Gabriel is an exemplary viscount and no one could fill his boots.'

'Because he's got feet the size of a barn,' Pierce noted to no one in particular, before taking a sip of wine.

His grandmother chuckled. 'I'm blessed to have such accomplished grandsons. They both take after me.'

"I thought I should spend more time here in case I missed anything,' said Pierce. 'And so I could visit my dear grandmother. It is wonderful to have a family gathering. We get together so rarely.'

Gabriel's mother glared, and his grandmother looked as if she'd just won the title of Grandmother of the Realm.

'I love these family dinners, too,' she said. 'We do not have them often enough.'

'They seem very entertaining,' Agatha said.

'Just ignore us,' Gabriel said. 'We test our wits instead of our rapiers.'

'You can ignore *him*,' Pierce said. 'But if Miss Marie would like to go with me on a carriage ride in the park tomorrow I'd be thrilled. Grandmother can be our chaperon.'

Marie tensed, then stammered, 'I—I would not impose upon your grandmother so.' Then she studied Pierce. 'And I think it would be best for me to avoid that.'

For a second her eyes locked with Gabriel's, and he reassured her with a glance.

His mother and grandmother saw it. His mother gave a soft gasp, and his grandmother grimaced.

'You have just reminded me,' his grandmother said to her daughter-in-law, 'I've never told Marie about your courtship with my son. I think it would be a wonderful thing to include in my memoirs.'

'Memoirs?'

His mother spluttered. Gabriel had never seen her do that before.

'Marie is writing the story of our family. I'm telling it to her.'

'What a thought! If you even get the facts right.' His mother tilted her head, and this time she gave a nod towards her mother-in-law and then frowned into her plate. 'And I suppose the odds are not in my favour on that.'

Marie took in a slow breath, and Gabriel didn't move.

'It's not completely decided to publish the memoirs.' Gabriel spoke softly but with emphasis.

'I can hardly wait to read Grandmother's recollections,' Pierce said.

'We'll see,' Gabriel said, easily enough.

'Gabriel. You must get this stopped. It's unthinkable!' his mother said, placing a palm flat on the table.

'I think you'll find it enlightening,' Gabriel's grandmother said, and then turned to Marie. 'We may need more paper.'

When they'd finished dinner his grandmother stood, tapping her lips with her napkin. 'I have so many stories to tell you, Marie.'

His mother rose, squared her shoulders, and addressed Gabriel. 'We need to discuss this.'

'We can talk in the sitting room,' Gabriel said.

'Did you encourage these…memoirs?' his mother asked, as soon as he and she were alone in the sitting room—or, as alone as they could be with his grandmother and cousin in attendance, both of whom had rushed in after them.

'No.'

'I should never have left this house… But my parents

need me.' His mother quirked a brow and stared at him, giving the napkin she still held a twist. 'One can only handle so much, and your grandmother is many times more than what is bearable.'

'You didn't have to marry into my family. I did warn you,' his grandmother answered.

'I like Marie,' Pierce said, his voice rolling like a cloud of cigar smoke. 'And I know I can speak for Gabriel. He likes her even more than I do.'

'She's fine for a tryst,' his grandmother said, 'as long as it's nothing serious. It is nothing serious, is it? You know I was jesting with that wager only because I really wanted those pearls.'

'Is that it?' his mother asked. 'Just a romance? Do be careful, Gabriel, you know how easily a woman can be hurt in a situation such as this.' She slid her index finger against her necklace, let it twist once, and then slid her finger back and forth several times. 'She's practically alone in the world, isn't she?'

'No. She has her aunt.'

'Sometimes it isn't so bad to be alone in the world,' his mother said.

'While I am friends with Agatha,' his grandmother added, 'Marie is better for Pierce. Because he needs someone like her. You need someone less adventurous, Gabriel. Like Rosalind. That's the perfect woman for you.'

'Marie should leave,' his mother said. 'I can tell this home is not the place for an unwed young woman.'

'She has nowhere else to go.'

I'll invite her to my parents' house,' his mother said. 'That will be best for everyone. We can leave at once.'

'No,' his grandmother said. 'We've hardly started my

memoirs. And I haven't yet told her anything about *your* family history. You'll find a few surprises there.'

His mother choked.

'Dearest Flora,' his grandmother said, nonchalantly tapping her finger to her ear. 'I hope you will enjoy reading about your parents—from my perspective, of course. Both interesting people, from what I could unearth. They need very little embroidery—so to speak.'

'You would not dare—' His mother's voice broke and her fingers splayed.

'If you will all excuse me,' said Gabriel, standing and taking a stride to the door. 'I'm going to go discuss your departure with Marie.'

He had to. He could not let her live here among the wolves—particularly the family ones.

Entering the corridor, he made his way to her room, knocking on the door.

'Marie,' he called out. 'I need to speak with you.'

She opened the door. 'I have my things ready to leave. I expected this. We will have to return to my uncle's hunting lodge and hope the servants there don't realise he doesn't know we're there.'

She stepped out into the corridor, looking the length of it. His mother had just stepped into view, and his grandmother was almost elbowing her out of the way.

Gabriel took in a long slow breath, then took Marie by the arm and backed her into her room, shutting the door behind him.

Almost instantly someone rapped on the wood. 'Gabriel. This is most untoward. Don't damage Marie's reputation.'

His mother.

The door rattled and he grasped the latch, holding it closed.

'Would you mind me visiting you tonight?' he asked softly.

'Just don't bring anyone with you.'

Marie stepped away from the door and Gabriel opened it. His grandmother and his mother stood side by side, guardians of their viewpoints, and Pierce relaxed farther down the corridor, leaning against the wall, arms crossed, one foot propped behind him, humour in his eyes.

'*This* is why I don't visit often,' his mother added. 'But it's clear this time that I have stayed away too long. My life is being destroyed right before my eyes. And my parents' health and happiness are at stake.'

'Grandmother, as I pay all your expenses, and the costs of all this household, I am telling you that you cannot write the memoir,' Gabriel said. 'Not only do I need to maintain dignity for the family, in order to help with my financial ventures, it would also cause grief to Mother. And to my other grandparents.'

'I would like to see Marie do as she wishes,' Pierce said. 'And I would enjoy reading Grandmother's recollections. Grandmother, just send your billing to my man of affairs.'

'The Duke will not be able to continue our friendship,' his mother said, wringing her hands. 'Not with his daughter about to be introduced in society. He does not know all the details of our family life, and to have them thrown out into the world... I will have to disappear—as I did before, when I was married.'

His grandmother shrugged and sniffed dismissively. 'I will be continuing with my memoirs.' She peered around

Gabriel's shoulder at Marie. 'You might want to get a copy of the signed document I gave your aunt and include it.'

'I should leave this house,' Marie said. 'It seems I am causing an upset here.'

'You're just acting like one of the family,' Gabriel said.

'She's a better listener than anyone I know,' said his grandmother. 'She's like a grandchild, only better, because she doesn't argue.'

'I do like you,' Marie said to his grandmother. 'And your memories are so interesting to me. This family's life. Except today is not good. I must hope this is an aberration.'

His mother groaned. 'I wish that were true.'

'See?' His grandmother held her head high and gave a dismissive look to her daughter-in-law before returning her gaze to Marie. 'It is nice to have a female in this house who is agreeable. And who can be trusted to do the right thing.'

Marie didn't know if she could be trusted to do the right thing.

Gabriel's mother made a choking sound. She was adept at that. And she had a nervous habit of tugging on her ear.

Marie sighed inwardly. Leaving Gabriel would be difficult, but it would be better to do it soon. He'd noticed her for all the wrong reasons. He'd thought he could make her into something exactly as he wished. And she didn't want to be used that way. Seen as someone lesser, who had to be dressed a different way and have her hair changed. A poor woman to be rescued. One who would deal with his grandmother—as if anyone could—so he could do his duty and then retreat from his family while attending briefly the social interactions they provided for him.

And she had almost no family to add to the situation.

She would be earning her keep.

She looked at him, seeing the weary look on his face. She was an orphan who had always wanted a family, but she could see now why to him her lack of family members might not be such a bad thing.

Chapter Sixteen

'**I**'ve missed you,' Gabriel said, after she'd opened her door that night.

'Did you notice me only because I have so little family?' she asked, stepping aside.

She indicated the sofa and he relaxed on the lumpy object, still amazed at how its wear seemed to create a welcoming hold, and how the room full of misfit furniture was the most welcoming one in the house.

He wasn't holding her, but inside her room, on the sofa, it was as if she was clasping him. He'd never been in a room that embraced him like this, and it was all because of her.

Looking around, he saw her reticule, some papers, her shawl, a cup, a flattened bonnet... He relished the moment.

'I shall have to find another place to live,' she said, moving beside him.

He put an arm on the back of the sofa, and after the smallest consideration she snuggled into the haven he'd made for her.

'Your grandmother has spent the evening trying to tell me all the family mishaps she can think of. And your mother has pulled me from the room and insisted I give to her everything I've already written. She says her mother-in-law is a bad influence on everyone, including you. She has even said I can move in with her parents if I leave the memoirs behind.'

'Are you going to?' he asked. Their lips were so close he could feel the caress of her breath.

'No. I would feel even less secure than I feel here,' she whispered. 'I don't know her at all. But I do feel I know your grandmother. If a thought is in her head, she has no problem with speaking it. But I will have to find some-where else to live.'

He didn't want to think of her alone in the world. True, she had her aunt, and she'd managed in the past. But he didn't want her to have to do that in the future.

'Are you sure you don't want to stay here?' He clasped her closer, surrendering to this moment of having her so near to him.

'I'm sure I *do* want to stay, but I don't want to be caught in the miasma of your family concerns.'

Her eyes begged him to understand, but he wanted her to understand as well.

'All families have hierarchies. Disagreements. Prob-lems. Resolutions.'

'A family should give you a safety net. A place to return to when you tumble. And I don't know that your family gives that,' she said. 'They don't enjoy being together. And none of them seem to have ever learned how to talk to each other in a nice way, just in commands. Even you.'

'That's not as uncommon as you'd think.'

And it didn't seem to matter any more. He needed to hold her. To have her close.

'Because you have such a large estate, you can sequester

yourself away from them for the most part. And that's what you do, isn't it? Sequester yourself away from your family.'

'My family is used to having its own way. They've been surrounded by servants their whole lives.'

He didn't see that as a bad thing. Servants were much better at pleasing his family than anyone else was.

'Now I see why I get on so well here. In a sense, I've been a servant my whole life.'

Her face blasted him like the coldest winter air.

'No, it's not that.'

'It would be too much of a commitment to be expected to keep everyone happy here. No, if I'm to be a servant again, it will not be in a house where my heart is involved.'

'I do care for you,' he said.

It was true. The way her eyes lit up when she saw the gardens thrilled him, and he enjoyed seeing her excitement. Her pleasure in the plants moving from bud to bloom. How she stopped to enjoy and inhale the individual flowers' blooms. So appreciative of being able to see the leaves.

'I believe you,' she said. 'You like me. But in perhaps the same distant way you like the other women in your family. I would be perfect to live here, in your mind, because I could be someone you only saw on occasion.'

Now he wondered if she was correct—very correct—in her intention of leaving.

But then another concern edged into him. One of fear. Of loss. He didn't want Marie leaving. She was safe in his home. Protected from other men who might not have her best interests at heart. If she fell in love with someone like Pierce it would only be a matter of time before he moved on to someone else.

And he knew he risked losing her, but he had no choice

if he wanted to keep his family intact. To protect his mother and his grandparents.

He would speak with the publisher and find a way to have his grandmother's memoirs stopped. But it mattered to him that Marie didn't seem to understand his distaste for having his family's misadventures shared.

He couldn't understand her willingness to embarrass his family. She was seemingly unaware of how much pain it would cause to people he cared about to revisit the problems they'd moved on from. It seemed she took his remonstrations much as she had his instructions for waltzing—she let them go in one ear and out the other. She seemed caring, but he didn't know if it went deep enough. Perhaps it was a façade she'd developed because she'd had to show a caring manner to survive.

She straightened her shoulders. 'I have been mostly alone in the world except for Aunt Agatha, and if I am alone again it will not be the first time. I can take care of myself. I will survive. I don't like being cold, but I can be, and I can make do with very little. In fact, sometimes I think I am happier with less. I don't have to worry about losing as much.'

He met her gaze. 'It's not a bad thing to have something you don't want to lose.'

Pondering his words, she saw the truth in his expression.

'It's safest for me not to take that risk,' she said.

'Is it?'

He reached out.

She clutched him, hoping she would remember for ever what it felt like to be sitting close to him, in this cosy room, with comforting things around her.

For this moment in time she wasn't poor, but wealthy

beyond belief. Being in this small room in this instance, near to him, enveloped in his presence, was the closest she had ever been to heaven. But like all wonderful things it could not last for ever.

'By fortune of birth I was given a viscountcy, and by that same goodness I was given the means to train for it. I have been a good shepherd,' he said. 'And I will continue to be a good overseer. It is my heritage, and I must pass on the best example of it that I can. Instead of writing those memoirs, you could marry me.'

Somehow the kind words hit her as a spear into her heart. 'I'm not blackmailing you into marriage. Not now. Not ever. And I am deeply offended at the thought.'

These were not words she would accept from a future husband. A future husband had to believe she was such a part of his life that no other would do, and know that he would slay emotional dragons for her—even if the dragons were inside himself.

He could not wed her to purchase her silence. To end his duty of finding a bride.

'You could find a much better wife,' she said, moving away. 'Daughters of dukes and earls and viscounts and barons are all about.'

In a marriage to her it would hurt to see him wonder if, perhaps, he should have chosen someone else.

'You are not being kind to yourself.'

'I suppose not. But I've not found much of the world to be kind either. And I have lived in that part of the world more than I have resided in your world. Really, I can only touch the fringes of your life. I stand just close enough to see in, but not close enough to stay in it. Not close enough for you.'

'With a marriage to me, you would.'

'I would always have to watch my footing.'

Not just with society. But with him. She would never know if he was thinking of the mistake he'd made. Of the society women who would have wed him. The grandparents and connections his children would have had.

'I will not be reminded, even with my own words, that I am not the jewel you would have hoped for. A poor man who might offer to share his only crust of bread with me is better than a rich man who tosses me a crust of his fine bread.'

She knew she placed a high value on herself—to walk away from a marriage that would give her money, but no promises of the heart. But she had seen what had happened to her aunt, and the belittling situation she had found herself in. The tension.

'You would rather risk so much than stay with me?' he asked.

'It will be better for both of us in the long run.'

'I am sure Grandmother's stories are interesting to other people,' he said. 'But I've lived them. Tried to discount them. I do not want them published.'

'Most people have things in their family that they would rather not be discussed.'

'This isn't about "most people". It's about us,' Gabriel said. 'In this room, it is about us. But I will always remember that your choice wasn't to marry me, but to disregard me. You have chosen the wrong path.'

No, she hadn't. Because she had chosen herself.

Quicker than she had ever seen anyone move, he turned away from her.

'You want to betray me, and I will not let you. Not under my roof.'

'Fine. I will leave.'

'But I don't want you to go.' He faced her again.

'Your grandmother has shared her stories with me. She trusted me, and you should, too.'

'You're planning to profit from your closeness to my family.'

'Yes. I am. I already do. And if it were not me, it would be someone else.'

'Let it be someone else, then. Not you.'

She was torn. Torn between the look she saw in Gabriel's eyes and the chance she had to support herself. If his grandmother's memoirs were published and did well, then her aunt had another friend who was considering having her story written.

It would mean a lot to her—having that opportunity and possibly many more—and not only that, listening to his grandmother's reminiscences had been fascinating.

But one thing bothered her even more. Gabriel did not trust her to do the right thing. He thought her to be betraying his family. And perhaps he was right.

Was she selling her integrity? The way she had when she had agreed to undertake the changes in her appearance that he'd suggested? Making herself into the person he wanted her to be. Someone just like everyone else.

He'd seen that she was different. Been fascinated. And then he had tried to remove the parts of her that he'd noticed in the first place.

She should never have agreed to be anything other than herself.

True, she had liked the hairstyle, and she had felt beautiful in the new dress. But he had remade her, and she didn't think she could remain as that person. She was more comfortable in clothing that didn't matter. That didn't make her seem above others. And, goodness, she was not. She was just herself. An orphan who had been fortunate.

She had no choice but to continue her journey and take care of herself.

'You would be giving up a fortune, children who will have the best of things, and a status few receive.'

'I have never had status. Nor a fortune. And I don't want either if it means I would be indebted to you or anyone else for ever.'

His eyes looked pinched, and she suspected that now he truly saw her. Not the woman he'd thought she could be, if she used just the right cosmetics and the best fashions and became an accessory to him. But a woman with a mind of her own.

She could see it in his face. His wonderment at how she could say no to such a thing. But status was not important to her. She had no children, and might never have any, but she had made peace with that. And a fortune would be wonderful, but once she accepted it she knew she would be encased for ever in a world that would not let her leave. It would own her. A world in which she wasn't quite sure she could measure up to expectations.

She put her hands on her hips. 'I could not do that.'

'What do you mean?'

'If you were the richest man in London or the poorest it would not matter,' she said. 'I would not sell myself even for millions. It is not about funds. It is about strength. Mine. To find my way in the world.'

'Being wed to me would give you a stronger place in the world, and yet you don't want to step into it.'

He touched her jaw with one finger, drawing her face up so that she met his eyes.

'Almost the first thing you did was ask me to change my appearance.'

'You had no qualms about asking me to change my cravat and wear simpler clothing. It doesn't matter to me. It's just colours and loops on the piece of cloth I wear around my neck.'

'It isn't. Not for me. You wanted me to be more appealing.'

'I wanted you to be the best you could be. Just as I suppose you did with me. It was not about changing who you are. It was merely a style of clothing.' He laughed softly. 'You wanted me to reflect the colours of the past, and I wanted you to stop dressing from the past and appear current.'

'If we can't agree about something so insignificant—though really it isn't—how could we agree about things like child-rearing?'

He studied her. 'We should leave that to the experts. I hire the best in staff, so there would be no concern.'

'Children need to be raised by their parents.'

'If you hire an experienced governess she will know much more about raising a child than you. A child's life is too important to be treated lightly. You should take care and find someone who has knowledge of the best ways to rear one.'

She tapped all four fingers to her chest. 'I would want to raise my own children.'

'A good governess would not keep children from their mother. And I'd expect to see my children often.'

Elbows tight at her sides, she faced away from him and made two tiny fists. She pounded them into the air.

'I didn't have my parents close at hand. If I should have them, I want to experience my children. And I wish for them to know I am at their side.'

'That would be easier with a husband.' He pointed a finger at his chest. 'Such as myself. Children need a father. To be created.'

'Yes. I know,' she said. 'But perhaps a father should be in their lives, not just visiting them.'

'My father wasn't in my life. And he was especially irritating when he was. I did nothing right. I annoyed him. He said it was a cruel twist of fate that a man couldn't pick his children, and that he didn't think he would have chosen me, or his father would have chosen him, but that my grandfather and I would have chosen each other. We were alike in many ways.'

'I cannot believe you would be that kind of father. A parent should not desert a child.'

'What makes you think that fathers are supposed to be close to their children? It's not natural. Remember in the Old Testament? The father had a favourite out of the two brothers and you know how that turned out. Best for fathers not to get involved.'

'I'm guessing the mother was not in those boys' lives.' She tapped her cheek. 'They probably had a governess.'

'Perhaps I should withdraw my proposal.'

'You don't have to.'

She moved, and tried to ignore the crispness of his waistcoat, the gentle masculine scent that would give any woman pleasant dreams for the rest of her life.

'My first proposal ended with an errant arrow, and now this. I am becoming adept at rejection.'

'Goodness,' she said. 'A little rejection is only a hiccup in life, or an awareness that you're trying something new.'

'Why would you say that?' he asked.

'Because it has been so in my life, and I assume it is the same for others. I've been rejected by relatives, by a school for young ladies—as both a student and a teacher—and by a seamstress for an apprenticeship…' She paused. 'I think Aunt Agatha is the only person who hasn't rejected me.'

'I haven't.'

'Is that how you see it?' She tapped her chin and put on the most innocent expression she could muster. 'Remember the first time you saw me? You were consumed with opinions about my appearance.' She mocked a male voice. '"Change your hair. And your attire. You'll be perfect if you're someone else. Someone I can change on a whim."'

'That's not what happened. I only wanted you to be the best that you can.'

'I *am*. I am the perfect niece for my aunt. I agree. She agrees.'

'So do I.'

'After just a few changes… A few hundred changes.'

'Didn't you enjoy the attention at the picnic? Being the most admired lady there?'

'Ho-dee-holily-dee…' She strung out the nonsensical made-up word. 'Talk about stacking the deck. There were no other women their age for the men to congregate around. Strange how that happened.'

'You were the object of notice.'

'Just because it was enjoyable, it doesn't mean it was the right thing,' she said, trying to mind her tongue.

'You are an extremely rare and wonderful person. But I won't let you cause notice for my family in society.'

She studied him. Since biblical times or before people had been writing down others' stories. She was only following in their footsteps. And keeping a roof over her head was important.

'My aunt must have a home. And if you had heard her arguments with her husband, you would see why it was best that we left.'

Lord Andrews had not always been so treacherous, her aunt had said. True, he'd never been perfect, but he'd not always been so insufferable. In his own way, Aunt Agatha had said, he'd loved her.

Marriage was such a disaster that she was amazed the practice had remained in society. The words of that silly promise—'I do'—were only as genuine as the person uttering them.

She appraised Gabriel carefully.

Solidness looked out of the eyes staring back at her. He didn't lie. He wasn't going to let his grandmother's stories be told.

She swallowed.

He wished to marry her, he said, but she wondered if that was only because he had reached an age where he thought he should settle and have children and she was right there in front of him. He could wed and get the memoirs quashed in one fell swoop.

'You are not the woman I thought you were when we first talked.'

Gabriel felt splintered. A part of him ferociously wanted to wed her, and another part of him warned him that he should hesitate. He should not commit himself.

He didn't know if he would be able to give her the permanency of heart she deserved. Perhaps he was too much like his father. Perhaps he truly didn't know what love was, or how to feel it.

'I'm trying to be more like your grandmother,' she said. 'At least in my fearlessness.'

'I don't know how the two of you get along.'

'We're managing well. I like her. She's sardonic when she wishes to be and it's amusing to me. I sometimes burst out into laughter when we're talking, and she ends up laughing also. Should I never marry, nor have children, as I expect, then I will try to become more and more like her. And should I marry—when I am in my older years, I expect—it will be to a man who wears a simple cravat.'

'There are a lot of men who fit that description. There is one in front of you and you are not taking a chance on him. You are afraid.'

Perhaps she was wise to be. He'd seen so many marriages fail, and most times, if not always, the first blow to the union wasn't from the woman, but the man. At least with the kind of men he played cards with at the clubs...

'That could be true,' she said. 'But even if it is fear, it doesn't mean I'm not making the right decision. In a short time you will forget the passion we shared in our moments together, and only remember that I needed a home. Now, you know I can leave. But if I couldn't, would my words still have weight? Everyone who lives here permanently is either in your employ or financially dependent on you. That is so much power and you don't even realise it.'

'You say that I don't realise it? Perhaps I do. And perhaps I treat them all with dignity, and you cannot see the true value in that.'

His grandmother was the worst possible influence.

Marie had been corrupted by his grandmother and by her aunt's free thinking. She'd been completely ruined in a most unacceptable way, but he'd given her the opportunity to redeem herself with an appropriate union.

And she had thrown it back in his face.

Tomorrow, he hoped to see her at breakfast, and he would make certain to have an elaborate neckcloth. She would notice, and likely have her hair in the most depressing knot ever. Not that he truly minded. She would still be Marie, and he felt bad for angering her.

'Well. Goodnight… And an apology.'

The moment between them lingered.

'I'm not apologising.'

'I am. To you. I don't like it that we disagree. I still want us to be friends. It means a great deal to me. *You* mean a great deal to me.'

Her mouth opened, and she stared at him. 'I'm still working on the memoirs.'

He flicked a brow. 'I still care for you.'

Chapter Seventeen

He had awakened early—if one could call it awakening. He wasn't sure he'd been asleep, because all night he had been considering Marie's views.

Even her thoughts on child-rearing were different from his. He'd never pondered Marie's perspective before. A man such as he had so many important duties to attend to. He'd never thought of children as being any responsibility of the father except for the provision of shelter, food, education and perhaps, as they grew, training in affairs of the estate.

But Marie might have a point, he thought. Although he wasn't sure that a baby would even notice its father's presence, and the nursemaid and the governess would probably be offended if he was present. A situation like that would take some consideration. The children might grow up disliking their father if they had to be around him continuously.

'You are joining us?' His grandmother squinted at him when he strode into the breakfast room.

'I thought it would be a pleasant way to start the day,' he answered.

'That's not what you usually say,' his grandmother replied, and then looked across the table at Marie. 'I suppose you wanted to see me.'

She laughed, in a way that said she knew she was the only one to find it humorous.

Marie greeted him civilly and he nodded to her, amazed at the awareness that washed over him.

Her hair was curled in almost exactly the style the maid had perfected on her. It framed her face and her glasses, and the looser knot she retained crowned the view.

'Did I tell you the story about the cutpurse trying to steal from my friend?' his grandmother asked Marie, interrupting his perusal. 'I want you to be sure to include that. That thief didn't think he would ever be able to get away from me. It hurts more than you'd think, you know…to pummel someone. I thought I'd injured my arm. Definitely bruised my hand.'

'How would you have handled that?' Gabriel asked Marie, genuinely wanting to hear her answer.

He supposed she fascinated him because she'd been raised as an orphan, and that made her different from the other women he knew.

'Well, I have no complaint with how your grandmother reacted,' she said, smiling at the older lady. 'She certainly got his attention. I don't know how I would have responded. I rarely know what I will do in a situation until presented with it.' Marie studied him. 'Your neckcloth is exceptionally bright today.'

He laughed, touching it. 'I know. I chose it just for you.'

'How sweet,' his grandmother said, rising and putting a hand on the table. 'It's ugly. And now I must go to my room to recover from the sight of it. I'm going to jot down some notes for more events I want Marie to include in my story.'

After she'd left, Marie said, 'I can see that she might not have been the best person to raise a child.'

'She was a better mother than it appears. When Father was young she made sure to see him quarterly.'

'That's true,' his grandmother said as she put her head round the door and looked back into the room. 'I really can't blame myself for your father's problems because I didn't raise him. Now, come along, Marie.'

She stood. 'I will be there directly.'

His grandmother cleared her throat and then left.

Gabriel's eyes met Marie's and he smiled. 'I suppose you should leave.'

She stood and walked closer to his chair. 'This is for trying to get me to blackmail you so you could marry me.'

She tied two of the loops of his cravat together. Then she put a hand on his shoulder, not taking it away instantly, but letting it slide slowly down his back as she meandered from the room.

He wondered if he had searched her out on purpose. Not in the house. But in life. If he'd managed to find the one person who would say no to him.

Then he saw the truth of her words hidden in his thoughts.

The one person who could say no.

He'd never thought anyone could refuse him. He had a title and a fortune.

Gabriel suspected that his father had had a constant battle within himself to remain within the bounds of proper society. That he had had so many mistresses as a way of living more adventurously. More dangerously. He had chased things which fired his blood and gave him an appetite for more. Not taking care of himself so things felt more rigorous. More dangerous. More daring.

Until he had been emboldened enough to attempt a boat crossing that caught him in a storm.

Gabriel purposely didn't race to the edge of things like that. He had worked hard not to continue the family lineage that way. His mother had spoken with him every time she'd visited, and the one thing she had requested each time was that he repair the family honour.

She'd claimed that his paternal grandparents had let down so many people—servants included—and several times he had been walking in corridors when the servants didn't know he was about, and had heard discussions of his father's mistresses or his grandmother's antics. He'd never liked that.

He'd asked his father, and his father had told him it was not his concern, said he would have the servants sacked for speaking when they should be working.

From then on, he'd pretended he'd heard the tales from a friend. In part, it was true. One of his friends had mentioned something, but he'd called him a liar.

His father had told him to get better friends.

He'd watched his father leave the room, wondering how one would get a better father.

Now he pondered if his father hadn't got the best of sons, either.

He didn't blame Marie for refusing him. It might have been the wisest thing she'd ever done. But that didn't change the fact that he cared for her.

He found he had no appetite, and without Marie in the room there was no reason for him to remain, so he moved back to his bedroom. The bed had not been made yet. A huge bed. Likely made to his grandfather or his great-grandfather's specifications.

Only one pillow had been disturbed. Only one pillow had ever been disturbed in this room since he had taken it. It was presumptuous of the maids even to think he would need two. He walked to the bedside and ran his fingers over the fabric, imagining Marie's head on the second pillow.

The fear of never having her at his side again clutched him.

Gabriel could see his father's errors. His father had chosen not to give his heart to his wife. He'd chosen not to give his heart to his son, either—which really hadn't bothered Gabriel at all. He'd had the best of nursemaids, and then the best of tutors.

He needed to seek out Marie. He needed to learn more about her. Perhaps a man should see a woman more than a few times before he proposed, but with Marie it wasn't necessary.

In that instant he suspected the footsteps he'd been determined to avoid had been the very steps he'd followed. He'd been just like his father—only he'd not left a wife alone at home. Or a family. He'd merely avoided having them.

At teatime, the butler entered his rooms and gave him a message.

He strode to Marie's room and knocked.

She was at a little desk and, stopped her scribbling when he entered. There were papers on top of the sofa, and she was still dressed in her singular dresses, reminding him of a doll from the past. One who'd had some trials, as evidenced by the smudge of ink on her cheek.

She appeared comfortable in her surroundings. And she made his house appear more lived-in. Less an elaborate shelter and residence, more a place of solace. A better home than it had been before.

But he didn't know if he was imagining a world like that because of his age and his desires. Perhaps he saw a different person than she truly was.

He reached out, bending to lift her hand. Bringing her knuckles to his cheek by way of greeting.

'Once you try to publish this book there's no going back.'

He wanted so much to hear her say that she would not risk hurting his family.

'There's never been any going back for any of us,' she said, standing. 'Life moves at a gallop when it is good, at a crawl when it is bad.'

He kept her hand in his. 'You could disguise the incidents, so no one knows who you are writing about.'

'We've gone over this. Your grandmother wants her story told, and I believe it is an important one. Inspiring to others.'

'It's easy not to realise the true value of things,' he said. 'Like privacy.'

But that wasn't what he truly meant. Trust. That was more precious. Priceless, in fact.

'But your grandmother wants her adventures noted. She wants other people to know of the trials she's had.'

'There are two sides to every story—if not more. Particularly where my grandmother is concerned. She's been lighting fuses all her life. And when she doesn't light them, she gets someone else to do so.'

'I agree that it seems that way, and probably is, but that's the thing that has made her fascinating. Someone sitting at home and having what appears to be a dull life could live vicariously through her, and see and appreciate the plainness of their life in a new light. They will thank her for it.'

'Is that what you're doing?'

'No. I have always been happy for the brief moments of peacefulness in my life, because I have seen so many people who do not appreciate them. Some of them create upset for the excitement of it. They fashion their own drama instead of traipsing to the theatre, but it is over a stocking or a bite of pudding or a hair ribbon.'

'You understand that my heritage and my obligation to my family name must come first?'

She clasped his hand. 'I appreciate that you're not ranting and railing against me.'

'That's not something I've ever done. My mother and father were quite businesslike as they discussed their differences, no matter how much was at stake. Both of them refused to be like Grandmother.'

'You are true to it,' she said.

'I asked you to marry me.'

'Because your family was annoying you.'

'Yes. But if a person knowingly lights the fuse, then they should be aware of the fragments that might fly about them. The destruction they could cause. Sometimes I can't keep explosions from happening. I could not un-break the window after Grandmother's first gunpowder explosion. It was destroyed.'

She nibbled her bottom lip again. For the rest of his life, if he saw a woman bite her bottom lip he would imagine Marie.

He wanted to be certain she knew he wished her no ill will, because he was going to make sure his grandmother's story stayed private. He could understand Marie's wish not to wed. To be able to take care of her aunt and herself. He hoped she could comprehend his duty to protect his family.

He would say goodbye, and she would see the sentiment in his gaze.

It seemed natural to kiss her, but as he was on his way to kiss her cheek she put a hand flat on his chest, stopping him. 'That will not cause me to change my mind.'

'I know.'

She stood and grasped the fabric of his waistcoat and pulled him close, but this time he stopped, just before their lips touched.

'I will not change my mind either, but you will always remain in my heart,' he said.

'I love you.' Her words were soft. 'But that doesn't mean I will be staying. It only means what I said. The book is almost finished, and my aunt is taking the pearls to be sold tomorrow.'

He knew the depth of his missing her would be great. Knew the emptiness that would follow him when she'd left.

He didn't know if he moved forward or she did, but their lips met, hungry, and their arms pulled each other close, and then closer. He ended the kiss, keeping his eyes shut, letting his lips linger at her cheek, and then enclosing her in a hug.

'Is this our goodbye?' she asked.

'No,' he answered. 'This is just our first step on a new beginning, away from each other.'

'I think a goodbye would be easier.'

A knock on the door interrupted them, and a maid entered.

'Miss Marie, did you know your uncle has arrived? He is talking with his wife.' She spoke quickly and left.

'I expected him to come. My aunt sent him a letter telling him we are not returning, and asking for the items she left behind to be sent to her. I doubt he has brought anything.'

Gabriel saw the sadness in her eyes, and knew he could not add to her struggles.

He would miss her. A lot. But it was for the best that he didn't care about her. That he distanced himself from her as soon as possible so it would be easier. Because he had recently visited the publisher. And it had been very cordial. Friendly.

The publisher had smiled and said, 'You scratch my back and I'll scratch yours.'

He would let the publisher tell her.

Chapter Eighteen

Marie was still in the little room, second-guessing herself, wondering if she'd let a lack of principles destroy her. She wondered if it was fair to Gabriel to tell his grandmother's story when he had done so much for her.

A crash of footsteps sounded outside her door and she raised her head, confused. Who would be running in the house?

Then the door burst open and her aunt rushed inside, arms splayed and chin quivering.

She stopped in front of Marie, tears forming. Pacing from side to side.

'What's wrong?' Marie asked, standing, feeling a knot in her stomach, knowing the news wouldn't be good.

'It's Reginald. He has left. And he has taken the pearls.' She clasped her hands, interlocking her fingers into a singular clasp and hugging herself. 'He asked me to prove I had not sold them. I was happy to do so. When I showed him that I still had them in my reticule, he ripped it from my hand. I told him I had promised them to you, but he wouldn't stop. He said I must go with him if I wanted them.'

She put a hand to her head.

'He wants everything to be unpleasant for me. He said they were only mine as long as I lived in his house, and he said I must return. I said I would never be forced. He stormed out, but I could not get him to leave the pearls.'

Marie gasped. The pearls were her aunt's security. Part of the marriage settlement Lord Andrews had given her before they wed, to prove he really cared.

Marie gave her aunt a hug. 'I will talk with Gabriel,' she said. 'He will help.'

Or at least he would help her aunt.

She touched the door, holding herself upright, letting her mind grasp the realisation that her thoughts had immediately turned to him and the belief that he would assist her. She comprehended that he was the only one she wanted to help her. The only one she truly thought could get the pearls returned.

She put a hand to her throat, considering whether or not it was fair to ask him for aid, but then she saw the tears rolling down her aunt's cheek.

She took her aunt by both arms. 'Don't worry. I will summon Gabriel.'

She rushed from the room.

Scurrying into the corridor, she ran to his rooms, hoping he was there, not knowing what she would do if he wasn't. At the door, she pounded on it, calling out his name.

Instantly, he opened the door, and the sight of him reminded her that he was not a dream. He'd been a real moment in her past. And now there he stood, tall, solid, not even wearing a plain cravat, but none at all. Waistcoat open. A ledger in his hand.

An imposing form. Rigid as a fixed blade.

He tossed the ledger aside when he saw her face.

'What's wrong?' he asked, grasping her arm. 'What has happened? Is someone hurt?'

'No. No. It's the pearls.'

He surrounded her with his arms, pulling her inside, hugging her close before he released her. 'They are just gems. Calm yourself.'

'They are not only gems. They are my aunt's security. Her marriage settlement. Our chance for a home. Please help us.'

She'd not seen him before like this. He was almost a stranger to her, and yet he was studying her with compassion, perhaps longing. Loss… And her heart tumbled a thousand times over, in less time than it took for her to say anything more.

She had to break the silence. Their eyes and bodies were speaking too much. Too simply. And she couldn't lose herself. She couldn't forget that she needed to be strong.

'Can you help us?' She rushed the words out. 'Uncle has taken the pearls. Aunt Agatha is in tears.'

He frowned, shaking his head. For an instant she thought he was disagreeing, and then she understood that he was reflecting on his actions.

'A wise man would only help you in return for a promise from you to give him the manuscript.'

'I can't. I've already promised it to your grandmother.'

He waited, arms crossed, stance wide. The blink of his eyes told her he was going to help her. He had already lost the battle within himself. He didn't relish it, but he would.

'And an even wiser man might do the right thing and help the people he cares about.'

He stepped away, reaching for the wrinkled cravat he'd removed and looked at it. He moved to the bell-pull and tugged on it three times.

'I can't let anyone else assist you.'

Almost instantly a servant arrived at a run. He told the maid to make certain the carriage was readied immediately.

'Do you need to take anything with you?' he asked, looping the fabric around his neck, giving it a simple tie, and doing up the buttons on his waistcoat.

'No,' she said. He was all she needed.

He fetched his coat and took her arm, and they waited at the front entrance until the carriage was pulled around.

She told him what had happened, and wondered what it would feel like to always have him at her side. Like a knight who would come to her rescue. A man who would thrust himself in front of anything that was charging at her. A protector.

The thought left her speechless. Only her aunt had ever seemed the least bit interested in protecting her. She'd never expected anyone else to come to her aid.

Now Gabriel was helping her. As if he was supposed to. As if she were his wife.

'Are you doing this for me?' she asked. 'Or for my aunt?'

'For you. But for her also. I have to. I won't turn away when you need help. I will always be here for you when you need me.'

'You don't have to. You promised me nothing. You owe me nothing.'

Then she saw something else in him. The reason his forebears were titled. The intractable promise.

He looked at her, and a smile wafted across his lips. 'Yes, I do.'

He looked across at Marie, sitting beside him in the carriage, prim little glasses perched on her nose. The outdated frock and the fringe of hair around her face gave her a rarity that soothed him. He'd never seen anyone who looked quite like her. Her mouth was pursed into a scowl, her eyes were tight, and her tiny brows rose above them.

He swallowed, shocked to realise the way his heart had wrapped itself around her. He couldn't help himself.

'Will you ever marry?' he asked.

Her lips thinned. 'I doubt it.' A soft smile flashed across her face. 'This would have been the time to take that direction. But…this book will be my marriage, I suppose.'

He squeezed her fingers, pleased she had not yet found out about his discussion with the publisher.

'I've been subservient all my life, in order to have food and a roof over my head. It has been my employment. But to have a husband… I would no longer need to be employed and yet I think that is what marriage would feel like. A job I cannot leave.'

'Many people leave it, even if their vows still bind them.'

'Like my aunt and her husband. And we are in the midst of that. It reminds me of how treacherous life can be after a simple vow.'

She studied the view as the carriage rolled on, and he reached and took her hand. He felt a light squeeze, and he pulled her knuckles to his mouth for a kiss before letting their clasped hands rest between them.

The carriage bounced and struggled in places, but continued on, and he supposed that was symbolic of their life. They were both going in the same direction, and would be feeling the ravages of life, but it would not be with any commitment between them, instead the knowledge of a deeper friendship in which disagreements would dissolve.

He hoped.

She wasn't going to take it well that his grandmother's memoirs would not be published. And now her aunt had lost the pearls.

When the carriage finally stopped, he took her hands after he'd alighted, helping her step out and tucking her hand inside his arm. 'How well do you know your uncle?' he asked.

She grimaced. 'He and my aunt had a terrific row just after I moved in, not long after their marriage, and not much has gone well since. He mostly kept to himself, and she and I kept to ourselves. Shouting wasn't good for him, my aunt claimed. And he did seem to disagree with everything she did.'

'Even people who don't appear to like each other may have a deep bond.'

'I've yet to see anyone whom marriage has made happy.' She wrinkled her nose and pushed at one of her sleeves, fluffing it. 'Not one person.'

He thought for a moment, more jesting with her than serious. 'It might be a clever ruse. People could just be pretending unhappiness so others are not jealous. A card game of sorts, with the winning hand kept hidden.'

She sniffed. 'Don't expect me to wager on that one.'

After stepping inside, he gave the butler his calling card.

The man read it, straightened his back, and took them into a room with drapes flowing into carefully arranged half-circles at their base, the fabric motionless even with the breeze bringing in the scent of meadowlands.

'I will fetch Lord Andrews immediately,' the butler said, leaving.

Lord Andrews' uneven gait announced his arrival, and his brows were knitted in a furrowed clump that looked difficult to contain on one forehead. He appeared like an ageing bull with a face damaged by years of running into hedges, other bulls, and possibly barn doors. He wore the narrowest cravat Gabriel had ever seen, and it was looped into a bouquet of knotted twists. Possibly about sixteen loops total.

He touched his cravat and gave Marie a quick glance. She responded with a smug nod and an overly polite greeting to Lord Andrews.

Lord Andrews stretched out a hand, indicating they both take a seat.

Gabriel relaxed against the sofa with Marie beside him. He spoke briefly with the man, complimenting him on the location of his house and the well-pruned hedges in front of it. Then he said, 'I wanted to talk to you about your plans for Lady Andrews.'

'Nothing to discuss if you're a friend of *that woman*. I have tried to be friendly,' he said, 'but I couldn't drink fast enough.'

Those eyebrows moved when he spoke of Agatha, and reminded Gabriel of a caterpillar struggling to remain in place while the ground moved around it.

'But you wed her,' Gabriel said.

'I was blinded by grief for my wife and *that woman* was already living here. I didn't grasp what I was doing.'

'You gave her the pearls, though.'

'It was a mistake. A huge one. I've taken them back. Even though they're fake.'

Marie gasped. 'You can't do that. You purchased them for your first wife, and you gave them to my aunt as a wedding settlement. They're rare—just as my aunt is.'

'They're fake. Just as fake as Agatha. And you.'

Marie crossed her arms. 'That is not true. They are real, and she is priceless. It's not her fault. She did what she thought best. And all because of a secret, everything changed. You're punishing my aunt but you're also punishing yourself.'

'Bah!' He waved a hand. 'Of course I'm punishing her. But they are fake. Probably why she likes them.'

Marie turned to Gabriel. 'We tested them. They're real.'

'How?' he asked.

'The tooth test,' she said. 'You rub them against a tooth. Real pearls are gritty. Fake pearls are smooth.'

'You heard the young lady.' Gabriel gave a shrug and rose, taking a step closer to the older man, knowing that few could ignore his words when he stood. 'She had tested them. They're real. Get them.'

'Paste,' the old man said, not retreating.

'I will come with you to retrieve them,' Gabriel said, 'or I'll wait here with you while Marie finds them. Tell her where they are.'

'Would you rather have the pearls?' the old man asked him, those caterpillar eyebrows stilling. 'Or would you prefer to have the letter in which your grandmother wagers you in marriage?'

'It was in the reticule,' Marie admitted, lips firm, lowering her head briefly before she lifted her eyes again.

Gabriel frowned. 'Get me the pearls. A piece of paper is only a piece of paper, and I don't care what it says.'

The older man went to a small cabinet and took out a folded piece of paper. He handed it to Gabriel. 'You can have it. It won't do me any good. Just a moment of amusing reading.'

Glancing at it, Gabriel put it in his coat pocket.

'Get me the pearls,' Gabriel repeated, commanding the man to move with his eyes.

'Fine,' the man said. He gave Marie another angry glance. 'She can get them. They're on my bedside table. But…'

His voice faded away as Marie ran from the room.

He glared at Gabriel. 'I should never have given them to Aggie.'

'Perhaps a wife is more important than jewellery.'

'You can see how well that is working out. Agatha brought my wife's daughter into my house without telling me who she was. A secret that would have been better kept for the rest of her life. She ruined the precious memories I had, and proved herself untrustworthy where I was concerned.'

'It's hard to keep secrets hidden.'

'Yes, but I would have been better not knowing. Just because something's true, it doesn't mean you want it splattered across your face.'

Gabriel agreed, but it would feel disloyal to say so.

Marie's returning footsteps sounded on the stairs, interrupting, and she entered the room with the pearl strands interwoven in her fingertips. Two strands, not overly large, with the outside rope having a larger pearl hanging from it. In her other hand she held an elaborate case.

'Agatha only wed me for a place to live.'

The old man studied Marie, challenging her to deny it.

'When I first found out about Marie I thought she was Agatha's daughter,' he said, taking a handkerchief and wiping his nose. 'I could understand that. After all, we all make mistakes in our youth. But the fact that they both kept the secret from me, and that Agatha brought her into my house as her niece… And then I discovered the truth.'

He pointed a finger at Marie.

'The courts would consider you my daughter. Don't you think a man has a right to know something like that?'

'Don't blame me,' Marie said. 'I should blame you for leaving your wife alone for two years.'

'I had to. I needed funds and I was helping a friend on a venture. I had no choice.'

'Maybe Agatha felt the same.'

'She should have told me about you before we wed.'

'Would it have made a difference?'

'I doubt it. I regretted it the moment I wed Agatha and turned to see the wrong woman at my side. It's true I gave the pearls to Agatha. I suppose I thought they would make her look more like my wife if she wore them. She was my wife's companion. Not mine.'

Now Gabriel understood Marie's viewpoint on marriage a little better. If she'd heard this man say that he'd turned and seen the wrong woman at his side...

Gabriel wondered if he would look differently at her after he'd read what she'd written about his family. If his feelings truly would change in an instant. They had when he'd fallen in love, and he wondered if people fell out of love just as quickly. He wondered if *he* would fall out of love that rapidly.

'Aunt Agatha is your wife now,' Marie said, moving to stand at Gabriel's side and holding the necklace so the light reflected from the huge pearl in the centre and the two huge bluish ones on each side of it. 'And I am not your daughter.'

Gabriel took the strands of pearls. He had no awareness of the stones, was only conscious of how close he was to Marie and the intensity of her eyes, thanking him. Again, his feelings for her intensified. Pounding strong within him. He wanted her to be happy, but he didn't know if his sincerity would fade as quickly as it had arisen. No feeling had ever intensified so quickly inside him. Not even hatred or compassion. He'd never had such strong emotions before. They were new to him, and they weakened him.

He'd raced here to retrieve the pearls for Marie and assist her. He'd helped others before. Many times. But it had never seemed that his life was at stake. That his happiness was in jeopardy. He was in her clasp as handily as the pearls were. But clasps could easily weaken. Could be destroyed.

Now Marie studied him, admiration in her gaze.

'We'll take them and leave,' Gabriel said to Lord Andrews. 'You're doing the right thing.'

Her uncle whirled around and one of his hands clenched, as if he could feel the necklace in his grasp, and his lips moved. At first he made no sound, then he spoke. 'I can't sleep without those pearls in my house. Last night I had my first night of good sleep since Agatha took them and left.'

'Perhaps there is a way you could have them back,' Gabriel said, an idea coming to him. 'You have a second house?'

'The hunting lodge. It's little more than a hut. I don't even like going there any more.'

'What if Lady Agatha would trade you the pearls for the lodge?' he asked. 'The law is that a man should provide for his wife,' Gabriel said. 'Whether you want her living here or not, that is a consideration.'

He levelled a stare at Gabriel. 'That would get two eyesores gone from my life.'

'The lodge desperately needs a new roof,' Marie said.

'I would have them both out of my hair?' he asked Gabriel, ignoring Marie.

'Yes, providing you pay the expenses for the lodge. A man should take care of his family,' Gabriel added.

'I'll do it for five years,' the older man groused.

'Ten.'

'Six, and I'll add enough to fix the roof and the floor. Trust me, it's needed. I will put aside the amount for that payment and the same for expenses on the property to be given to my wife in full. I want the paintings from the walls, but the furniture is of no consequence.'

Gabriel looked at Marie. Saw the quick upsweep of her chin.

'I'm sure she would be happy with that,' Marie added.

'Until everything has been agreed I will make certain to hold on to these.' Gabriel lifted the pearls. 'Plus, I will employ someone who will make sure the paperwork which allows the lodge to change hands is completed. The pearls will be returned when the papers are signed and the repair money is received. Until then, I will have them stored in my safe.'

Gabriel slipped them into his pocket beside the paper.

The property would still belong to Lord Andrews, so they would have to be careful in putting it in his wife's name. He didn't know how it would be sorted out, but his man of affairs would.

The older man thumped over to stand beside Gabriel.

'Let me touch them.'

His voice wasn't a command, but a request. Gabriel held them out, and Lord Andrews ran a gnarled finger over the pearls.

'If I release the funds immediately, will you have paperwork ready to be completed?' His voice softened. 'Without these, I have nothing. I never knew how much my wife meant to me. I never knew how alone I would feel when she was gone. That's why I wed Agatha. But after I wed her I was still alone. And then I discovered how I'd been betrayed.' His hand fell to his side and he shook his head. 'I thought marriage would bring back my world, yet I felt more abandoned than ever. What a jest.'

With that, he turned to leave.

'Why don't you try to talk with my aunt?' Marie asked, interrupting Lord Andrews' exit. 'She was a good companion to your wife. The two of you could talk about her. If you don't think of Aunt Agatha as a wife, but as a friend, perhaps you would get on well.'

'Do you think she would want to live here if she had anywhere else to go?' he asked. 'I don't.'

'I can't say. But she might want to live here if you were friendly to her.'

'I do need someone to advise the housekeeper,' he said. 'But I want the pearls back in my house first.'

'Then you will have no trouble with our men of affairs meeting and getting the particulars in order,' said Gabriel.

'The sooner the better. Tomorrow, even.'

'The hunting lodge will be set aside so it belongs to Lady Agatha and her niece,' Gabriel said.

'It will.'

Marie saw satisfaction in Gabriel's regard. They'd secured a house for her aunt, and funds for a time.

She only felt sadness. She didn't want to leave his house. But she didn't want to wed a man who might look at her after the wedding and see the wrong woman.

'We'll begin on the particulars today, after I have talked with Agatha to make sure she's happy with this, and I will get everything done quickly,' Gabriel said.

Her uncle gave a quick upsweep of his head. 'Send me a note if she is agreeable, and I will arrive at your house with my man of affairs to complete the transaction.'

'And will you talk with Aunt Agatha?' Marie asked.

'If I've time to spare, I might.' He glared into the distance. 'It seems, since she left, I don't know which direction is up and which is down. I was so angry with her. *So* angry. But living without her… She was…useful to have around.'

Gabriel gave him a nod, and they made their farewells.

'Useful to have around?' Gabriel said once they were alone. 'Faint praise.'

'More than she usually heard from him, I assure you.'

Once they were in the carriage, and it was rolling away, Gabriel said, 'We'll go via my man of affairs' office. His brother is very knowledgeable about property transactions. The sooner it is completed, the better off you'll be. We don't want to give your uncle a chance to change his mind.'

'He's not truly my uncle. Not even by marriage. Agatha worked as a companion to her distant cousin. My mother. When my mother discovered she was going to have a baby and knew it couldn't be her husband's, because he'd sailed from England months before, she decided to keep it a secret. Aunt Agatha helped her to conceal me, thinking eventually my mother would be able to take me in as a ward. But my mother didn't. And would become furious when reminded of me.'

When Marie's mother had passed away, Agatha had consoled Lord Andrews in his grief.

'After Lord Andrews asked Agatha to wed him, she said she wanted her niece to live with her, and he agreed. At first.'

'You don't hold a grudge against your mother?'

'No.' Marie gave a one-sided shrug. 'I would have hated to live with a mother who didn't want me. I would always have been thinking something was wrong with me.' She tapped under her chin.

'You must have had a miserable childhood.'

'No. A mostly happy one. I worked a lot. Laundry and cleaning and cooking and so on. I didn't really mind. The local shopkeepers were generally nice.

She moved closer, surrendering again to the joy of feeling that he cared for her.

'I couldn't change the fact that the woman who raised me often resented me but needed the funds.'

Then she paused.

Shaking her head, she said. 'A lady would visit me occasionally. A nice lady, who worked as a companion. She would always bring funds for my care. I suspected she was my mother, and I asked her one day, but she said she wasn't. The lady whom I lived with verified it. My mother had stayed in her house since before I was born, so the servants wouldn't know she was going to have a child.'

Marie had been disappointed, but the lady—Agatha— had done her best. Even if her visits had only been for a few quick moments when funds were delivered, or an occasional half-day.

Agatha had taken her on her first carriage ride. Such an adventure. A present for her thirteenth birthday. Marie had enjoyed having someone who cared about her, and when

Agatha had come to her after her marriage and invited Marie to live with her she'd been overjoyed.

Aunt Agatha had asked if she wanted to bring her clothing, and she'd said that she would like to leave it behind for more unfortunate people. But really she'd been wearing her best dress, and the only other had been too small for her and pinched painfully under the arms. They'd thanked the woman who'd cared for Marie, and Agatha had promised to visit.

When Marie had arrived at Lord Andrews' she'd been given a frumpy old dress that her aunt had apologised for, and bathwater. Bathwater in abundance. And soap. Soap that had smelled like a flower garden. That had been the only thing she'd asked for more of, and she'd kept the excess fragrant soap at her bedside, waking up to a room that smelled of bliss.

She'd felt like a flower arrangement when she'd stepped out of the bathwater and dressed in the old dress, which had hung off her, but it had been so pleasant to have a dress that was too large instead of too small, after a childhood of trying to squeeze into dresses she'd outgrown.

Getting to know the maids had been enjoyable, and soon they'd all insisted she must let them assist her and clean for her, or they'd be out of a job. She had pinched herself. And not awakened. She'd felt richer than any Midas.

She'd decided it was too good to be true, and that she would do her best to go along with whatever arose and be a wonderful niece…or, secretly in her heart, a daughter.

'Agatha gave me some mementos. She showed me a painting of my mother. Her husband had put away all her jewellery, but she gave me some handkerchiefs my mother had had. Showed me books she'd read. But really only the portrait meant anything, and I would try to see my resemblance in it. The rest of it—the handkerchiefs, the books, the rooms she'd lived in—didn't mean much to me. It made me angry more than anything. That she could have had so much and keep me a secret.

'I told Agatha I'd rather have mementos from her, and that, even better, I had memories of the happiness I always felt when she visited. Of the few times she was able to take me on a carriage ride or spend half a day with me.'

'You were fortunate to have her.'

'Your grandmother was the only person who would take in my aunt, and she encouraged her to leave a man who was unkind. She wants her story told. And I would like it to be told also. If being wayward is the only way to have a heart, then perhaps people should know it.'

'Are you including your own history in the memoirs?'

'No, this is your grandmother's book.'

'You could put a note inside,' he said, 'and tell your story…and Lord Andrews'.'

Her body tightened and she couldn't speak. His words had hit her with the force of a slap. Lord Andrews would never forgive appearing in a book like that. He would be furious at Agatha. The marriage would be destroyed with no chance of repair.

She unclasped her arms from around herself. 'Agatha is provided for, and I will not risk anything ruining that. It's the least I can do to help her procure a home of her own. I'll be able to take care of myself.'

She tried not to think of the words he'd said at the last. The duplicity of not wanting her own story in the memoirs.

Chapter Nineteen

The horses had seemed full of life when they'd begun the journey home, but they soon slowed, relaxing their pace. The excitement Marie had once felt at being in a carriage had faded, overridden by the need she felt for Gabriel.

'Can I see the pearls again?' she asked. 'They really don't mean much to me…except for their value in gaining Aunt Agatha her freedom. That is everything. She'll have a home now. A place of her own.'

He studied their bluish tint. To him, they looked as if they were worth little, but everyone else seemed impressed with them.

'They're just baubles,' he said.

She grasped them, letting her fingers dance over the orbs. Looking at the clasp. A piece of jewellery worth more than she'd ever owned in her life—probably more than Agatha had ever owned.

She returned them to him, anxious to get back to his home and tell Agatha the good news.

Then she looked at his face, and felt a river of emotions pass between them. She would be leaving his home, and she had to make plans.

She clasped his hand the rest of the way back to his

estate, and released it only as the carriage stopped at the entrance.

When they walked into the house, the light was already fading from the sky. She rushed inside to spread the good news and tell her aunt that the hunting lodge would soon be hers.

Her aunt clapped her hands in joy at the opportunity to live in the lodge, and agreed that she would prefer to exchange the pearls for a home.

'I'll put them away,' Gabriel said, and Marie followed him.

Once in his room, he locked away the necklace, and then, with just a look in his eyes, he seemed to be able to pull her into his arms. His hug was tender. His touch on the back of her neck consoling.

She wondered if he was caring for her, or just for a woman who had had so little affection in her life.

'You don't have to show me extra tenderness because of my past.'

A small line appeared between his brows. 'I wouldn't caress you at all if I didn't want affection between us.'

She felt cosseted. Consoled. Her heart expanded to the point of almost filling her eyes with tears.

She hugged him in return, wishing she could give him the same feelings he was giving her.

Staring up into his eyes, she felt her knees weaken, and yet she didn't fall away. He held her. His arms were cradling, soothing, lifting her.

She moistened her lips, wanting his kiss more than she wanted air.

He must have seen it in her gaze. Their lips met. A taste

reminding her of wine. Of comforting nights. Of dreams too good to wake from.

He pulled away, reaching to touch her hair, her cheek, running his fingertips over her face.

'This moment is my whole life,' he said, touching her bottom lip. 'You are the sunrise, the sunset, and all the hues in between.'

She reached for his cravat. 'A simple knot is so much easier to take off.'

'Prove it,' he whispered against her lips.

And then her fingers slipped, and she accidentally tightened the knot.

He reached up and put his hand over hers. In an instant the neckcloth was loosened, and fell to the floor.

'Nothing to hurry about,' he said. 'Nothing to worry about. We have all night, and I want this to last at least that long.'

He took her into his bedroom. Effortlessly.

Then he let her stand beside his bed, and he dropped a soft kiss onto her lips. The softest kiss she'd ever had. So much lightness from someone so much stronger than she was. She realised she'd been asleep her whole life.

He touched each hook on the back of her dress and she felt them undone, but he didn't remove the garment.

Instead, he stopped and slipped his waistcoat from his shoulders, dropping it. He pulled his shirt from his trousers, and then stopped moving.

'Since we have the whole night,' he asked, 'do you mind if we go slowly? If I hold you in my arms? If we just sit and feel the night?'

'I'm not sure,' she said, not certain she could wait, feeling her body crave him. 'But we can try.'

She sat on his lap, felt his arms around her, and he held her hands, moving his fingertips over them, watching them as if he'd never touched anyone's skin before and could hardly believe the tenderness of it.

She had never seen anyone's hands in the way she saw his.

Capable, strong, and yet so gentle.

He put his cheek against hers and somehow shut everything away from her. It was a gift he had—enclosing the world around them and making everything and everyone else disappear. Even if they were only together for this one night, he made it feel like a for ever moment. Stopping time to hold her close.

He ran his fingertips over her shoulders and pushed her dress aside, his lips capturing the soft skin underneath.

Helping him remove his coat, she pulled him closer, burrowing into his arms, and he wrapped her more warmly than any covering that had ever touched her.

Removing his clothing, and then hers, he pulled her onto the bed with him.

'Marie…' he whispered, and he made her name sound exotic, intriguing and intense.

Their kisses deepened and she tasted the moist miracle of Gabriel, marvelled that all was right with the world.

When his fingertips brushed over her breasts, holding her nipples before he gently grazed them with his teeth, she gasped.

Then she ran her hand over every plane of his body, memorising it, though she knew she would never be able to totally recapture the feel of him in such a way that it would remain with her for ever, as she wanted it to.

Kisses rained on her face, and then he rose above her,

asking her with just a slight change in his countenance if she were ready. She answered by reaching up and pulling him closer with all her strength.

A flurry of passion ignited within her and rose quickly to its peak. She clutched him, hanging on for life, and he responded, holding her against him.

'You don't have to rush away,' he said as she lifted her dress from the floor.

'I really should get back to my room.'

'Stay a little longer.'

She sat on the bed, her hand resting on the covers, and he moved closer, so he could interlace his fingers with hers.

'It pains me to think of you, a child alone in the world, with no parents for help. What if Agatha hadn't cared for you?'

He gave her hand the smallest squeeze, and she felt protected. Touched.

She stood. 'She did, though. And, really, almost everyone around me did watch over me.'

'A child shouldn't have to think about such things.'

'I didn't. I just survived. And I knew if I did all the right things, one day I would have a chance at something better. Aunt Agatha told me that over and over. I had all the answers. Truly, I did. I only needed one. I was simply to survive until I could get to a point to thrive. And now I have the luxury of choices. Not a tremendous amount, but more than I had before. I'm not finding the decision as easy as I would have hoped, though.'

'Do any of us truly have choices? Or must we just try to decide on the best option that might take us in the direction we should go?'

She understood how he felt.

'I don't want to be missed,' she said. 'I must get back to my room. It will be morning soon, and you are the only one in this house who isn't an early riser.'

'Let me help you dress,' he said. 'It will be an honour.'

'To be a lady's maid?' she asked.

'For you. Yes.'

She held herself away. 'You don't have to be so concerned. I was fortunate.'

He held her close and rested his cheek against hers. She knew her height was taller than usual for a woman, but she was still smaller than he was.

'What are your plans?' he asked.

'I will live with my aunt at the lodge and I will study botany. Or birds and flowers and weeds and nature. It will be grand to have such a world around me.' Then she whispered. 'And we will have a cook. And a gardener. What rapture.'

'I have a cook and a gardener and a vehicle.'

'You have so much,' she said.

'Yet you refuse to consider the impact those memoirs will have on me, even as you know what it would mean for your aunt to have her story included. Her husband would not take it well.'

He lifted her fingers and brushed them against the skin of his cheek, following the downward line of his skin.

'As I said, I will not be including Lord Andrews. It is too risky. He might rescind his offer to Aunt Agatha. And besides, their marriage has already been hurt by the past. That is enough pain for a lifetime. It is different for your grandmother, because your grandfather is no longer with you.'

'My mother is courting. Her new beloved has a young

daughter. A young daughter who may not be as strong as you. Who *can't* be as strong as you, given she has likely been sheltered by her father. She has already lost a mother, and her father will not want more grief in his family.'

'If your mother's sweetheart cannot deal with the truth of your mother's past, and she can't persuade him before they marry, then perhaps they shouldn't wed. It was horrid to see the upset when Lord Andrews discovered my parentage.'

She hesitated.

'The rows were horrible. Living in such an atmosphere was terrible. He might have been able to forgive Aunt Agatha if they had not wed. Marriage causes people to stop being sweethearts and become two rivals under the same roof—or, in your case, a person who is determined to retreat from everyone else.'

'I'm not retreating. I just have too many duties to be able to loll about all day, or spend large amounts of time going on about the weather, or playing cards, or chasing after a new sweetheart.'

'I have just realised that you have so many people who care for you that you do not even consider them. You take their affection for granted.'

'What do you mean?'

'Your mother, your grandmother, Pierce…' She shrugged. 'Even the butler cares for you. And your valet. The housekeeper. The cook. And it is not just because you pay their wage. They genuinely like you.'

'I try to be kind.'

'Did you know that some people have their servants face the wall if they happen to be in the corridor at the same time?'

'No. That's ridiculous.'

'Not to them, but to you it is. But now, in your own way, you are the one turning your back. You provide, but you retreat to your rooms. You let them walk by. You are kind and considerate, but do you really see them as people?'

'Yes. I do,' he said. 'I truly do. I am close to my valet and my butler, and the butler takes care of the rest of the staff. I don't spend much time with the female members of my household, but the butler sees that everyone is treated fairly.'

He moved to lift his cravat from beside the bed, wadded it, and arced it across the room.

'Perhaps you are the one who is inexperienced in this. Not showing feelings doesn't mean you don't have them.'

Gabriel studied her.

They had shared an intensity within an intimacy. He understood that she wanted to have a place she could retreat to, and he had given her that. She had options. A plan for her life.

She was looking at the backs of her hands and seemed to be rubbing something away from herself. Guilt, perhaps.

'I want to tell your grandmother's story, and that will give me the means to be on my own.'

'A noble goal. To control your fate,' he said. 'But at the expense of others? I'm not so certain.'

Just as she'd lit that fuse in the gardens, another was lit inside him, sizzling forward at a fast pace, leaving him speechless. The intensity of their lovemaking had deserted him, and in its place was a feeling of being used.

He'd done all he could to provide her with a way around publishing the memoirs, and yet she persisted in continuing on that path, claiming she needed to be on it to provide a roof over her head.

That, he could understand. A roof.

But she didn't need to destroy his roof to obtain it.

Damaging his family and his reputation was not something he could fathom.

She gathered her things, and he helped her dress, and then opened the door for her to leave.

Later, he missed Marie so much he wanted to search her out. But he didn't want her to know how much he missed her, so instead he went to his grandmother's sitting room. It was better that he did not see Marie again before she left.

His grandmother sat at her desk by the window, her pen in her hand and a small stack of paper and a perfume bottle in front of her.

'Just making some notes for Marie,' she said.

'Where is she?'

'I only know she's not in this room,' she said, sorting the papers and raising one so he could see it. 'A love letter your grandfather sent me.' She sniffed. 'He was always calling me his little frog. His favourite endearment. But he was the one who had to jump . I miss those days. I miss him.'

'Have you told Marie about those endearing names?'

'Of course.' Her face formed a mound of happy wrinkles. 'You should be proud of these memoirs. Yes, I embarrassed you, and I embarrassed my husband's family, but I had fun. Marie needs to learn about adventure.'

'No, she doesn't. It was providential that more people didn't get angry with you for the things you did. And your fortune was used to help smooth things over. You should stop this now. You're hurting too many people.'

She used the back of her knuckles to smooth the skin on her neck. 'My fortune was a smaller amount after your grandfather got a grasp on it, but you should thank me for that marriage. It gave you a title. And my father helped his grandson—your father—to rebuild the family finances, and taught him how to manage a ledger and tenants and everything but women. Probably easier to teach a cat to sing.'

'Don't judge all women by your actions.'

'It will be a mistake on your part if you don't take my actions into account. A mistake. If you wed some little flower petal like one of those women I invited to the soiree they will decorate your arm, and your house, and you will get on well. You don't need to wed a woman with my sensibilities. She would cause you no end of worry, and you'd be just as alone as you are now, but with a wife as an additional burden.'

'Do you consider the women in my family are burdens to me?'

'Aren't we? In your opinion?' She smiled to take any sting out of the words. 'Your mother keeps to herself...as you do. She stays away from London in order to hide from everyone. Now she watches over her parents, but she left Town originally while my son was still alive. She left you behind to keep an eye on your father. And you're still trying to make it up to her because you couldn't control him either. They both deserted you, and it still upsets me. And, no, I'm not putting that in the memoirs.'

She moved her foot and let her slipper dangle from her stockinged toes, then she gave a kick and the slipper hit the wall.

'You could quash the memoirs.'

'I could. But they will be published. Marie needs the

money. So does Agatha. And even if it I did stop it, Marie still has ink on her hands and wears those frightful frocks. Yes, you dressed her up well once. *Once.* But she went straight back to looking like a ragamuffin.'

His grandmother's eyes had never appeared so cold. 'It's for the best that nothing further developed between you, because you will always know that Marie was willing to sell your family to the highest bidder, so to speak.'

He didn't waver.

'Your choices are your own,' she said. 'Mine are mine. I gave this family funds through my father. I wanted the title of Viscountess. I charged my way into society and then I did as I pleased and let the men clean up after me. But I certainly looked the part. She doesn't.'

He clamped his teeth before speaking. 'She is beautiful.'

'I don't want you to wed her. Rosalind is perfect for you. The only way I can make certain you don't wed Marie is to show you how mercenary she is.' She waved a hand, dismissing his words. 'It has nothing to do with Marie's face, and everything to do with her presentation. She doesn't present herself well.'

One brow rose. She tapped the side of the perfume bottle.

'Marie is nearly a child of the streets. She truly is. She doesn't want it known—and that is to her credit—but Agatha talks too much—as do I—and she has told me the truth of Marie's birth, and how Lord Andrews found out and was incensed. She shouldn't have told me.'

'Grandmother, do you only allow friends into your home so you can gather information to hold against them?'

Anger tinged his voice, but her smile only grew.

'You and your grandfather and your father learned commerce one way—I another.' She still smiled. 'Besides, I do like Marie, but she isn't viscountess material. She doesn't give a fig about—' Then she stopped.

He controlled his temper, waiting to see what she'd say.

'Perhaps I am wrong. Perhaps Marie craves attention as much as I do. She is willing to write the memoirs, and she does get noticed with her spectacles and frightful frocks…' She hesitated. 'I don't think you will treat her right. If you wed Rosalind, I won't care. But if you wed Marie and chase after other women it will kill her. She doesn't trust marriage anyway. And I don't trust you to be faithful. Marie needs someone she can count on. And based on my experiences, and the people around me, I think she will be happier unmarried.'

'It is not your decision.'

'If you say so.' She shrugged, then changed the subject. 'Will you pass me my shoe?' she asked.

He didn't move.

'Fine. Ring for a maid to fetch it.'

He walked to the door, putting his hand on the cool wood.

She called out, interrupting his retreat. 'It's best she goes. Because you're noticing her too much. And you're too much like your father. You do have your father's smile after all.'

He flashed his teeth.

'Again, I do like Marie. But society will not forget the part she played in the inevitable scandal of my memoirs. Society is vengeful, and no one would ever be able to convince it of her being virtuous once she goes through with the publication. Society has to be respected in order to give its respect.'

'How could you do this to Marie?'

'I'm not doing it to her. She's doing it to herself. She's choosing commerce over love. Your grandfather had a title, and yet still, even to the end of his days, it was in everyone's mind that he wed for money. That's how I know that it never goes away. Never. It was always with him. I couldn't erase it. He couldn't erase it. It didn't matter how much we loved each other, it was always there. And even now, as his grandson, you are aware of it. Those secrets don't die.'

He walked out of the room. He couldn't dispute his grandmother's words. He agreed with them. The fact that Marie had shared his family secrets would always be between them if they married.

They would never be able to escape it.

Chapter Twenty

After his man of affairs finished the documents Gabriel stood with Marie and her aunt, and watched as Lady Agatha took the jewel case and gave it to her husband.

'I hope these make you happy,' she said.

With a flick of the latch, he opened the box, staring inside. He didn't raise his eyes from the pearls. 'If you've left anything at my home, you can ride in the carriage to get it, and it will deposit you both at the lodge afterwards.'

'Thank you,' Agatha said. 'I did leave behind some sketches. And a few mementos. But I must collect my things from here first.'

He raised his eyes, holding the pearls in his left hand. 'I've had a lot of time to think about it. I've watched everyone around me go on with their lives since my wife died, and I need to do the same. I want you to do so as well. I would like to see you and Marie settled into the lodge. And I might like to visit from time to time.' Then he took her hand and lifted the back of it near his lips, gave it a kiss. 'But only if there are no more secrets between us.'

'I hope you can forgive me for not telling you the truth about Marie. I had kept it private for so long I didn't even think about it any longer. And it didn't seem my truth to share. Plus, I didn't want to hurt the memory you had of your wife.'

'Can we take a carriage ride and talk about it?'

'That would be wonderful,' she said, taking her lavender-scented handkerchief from her reticule and giving it to him. 'Please let me speak with Marie a moment and then I will join you.'

Lord Andrews gave Gabriel and Marie a nod, and then left.

'That was the most compassion I have ever seen from him,' Agatha said. 'I hope it isn't a temporary state.' She interlaced her fingers. 'His wife truly did love him, and regretted that she had erred, but I could not regret it because it gave us you.'

She focused her entire attention on Marie.

'I am sorry for the grief it has caused you, and sorry that you didn't grow up in a grand house. But I saw your birth, and I held you, and I have loved you as my own daughter since that day. You were the best card I'd ever been dealt, and I wanted to hang on to you. Remaining as companion to your mother was the best I could do for both of us. I hope you understand.'

'Most certainly. Over and over. We cannot undo the past,' Marie said. 'And I am pleased about my birth. In my childhood the winters were cold, but I did have a grand time.' Marie smiled. 'I doubt I would have enjoyed growing up in Lord Andrews' house—plus, it was always like my birthday when you came. The other children around me never got such grand treats and adventures as you gave me. Sometimes I shared the treats with my friends, and on those days I was the most important person in all London.'

'You always will be to me.'

Agatha gave her a fierce hug, and scurried from the room, sniffling.

'I'm sorry for the grief that keeping me a secret caused her,' Marie said to Gabriel. 'But at least I knew who my birthing mother was. I had a good childhood. Not perfect, but good enough. And even if I think of complaining, then I wonder whom I would be trying to make sad.'

He noticed she ran her fingertips over the sides of her skirt when she said that. She'd spent her whole life wearing others' cast-offs and making herself happy with what life gave her.

The expression on her face changed. 'It almost made me feel special to be an orphan when I was growing up, even though I missed tales of my heritage. I could imagine my parents as I wished them. I have been fortunate. So very fortunate.' She smiled at him, but it didn't reach her eyes. 'And so have you.'

'It didn't always feel that way.'

He'd had so many duties that he'd had to study, hour after hour, and at family meals he'd had to listen to his parents bickering about his grandmother's antics. While neither had approved of them, they'd definitely not agreed on how she should be handled. But he'd known he was fortunate. Perhaps he'd looked from the window of his parents' coach and seen little Marie running errands and felt sorry for the sad child whose parents didn't have the wealth his did.

And now she was willing to turn her back on it.

'Do you like poverty?' he asked.

'No.' She laughed. 'I have seen it reflected at me from murky bathwater. It's not pleasant. But thanks to you that is no longer my fate. I want to thank you for helping me and my aunt—my very precious Aunt Agatha—and for making sure she has a home.'

'I am pleased to do so.'

The words burned his throat. He *was* pleased she had a home. Pleased Marie could be with her aunt. But he wasn't happy that he had given her the resources to walk out of his life. He had had no choice, truly. It had been the correct thing to do. The right thing. But he knew he would ponder over the choices he had made for a long, long time.

'I have enjoyed having you in the house,' he said. 'You've been a friend to my grandmother and she's been happy to have an audience.'

And he had been pleased to have her with him—even if he was disappointed that she had chosen to write his grandmother's story, and upset with the feeling of her betrayal.

'I am finished with my account of your grandmother's life.' She put a hand on his arm. 'I was shocked in places. She's not always been virtuous. I don't know that you should read it. She has said she has started making notes for volume two, and will contact me at the lodge.'

'I understand,' he said.

The publisher had reassured him that no one would read the memoirs. He would expect contact from the man soon—just as soon as the manuscript was submitted.

Chapter Twenty-One

The butler gave a light knock and walked inside the library. 'Lady Agatha only needed a small amount of help with her departure, and was happy to be on her husband's arm. Miss Marie seemed unsure about it all, but she left in the carriage with them.'

Hawkins held a parcel in his hand.

'And this arrived.'

Gabriel didn't move, his eyes on the bulky rectangular package.

'Would you like it on the table?' Hawkins continued.

'No.' Gabriel held out his hands. 'I will take it.'

Without excess movement, the package was placed in Gabriel's grasp and the servant left, making almost no sound. The door clicked shut, and the silence in the room oppressed Gabriel.

He held the story of his grandmother's life. The family's history and its escapades detailed for others to read for their amusement.

His jaw locked as the thing that had caused such a whirlwind in his life officially ended.

When his friends had asked about the rumours of his grandmother's behaviour he'd shrugged away the reports as exaggerated, and hoped they were. And after his grandfather had passed on he'd even hired people to keep watch over her, and to keep other people from hearing about her exploits. He knew they'd not be able to contain her completely, but they'd been able to keep others away from anything trying, and alerted him to her adventures. He'd even paid the scandal sheets to keep quiet.

Now the story sat in front of him. Knowing the details of his family life had been exposed in such a way angered him. But it was the fact that Marie was willing to profit by it that gave him a kick to his stomach.

He expected such a thing from his grandmother. She never found a pot she wasn't willing to stir. Dust she wasn't willing to kick up. An event she wasn't willing to make ribald. But he had expected more from Marie. He had thought her reserved, reticent, retiring.

Somewhere under that demure demeanour she had a cache of explosives.

Gabriel reached out and pulled at the string binding the wrapping paper and it came untied. The papers seemed to fall open to their title page: *The Memoirs*.

He ran his fingertips over Marie's name, written in small print under the title in tight, cramped handwriting. He could imagine her hand dipping the pen, then tapping it on the side of the bottle of ink, carefully putting her name to the title page.

His grandmother's reminiscences had been written clearly.

The chapters were sewn together in clusters, with one big stitch at the top left-hand side and threads hanging loose. Marie would have bent over the binding, her eyes studying it as she pushed a sewing needle and thread through the papers and then snipped it off and tied the strings.

He envisaged her working hard, putting her heart into his grandmother's story. Possibly sometimes amazed by the risks taken by the older woman. The events the older woman had attended. The men she had entranced.

He'd thought nothing inside should surprise him, but he read the first chapter and discovered he had not really known of his grandmother's past. These stories had been successfully hidden from him.

Then he wondered if the only person truly in the dark had always been himself. If he'd done all that work to protect his family's reputation so he didn't have to face it. If the rug he'd been brushing things under had been his own.

He could read no more.

He put the papers aside and looked into the empty fireplace. He would have to have it lit, just like that fuse had been.

And he fought the explosions inside himself.

Gabriel stood at the window, looking out over the perfectly tended grounds. Perfectly tended because his gardener had a love for nature. A wish to see things grow. But it was more than that.

He'd spoken to the gardener. Seen the man's face when he'd talked of getting a new plant he'd heard about and hoped might grow well.

He doubted the man even knew of the emotion that shone through his eyes.

And now he understood. Understood how the man would feel if he went to the garden and discovered all the greenery gone. Everything. Nothing left but ground. Barren earth. A place without growth.

He'd seen what loneliness did to a man. He'd seen it in Lord Andrews. A man who claimed he couldn't sleep without a specific piece of jewellery nearby because he hoped to feel closer to someone he'd cared about and lost.

Striding inside, he moved to his rooms and found the safe that was years older than he was. Using the combination that had been handed down, just as the house had, he opened the lock. He pulled out a box that had been in the safe for a long time.

Jewels not wanted by the women in his family. Left behind, more or less, by the women who'd owned them. Not worthy of them. Too insignificant in their eyes to matter. Too insignificant to be worn. Forgotten about.

But he'd never completely forgotten the ruby ring. It had meant more to him than any of the jewels he'd seen worn by the women in his family or anyone else.

He opened the box to look again at the ring that had once been his great-grandmother's wedding ring. And then at the other piece of jewellery she'd owned that neither his grandmother nor his mother had wanted—a gold necklace with one small misshapen pearl hanging from it.

The pearl was a baroque. Considered exquisite in former days. Different from the others.

He returned it to the safe and shut the door as he heard the lumbering crash on the stairs.

He knew what was to happen next and, as expected, Pierce walked in and found himself a spot on the sofa.

Gabriel informed him that if he wanted to keep his boots, he'd better take them off the furniture.

Pierce took a handkerchief from his pocket and daubed

at a spot on his coat. 'You have the clumsiest servants I've ever seen. They could spill air.'

'Why don't you stay a while?' Gabriel asked. 'You can drink here as easily as at your club.'

'I agree,' he said. 'Would you pour me a drink?'

'No.'

Pierce laughed, and rose to fill a glass, and then half filled a second one and gave it to Gabriel.

'Don't overdo it,' he said.

'I never do,' Gabriel answered.

The nights were interminable, and sitting with Pierce would be better than listening for Marie's footsteps.

After a half-hour or so of sharing tales they'd both heard before, Pierce said, 'So, why the air of melancholy? Have you finally realised you are in love with the errant archer?'

'That is not your concern.'

'Ah,' Pierce said. 'I saw the determination on your face when you pulled the bow string and aimed that arrow. You might not have known you were in love, but I did.' He checked the stain on his waistcoat again. 'Of course, that didn't change my plans to woo her away from you. No sense in making it easy for you.'

Gabriel let out a deep breath. 'She means more to me than anything else in the world.'

'So why is everyone tiptoeing around as if they're afraid they'll wake someone?'

'The household has divided into two camps. The females are congregating on one side, and the males on the other. The maids dart about and rush so they can do their jobs but are not seen as disloyal. The male servants are distressed with the maids, and extra-solicitous of me, if that is possible.'

'Servants divided in your household?' Pierce asked, his voice high, and then he lowered it. 'Well, Grandmother *does* live here. And I did speak to her just after I got here. Somehow her maid misunderstood my request that she water my horse…'

'I told the butler to gather the servants and tell them that they must all work together. He returned and told me the housekeeper agreed completely, and yet nothing has changed.'

'What is the disagreement?'

'I'd rather not discuss the particulars.'

'Oh, I'd rather you do. And don't be surprised if I already know. As I said, I did see my adorable and retiring grandmother before I came to you. She says what is on her mind.'

'I prefer diplomacy.'

You're too respectable. It amazes me that we get on at all.'

'We all need a roof over our heads, and coal and flour, and soap and meat, and puddings and breads…'

'I try to let my man of affairs take care of all of that. You should take a lesson.'

'From you?'

'Yes. And, since Marie isn't here now—I asked, so I know that it is her absence that is dividing your household—I suggest that I court her. Simple enough. We all get what we want.'

'Touch her and you will go out through a window head-first.'

'From what storey?' Pierce looked at his glass. 'Because she might be worth a few bruises. I can just imagine her at my bedside…coddling me. Holding my hand. Holding my—'

'You really want me to kill you, don't you?'

'It sounds to me as if you've already made some sort of commitment. Maybe you've decided you'd rather risk unhappiness with her than risk happiness with anyone else. I think Grandmother's phrase is *Better the pestilence you know than the one you don't.*'

Pierce stood, and claimed it was time for him to find more enjoyment, because being with Gabriel was about as much fun as watching a horse's tail swat flies.

Then the room became silent. Tomblike.

Gabriel stared at the walls surrounding him. The silence was too quiet. A night stretched ahead of him that would consist of hours broken into minutes…broken into seconds pounding inside him.

He was hungry, but not wanting anything to eat.

Tired, but unable to sleep.

Lonely, but with Marie all around him.

Chapter Twenty-Two

She crumpled the paper in her hand. She'd been betrayed. By the publisher.

Turning to her aunt, she said, 'I must return. Gabriel has the memoirs.'

Her aunt studied her face. 'I thought you'd sent them to the publisher.'

'Yes. He did have them. But now Gabriel has the only copy.'

'I tried to warn you. He is his grandmother's grandson. She is a good friend, but we agreed not to trust each other a long time ago.' She hesitated. 'I'll send someone on a horse to ask if you can borrow my husband's carriage.'

Marie agreed to wait, letting her temper simmer. She should have known this would happen. Gabriel had power and authority and he would not hesitate to use them.

After the carriage had arrived, Marie rushed out to it. It seemed to take for ever for the vehicle to travel to Gabriel's.

She ran to the entrance she'd always used—the one on his grandmother's side of the house. She rapped loudly, and a maid opened the door.

'What is the rush?' Gabriel's grandmother said, stepping into the hall, directly in front of Marie.

'He has the memoirs—Gabriel.'

Her mouth formed a huge O, and so did her eyes.

'Gabriel? He has done that? Oh, my… I never thought he would do such a thing.' She blinked. 'But while you were writing I did keep remembering things that needed to be included, and I did jot down a few notes of what I'd told you each day before I went to bed at night. You will have to stay here and rewrite it.'

'I can't stay with Gabriel here.'

'Why not? Just tell your feet to stay put. Don't open the door if he knocks. He's rather opinionated, anyway. He won't bother you. You won't have to see him. And I may invite Pierce to help you. He's so helpful…'

She could not live under the same roof as Gabriel any more. Their rooms would be too close. It would be too tempting.

'I don't have any clothing here,' she said.

His grandmother squeezed her eyes tightly shut. 'Goodness, I have an old dress or two you can wear. It's not as if you normally wear anything other than a frightful frock—except for the picnic dress. I'm sure you and the maids can sew a few flounces. You appear to be good with flounces.'

She sighed, more dramatic than any actress Marie had ever seen on stage.

'You think you are saving funds by dressing comfortably. But you're also doing something else. You're saying you are your own person, and you want to keep people at arm's length.'

Marie shook her head.

'You're good enough at sewing to make those dresses fit you better. You know how to rip out a seam, take out things and change them, and then sew the seam back. But do you do it to make your dresses more fashionable? No.'

'They're comfortable.'

'Naked is comfortable. Wrapped in a blanket is comfortable. Dressing in nice clothing can be comfortable also. Both of us get on well—and you know why? We're stubborn, and we don't really care what others think of us. But really, the one person we should both treat well...the one person we should both consider...is the only one who is being hurt by our actions. And that is something we should think about.'

She *did* think about Gabriel...about how the lines at his eyes had tightened and he'd appeared to be finding her wanting.

'People don't change much,' his grandmother said. 'They keep making the same mistakes over and over and over...for years. You think I haven't messed up that trick of hiding cards in my reticule many times before? Well, I have. But I keep on thinking that I'll get it right the next time, instead of realising I should get it right by playing within the rules.'

Perhaps it was true. What if the actions that had been the right ones for her in the past were no longer moving her in the direction she should take? What if she should change now and become an even stronger person.

'Your story means a great deal to me,' Marie said. 'I believe in what you said. The risks you took. I think you were being true to yourself.'

'I was being true to myself. But *only* myself. It took me years before I realised that I should be true to my family. And that is when Gabriel saw his grandfather and I together. That is when I learned that my husband was more important to me than anyone else.' She lowered her eyes. 'Sadly, we did not have a great many years left together at that time. But I treasured each day. Each moment with him.'

She studied her hands and patted the top of one.

'Perhaps I sometimes still make the same mistakes. With my family. With Gabriel's mother and with him. I need to tell the whole story—not just the part of it where I am uncaring and sometimes spiteful,' she said. 'I seem to have no trouble owning up to my mistakes, but perhaps I need to own up to the things I've done right also.' She lifted her chin. 'Perhaps you should examine your own motives, Marie. Don't wait until it's too late.'

'My only motive is to support my aunt.'

'True. True… And I'm sure you're not afraid of marriage. Your aunt says you've not been around many people who were actually married to each other in your life. She said that when you were growing up the woman who cared for you might have a different man entering the house every time she visited. She was thankful that the woman kept telling you about the dangers of losing your heart. That kept you on the right path.'

'I was on my own path. She told me that too. Time and time again. I have always been on my own journey.'

'True. And it is not a society one, like Rosalind's. She's perfect.' She enunciated the word with a little purr at the beginning. 'Have you seen the way she dresses? A veritable fashion plate. An asset to any family. She will let Gabriel do as he wishes. Over time, they'll both likely stray in their marriage, but on the outside it will appear perfect.'

She shut her eyes and her lips thinned.

'Rosalind won't take it personally, like his mother did.' She cleared her throat. 'I thought it was going to kill her until she swept her husband out of her life. And then it killed him. Because he just let himself go. To drink. To brothels. To chapel… But that was only the once. The last time…'

In that moment, as his grandmother watched her, she saw no laughter. No jesting. Just loss.

Marie took the woman's hand, but his grandmother tugged her hand away. 'Don't let me get all weepy. I want those memoirs published. They are the record of my life.'

'But you can keep a copy for your family to read.'

'Oh, now that you have a home in the country, my life has lessened in importance for you. Go and enjoy your weeds. You won't have any thought of what Gabriel is doing here in Town. He is a good man, and he knows his duty. His duty is Rosalind. She's spent her whole life learning to be the perfect wife.' She shivered. 'Not like you. Agatha said you were basically trained to clean. That's noble. Cleaning. But not for women like me or Rosalind or Gabriel's mother.'

Then she lifted the perfume bottle on the table beside her and stared at the ceiling. She sprayed the air, the rose scent cloying.

Marie stepped away.

'The manuscript must be with him. Make sure he hasn't burned it.' His grandmother lowered the perfume and kicked out a foot, causing her skirts to fly out at the sides. 'It will be such a trial to tell you all those stories again. But I will if I have to.'

'I will speak to him,' Marie said, and then she stopped and examined his grandmother. 'Rosalind may be perfect, but we both know that you don't really like her, and you yourself said that weeds are stronger than hothouse flowers.'

His grandmother crossed her arms, shook her head, and this time her purr sounded more like a growl, seeming to underscore her words.

'So? What's it to be? Are you a weed or a hothouse flower?'

Chapter Twenty-Three

Rapping briefly on the door, Marie heard him call out, 'Enter,' and she gripped the door handle and opened it.

Gabriel studied her. There was no warmth in him other than the demanding blood that ran in his veins. She'd misjudged him earlier. She'd thought he would eventually understand that it was important to his grandmother to have her memories shared. Important to Marie to be able to support herself. She had hoped other women would want their anecdotes shared as well. That women would learn of their heritage and want others to comprehend the trials they'd endured.

'You have my manuscript.'

He stood, tossing the pen he held to the blotter. 'Yes, I do.'

She moved until only the table was between them, feeling as though she were on some imaginary gigantic chessboard and she didn't understand the rules of the game or her opponent. She didn't even want to play.

'I want it back.'

'You were going to tarnish my family name,' he said.

'Your grandmother agreed,' she said. 'It was her choice.'

'Fair enough. Just as it is my choice to stop it.'

'I will just write it again.'

'And I will stop it again—and again and again, if I have to.' He moved around the desk. 'You can live in the lodge. You have your expenses paid for some time. You don't have to publish.'

'It is the truth as told to me by your grandmother.'

'I don't care if it wis carved in stone, embroidered on silk or written on a pearly gate. It is my family you were trying to destroy.'

'It's your grandmother's story. Her life. Her history. I would think you would want to know that it has been recorded.'

'And if you can profit from it, all the better?'

He moved back to the other side of the desk, opened a drawer and pulled out a few pages from the beginning of the book. He tossed them between them.

'Would you be so kind as to read it aloud?'

'I know what it says. Your grandmother and your grandfather had a fiery marriage. They lit each other's fuses.'

'Did you make this up? About Grandmother and Grandfather trying to throw each other out of a rolling carriage? Calling it "a little marriage disagreement"?'

'No. That's true.'

'This cannot be published. It cannot. And you claim she was betrothed to two men at the same time? This is a travesty for our family.'

'You see what I mean about marriage?' Marie said to him. 'Not one single person I have ever heard of has had a truly good marriage. Not one. Except perhaps your grandmother and grandfather. And even so they nearly killed each other.'

'You're right. I have just realised it. Marriage is a sham. This proves it.' He let the pages flutter to the rug. 'Marriage is best conducted with separate houses. Just as your aunt and her husband have discovered.'

'We do not disagree on that.' Marie gathered the jumble of papers, straightening them.

He stared at the desk, and at the crumpled brown wrapping paper. He held on to the string, twisting it around his fingers before wadding it into a ball and dropping it.

'I wish you weren't so upset,' she said, moving to stand near the desk.

He let out a puff of air through his nostrils. 'I don't know what I should do,' he said, looking at the papers on the desk in front of him. 'My other grandparents are frail, and I don't want them upset. However, I doubt they would even hear of these stories. But my mother is hoping to wed again, and her sweetheart often stays in London and is a stickler for propriety.'

He paused, and then sighed in defeat.

He opened the drawer again and took out the unbound papers. He ran his hand over the top and then gave them to her. 'Do as you wish with it. I will not interfere or speak with the publisher again.'

She put the previously tossed papers on top of the stack and lifted it without speaking.

'Grandmother has the right to live her life as she chooses, just as I do,' he said. 'Without her funds added to the family coffers and her father's tutelage we would likely have the title and little else.'

'Did you read any more of than the first few pages?'

'No.'

'Are you sure you are willing to let this go to the publisher?'

She had to ask. He could still change his mind.

Instead of answering, he shut the drawer.

'I knew my parents did not have the best match,' he said, 'but Grandmother, with all her flaws, always spoke lovingly of her union with Grandfather. And I remember her caring for him when he was ill. He might have been exasperated by her—many times—but they were always supportive of each other.' He met her eyes. 'Is that what you found? That they loved each other?'

'Yes. She has the fondest memories of him, and she says she misses him every day.'

'Does that not change your view on marriage?'

She cradled the pages in her arms and moved to the door. 'I hadn't really considered what I was writing…what it meant.'

'Perhaps you should. Perhaps I should. And…' His pause was a lengthy one. 'And perhaps everyone should. My parents had a distant marriage, and my mother never said anything about missing my father after he'd passed away. She didn't live with him most of the time.'

'I know.'

'Father shouldn't have strayed. Or perhaps Mother shouldn't have married him. Perhaps you're right about marriage.'

She clasped the papers closer.

'Let me write a note to the publisher,' he said, sitting at the desk, dipping his pen in the ink. 'I will tell him that he may go ahead.'

'You will?' She took a hesitant step towards him.

'Yes.'

She heard the scratch of his pen sliding across the paper and walked to his desk, watching him blot the ink. She put the manuscript on top of the wrapping paper and read Gabriel's note allowing publication.

He indicated she should place the letter of agreement on top of the stack, and after she did slipped the heavier cover over them and tied it.

She picked up the parcel and started to the door, pausing to look back at him.

Then she walked to the fireplace and tossed the papers inside the burning flames. Immediately the scent of scorched paper reached her nostrils.

In a flash, he'd jumped from the chair, hurled himself around the desk, grabbed a poker, and pulled out the smouldering, charred package.

He stamped on the burning spots. Then he stared at her.

'I can't do it,' she said.

'I understand.'

He lifted the papers from their burned packaging, avoiding the smouldering areas, kicking the string and the heavier covering back into the flames.

'But you're correct in that secrets can't be kept. And Grandmother has a right to tell her side of the story.'

She took the papers from him. 'You don't understand.'

Again, she held the pages towards the fire, but he slapped them away, sending them flying into the room.

'You don't understand,' she said again. 'I can't risk hurting the young women who might read this, and I can't risk hurting someone who might believe that living such a life without care can be safe or healthy. Your grandmother had a fortune at her disposal, and still she was scarred in the leg, almost fell out of a carriage, and missed out on much of her child's life because she was chasing adventure.'

She shook her head. This was not about his grandmother's story. It was about more than that. She didn't want any young woman finding herself in the predicament her mother had faced. And she definitely didn't want them to think that pretending lawlessness would lead to a romance.

'And I can't risk hurting you,' she said.

He put a hand to the back of her head and pulled her to him so he could kiss her forehead. 'Sweeting... This is not something that has to be decided now. Why don't you stay here again, try to keep Grandmother from lighting any more fuses, and give us a chance to get to know each other better?'

Gabriel woke from where he had dozed on the sofa as the dawn light began to show through his window.

He opened his eyes. His valet had arrived and left after opening the curtains.

Then he heard it again. A rap at his door. A light rap. A Marie rap.

He stood, straightened his cravat, and called out for her to enter.

She peered around the door, her spectacles firmly in place, in a fluff of curls and a sad dress that had seen better years. And still she was the loveliest woman he'd ever seen in his life.

This was the sight he wanted to wake up to every morning.

Then he saw the thin manuscript she held in her hands.

She held it out to him. 'This isn't the original. We've changed a few things,' she said. 'I left in the carriage incident—how could I not?—but we've added an explanation of how your grandmother regretted her actions and tried to learn from her mistakes and be a better person.

And how much she loves her family…and how much they mean to her.'

'Including my mother?'

'Yes. It took her a while to remember that, and she may have embellished a little. But she says she truly does like your mother.' She ducked her head. 'In short doses and from a great distance—which I didn't include. She says it has been her goal in life to give your mother long earlobes…but not with these memoirs.'

Gabriel took the papers and moved to his desk. He pulled out the wrapping paper that the publisher had used to cover the original manuscript. He took the string and wrapped it, and then he gave it to her.

'The butler will be able to have it delivered for you.'

She hugged it to her chest. 'You do not want to read it?'

'I think it is best that I don't.'

'I have talked with your grandmother, and she told me she does not want to damage your mother's romance.'

'I appreciate that.'

She ran her hand over the parcel. 'This is to be her chance to set the record straight. To offer an explanation of her errant ways. Not to embellish her adventurous ways, as it was at first, but to say how she has learned from them, and would now recommend only the straightest and narrowest path to everyone. And she has passed that on to you.'

'That's not exactly how she taught me to be upstanding,' he said. 'I learned to be so by dealing with her disasters.'

'Which she credits you for many times over. In writing.'

'You and your aunt became a family with no ties to bind you at all…except one. The heart. It is a familial love, and that is what I want to form with you at my side. The love of a family between us. Even if we never wed. Even if it is only friendship.'

He touched his neckcloth, and the simple knot at his fingertips reassured him. Made him feel closer to her.

'I liked it when you returned to the way you prefer to dress,' he continued. 'Still the beauty in you shone. I liked it when you told me the truth about your relationship with your aunt—how you appreciated the good things of your childhood and didn't weary yourself over the things you couldn't change, but celebrated the things you had, and worked to keep them. Not just for you but also for your aunt.'

Her eyes didn't give any evidence of what she was thinking, but it didn't matter. He had to speak what was in his heart.

'I like you tremendously. More than I've ever liked anyone before. *Anyone.* You are the family of my heart. The family I would choose if I had all the people in the world to choose from and the person whom I want by my side. This feels more like love than anything I've ever felt before. I adore you. And even if we're apart for the rest of our lives I always will. You are the one person I know I can love for ever.'

She hugged the parcel even closer, before putting it on the table close to the door. She walked forward and took his hands.

'I wanted to ask you something,' she said.

He waited.

'Will you marry me?' she asked, reminding him of a lost child.

But she wasn't lost. Because they had found each other.

'I thought you would never ask.'

'You are a risk worth taking,' she said. 'Though a very minor one. In fact, I would say I am the bigger risk.'

'You are no risk at all.'

He walked around the desk and hugged her close, shutting his eyes for a moment and enjoying the knowledge that they were standing together and she wanted to marry him.

'As I listened to your grandmother recount her tales again,' she said, 'this time telling me how you worked so hard to keep her safe and protect the family, doing all you could to make life the best it could be for her, I realised that you were the one person I want by my side always. Someone who truly cares about the people around him and lives a strong life, with all the actions everyone claims are important, but who also does all he can to make them happen.'

'You could have just said you like the way I tie my cravat.'

'There is that as well.'

He placed a soft kiss on her lips. 'We cannot wed soon enough for me.'

Chapter Twenty-Four

They'd waited three weeks before the banns were read. Gabriel claimed he was giving her time to change her mind, but that wasn't true, and he had reminded her every night how much he loved her.

And when she had told him her only regret was in being born out of wedlock he'd taken her by the shoulders and shaken his head.

'No decent person is a mistake, regardless of how their life started. Your parents had nothing to do with the way you turned out. You made the choice to be good on your own, and you make my life better. I need you.'

Then he'd paused, considering.

'In our years together I want you to accept that a person doesn't need to try to live life so cautiously that they may never have regrets, because then you will regret the adventures you didn't have. And I don't want you ever to regret our marriage.'

She'd hugged him with all her might.

He had put all his worry about the memoirs aside. Nothing mattered as much as having her for his wife.

And now here they sat on the sofa, side by side, and suddenly all his concern about what she'd written about his family dissolved. Nothing mattered except her, and she was curled beside him in a dressing gown, with her hair beautifully askew, loosened from her knot, and her eyes peering at him with love through her spectacles.

'What did you do with the remains of the original manuscript?' he asked.

'It's in a safe your grandmother has. She says she has mainly written it for future generations she might never know. She thinks if they read the published memoirs first, they will not be so shocked at what she calls her "true story". And she says she planned this all along, but who knows?'

She shook her head.

'She also says she hopes we have a little weed soon. And when I know I am going to have a baby she wants me to tell her before I tell your mother. I told her we would tell them both at the same time, and now she's pouting, but she'll be over it by morning.'

He wouldn't have believed it was possible for a person to love another as much as he loved her. He loved the way the spectacle frames encircled her eyes and the lenses seemed to magnify her gaze, and he loved her love for him.

She had seemed to bloom since their marriage, and she wore the ruby ring from the safe and the misshapen pearl, which she claimed to be the most amazingly beautiful one she'd ever seen.

His grandmother had made it her mission to get Marie to become the most fashionable woman in London, and in Gabriel's opinion she had succeeded roundly—though Marie had complained, laughing and saying, 'Once a weed, always a weed.'

Then his grandmother had said, 'Weeds survive.'

She and his grandmother had become even closer, and

he knew Marie kept his grandmother from needing any more fuses of any kind ignited.

In fact, his grandmother and his mother could now even manage to share an occasional cup of tea, if Marie cajoled them into being nice to each other.

'You will not believe what Aunt Agatha has told me,' she said, and didn't wait for him to answer. 'She doesn't want to stay at the hunting lodge. She believes her husband is falling in love with her. He has bought her a new strand of pearls. Her own, he said, because he wants her to create memories with them.'

Then she reached under the sofa and pulled out a book.

'The publisher has sent this. I want you to have it.'

'Let us read,' he said, and held out an arm.

She leaned into him.

He read the first few pages and then began the second chapter. He would never have recognised his grandmother. She'd been a hellion, always fighting to be the centre of attention, even in duels, and she was honest about her disguised efforts on the stage with a horrible rendition of an unfortunate song, but the repentant woman was dedicated to her family, had chosen the right man to wed at the last moment—and, through a series of misunderstandings and fortunate events, had managed to save the day many times over.

That was not how he remembered hearing the stories from his mother, but now he understood that his grandmother's memories would never be the same as his mother's.

'Is this Grandmother's true story?' he asked.

'I'm not sure. But it's the one she told me the second time, after thinking long and hard about it. And your mother helped us take some things out, and added a short prologue at the beginning, which says that some of these tales may not be exactly true, but parts of many are.'

Marie relaxed against him, settling in, and he continued reading. As he finished each chapter he saw his family through her eyes, and he felt closer to it and closer to her.

When he'd finished, he gave it back to her. 'It's flattering to my grandmother. It's flattering to my family.'

'I enjoy listening to her stories. She's different when she's with my aunt, and she's different when we are alone. She just reminisces and recalls the past.'

'You have succeeded in correcting the family history. I like it.' He lifted the book, but couldn't take his eyes from her. From the radiance he saw. He wouldn't have thought a simple compliment would mean much to her, but it seemed to mean the world.

'Gabriel… Gabriel?'

He heard his mother shouting in the corridor, and then she stepped into the room.

'You will not believe what that woman has done. She's wagering again. This time on *my* betrothal.'

His grandmother strolled in behind her. 'I don't know why she's complaining. The Duke himself wagered he'd wed her within six months.'

'Yes! She asked him when he was going to propose, which is entirely not her concern. And now she has talked him into letting her play the harp at the wedding breakfast.'

His grandmother nodded. 'I am very kind that way.' She clasped her hands. 'I like him. He's a little young, in my opinion, but that's not my concern. He'll make a good… um…son-in-law.'

'He's not going to be your son-in-law.'

'Well, I will be his mother-in-law by proxy, then. And

you can be my daughter-in-law again.' She tugged at her earlobe. 'I've missed having you as a daughter-in-law.'

Gabriel's mother groaned. 'Trust me. In my heart, your position has never changed.'

Then his mother saw the book in his hands. 'What are you reading, Gabriel?'

'Oh, dear,' his grandmother said, swooping closer. 'Is that…? Is that mine?'

Gabriel held it out to her and she clasped it in both hands. 'Finally.'

His mother coughed, but it sounded more like a squawk, and then both women left, arguing over who would read it first.

Gabriel interlaced his fingers with Marie's. 'That is the best I've seen them together in a long time.'

'We're so fortunate we have a big house.'

Gabriel stood. 'With a good lock on our door,' he said.

After latching it, he returned to open the bedroom door. Then he took her hand and lifted her to her feet, sweeping her into his arms and carrying her from the room.

'I'm so grateful to have you,' he said, giving the bedroom door a kick to close it after they'd gone through it. 'I look forward to spending many nights watching the stars with you and many mornings waking with you at my side. But now what I want most of all is to tell you how much I love you.'

'I love you too,' she said. 'You're the man who has made me believe in marriage and happy endings.'

* * * * *

HISTORICAL

Your romantic escape to the past.

Available Next Month

How Not To Propose To A Duke Louise Allen
The Marquess's Year To Wed Paulia Belgado

....

A Season With Her Forbidden Earl Julia Justiss
A Wedding To Protect Her Fortune Jenni Fletcher

Keep reading for an excerpt of a new title
from the Historical series,
ALLIANCE WITH THE NOTORIOUS LORD
by Bronwyn Scott

Prologue

February 5th, 1852

There were some among society—mainly jealous old biddies with unmarried daughters—who would say Antonia Lytton-Popplewell was simply born lucky. Antonia would disagree. She'd been born with something much better than luck—optimism. Luck was haphazard at best and held one at its mercy without any indicator of when or where it would strike. But optimism was constant and that constancy made many things possible—like allowing oneself the pleasure of trusting others and believing that life would work itself out, which it invariably did.

Just like this current hand of whist. It had started out as an ordinary hand, but was working itself into a grand slam one trick at a time, thanks to her partner's extreme skill. If anyone could turn a mediocre hand into something spectacular, it was her friend, Emma.

To Antonia's left at the table, her other friend, Fleur Griffiths, gave a pre-emptive sigh of defeat. 'Four tricks to go. You're going to make it, Em. I can't stop you.' She tossed the seven of hearts on the pile.

Their hostess, Mrs Parnaby, matched her with a grimace and played a powerless card. 'Me neither.'

Fleur played her last heart and cast a wry smile in Antonia's direction. 'Once again, you have all the luck. Emma did all the work, but you'll win the night.' They'd played a round robin, rotating partners so that everyone had a chance to play with each other. As a result, Antonia had accumulated the most individual points for the evening, which had started hours ago after dinner. They'd sent their husbands home at nine. It was now after midnight.

Antonia laughed at Fleur's begrudging congratulations. 'I had complete faith Emma would see the potential in my little hand and maximise it.' Optimism always saw potential. Just as Antonia had seen the potential in the trio's friendship eight years ago when they'd been three new brides married to three powerful, older men who adored their young wives. Antonia had turned the wives of her husband's two best friends into her own best friends. Now, the three of them were as inseparable as their husbands, their bonds just as strong. The only bonds stronger were the bonds of their marriages.

'Well done.' Antonia applauded as Emma took another trick. She was genuinely enjoying herself. This evening was exactly what she'd needed. No matter how much she loved her husband, Keir, it was good to have some time with her friends, sans husbands. The last few months, she and Keir had been immersed in his latest business venture, an abandoned building in London he wanted to turn into a first-rate department store to rival the *grands magasins* of Paris. They hadn't had a moment to themselves since the project had got underway and it had taken a toll on them.

When Emma's husband had asked Keir to accompany him to check on the soundness of a mill in Holmfirth as a potential investment, Antonia had jumped at the chance to mix a little business with pleasure and turn the trip into a partial holiday. She hoped to rekindle a little romance between her and Keir. Between overworking on the new project and the looming disappointment of eight years of marriage in which he'd amassed a fortune but no family, Keir had begun to struggle in the bedroom of late. As a consequence, she'd felt the stress, too.

They'd begun to wonder if time had run out for them when they hadn't been looking. Where had the years gone? Keir had been forty-nine when they'd wed, a man who'd been determined to have a financial empire *before* he committed to marriage and a family so that his wife and children wouldn't struggle as he'd struggled growing up. She'd not been bothered by the age of her husband. Instead, she'd been optimistic that children would come eventually. But now, she wasn't so sure. The business and pleasure trip was going well in restoring her hope, though.

Antonia's cheeks heated at memories of last night. Perhaps she'd wake Keir up when she got back to their rented home on Water Street, crawl under the covers, slip her hand beneath his nightshirt and…

Someone banged on the front door, shouting, 'The river's in Water Street!' Emma's last trick went unplayed, their hands forgotten as the women exchanged a look of consternation and ran for Mrs Parnaby's lace-curtained windows. There was nothing to see, only to hear. To Antonia, it sounded like the whoosh and whirl of a roiling wind. But that made no sense…

'The dam!' Emma gasped, grasping the situation, wild panic lighting her grey eyes. 'It must have burst and the river's flooded.'

'The men!' Antonia cried, Emma's panic contagious. Their husbands had gone back to their Water Street quarters after dinner at the Parnabys', determined to make it an early night before the business meeting about the mill in the morning. Emma's gaze clashed with hers for a horrified moment.

'Garrett,' Emma whispered and then she was off, racing for the door.

'No! You mustn't,' their hostess cried. 'If you go out now, you'll be washed away, too.'

Washed away, too.

The terror of those words galvanised Antonia into action. She and Fleur grabbed for Emma, dragging her bodily from the door, Mrs Parnaby assuring them they would all go out in the morning for news. There was nothing more they could do at present.

Except to wait.

Except to think about the horror of Mrs Parnaby's words. Mrs Parnaby thought it was hopeless. She'd already consigned their husbands to death along with the other residents of Water Street, aptly named because of its location to the River Holme where Hinchliffe Mill preceded the town of Holmfirth.

The four women sank into the stuffed chintz chairs of Mrs Parnaby's parlour. A frightening silence claimed the room. No one wanted to speak the truth. No, it wasn't truth. Not yet. Antonia stopped her thoughts. She would not let herself go down that path—a path that led to the conclusion that Keir, Garrett and Adam were dead, drowned in a river that had flooded its banks when the dam above it burst. Antonia reached for Emma's hand. 'They're strong men. They can take care of themselves.' The idea that perhaps they could not was unthinkable.

Antonia let those words sustain her throughout the long hours ahead. She called on images of Keir in her mind as he'd been tonight. Happy. Laughing. Content. The way he'd looked at her from across the table had assured her that no matter what they faced in life, they faced it together and his love for her had not, and would not, diminish. Nothing could mar their happiness. Nothing could intrude into their private world.

But the world, like water, had finally found a way to seep in. When morning came, Mrs Parnaby led them through waterlogged streets choked with mud and debris. Animal carcasses, iron machinery wrested free of its anchorage, household odds and ends—nothing had been spared the river's wrath. Antonia had never seen anything as thorough as this destruction, all of it proof of how violent the flood had been and how dangerous. Waters strong enough to break down a building, to wrench iron equipment from its restraints and dismantle it, would have been unnavigable for even the most capable of swimmers. Her heart sank as they reached the Rose and Crown Inn where the displaced were gathering. If tons of steel had not survived, how could mere flesh and bone? And yet some had.

James Mettrick, one of the men they'd come to do business with, who was also a Water Street resident where they were renting, had survived. He was battered and bruised, but alive. He'd found his way to shore. If he had, perhaps Keir had as well. Perhaps Garrett and Adam, too. Antonia exchanged a glance with Emma and knew she was thinking the same thing. There was still hope.

Antonia clung to that hope as she threw herself into helping the bedraggled. She served hot drinks and food, wrapped warm blankets about shaking shoulders, toted lost children on her hip who'd come looking for parents, and held strangers' hands as they struggled to process the magnitude of the flood. Jobs, lives and homes had been washed away. Many were just starting to realise there was nothing and no one to go back to.

She stayed busy, but each time the door opened, her gaze strayed towards it, her heart hoping Keir would walk through it. Each time she was disappointed. She consoled herself in knowing that *when* he did come, it would be late. He would be out helping others, putting others first. He would not come until all who needed him had been helped. Then they would go home to London, to their town house, and this nightmare would be over.

At ten o'clock in the morning, it was not Keir who walked through the inn door, but George Dyson, the town's coroner. He was grey and obviously fatigued. Antonia's heart went out to him. What must the poor man have endured in these past hours! He'd spent the time since the flood bearing the worst news to friends and neighbours. She froze as she watched him approach Emma, a polite hand at her elbow as he said something to her in low tones. Colour drained from Emma as she gestured for Antonia and Fleur to join Mr Dyson in the inn's private parlour. For the first time Antonia could recall, her optimism faltered.

In the parlour, she gripped Emma's hand, the news falling like a blow despite Dyson's attempt to soften it. 'Lady Luce, Mrs Popplewell, Mrs Griffiths, I wish I was not the bearer of bad tidings. I will be blunt. Water Street never stood a chance. The river hit it from the front and the side, absolutely obliterating the buildings.' The man paused; his Adam's apple worked as he swallowed hard. She wondered how many times today had he already made the same speech? Antonia gripped Emma's hand tighter as if that grip could hold back the inevitable. Perhaps he only meant to tell them hopes were slim because of that damage? She did not care how slim the hope was as long as that hope still existed.

Dyson recovered himself and continued. 'James Mettrick's family and the Earnshaws, both acquaintances of yours, I believe, are gone. Their homes were entirely destroyed.' Antonia bit back a cry, her sliver of hope all but extirpated.

'James Mettrick survived. He was brought in this morning,' Emma argued, the jut of her stubborn chin saying plainly, *Don't tell me there are* no *survivors when there were*. Antonia had never loved Emma more than she did in that moment. Emma, who was willing to stand between them all and the Grim Reaper with her arguments and quick mind. But Emma could not out-argue, could not out-reason this. At the realisation, something turned cold in Antonia. She felt as if the very life of her was seeping away as she waited for the *coup de grâce*.

Dyson gave a shake of his head, his tone gentle with Emma despite her scolding. 'The bodies of your husband and his friends have been recovered, Lady Luce. Your husband was found in the Victoria Mill race. I *am* sorry.'

'No!' Antonia let a wail. Not Keir. No, this wasn't real. The world became a series of fragmented moments. She was on the floor, sobbing. Beyond her, Fleur yelled her rage and smashed a plate against the parlour wall. Then Emma was beside her and they were in each other's arms, each of them trying to support the other against the unthinkable. Fleur came to them and they clung together, crying, consoling, rocking, reeling, until they found the strength to rise and do what needed doing: identifying the bodies.

One of Dyson's assistants stood with Antonia in a tent acting as a makeshift morgue behind the inn. He drew back the sheet and Antonia gave a sharp cry at the mottled, cut face of her husband. She'd thought she was prepared. She'd seen death before. She'd been at her grandmother's bedside, her grandmother's passing peaceful, her hand in her daughter's, a serene smile on her face as she left the world. But *this* was nothing like that. Keir didn't look peaceful. He looked…angry, like a warrior who knew the forces arrayed against him were too many, that his best fight wouldn't be enough, but he'd fight anyway.

Out of reflex, Antonia reached to smooth back the dark mat of his hair and gasped at the gash revealed on his forehead. If she needed further proof, there it was. This had been a violent death. Something had struck him. She thought of the heavy machinery she'd seen in the street this morning. Had one of those pieces hit him? Had he been knocked unconscious? She reached for his hand. No, his hands were cut and scratched. He'd clawed at something, gripped something. He'd fought. Perhaps he'd clutched at a piece of furniture as he'd been swept into the current. Perhaps he'd clung to a branch at the riverbank, trying to hoist himself ashore.

She wanted to push the images away. She didn't want to think about Keir's last moments and yet she must. She would not be a coward, not when he'd been so brave. Had he been afraid? Keir had never been afraid of anything. No risk, no enterprise was too daunting for him. Her thoughts went to the inevitable. Had he thought of her at the last ? Had there been time to whisper a silent goodbye as he'd gone under? Had she been with him at the end at least in his mind?

'Ma'am? Are you all right?' the assistant enquired nervously. He was young and no doubt the day had been overwhelming for him, too.

She nodded the lie. How would she ever be all right again? All the light, all the love in her life, had just gone out. 'I'd like a few moments alone, please.' She'd always be alone now. It was a sobering thought.

The tent flap closed behind the assistant and Antonia

sank to her knees, Keir's limp hand still in hers. This would be the last time she saw him, held him. She willed the memories to come with their bittersweet comfort. 'I remember the first time I saw you,' she murmured. 'It was at the Gladstone Ball and you were my knight in shining armour.' She felt a soft smile cross her lips at the remembrance. 'We surprised everyone,' she whispered.

She'd come to London that Season armed only with a wardrobe that flattered and the Lytton optimism that her looks would be enough to save her from genteel poverty and spinsterhood. She'd done more than save herself. She'd married Keir Popplewell and lifted not only herself up financially, but her family as well. Keir had paid her father's debts, relieved the country estate of its burdensome mortgage, and purchased an officer's commission for her brother. More than that, though, she'd married a man she loved and who loved her in return.

As for Keir, he'd gained a foothold in society with his marriage to a baronet's daughter, something many had thought impossible. Who would tolerate the rough-mannered, blunt-spoken businessman despite his fortune? He didn't *act* like a rich man. He was notorious for talking to servants—his *and* the servants of others. That was just the tip of the *faux-pas* iceberg. He paid attention to the poor. Keir Popplewell had a heart for the outcast.

Antonia had fallen in love with that kindness. It was a rare man who knew when to be ruthless in business and kind in life. Now, that rare man was dead. Tears smarted in her eyes. He was gone and there was no heir left behind, no piece of himself, no legacy. There was no one left but her. She and Keir had indeed run out of time.

'I think it's time to go.' Emma's words pulled Antonia out of her own reveries by Mrs Parnaby's front window four days later. Most of those days had been spent in front of that window, thinking, remembering, crying, railing at a fate that had left her a widow before she was thirty, before she could be a mother. Keir was supposed to have died of old age; they were supposed to have had more time.

Antonia looked between Fleur and Emma in the silence that ensued. Emma's words were not far from her own thoughts. Somewhere in the sleepless darkness last night, Antonia had come to the twin conclusions that she had to pick up the pieces of this tragedy and, secondly, she had to carry on. She couldn't do either of those here in Holmfirth surrounded by strangers. She needed to be home, in London. Keir's business and his employees would be counting on her to continue the work.

Perhaps Keir himself was counting on her, too, from the Great Beyond: to go home and finish their dream. She nodded when Emma finished speaking. 'I need to return to London and see how things stand. Keir was in the midst of restoring an old building. He had plans to turn it into a department store.' Antonia drew a shaky breath, debating her next words. If she said them aloud the dream would become real.

'I think I'll finish for him. I think it's what I must do, although I'm not sure how. I'll figure it out as I go.' She looked to Fleur. 'Shall we all travel together as far as

London? It's a long train ride from west Yorkshire when one is on their own.'

Fleur didn't meet her eyes. 'No, I think I'll stay and finish the investigation Adam began on the dam for Garrett. There are people to help and justice to serve. People deserve to know if this tragedy was a natural disaster or a man-made one.' Eighty-one people had died that fateful night. It wasn't only their husbands that had been lost. So many families had been affected by the loss of loved ones and livelihoods.

Across the room, Emma spoke sharply. 'Do you think that's wise, Fleur? If it is man-made, there will be people who won't appreciate prying, particularly if it's a woman doing it. You should think twice before putting yourself in danger.'

'I don't care,' Fleur snapped and Antonia's head swivelled between her two friends. Something more was going on here. What had she missed? Fleur's tone was strident. 'If Adam died because of carelessness, someone *will* pay for that. I will see to it and I will see to it that such recklessness isn't allowed to happen again.' Antonia wished she had half of Fleur's courage.

'And Adam's child?' Emma shot back, the remark catching Antonia by surprise. She'd been so wrapped up in her own grief, she'd thought nothing of Fleur's hand finding its way to the flat of her stomach, a gesture she'd made several times over the past days. The thought of a child struck a chord of sad longing within Antonia. How wondrous it would have been for her to have one last piece of Keir, but there was no chance of that. Her courses had arrived that morning, not that she'd been expecting it to be otherwise.

Fleur shook her head, her voice softer when she spoke to Emma, her earlier anger absent. 'I do not know if there is a child. It is too soon.' But not too soon to hope, Antonia thought privately. Fleur suspected there was a chance.

'Just be careful, dear friend. I do not want anything to happen to you.' Emma rose and went to her. Antonia joined her and they encircled each other with their arms, their heads bent together.

'We're widows now,' Emma said softly.

There would be enormous change for each of them over the next few months—the death of their husbands was just the beginning. Widows lost more than a man when husbands died. Society did not make life pleasant for women who hadn't a man beside them even in this new, brave world where women were demanding their due. But amid the chaos of change, Antonia knew she could depend on two things: the friendship of the women who stood with her now and the realisation that, from here on out, nothing in her life would ever be the same again.

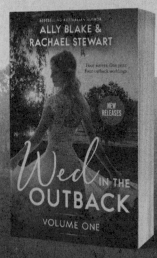
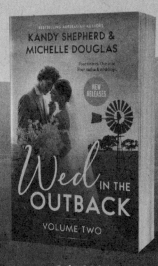

ubscribe and
all in love with
Mills & Boon
eries today!

ou'll be among the first
o read stories delivered
o your door monthly
nd enjoy great savings.

WE
SIMPLY
LOVE
ROMANCE

MILLS & BOON

JOIN US

Sign up to our newsletter to stay up to date with...

- Exclusive member discount codes
- Competitions
- New release book information
- All the latest news on your favourite authors

Plus...
get $10 off your first order.
What's not to love?

Sign up at **millsandboon.com.au/newsletter**